A
Different
Matter

EDENGONE

J.P. Dold

Book One

A Different Matter: Edengone

By J.P. Dold

"Relax, Anna," the controller said. "All field crews in. You're the last. Seth's been asking after you."

A weight lifted off her mind. "Thanks, Control. Let him know I'm in, will you?"

"Will do." Was that a hint of laughter in his voice? "Control out."

Final checks completed, Anna transmitted a snag list to the maintenance chief and clambered down to the garage deck. A crew was already swarming up ladders and onto the drive units, checking strain gauges and lubricants. A tanker truck trundled past and aimed a nozzle at the towering wheels. A needle jet played over the mesh, washing away the detritus of a day's travel.

"Just routine stuff today." Anna waved to the maintenance chief and called out above the hiss and rush of water. "Nothing needing repair or replacement, thank the skies. I need an early start tomorrow."

He huffed. "Not a chance. Control says storm's set to last through tomorrow at least."

"Kak! It's bad enough that it's too dangerous to stay out in the field overnight." Anna's shoulders sagged. "We'll never get finished at this rate."

"What's left out there? A few beacons now?"

"And the last harvest site is shutting down."

The chief whistled. "I didn't realize they were still working a site. Thought it was just clean-up."

"The padres wanted to work as much as they could until the last minute."

"This is cutting it fine by any measure of sanity. How're they managing the nights?"

"The rigs have to come back of course. Everything else is lashed down hard against the storms." Anna shuddered. This time of the season, the planet's hypersonic jet stream dipped and hugged the nighttime terminator. For all the planet's unpredictability, this feature had been a constant threat for weeks now. "Seems they've been lucky not to lose anything. I've got at least a dozen beacons unaccounted for. Broke free and blown away."

"Sponge gives ..."

"And Sponge takes away." Anna finished the ritual saying.

Jennifer now saw stairs as a personal challenge. She kept a steady pace, breathing deeply and evenly, up the last steep companionway to the flat roof of the habitat. Her thighs and calves burned, but the sweat rolling down her face was due less to physical effort and more to the furnace heat of this damnable city.

The weather dome arched a few meters above her head, vanishing from sight beyond the railing that marked the edge of the roof. A luminous orange glow at eye level brightened to the outline of the planet's giant star that seemed to loom across a quarter of the sky. A forest of clear mushroom caps stood shoulder high around her. Light wells, funneling daylight into the heart of the habitat.

The dome overhead creaked against a fitful background of breathy bass tones. Jennifer stared upwards at the carved ribs that met in the center. After a few seconds, she tore her gaze away and swallowed a fit of vertigo. The dome was swaying, but it gave the overwhelming sensation that she was the one moving, in direct contradiction to her inner ear. She focused on the rock-solid floor and regained her balance.

A movement in her peripheral vision announced Simon Galloway's arrival. Today he favored a canary yellow shirt tucked into avocado green fitted breeches. Voluminous sleeves billowed as he emerged through the opening in the roof.

Jennifer noted he'd barely broken into a sweat. His eccentric dress sense might lull some people into thinking him an easy mark, but it seemed he maintained his physical fitness with the same ruthless efficiency as his career climbing.

"Nice view." He sniffed.

"You've left us with one hell of an uphill struggle."

"So, straight to the point? No 'how are you?' No 'isn't it warm today?'" A smirk. "As I said before, the President places great faith in your abilities to get her what she wants."

"Shares in pharmaceutical profits are the cornerstone of Elysium's colonial agreement." Jennifer worked hard to keep the snarl out of her voice. "They'll safeguard those to their dying breath." There had to be more to this deal. She fumed. Galloway was holding something back. Had she been offered an impossible task? Was he setting her up to fail?

"We're not asking them to surrender any existing income streams, just future discoveries. I'm sure there's some leeway to offer short term gains in exchange."

"What rationale could I possibly give for offering those kinds of concessions? They'd be suspicious, and rightly so."

"Everything hinges on medicinal exports, doesn't it? Bioactive compounds not found naturally in any Earthly species. A unique resource." Galloway inspected his distorted reflection in the polished cap of a light well. He smoothed an eyebrow, reminding Jennifer of a cat preening. He sighed, an elaborate and theatrical gesture. "I admit it's a tough assignment, so I'm authorized to give you bit more motivation."

Jennifer arched an eyebrow, but refused to rise to the bait.

Galloway smiled. "This new discovery–"

"*Potential* discovery, I think you said. To be confirmed."

"Indeed." His face betrayed only a hint of annoyance at her interruption. "I understand you have a little staffing issue in your senior ranks."

Jennifer blinked. The non-sequitur left her fumbling for a suitable response. Galloway saved her the bother. "Remind me what happened to the not-quite-late but still unlamented Don Kozyr."

Dammit, he was toying with her. "His mind failed during the last transit. You know as well as I do that's a known hazard of space travel."

"Despite the drugs we take to ease the mind?"

"The drugs are a necessary buffer, and it's still safer than crossing a busy street. And you improve your odds greatly if you look after your physical health."

The slob had brought it on himself. The thought hung unspoken in the air between them.

"Yet even with the best drugs, our range in a single transit is severely limited."

With a grimace of distaste, Jennifer thought back to the series of hops they'd endured to reach this distant backwater, and the lengthy return journey to proper civilization.

"Imagine if we could extend that range–safely, mind you–a full order of magnitude. Maybe two."

Jennifer's heart seemed to pause mid-beat. Her breath stilled. Her mind raced to encompass the possibilities. She realized Galloway was peering intently at her.

A corner of his mouth twitched in a wry smile. "I see a light bulb glimmering."

"Indeed," she murmured. "Imagine what it would mean for the company that held sole control of *that* key."

Galloway caressed the smooth polymer of the light dome in front of him, gazing deep into its depths. "The future would be bright." His voice seemed wistful.

"The stakes are way beyond any simple new medicine or recreational drug. I can see the Company's interest."

"It's not simple greed, of course. Not the Company begrudging the colonists a share. But if Elysium retained their normal share of the profits, under the kind of agreement they have in place at the moment, they'd be able to clear their historical debt within months."

Jennifer felt a cold hand squeeze her heart. She knew the way traditional colonial agreements worked. "And once they'd met the financial terms, they'd become a fully independent entity ..."

"And all rights would immediately revert to them. Our income stream would be cut off entirely. That cannot be allowed to happen."

"So when this becomes official, we need to keep their hands off any part of the proceeds." Another thought occurred to Jennifer. "And that's why your current mission has to remain a secret at all costs. This needs to be a *future* discovery."

"So, I can leave this matter in your capable hands."

"I still need a strategy to persuade them, without raising any suspicions, to surrender rights to future discoveries."

Pale eyes glinted. Dammit! The slimy creature was still hiding something.

Galloway drew out the moment, the silence between them accentuated by sporadic buffeting of the weather shield. Finally, a sly smile crept across his face. "If you need a helping hand, you might like to know that the colonists are planning to propose an alternative agreement. Something that would be highly beneficial to them."

Jennifer stared. How in the Nine Hells would he know *that*? Sensations of plots moving unseen just beyond her reach made her head spin. She mentally shook herself. As much as it pained her to accept Galloway's help, her mind suddenly latched on to the implications of what he'd just said. "So, they would expect to give away some significant concessions themselves."

"You've a reputation for seeing the possibilities in a situation. Why do you think the President insisted on assigning this negotiation to you?"

Chapter 3

Jennifer Steel paused on the threshold to the conference chamber. The sneer, which was as much a part of her public persona as her sharp-pressed suit and dazzling white cropped hair, had to be reminded of its place. In full view, front and center.

She was on display and the senior representative of the Company on this inhospitable world. These colonials had to know that their best efforts to impress were doomed. All the same, she was unnerved to find that her habitual sneer had needed prompting.

Most colonies she visited made strenuous efforts on her behalf. Their efforts were laughable. Nothing off Earth could compare with the decadent ostentation she was used to. They tried, nonetheless. Hence the trademark sneer.

These people had deftly sidestepped the problem. The auditorium was large, but not overwhelming. The round floor could easily seat a thousand people. But it was also clear this space was entirely functional, used by the townsfolk here for everyday purposes and not created specifically for their visiting dignitaries.

Agreed, living in airtight domes they couldn't simply erect a few walls and a roof just for the occasion, so they were making do with what they already had. But even so, some of the outlandish attempts at extravagant decoration she'd seen elsewhere had tempted her to laugh out loud.

Not so here.

Two long tables faced each other, for the Elysium and Company delegations. A third, smaller table closed the gap at one end. The Earth Nations Committee for Offworld Affairs observers, here to chair the proceedings and ensure legalities were observed.

Legal. Not necessarily fair.

Behind each of the three tables, a huddle of screens and smaller desks accommodated each contingent's support staff and advisers.

A respectable distance away, facing the observers' table, a handful of media vultures sat on a small podium, ready to spread their edited biases to the worlds outside. They had their uses—the Company made as much use of public misinformation as any politician—but they were fickle. Jennifer was keenly aware of the cameras on her right now, and the commentators in the background looking to find hidden meaning in the tiniest clue: an unguarded glance, a micro-expression, the color of her suit buttons.

What took her by surprise was that everything was clean and comfortable, places at tables set out with precision, but all entirely business-like. Jennifer breathed silent relief that she'd resisted suggestions that these people needed a show of wealth to remind them of their place in these negotiations. Her suit was smart, but not showy, and completely unadorned. Even the clasp closing the shirt at her neck was a simple Company crest.

She also noted the subtext here. The Elysium delegation was all about business, and was not cowed either by the Company itself or by her status.

She waited on the threshold, to be invited in by the Offworld Affairs chief facilitator.

The observers were already in the room, seated. They were the official hosts, so they were in place to formally welcome the combatants to the arena. There were no guns or swords in sight, but Jennifer saw this as gladiatorial combat all the same. There may be no blood shed, but financial hemorrhage and corporate slavery were as real to her as the corporeal variety.

The colonial delegation had also paused in a doorway around the circle to her left, easily identified by their pasty, bluish complexions. One face among them stood out. Maximillian Kyari, midnight-skinned legal counsel to the Elysium government, such as it was.

Kyari was certainly a renowned expert in interplanetary legal affairs and colonial resource agreements. As such he was a fine choice to advise Elysium on the delicately brutal negotiations about to commence. That he was also one of Jennifer's secret weapons was their hard luck. They should have done more due diligence before appointing him. Admittedly, that was hard to do from eighty parsecs distance, especially when all travel and communications went through the Company's hands.

That was not Jennifer's problem.

The chrono, meter-high orange numerals projected onto the wall behind the observers, ticked to 10:00. The chief facilitator and all his contingent stood.

The chief facilitator raised his hands, arms outstretched to greet the two contingents. "As appointed representative of the Earth Nations Committee for Offworld Affairs, I recognize the representatives of Elysium, and of Heron Baywater to the room."

Jennifer took her cue and advanced towards her table. The rest of her team followed, in strict order of rank, and arranged themselves behind their assigned seats at the table. A larger gaggle of support staff spread themselves out behind her. The colonists mirrored her team's movements on the far side of the room.

Silence fell. Everyone remained standing while the facilitator clasped his hands in front of him. "With heavy hearts we note the absence of Company negotiator, Don Kozyr." He gazed at Jennifer. "Do you wish a delay in proceedings in light of this misfortune?"

Jennifer grimaced and hastily turned the expression into an appropriate blend of sadness and resignation. "We do not. Don Kozyr's deputy will take his seat at the table."

The facilitator nodded and began his welcoming speech. Rich, deep tones belied his frail appearance.

Inwardly, Jennifer wondered at this subtle jab, dressed as it was in conciliatory tones. Losing a senior adviser in transit like that was considered a bad omen, to those who believed in such things. Jennifer didn't believe in omens, but this could easily be a ploy to unsettle her team.

The head of the ENCOA delegation droned on. Formal introductions, person by person. Name, background and qualifications, position and role in the negotiations. Then a summary of the history of Elysium, the legal components of its colonial charter, and the framework within which the current review had been invoked.

Nothing here was saying anything new, but Jennifer used tried and tested mindfulness techniques to maintain her mask of attention. It didn't help that the oppressive heat in these domes was drawing a trickle of sweat down the small of her back, and her throat felt raw and inflamed from the traces of native chemicals that the air filters couldn't completely erase. At first, the slight spicy tang in the air was an exotic curiosity, but after a few days it made her feel sick. She longed to reach for the water glass on the table in front of her, but nobody was stepping out of line until the opening formalities were over.

The facilitator moved on to a reminder of the five-hundred-year-old ENCOA resolution limiting hereditary indenture. *That* caught Jennifer's attention. Welcoming speeches by non-partisan chairs usually followed a standard format and *never* contained partisan messages. Here was a blatant reminder to the world outside that the colonists were legally entitled to freedom from Company control. A clear appeal to the wave of popular sentiment now riding high across the young worlds beyond Earth.

In theory, she could halt proceedings and make a formal complaint against the observers' neutrality, and yet, Jennifer seethed to herself, this was the main reason for the negotiations in the first place. That was public knowledge, so they would argue that a mention at this point was perfectly natural, even required, as part of the context-setting.

All the same, it placed her team on the defensive before talks had even begun.

That could hardly have been accidental.

Mikel 't Hooft glared at the tutorial program in frustration. Ninety-eight percent? Shame and disappointment briefly dulled his thinking. He rocked gently back and forth on the study bench while he stared at the screen. Where had he dropped those marks?

He stole a sidelong glance at his neighbor, thankful to see she was too busy wrestling with her own test to have spotted his embarrassment. While other kids in their early teens were plowing through the basics of organic chemistry, Mikel had progressed to subatomic interactions at binding sites in neural synapses.

C'mon Lotte, you're bright enough, that one's easy! Mikel felt the urge to message her a hint. The urge built swiftly to an overwhelming need to help, to be liked. He closed his eyes and acknowledged the sensation, like he'd been taught, allowing it to flow through him until he could let it go. "No-one likes a smartass," senior educator Georgina had repeatedly told him. Mikel's lip curled, and he returned to his own screen to track down where he'd made a mistake.

Rock. Rock. Rock.

A tap on his shoulder broke his concentration. He looked up, startled, then smiled up at aunt Karin.

"Deep in thought, Mikey?"

He sighed and shut down the tutorial. He'd gone over the errant question in fine detail and was confident his own answer was more correct than the stock answer the program was expecting. Stupid program!

"Time to go home."

He was vaguely aware that the classroom had emptied out without him noticing. Nothing unusual in that, other than a twinge of disappointment that Lotte had left without saying goodbye.

He hopped off the bench and followed Karin out the door.

They wound their way from dome to dome through bright-lit halls and tunnels. The corner where the Bartolini clan normally hung out was strangely quiet. That was a welcome relief—on his own, Mikel usually gave that whole dome a wide berth—but it only added to his unease tonight. In fact, the town as a whole felt wrong.

With a shock, Mikel noticed that the walls here were bare. This passage was normally alive with vibrant marquetry panels. Now, it was hard to tell where he actually was. Without decorations, the halls all started to look the same.

Despite the lack of crowds to push through, he edged closer to Karin's side.

For once, Mikel was relieved to find their common room alive with excited chatter, loud, distracting. Not quite threatening—Mikel felt safe here—but close to overwhelming. But at least it was normal.

More or less.

And at least here, he could put a name to most of the people. There were just a few he got mixed up, adults on the edge of this group of families who were around sometimes but not often. In fact, in some cases Mikel was never entirely sure whether they really were the same person back again after a week or two, or simply another stranger who *looked* like someone who was here before. Faces blurred together in his mind, so he was rarely confident he actually knew who was talking to him.

Regardless, they always seemed to know *him* and seemed to want to say hello. He got away with nothing more than a shy smile. Words formed in his mind but never made their way to his mouth. It just seemed safer that way. The world of people was a bewildering place, full of unfathomable rules that he seemed to trip over by accident.

Voices raised on the other side of the room boomed through Mikel's head and made him flinch in panic. Arguments scared him. They upset the balance of the world and the noise *hurt*. A quick scan around the room reassured him that this was nothing to worry about; it earned nothing more than a few casual glances from others in the room. Forcing his hammering heart to calm down, he reminded himself that people argued loudly all the time, but they seemed to have ways of resolving their differences. The world of speech, of interactions, was fraught with hidden traps. People–other people, that is, even children and other teens–must have some hidden sense that Mikel felt blind to. Retreating into silence had become a way of life for him.

A new commotion near the entrance. "Where's my boy?" Mikel's heart leapt at the warm, familiar tones. He left Karin's side and rushed to meet Anna, wrapping his arms around her and snuggling his face into the curve of her neck. Not for the first time he wondered how he could now be taller than her, or had she shrunk? It seemed wrong for a boy to be bigger than a grown up. She was swamped in layers of outdoor clothing that smelled of sweat and sour plant sap, and the strap of the face mask dangling around her neck cut into his chin, but he didn't mind.

"Hey, Mikey love. I missed you." She held him at arm's length. "But then, what's new?" She gave that beautiful lopsided grin and he stuck his tongue out.

I love you, mom. The unspoken thought radiated with such intensity that, somehow, Mikel just knew she felt it.

He gave a quick wave to Seth, hovering behind Anna, one of the few people outside their clan that he could recognize. Hardly surprising. Seth often seemed to be around even though his clan's quarters were several domes away.

They took their places at one of the long tables–it seemed emptier than it should be–and helped themselves from a steaming pot of wild rice and bean risotto.

Karin joined them and sat on Mikel's other side. "How's it going out there, Sis?"

Mikel concentrated on his food while voices babbled around him.

"Daytime storms are holding us up," Anna said, "but just a few more days in the field and we're all done."

"That's good to hear." Georgina, Mikel's teacher, plonked herself down opposite. "We've stayed late this season. Nights have turned nasty."

"Company quotas," someone else grumbled from down the table. "It's been a rare lean season."

Mikel glanced that way. The gravely voice was instantly recognizable. He usually tried to avoid the clan's fearsome patriarch, even though his equally fearsome twin daughters had always treated him well. Clara met his gaze and flashed him a flicker of a wink. He smiled.

Nick de Jong, one of the town's leaders, took a seat next to Georgina. Mikel shuddered and focused harder on his food. There was something indefinably *off* about Nick. Like another creature, something cold and slimy, inhabited his skin.

"Are you all packed up, Mikey?" Nick's voice grated on his mind. "The trek's a big adventure. I don't suppose you remember the last one. You were too young."

Mikel ignored the question and carefully separated out the beans from the rice, so he could judge how much of each there was. It was important to balance the mouthfuls so he didn't end up with too much of one or the other to finish off at the bottom of the bowl.

"It's going to be a lot quieter here tomorrow." Karin's voice was soothing after Nick's, but her words turned his stomach to ice. What was going on? Why was everything so strange?

A simple protein structure built in his mind, meticulous, atom by atom. Flexing his mental muscles, Mikel imagined the acidity of the solution increasing. He pictured the effect on electron distribution across the molecule, and tried to imagine how its folded structure would adjust as bonds *here* strengthened while those *there* weakened.

Time and time again, he wrestled with his inner world. He never managed to go more than a few steps before the complexity became too much, but the exercise kept the outside world at bay.

———•—•———

The ENCOA facilitator stirred in his seat and glanced back and forth between the Company and colony delegations. After the opening formalities, ceremonial strictures were relaxed and sleeves rolled up for the real work. "So, we have before us a fairly standard agreement renewal. Areas for negotiation are well-understood by both sides, thanks to the diligent preparatory work of Company and Elysium lawyers and accountants over the past year."

Past the auditorium's doorways, children's laughter intruded. The facilitator drummed his fingers on the table, as if wrestling with an inner conflict. Jennifer held her breath and found the palms of her hands sweating. This man was an unknown quantity. The ENCOA choice to lead the congress had remained a closely-held secret until after they'd boarded the longship in Earth orbit, and Jennifer knew little about him other than he was known to be a stickler for protocol.

"I understand the Elysium authorities wish to table an alternative and"–he cleared his throat with a slight crease of a frown–"somewhat unorthodox approach, to be considered in parallel."

Jennifer let out the breath she'd been holding. This was the avenue Galloway had talked about, the one that she was pinning her hopes on for securing the concession the Company needed.

Some part of her had wondered if Galloway had been mistaken, or bluffing. That there was no alternative agreement to be tabled and that she'd somehow have to work miracles within the standard framework. Beyond that instinctive paranoia, her worst fear, that the facilitator would dismiss the motion out of hand, had not materialized.

She eyed the head of the Elysium delegation sitting opposite. Chubby and relentlessly cheerful Josiah Handel. He'd smiled and nodded through the interminable introductions and opening speeches with boyish enthusiasm. Jennifer had trouble reining in her gag reflex.

Josiah stumbled to his feet, and bobbed his head, ingratiating. "Aye, indeed. Groundwork for a substantially revised agreement has been laid alongside the more traditional agreement."

"And you feel you have good grounds for this alternative to be tabled?" The facilitator looked bored. He was going through the formalities.

"There is precedent, to be sure. The colony of Harper's Forge was fast-tracked to independence from its founding corporate monopoly. Although the context is different, the legal framework has formed the basis for our proposal."

"True." The facilitator looked thoughtful. "In that instance, the United Earth Nations deemed the planet's abundance of scarce metals was a strategic resource too valuable to humanity's future to be monopolized."

"Granted, the situation is not comparable, but we believe we have a compelling case for this path to be considered."

"And does the representative of Heron Baywater object to the tabling of this proposal?"

Jennifer took a sip of water, drawing out the moment before responding. This was the option the Company needed in place if Galloway's endeavor bore fruit, but at the same time she could not afford to appear eager. For the first time, she became aware of the faint background rush of air from the dome's filters, and the creak of seats as people all around the room shifted, leaning forward to catch her words. Folders of neatly-indexed data popped up on the tablet in front of her, supplied by the small army of analysts at tables behind her. Facts, figures, news snippets, speaking points, all ready to support any argument she wished to make. She ignored them.

"My team is reviewing the proposal, but the general intent is clear enough. I maintain that I do not believe this to be in the colony's best interests."

"I think we should let the Elysium contingent speak for Elysium." The mild rebuke from the facilitator was exactly the response Jennifer had been angling for. She'd subtly nudged him into favoring this departure from normal procedure. He pointedly turned towards Josiah, who again rose to his feet.

"As appointed representative of the collected cities and townships of Elysium, I can assure the gathering here that we take our wellbeing very seriously indeed. We thank the Company for its stewardship over the past four hundred and thirty years. The exit conditions built into the charter agreement are intended to protect a fledgling colony from financial ruin until conditions are met for it to cut exclusive financial ties to its founding corporation. In our case, we believe those criteria have now become more of an obstacle than a safeguard."

Jennifer decided that some form of protest at this would be expected. "And I understand our respective teams have found substantial common ground in addressing many of the Elysium concerns in the revised *tradi-tional* agreement."

"True enough, but it still binds us to Company terms and conditions for access to resources vital to our future. Elysium has a stable internal economy, a carefully managed population, and huge potential for growth. We aspire to full self-determination, with the freedom to strike independent trade deals with other worlds, and transport contracts with any or all of the spacefaring corporations."

He looked up and down the table at his colleagues, and gestured with an expansive wave of an arm to indicate the room and the city around them. "No colony has been held in thrall for so long, or been held to such stringent demands from its founding company."

"And yet," Jennifer murmured, "without managing to meet the agreed-upon repayment schedules."

For the first time, Josiah scowled. "The nature of the traditional agreement ties repayments and costs to indices in the prevailing marketplace. The intent is to shield both colonies and corporations from premature independence in unpredictable futures, but it also acts to move the target in ways that can be detrimental to the colony. Indeed, despite the vagaries of market forces ..." Josiah entirely lost his jovial demeanor. He paused and speared Jennifer with a glare far sharper and more calculating than she would have believed possible. "... By our own calculations Elysium has been entirely self-funding for over a century. It is time for Heron Baywater to acknowledge that fact."

Josiah sat. At a nod from the facilitator, Jennifer rose to her feet for a formal rebuttal. "The Company's position has always been to protect fledgling colonies from harm. We placed people here, four centuries ago, on an inhospitable world. We owe their descendants a duty of care. Your situation is unique, in that this world cannot be terraformed without destroying the indigenous life present here. You will always be dependent on protected, enclosed habitats and the technology needed to sustain them, and your external economy is dependent on the plant products you can harvest. A precarious position."

Her speech was impassioned. The Company's opposition had to appear genuine. "People remember the unique claims made for Harper's Forge. Yes, it was placed on a fixed-term agreement, basically a time-bound transition to independence from the corporation. What people gloss over is that it was tied instead to the Council of United Earth Nations. It was *too* strategic an asset to ever be free."

"That is not a claim we would wish to make."

Jennifer inclined her head, acknowledging Josiah's interruption with good grace. "That was merely scene-setting to my point. What people forget is that the economic case for Harper's Forge fell apart fifty years later, when accessible deposits of those scarce elements were discovered on moons in two separate systems within months of each other. The bottom fell out of the market, and the United Earth Nations found themselves bailing out their white elephant for the *next* fifty years. If the colony had been truly independent, it would have died a lingering and impoverished death."

She drew herself up to her full height and her gaze roved across the tables of facilitators and negotiators, before facing the media gallery full on. "That is not a fate I would wish on the two million people of Elysium."

As Jennifer sat, the facilitator beetled his brows at her. There was a long pause before he cleared his throat. "If that is the extent of the Company's objections, I see a great deal of concern and *protectiveness*"– Jennifer allowed a flicker of a grimace to cross her face, well aware that sharp observers would understand the Company was protecting more than colonists' well-being–"but I see no *legal* argument presented. I will allow the second proposal to proceed alongside the main business of the negotiations."

Jennifer willed the hammering in her chest to subside before she trusted herself to speak. So much had hinged on that decision. "I will, of course, bow to the facilitator's ruling. However, I ask two things of this assembly. First, that we *all* negotiate in good faith on the terms of *both* proposed agreements, until such a time as one or other becomes either obviously untenable or the obvious path forward."

The facilitator sighed and gave an irritated wave of his hand. "That should be taken as read. I will have no patience for any signs of obstruction ... from either side."

"Second, that the representatives of the Company be permitted some direct observation of Elysium's industrial capability, to ease our misgivings."

Chapter 4

From the roof of the storage pod, twelve meters off the ground, Anna guided the last of the salvaged marker beacons into its cradle and returned the cargo crane to its stowed position. She checked the beacon's serial number against the inventory on her tablet, and heaved a deep sigh. Despite the dusk chill, a stray trickle of perspiration stung the corners of her eyes under her face mask. It would be good to return to the breathable air of the crawler's cab and strip off her bulky outer clothing. This had been a long and hard day, but *finally* she was done.

Despite the lure of home comforts, she rested a while longer to take in the panorama. Next time she came out this way, once the years-long night in this hemisphere ended and people could return, the treacherous landscape will have shifted beyond recognition. They'd have to start over, sounding the kilometer-deep organic mass for new lodes to harvest, laying out a new network of markers to guide the harvest crews safely.

But for now it was time to abandon their home as the north pole turned its back on the sun through half the planet's thirteen-standard-year orbit.

Polished copper overhead darkened to chocolate in the north. The clear sky didn't fool her. Already, pewter thunderheads smudged the eastern horizon, heralding the lengthening nights' storms. The most predictable feature of the weather at this turn of the season, nightfall brought howling destruction down from the sky. A good time to be under shelter.

Anna swung herself out of the crane's seat and down into an airlock. She murmured the ritual of entry under her breath, fingers on controls following the familiar words, and counted while the lock flushed the world's native toxins from the air.

Through the tunnel between the crawler's forward pair of seven-meter wheels, she clambered up into the driver's cabin and settled into the center seat. A triangular clan sign hung from the back of the seat, with Anna's personal signature. A warning to anyone entering the cab that this was her turf, her sanctum. She murmured a brief homecoming, eyes glancing over the faded photo of baby Mikey and dear departed Luuk. Her fingers brushed a homemade dreamcatcher before resting on the crawler's drive controls.

A schematic of the vehicle glowed in semi-darkness. Anna recited the startup checklist as her eyes and fingers danced over the panel, bringing power and drive online one segment at a time, checking each yoop in turn for status replies, confirming hitch and hull integrity down the length of the train. A visual check from roof-mounted cameras compared the orientation of the insect-like vehicle with the reports from the hitch sensors.

Another ritual, one which was personal to Anna, and the crawler eased forwards a few meters proving she really was powered up and mobile. Not always a given, out here.

The sounds from the shortwave radio at her side weren't so reassuring. Anna scowled and thumbed to 'transmit'. "Serendipity Control, this is Charlie Tango seven niner, respond please."

Static answered her. She grimaced and gave a three-fingered sign of defiance to the futzed-up radio. She smacked the top of the casing for good measure and was rewarded with a faint but understandable signal.

"Serendipity Control, how's it going, Anna?"

"All cleaned up. On my way in."

"You're cutting it close." Even through bursts of white noise, worry was evident in the tone. "Any word from Seth's crew? They haven't checked in yet."

Anna stomach lurched. She and Seth were the last two crawlers out in the field. The few remaining drive cabs back home were by now hooked up to their trains, ready to evacuate the last of the town's population. "Nothing from where I'm sitting. I'll check it out."

"Negative, Charlie Tango seven niner"–the sudden formality told Anna the field controller was serious–"you don't have time for a detour."

Anna already knew that, but it was the same old tension between company policy and *the right thing to do*. "Say again, Serendipity, static … losing you …" She killed the radio. You could hardly be hauled up for disobeying an order you never received.

The crawler surged forwards under Anna's guidance. She brought the segmented vehicle around in a wide arc, sticking to the relative safety of smooth, high ground, and angled towards Seth's last known position.

Bright floodlights lit the darkening ground, dispersing shadows cast by almost horizontal orange rays. Anna's gaze flicked from the chart at her side to the ground in front of her. She pushed the crawler to its maximum. At forty kilometers an hour the ride lost its lazy riding-on-air wallow and jarred her through the seat frame. A forest of leafy growths loomed ahead, square kilometers of Sponge's photosynthesis factories. Drivers normally avoided them. A crawler could get entangled, but Anna knew the trunks were shriveling, their job done for the season as the hours of daylight dwindled. She knew this, but old habits were hard to break. She gritted her teeth and kept her hand firmly on the throttle.

The forest succumbed, but nobody'd mentioned the rough and rutted surface underneath. She was almost thrown out of her seat, and it felt like she'd cracked a tooth on that first bounce. She eased back a bit, but it was still faster than going around on the higher ground.

Time mattered. It wasn't like Seth to not check in.

The crawler thundered through the dying forest like vids she'd seen of a snake slithering through grass.

Cresting the next ridge, Anna gasped and brought the crawler to a halt. She checked and re-checked her charts. The landscape for a hundred klicks around town had been thoroughly mapped. Her updated charts, only a standard year old, had been annotated over and over by hand to keep up with shifting conditions, but the next few kilometers had always been a safe point to cross between one ridge and the next. Clearly the chart needed updating again.

Seth's crawler lay a klick away. Even from here, she could see the massive vehicle was in trouble. On supposedly level ground, the rear sections dipped at an impossible angle.

Anna wracked her brain. Seth had just cleared a northern harvesting camp, the closest to town, the most consistently productive, and the last to be shut down. His train had a crew car and, she was pretty sure, five cargo pods. After today it was to be hooked up to another waiting train for the trek south. No need to unload, its precious cargo of harvesting machinery was already packed away for the journey.

She could see the driver's cab, and counted the pairs of wheels back. Had she remembered right? He was a pod short. She lifted a pair of binocs to her eyes and confirmed what she feared. The last pod and rear pair of wheels had sunk almost out of sight.

The ground was rotten.

The binocs also picked out the crew in the distance desperately trying to sink anchor points into the fragile surface to haul themselves out.

She turned the radio back on but static blasted her ears. The electrical activity here was so intense she was cut off from home. Not that they could help. It looked like the crawler would be lost inside the hour.

She pulled on her mask and scuttled down steps at the back of the cab to the cramped equipment bay. The kit she wanted was readily to hand in storage clamps. Neatness out here was not an obsession, it was the key to a useful lifespan.

Out through the lower airlock and on the ground, Anna instinctively checked the near wheels for signs of settling before stepping cautiously away from the crawler.

She thumbed a switch on her lapel and hailed the distant crew. "Seth, it's Anna. What's your status?"

"Tread careful, Anna. Ground's fragile."

Shit! Even the line-of-sight signal was badly distorted. Seemed like Sponge was having an epic hissy fit.

"Didn't look any different from when we crossed a week ago, but it's dicey now. Just blind luck we got as far as we did before the crawler broke through."

"Okay on foot?"

"No guarantees there, even."

Anna choked back a panicked response. This was every field crew's nightmare. She studied the surface at her feet, unslung a probe hanging over her shoulder, and poked the ground. The probe slid into the spongy mass far more easily than she liked.

She returned her attention to the activity around Seth's vehicle. "You'll never get a firm anchor to haul the crawler out."

"Tell me something I don't karking know."

"Can you unhitch the last coupla cars? Drive the rest out?"

"Already tried. *Nutloos* hitch is jammed at that angle and ground's breaking up even as we speak. Won't take the weight of even a small train."

"Then the crawler's lost. Get the kak out of there!"

Anna tried to keep growing desperation out of her voice. It was Seth's call as the crew boss, and there would be hell to pay for the loss of the vehicle, but surely he knew a lost cause when he saw one. Sometimes you just had to hear the bleedin' obvious spoken aloud.

Through the binocs, she watched Seth gaze around. She could feel the anger and helplessness from here. He gave an exasperated hand signal and his crew started hitching up to a safety line.

Anna hurried back to her own crawler and clambered up outside ladders to the top of the cab. Along the way, she unclipped the end of a lightweight line from one of the cable drums mounted on the front, and kicked the clutch. The end of the line clipped to a heavy piton which she loaded into an airgun mounted on the roof.

She checked the line for snags, and aimed. Urgent squalls whipped at her jacket and tugged at the line. She blinked salt from her eyes, wishing she'd thought to pull on a sweatband when she hustled out of the cab, and adjusted for the wind howling across the ridge behind her.

The gun kicked. The line streamed out towards the four figures now struggling away from their doomed vehicle.

Anna tracked the line with a roof-mounted spotlight. It covered little more than half the distance, but would give the crew something to hold on to. Something connecting them to safety. If they made it that far.

She grabbed another piton and climbed back down. There was little she could do to help now, but she had no time for idleness. With a queasy feeling in the pit of her stomach she noted that the nearest wheels showed signs of settling. If she wasn't quick, she'd be in the same mess as Seth.

The piton sank most of its length into the ground without Anna even having to put her full weight on it. Kak! She picked up the slack line and threw a clove hitch over the protruding pole. Lucky it wouldn't need to hold much weight.

Back to the cab, Anna checked on the crew's progress towards the end of her safety line. She engaged the crawler's drive and reversed carefully up the ridge to firmer ground. The piton in the ground in front of her provided just enough hold to pay out more line from the drum as she reversed.

Through the equipment bay once more, it was times like this that Anna questioned her insistence on working without a crew. Times like this, extra pairs of hands and legs would make things so much easier.

Times like this happened once a season. The rest of the time, solitude helped Anna preserve her sanity.

She was strange like that.

This time she went out with a long spike, more pitons and guy lines, a hand-held pneumatic gun, and a low-power radio beacon. Under normal circumstances, she'd use a heavy pile driver to hammer the spike into the dense, woody shell that coated Sponge's planet-girdling network of structural veins. These were not normal circumstances. The pneumatic spike gun jerked in her hand as it pumped a circle of shorter pitons into the ground. She stood the spike in the middle and belayed it with a series of guy lines strung taut to the pitons. Not as secure, but, with luck, it would survive the standard-years-long night and allow them to locate the crawler when light returned to this hemisphere. Equipment was precious.

Beacon in place, with a note of direction and distance to Seth's crawler, Anna returned to where she had first stopped her own vehicle. She unhitched the line from the piton and, using a compact remote control panel on her lapel, started reeling in the slack.

The first of the crew was now only a hundred meters away, with the rest strung out at thirty meter intervals. They all seemed to be slogging through increasingly soft ground, sinking calf deep with each step. This was insane! This patch had been firm all season. Sponge was fickle, but Anna had never seen the surface rot away so fast.

A faint but ominous ripping sound caught her attention. She glanced up to see Seth's crawler sink up to its axles.

"Keep moving!" Seth roared from his position at the rear of the column.

The first man reached Anna, and unclipped himself. It was John, one of Seth's lead haulers. She jerked her head towards the piton at her feet. "Grab my gear and get it stowed away."

The next along–a woman, Anna saw, despite both their fogged-up masks from over-exertion–was sinking to her knees. "Hold tight!" Anna fed more power to the cable drum to haul on the line.

The woman stumbled a few more paces, then reached firmer ground. Anna reached out to help her, and noted she also had a control panel sewn into her jacket. Belatedly, Anna realized this was Sarah, Seth's driver. Good. "Patch yourself into my network and take over the drum controls. I'll keep both hands on the line."

Anna noticed she was now calf deep herself, and hastily backed up a few paces.

The line yanked almost out of her hands. The man in front of Seth disappeared. Seth cried out and leaned back to take the weight. Anna clipped herself onto the line and braced, sinking knee deep into the treacherous surface.

Seth crabbed sideways to skirt around the hole, keeping up tension on the line. "Ambrose! Can you hear me?"

A faint call that Anna took to be an affirmative.

Another ripping sound, this time deafening like a nearby electrical storm. Seth vanished with a yell. The line tightened.

Anna watched, helpless, as the surface disintegrated. A gaping chasm spread towards her faster than a man could run. The ground at her feet opened up and she fell into the depths.

A dizzying tumble. The air *whuffed* from Anna's lungs as the line halted her fall. The nightmare innards of Sponge flicked in and out of view in the beam of her strapped-on headlamp. A labyrinth of Byzantine columns in green and tan stretched into the distance, arching overhead. A strip of paler chocolate sky showed the gash that had opened up in the surface.

Below, the tangle of plant life seemed to writhe in the lamplight. Pure optical illusion. Nobody had ever *seen* Sponge move.

A wall of twisted trunks loomed close.

Thorns!

Anna stretched out her feet, aiming between the meter-long spikes but, spinning helplessly, any kind of aim was a forlorn hope. She let out a scream as a needle-sharp point pierced her left boot. She came to rest, her sleeve ripped by another gleaming tip.

While she panted through the pain, a bubbling scream from below was cut short with shocking abruptness.

Feebly, Anna tried to push against the trunk with her good foot to free herself from the spike, but she couldn't reach.

Through a haze of pain, she felt the line tug at her waist. A tiny spinning figure flashed into view sixty meters below. It looked like Seth had missed the deadly trunk and was starting his pendulum swing in the other direction.

The line hauled Anna away from the trunk. She caught a glimpse of a blood-slicked spike before she twisted free and into open air.

Don't be sick. Don't be sick. Don't be sick!

She spun in mid air, feeling faint. She was hallucinating, she was sure of it. Shock maybe? Some harvesters talked about poison down in the depths. Was that needle poisoned? Why would a single worldwide super-organism, a plant with no predators, need poison?

Why would it need thorns?

She swung back towards the trunk, too weak to do anything to protect herself, but the initial momentum of her fall had been damped by her impalement and release. The spikes menaced from a meter away before receding again.

Anna became aware of a dim glow in the depths. Bioluminescence. Some harvesters talked about that, too. A danger sign.

Lights moved in the depths, at least a kilometer down. Fuzzy, green and blue, like a colony of fireflies on the move.

Where did she read about fireflies? Something from Earth.

The surreal glow silhouetted an outlandish fractal of twisting stems and intertwined branches reaching towards her.

Her mind traced patterns in the shadows, inventing faces in the random light and dark.

Strong arms gripped her shoulders, and hauled her out onto firm ground.

Don't be sick. Not in your mask.

John helped her to her knees and gazed into her eyes. She gave him an 'all right' sign and he turned his attention back to the line.

With a shock, Anna saw he'd found both the time and secure enough footing to rig an A-frame and running tackle for the line over the lip of the chasm.

How long was I down there?

The next head appeared above ground, followed by a torn and bloody torso. Poor Ambrose. John tore off his gloves and felt for a pulse. He shook his head. Anna gagged and decided she was not as all right as she'd made out. She swallowed acid and staggered to her feet. They were still in grave danger and time was ticking. There was no place for *nutloos* lightweights out in the field.

At last, they brought Seth to the surface. Anna's knees weakened with relief to see him emerge unharmed.

They laid the A-frame flat and used it as a makeshift sled to haul Ambrose back to the crawler.

The sky was almost black overhead. The vanishing sun on the horizon lit the roiling underside of clouds in ruddy streaks between pools of ink. Fierce-driven gusts buffeted the high-sided crawler and the gale played a banshee shriek through gaps between machinery, nothing more than an overture of the ferocity to come. Vehicles were not designed for this kind of punishment.

By the time they'd brought Ambrose's body on board and cycled themselves through the airlock, the crawler was bucking under a relentless onslaught.

It would take two hours to reach home.

They didn't have two hours.

No words were needed, the looks between them said it all.

Anna beat her sluggish mind into gear. This was her vehicle, they were looking to her for leadership, and she was a karking surveyor, dammit! She knew this ground better than her own face.

Sheet lightning cracked the sky beyond the cab's panoramic windows. The concussion was immediate and deafening. It jarred Anna out of her torpor. "Only a klick or so." She pointed to the chart. "There's the North Seventeen outflow. I know that one. On the west side, the third guide vane out has enough flat ground in its lee for a small train." She clung to the console, too weak to step up into her seat.

"You can't drive, Anna." Seth's voice was kind but urgent. "And who the heck sets up their sanctum in the driver's seat?"

Sarah held back, eyeing Anna's personal items decorating the control panel. A manic giggle escaped her lips. Driving solo for so long it was something she'd never even thought about, but intruding uninvited into someone's private space was one of life's strongest taboos. With the last of her strength, Anna mumbled, "I welcome you, Sarah, as a friend. Welcome to my home. Welcome to my home. My space is yours. My friendship is yours. Treat this space as your home. Welcome to my home."

Even as Anna croaked out the last words of invitation, Sarah leaped into Anna's seat and began murmuring the starting ritual. Her fingers flew over the control panel, bringing the vehicle back to life. Despite the extreme urgency, their lives depended on a fully functioning vehicle.

Anna collapsed to the floor, dimly aware of arms helping her settle. She had just invited a newcomer into her personal sanctum. They were in a dire situation indeed.

Chapter 5

The translucent structure in front of Mikel glowed with an inner light, mesmerizing in its delicate intricacy. Horizontal and vertical pieces in green, tan, blue and silver, branched and interlocked in a three-dimensional web that covered most of a work table.

The model seemed to darken and thicken, gaining substance through a haze that blurred reality and imagination. *Not now! I'm nearly finished!* But Mikel knew there was nothing he could do but let the hallucination pass of its own accord. He clutched the edge of the table to stop the room from spinning. He released one hand to scratch at a ferocious itch deep under the skin of his other forearm. *Huh. That's new.*

The dizziness passed after a few moments and Mikel returned to his work. Just a few more pieces to go. He rummaged through the tray at his side. Frustration burned across his mind ... had someone been moving the pieces around again? He'd had everything ordered. Without familiar order, everything blurred into a confusing mess. It could take him hours to find what he was looking for amongst the myriad multicolored shapes.

He stopped and breathed like he'd been taught. In ... out ... calm. Patience. His gaze scanned the tray, front to back. Things came into sharper focus, recognizable again. He just needed to find ... *there!* A medium-bore aquifer cross-connector, mixed in with the vertical single-branching trunks. That's why he'd gotten confused. He must have knocked it out of place.

He slotted the last component into the model, massaging the smart plastic until it formed the right connections to its neighbors. He reached up and switched on an overhead sunlamp, shining it on one end of the model. Lights flowed in the depths. He moved the lamp to the other end, and the river of light did a complex turbulent dance before reversing direction.

Mikel glanced up, a sick uneasiness dispelling the glow of satisfaction brought on by the orchestrated light dance. He pushed it aside. Karin would be here. *Should be here by now, surely?* The room seemed unusually quiet. The quiet didn't bother him. It made it easier to concentrate without a lot of noise and bustle in the study room, but noise and bustle was *normal*. This quiet wasn't. Where had everyone gone? And where was Karin?

Fragments of memory intruded. Anna, telling him that Karin was leaving. *They were all leaving* ... that memory got quickly squelched with barely a thought. His mind shied away from dangerous territory and even the memory of that evasion disappeared along with ... where was he?

Karin.

Anna had said she wouldn't be here today, but that thought had been held in quarantine while Mikel worked out how to resolve the paradox. On the one hand, Anna was his mother and mothers always knew what was happening. But on the other hand, Karin *always* came for him. Mikel couldn't picture a world where she didn't. There were too many incomprehensible novelties to make any sense of it.

Now, faced with disturbing clues, it seemed like Anna may have been right all along. The implications threatened to drown him. His mind rebelled.

Karin would be here.

He turned back to the model on the table in front of him.

"Mikey, it's time to go." Senior Educator Georgina van Buren tried to keep the impatience out of her voice.

The construction on the table both fascinated and disturbed her in equal measure. The educational building kit was meant for much older students, a hands-on tool to model the intricacies of the Sponge super-organism.

Mikey had gone far beyond the standard models of known Sponge constructs, and was inventing novel configurations. But these creations seemed far from random. They were unknown, but oddly credible. That was the disturbing part.

Georgie shook her head and gave an anxious glance at the chronometer on the wall. "Mikey! Remember what Karin told you yesterday?" No reaction ... or was that a slight hunching of the shoulders? She tried again. "Karin isn't coming today. She's left. You're a big boy now and can make your own way home."

And I have my own last packing to do before we leave at daybreak tomorrow. She buried her impatience. The last of her family here was clearing out their quarters, collective possessions loaded into their assigned crawler and a family sanctum set up in one of the crew pods.

She cast an eye over Mikey's work. It would take her at least an hour to dismantle it all and pack the pieces away properly. A tote box of educational material lay open on the floor beside her, the last item she needed to account for and haul to the waiting crawler. There was plenty of room still in the top. Maybe she would just break it down far enough to fit, and sort it out properly on the way. Two weeks in the crowded confines of the crawler tested people's patience to the limit. Even minor distractions would be welcome.

Georgie wondered sometimes how much Mikey actually understood. Most of the time he seemed simple, and many people dismissed him far too readily. She knew better. He was just locked into his own world. Intelligent, beyond doubt. Maybe even beyond normal measure. What she questioned was how much of the real world intruded through his filters and made an impression on his inner state.

Mikey wasn't entirely unique. In her years educating the young, Georgie had seen more kids growing up unusually quiet, withdrawn. It took a while to notice, over passing decades, but eventually Georgie's curiosity won out. Patient research in the colony archives told an inconclusive but tantalizing tale. Something in the gene pool was setting the colonists on their own path, drifting away from old Earth norms.

It couldn't simply be inbreeding. The planet's population numbered near two million, and the planners ensured a slow but steady mingling of family lines with each trek across the equator. And yet, over the centuries the planet was making its mark. Their pale skin tones reflected a cloistered life behind domes and masks, and a faint blue tinge revealed subtle shifts in biochemistry as they slowly acclimatized to the native toxins that tainted even the best-filtered air. Along with that went an imperceptible drift towards insularity, with Mikey as an extreme example.

She made a note to talk to Anna about Mikey's future. He was at the age when young teens began vocational training. He would need to find a niche somewhere in Elysium society where he could make a contribution. Right now, she had no idea what that might be, but the planet couldn't support freeloaders.

Her tablet pinged. Georgie glanced at the screen and stiffened. There was trouble out in the field. It looked like she wouldn't be joining her own family tomorrow after all.

In the kind of circles Jennifer inhabited, official receptions on Earth were exquisite affairs. More for the benefit of the hosts than the guests supposedly being honored. Opportunities to be seen and to impress.

Yet, once again she was struck by the everyday lack of self-importance of the setting, the food, the clothing. Just like the conference hall where the negotiations were held, she got the disconcerting impression that the richness and gaiety on show this evening was nothing special, nothing more than these people would be putting on for their own benefit anyway.

She circulated, fielded questions about Earth, other colonies, and the latest shows from the entertainment channels. New releases, it seemed, took weeks to make their way to far-flung worlds like this.

As the official host this evening, her colonial counterpart Josiah Handel made introductions with relentless humor and cheer. Her personal aide, Nikolai Shevchenko, shadowed her. Reserved, discreet, observant, Nikolai would normally fade into the background poised to catch people in unguarded moments, filing away glances and expressions for later analysis. No chance of that here. The visitors were conspicuous among the deathly pale locals, who all looked like they'd just walked out of a deep freeze.

While she talked, she studied the people milling around her. The hall was ablaze with color, nothing at first glance too far different from events back home. But the impression was quickly dispelled on closer look. She guessed the company here was decked out in what passed for finery, but it would be grotesquely out of place on Earth. Foreign and quaint were the most charitable words that came to mind.

For starters, the color palette was too dark and bold for refined Earthly tastes. It favored deep blues, greens, earth colors and burgundys, eschewing pastels and metallic tones. At least the assembled guests had dropped the gaudy patchworks and patterns of their work and casual clothing. A primitive African/South American fusion, Jennifer thought sourly, with more than a touch of Viking.

And then, there was no sign of jewelry anywhere. Instead, it seemed that formal wear on Elysium demanded intricate embroidery in shimmering thread. A cold and calculating part of her admired the artistry. Just not the context. In Jennifer's view, as she gazed in polite attention at the vegetable grower in front of her waxing lyrical about hydroponics and cross-breeding programs, flamingos in flight had no business adorning a woman's chest.

Jennifer's own tailored suit, a deep bronze in color, plain and buttoned to the neck, probably appeared exotic in their eyes. Some of her retinue, decked in medals and awards, gold piping and glittering jewelry, came across as tacky in comparison.

Only her security detail, in uniform navy blue tunics and breeches, came close to blending in.

Loose-fitting cloaks, wraps and tunics obscured but never completely hid the ubiquitous bulges at hips where lightweight emergency masks sat.

Ever-attentive Josiah followed her line of sight. "Aye," he murmured, "even in here. You have to remember that this is an enclosed environment unlike any other. Normally, sealed habitats keep vacuum at bay. You get immediate warning of even the smallest hull breach. The shriek of wind whistling into vacuum is not something you ever forget."

Jennifer glanced down at him in surprise. When had *he* had the opportunity to travel off-planet?

"But," he continued, "Sponge is sly. A door could be left wide open to the outdoors, and—without the sensors and alarms, of course—the first you'd know is when you walked into a bubble of tainted air. You have scant seconds to get clean air into your lungs before the damage is irreversible."

Jennifer kept her expression neutral, wondering just how much he was joking. *Or*, a furtive voice whispered in the back of her mind, *was that a* threat?

He laughed and patted Jennifer's arm. "Come. Try some of our local delicacies."

She drifted after him, stopping for a word here, an introduction there. The reception, such as it was, centered in one of the community domes a few hundred meters from the conference hall, but the party seemed to have no clear boundaries, spilling into adjacent domes like an amoeba. After a few speeches of welcome to the Company and ENCOA representatives, with bland well wishes for a successful conclusion to the negotiations, people flowed back and forth. Conversation and laughter was loud and uninhibited, another jarring contrast to polite society.

In fact, the more Jennifer observed, the more it seemed like the Company delegation was little more than a pretext to party. On her forays between her team's quarters and the conference room over the last few days, there was an increasing undercurrent of excitement that was entirely private to Elysium, that had nothing to do with the Company at all. The shouts, the laughter, people greeting, were usually in the distance ... the far end of the hall, echoing from the next dome over ... but here it struck her full force. The city was celebrating some-thing big, and *she* was not the focus of attention. Not even slightly. She bristled at finding herself so much on the periphery, even in the midst of a vast crowd.

Granted, people nearby plied her with questions and listened politely when she spoke. She was accustomed to a constant press of people com-peting for her attention, but tonight there seemed to be unseen com-petition that she couldn't identify. More than once, people approached her circle and, instead of joining the throng, they spoke with suppressed excitement and drew a knot of people away with them.

This was unheard of.

She decided to test her impressions directly. In an unexpected lull, she caught up with Josiah. "I get the feeling there is more going on here beyond a welcoming reception."

Josiah had the good grace to flush slightly. "This was announced and planned as an honor for our Company guests, but given the timing I had little hope that would remain the focus."

"How so?"

"This is the time of the trek. Did you not realize? Whole townships are arriving from the northern towns. People are meeting up. In many cases families are reunited who haven't seen each other for six standard years."

Jennifer exchanged glances with Nikolai. They edged aside as a squadron of shrieking children flew past, arms wide, to surround an elderly couple.

"At this time of the season, even the smallest gathering is like a match to tinder. Clan quarters open up, and any gathering of more than a dozen is likely to explode into an all-night party that takes over the whole dome."

Jennifer eyed the movements of people with new insight. Knots coagulated, then moved as one to swallow new arrivals with new crescendos of joyful sound. Her head span. It was threatening to overwhelm her senses.

Josiah lowered his tone in mock conspiracy. "This is a sight few off-worlders are privileged to see."

At last, Jennifer found herself in a dead zone to one side of the hall. Josiah had vanished into the crowd.

Tables around the edge of the room bore an ever-changing spread of dishes. As one emptied, its place was taken by another in a seemingly random order. Soups and stews predominated, interspersed with aromatic rice, pulses, vegetables raw, steamed, and fried.

She took a bowl and lifted the lid of a tureen. A wash of cinnamon and ginger enveloped her. The creamy chowder—somehow seafood came to mind, even though Jennifer knew the local diet was exclusively vegetarian—must be popular. The tureen was fresh, still piping hot, but only a third full.

"That's my Gramma's recipe."

Jennifer stared down at a young boy smiling up at her.

"Really? Is your Gramma a caterer then?" She tried to match the urchin's smile.

"Huh?" He screwed up his face. "Nah, she drives the trains, but she's a *heerlijk* cook too!"

She stared after him as he scurried off into the crowds, feeling like she'd just missed an important clue about Elysium society.

Another oddity struck Jennifer full force as her security chief emerged with a relieved expression. The atmosphere was informal, people curious but at ease, and an unsettling absence of any kind of security other than Jennifer's own retinue surrounding her again with veiled belligerence. On the pretext of needing a break from the milling crush of bodies, she drifted towards the nearest entrance and out into the perimeter corridor.

In the few meters between the outer skin of the dome and the building behind her, couples and small groups of people meandered, chatted, greeted and hugged. Jennifer strolled casually, but her attention was focused on the entrance and the people coming and going.

She was used to being the guest of honor at receptions like these, recognized and admitted without hindrance, so the anomaly hadn't struck her at first. But for most people admission to an event like this was usually subject to fierce competition, wrangling, string-pulling, bribery and outright blackmail. Nobody got through the doors without strict identity checks and verification against the official guest list.

Here, people seemed to wander in without any kind of checks. There was no guest list. No security. She shuddered and sought to hide her confusion, and yet it seemed to fit with the anarchic society she'd glimpsed already.

She cast her gaze up, tracing the line of a massive structural rib arching above her, vanishing from view behind the lip of the building's roof.

"Most people take it for granted." A voice at her elbow startled Jennifer. She looked down to find a short, white-bearded man at her side also gazing up at the inside of the dome. "Quite the engineering marvel, though."

Jennifer flicked a glance at her security contingent closing in, and gave a tiny shake of her head. This man didn't appear threatening. "Most of this structure is made from local materials, I understand."

"Remarkable materials. We barely understand them, but we've learned how to use them." Jennifer was used to screening out sales pitches, the forced undertones of false belief. She could sniff out that falsehood in an instant, but her hackles didn't rise today. He sounded genuinely enthusiastic as he gestured to the polished rib. "Lightweight, but strong enough to hold up against thousand-kilometer-an-hour winds. Flexible to give just enough in gusts, but not too much. A lot of study went into these structures."

Jennifer recovered from her shock at being addressed as an equal. The man's utter lack of self-consciousness was disarming. It was also dangerous. She had to remember who she was. She was here to do a job, and these insights might prove valuable. Belatedly, she remembered the protocols that normally ruled her life. "My apologies. I believe introductions are in order." She held out a hand. "Jennifer Steel."

He glanced down at her outstretched hand but made no move to take it. "Frederik Johansen, habitat engineer."

Jennifer wondered if her briefing notes on accepted customs were leading her astray. She let her hand drop.

"And I know who you are." His eyes flashed, bonhomie gone. "You're the one trying to hold us back in the dark ages."

Chapter 6

It was only a short drive to the outflow, one of many broad pits pockmarking Sponge's surface, ringed by tall ridges that Anna hoped would shelter them from the swelling storm.

Ten minutes, battling against the elements. Rain lashed the wraparound windows of the cab in a thunderous torrent. Through the fog of pain, Anna fought repeated impulses to leap up and take back control of the crawler. Only Seth's soothing hands on her shoulders stopped her. "Sarah's a good driver," he murmured in her ear. "Dare I say it, almost as good as you? Rest a while. We'll need all hands shortly to secure the train."

She barely heard him. Lightning split the sky in a continuous barrage. Sarah hunched in the center seat, surrounded by glowing screens and drive controls, a picture of concentration.

Anna stretched out on the narrow strip of floor behind the row of three seats and consoles. Her hands tingled at the scratchy feel of the fibrous floor matting, woven from coarse Sponge flax. The tingle pulsed in time with the throbbing of her foot. While Seth cradled her head, John pulled off her work boot and dressed her foot. He patched her up as best he could, and pumped heavy duty meds to deal with shock and pain. Her body would pay the price later, if there *was* a later.

The sharp tang of antiseptic cut through the heavy cinnamon scent that pervaded her cab. Her thoughts drifted to the compact galley upstairs. She had guests for the night. What provisions did she have left? She normally kept a well-stocked larder for her weeks-long forays across the surface at the height of the season, but as the days shortened and the nights grew wild, field crews' travel radius shrank. It must have been a week since she last cooked herself a proper meal in here.

Ten minutes driving, then it took Sarah another ten to maneuver the vehicle around and reverse it as far as it would go into shelter.

Anna was barely aware of John rolling up her sleeve, and a tiny scratch on her arm.

The stimulants kicked in and she gasped. The world around her, the violently rocking cab, the howling strobing lightshow outside, came into sharp focus. She winced as she eased her boot back on, but at least the pain had dulled to a manageable nagging.

With Seth's help, Anna struggled to her feet. She clung to him a moment longer. "Be careful out there."

"I'll be on solid ground," he muttered. "Mind you don't get blown of the roof."

Anna limped up through the cramped living quarters and reached out of the top airlock. She clipped a safety line to the guardrail running around the roof of the cab. Most of the crawler's eighty-meter length nestled in the lee of the natural outcrop. Half of the first car, the forward yoop, and the drive cab bore the brunt of the gale. Icy droplets hammered her mask, running off and down her chest in a steady stream. Even as she grasped the stock of the heavy duty airgun, a damp chill seeped through the seams of her jacket.

John had the toughest job acting as go-between, clambering up and down the side of the drive cab, almost pinned in place by the battering-ram force of the wind. Anna took the belay lines he passed her, clipped them to pitons, and manned the rooftop gun. With John guiding her aim and checking for snags in the line, Anna fired anchoring pitons into the wrinkled face of the ridge.

She eyed her next target, straining to make out John's directions over the static of the line-of-sight radio. Blustering swirls of air tugged at the gun and the line. She braced herself in her safety harness and focused on a patch of the veined wall fifteen meters away. The material of Sponge was tricky. These guide ridges were formed from structural fibers, riddled with sinews too hard even for her tempered nickel-steel pitons to pierce. She aimed for the crevices between protruding veins, but even at this short range, the howling storm made it more luck than judgment.

"All clear," John yelled.

"Clear, aye." Anna fired. "Kak!" She ducked as the piton glanced off a strand as hard as steel and went clattering down the gully between ridge and crawler.

Wordlessly, John handed her the next line. The next piton held fast, and Seth and Sarah down below cranked the line tight to one of the many anchor points on the cab's side. Anna hit more often than she missed, and that was all anyone could ask for under the circumstances. With each line anchored, the cab's bucking motion lessened despite the ever growing ferocity of the night's storm. Anna shivered in the icy deluge. A river boiled around the silvery mesh of the seven-meter wheels.

At last, they judged they could do no more. The cab and leading car were anchored firmly against the night's rage, and they risked getting swept off their feet, with or without safety lines.

It was a soggy crush on the crew deck at the top of the cab. Four exhausted companions helped each other out of drenched clothing to be hung from a drying rack in the narrow galley.

"That was close." Sarah slumped onto the dinette bench next to the galley and ran her hands through sodden hair. "We owe you, Anna."

Anna eyed the door to the washroom where Seth had just disappeared from sight. As the host, she was last in line for the cab's one shower. The others had drawn lots for the privilege. She shook away the afterimage of Seth's hard-muscled back and rummaged in a locker for more towels.

A stab of pain from her foot drew a stifled gasp which Anna masked by tossing the towels onto the dining bench. "It's all part of life out in the field."

"True that." Sarah glanced at John. "And to think, you gave up the chance to fly free instead of slugging it out with us ground huggers."

John gave a sour smile. "Believe me, we're better off down here."

"Even with all the grunt work of lashing down a ground rig every night?"

"Even so." He caught his balance as a vicious gust rocked the cab, and gazed upwards as if studying the sky beyond the ceiling. "Up there, the dangers come with less warning and even less forgiveness."

"Besides," Anna added, "shuttle pilots get a spell of work once in a while when a longship comes calling, then what?"

"Exactly," said John. "Working in one of the big cities in between times? Not the life for me."

A steaming shower and dry clothes restored life to Anna's frozen limbs, and she wedged herself in the starboard navigation seat, feet propped on the console. She'd directed the others to the crew bunks in the living quarters upstairs, but she kept her own company in the comforting multi-hued twilight of the consoles.

She wondered how Mikey was coping. He was used to her being out in the field, and the extended family of the clan took care of domestic needs, but he was expecting her home tonight. Any departure from the expected upset him. He couldn't voice it, but she felt the pain in his eyes when his ordered world broke down. She ached to get a message to Serendipity. They'd tried, of course. They were still cut off. Alongside the driver's seat, the *nutloos* radio hissed and spluttered softly to Sponge's electrical tantrum.

As she tried to arrange herself more comfortably, seeking an angle that would lessen the throbbing in her freshly-bandaged foot, a cold spasm wracked her. In the midst of the blustering hurricane still trying to rip the crawler free from its restraints, the enormity of their situation hit her. A man lay dead in the storage bay beneath her and they were lucky it hadn't been worse. They had all come close to losing their lives and they were still in a precarious position.

The others should have been lost along with their crawler, victims of Sponge's fractious nature, but *she* had put herself in harm's way. The decision had been instinctive, unquestioning, and although some high-and-mighty bureaucrats might disagree, *she* knew it had been the right thing to do. Even if it hadn't been Seth and his crew, she'd have done the same. But what would happen to Mikey if she didn't come back?

She pushed those dark thoughts away. As she'd said to Sarah, it was a part of life in the field. Nothing out here was certain. They relied for survival on themselves, their equipment, and deeply-entrenched procedures.

The hours of darkness ticked by. Through a fitful doze she was dimly aware of the wind slackening off.

Seth shook her awake and handed her a steaming mug of sweet char. For a moment, a sense of unreality gripped her. The absurdly domestic scene felt like a dream, Seth smiling down at her, smooth skin crinkling around eyes that appeared black in the dim nightlight.

Burning fingers broke the spell. She had no idea when she'd finally fallen asleep, but it was still dark outside. Anna smiled her thanks and set the mug aside.

"Two hours to dawn," he said. "We need to loosen off the anchors and retrieve as many pitons as we can."

Back to business. Safe territory. She pulled her boots on, gritting her teeth against a fresh stab of pain. She took an invigorating slurp of char while Seth's words seemed to dance over and over through her sleep-fuzzed mind. She'd heard some of the engineers over at Jorvick were always looking at new ways to use the materials plundered from Sponge's depths. Surely something as simple and commonplace as pitons could be fashioned from the rib material rather than from precious imported metal?

But pending engineering miracles, they needed to salvage as much as they could under the crawler's floodlights. Her heavy jacket had mostly dried out in the warmth of the galley. She shrugged into it and hobbled up to the roof.

Anna drove the cargo crane with John dangling from a safety harness. Poor John! It seemed he was always slated for the heavy work. Anna was as gentle with him as she could be, following slackened-off lines up to their buried pitons and bringing him close to the ridge face. There, feet braced against the ridge, he swung a heavy mallet to loosen the piton from Sponge's grip.

One by one they succumbed while Seth and Sarah gathered and stowed the equipment.

Sweat sheened John's face by the time they were done. Anna, on the other hand, had to massage life into numbed fingers and she lost all sensation from the waist down in the icy pre-dawn.

With the vanishing storm, the blanket of static had lifted too. As soon as they were underway, Seth hailed Serendipity and reported the mixed news. Relief at their survival was muted by the loss of Ambrose and the crawler. Regardless of the human cost, when the time of reckoning came between the town's planners and the Company accountants, the equipment would weigh heavy on their minds.

Thankfully, that was not Anna's department.

John inspected the dressing on Anna's foot and applied a potent balm of analgesics and antiseptics from the medical kit. He re-bound the foot and Anna grimaced as she worked it back into her boot.

She gestured to the punctured boot. "Shame work gear doesn't repair itself like people." John grinned up at her, and packed supplies carefully back into the medical kit.

As the domes of Serendipity appeared in the distance, sheltered in a hollow between two steep ridges, Sarah halted the crawler and climbed down from the driver's seat. "If you're up to it, you should do the honors."

Anna tested her weight on her injured foot, and took her seat with a grateful smile. She stretched and flexed her fingers across the controls. "Serendipity Control, this is Charlie Tango seven niner, coming in to dock."

"Hello Anna, this is Serendipity Control, we have you on visuals. Welcome home." A pause. "Reverse into South Two, lock beta. The rest of your train is lined up ready for you."

"South Two beta, aye. Reversing to hitch, aye. Pass the word to the ground crew, I'm coming in. Charlie Tango seven niner out."

Anna drove past the outskirts of town to the row of southern garages, and brought the crawler around in a wide arc, lining the rear car up with one of the massive vehicle tunnels. She switched the crawler into reverse drive, concentrating now on the screens around her. Checking the crosshairs of the rear camera she huffed to herself. A meter and a half off center. She ascribed that margin of error to the drugs and hoped Sarah hadn't noticed. A twitch of the master joystick adjusted her line as she eased the vehicle back. With only a meter clearance either side through the lock tunnel, too little for even a small course correction once she was committed, she had to be spot on or she'd have to pull forward and try again.

She swore she'd never live down the humiliation if that happened.

As the wheels of the rearmost yoop nudged their way into the lock, Anna checked her readouts. Ten centimeters off center. She could live with that, especially as her line was plumb straight. This kind of maneuver would be impossible under solely manual control, but the drive computer fed commands to each of the drive wheels to keep the bulky vehicle on course.

Heavy strips of fibrous hangings guarded the entrance and brushed over the roof as the crawler eased its way down the tunnel. Three sets of hangings, and a slight overpressure inside the garage itself, kept the outside atmosphere at bay with little leakage while vehicles maneuvered in or out.

The camera brushed past the inner curtain and Anna paused to locate the head of the waiting train a hundred meters back. A small garage crew was already assembling alongside, ready to help hitch her up.

A flood of relief swept through Anna, momentarily overwhelming the fatigue. She was home.

Chapter 7

Mikel arranged a meticulous wall of crisp fries, corralling a spoonful of mushroom stew. A small heap of green salad stood guard to one side. The trick was to eat the innermost fries before they got too soggy, and rearrange the circle before the stew leaked out onto the rest of the plate. Mushroom stew and green salad didn't mix. Mikel couldn't explain why, it was just one of those *unhappy* combinations that he avoided at all costs.

Like the school room, the clan dining room was unusually quiet. The adults' voices were odd today. They talked in hushed tones about someone called Ambrose. Something bad happened. When he looked close, there was a trail of damp down Anna's cheek and a strange catch in her voice. He tried to ignore it. Wishing it away. *Anna was crying.* The strangeness stabbed deep into his mind. Children cried. Anna didn't. Anna was strong. It would be okay.

Mikel had no idea who Ambrose was. Maybe he'd met him, maybe he hadn't. Grown ups all looked the same, apart from a few that he knew well, so the talk was not relevant. Not interesting.

Memories crept cautiously to the fore, memories of pain and panic that he'd kept safely tucked away since he was young. It was happening again. Anna hadn't come home last night. That wasn't unusual, except that she was supposed to be here. Instead, Georgina had brought him home and looked after him. Georgina, not Karin. Too much happening that shouldn't be happening.

Last night, long after lights out, Mikel had crept into the family room and spent hours on a tablet trawling the town library, trying to make sense of what was going on. Something in conversations around him had given him a starting point.

The trek.

Of course, he knew all about orbital mechanics. The world–*his* world–spinning on its side, one pole facing the sun, then the other.

Orbital period thirteen Earth standard years, axial rotation thirty Earth standard hours. Odd. Clocks were set to the Elysium day/night cycle, and yet the calendar was tied to Earth standard. When people talked about a year they meant an Earth year, not Elysium. Why the inconsistency? An anomaly, but not interesting enough to pursue right now.

Here was the relevant bit. People on the surface forever chasing summer, escaping the deep freeze that came with long years of darkness at this latitude. Hence the trek. The migration from autumn in one hemisphere to spring in the other, then back again after another six years.

It made logical sense, but Mikel baulked at the implications. Leaving his home. Leaving familiarity and security behind. On an intellectual level, he could understand the idea of other towns, other domes with other rooms, but he couldn't *picture* it. Couldn't place *himself* there. His home was *here*.

This was what he'd locked away. This had happened before. He was fourteen years old now. Earth standard years, that is. He would have been maybe eight then. It figured. He couldn't remember much from then, but the terror had been real enough to leave its mark.

The conversation around him seemed to have moved away from Ambrose, away from things that made his mother cry. Back to the trek. The terrifying *unknown* reached out to engulf Mikel, but he needed to listen, to learn how to deal with this impossible threat to his stable life.

"The Company will send new equipment."

That was Georgina. She always seemed to *know* a lot of things Mikel didn't, but then she was so slow at seeing the connections between the things she knew. Once he had the facts, Mikel was always faster at solving problems and drawing conclusions than Georgina. That troubled him, too. Teenagers weren't supposed to be better than grown ups.

"It's hell trying to get even a handful of spares to keep things running, but they always seem happy to replace whole units when they finally fall apart."

Another anomaly. Somehow this one seemed important, but Mikel couldn't see where it fit into the pattern of life, home, and safety. *Why is it easier to replace a whole rather than a part?*

"Sure," Nick snorted. "Once we've completed a meter-thick wad of loss claims paperwork."

"At least that'll be easy this time," Georgina added. "It may be hard proving a unit sitting in the garage can't be patched up any more, but one that's lost below the surface must be a bit of a no-brainer."

"Actually," Anna seemed hesitant. More strangeness. "It was still on the surface when we left it. Kinda. Will that be a problem?"

Nick closed his eyes briefly. "We'll be careful what we state in the reports. It's lost to us for the coming season. Leave it at that. Once we've done the paperwork right, they're happy to send a replacement. I think the loss claim allows them to set it off against tax or something."

Mikel filed the strange words away for future reference. Here was a whole world of connections, causes and effects, that seemed to hover on the edge of understanding.

"What they don't tell you," Nick continued bleakly, "is the cost of shipping new units out here."

Anna stared at him. "Then why not simply ship the parts we need to keep things running? I know nothing about costs, but even I can see that a few crates of spares is smaller and lighter than a whole car or yoop."

Nick grinned. Mikel had trouble working out expressions, their range and subtlety confused him, but some screamed loud and clear out of the background clutter. Nick's grin held no amusement, it was pure animal ferocity. Mikel winced. Neither Anna nor Georgina seemed to have noticed the feral threat Nick suddenly seemed to pose. "And yet, their shipping rates always seem to rise for anything useful. Or, as they put it, they give us a *special discount*"–those words were spat like a curse– "for something as vital as a replacement car. But that's another purpose for the paperwork. To avoid us abusing their generosity, as they put it."

"Rather than letting things fail, isn't it in their interests to give that special rate for the occasional crate of spares instead? Surely it must make more sense for them?"

Georgina sighed. "You should have paid more attention to your social and politics lessons, Anna. The shipping doesn't cost the *Company* anything."

"It's all part of our colonial agreement." The animal had vanished from Nick's face. He just looked like a tired old man again. "Everything they ship us gets charged against our colonial debt."

"So if we're paying the cost anyway, why is everything so difficult?"

Connections clicked. *It's not easier to replace a whole unit. It's more beneficial to the Company to keep things run down! Why?*

———•◦•———

Anna settled Mikey into bed and returned to the dining area. Most of the few remaining people had left for their family quarters. One of the clan's caterers busied himself at the far end of the table, clearing the remaining scraps and dishes.

Georgie made her excuses, but Nick was still seated, picking at his teeth. It looked like he had something more serious on his mind.

"We're a drive cab short now," he muttered. "Anna, apart from the final shut-down crew at North One, the last four trains are lined up in South One and Two. What'll it take to shuffle things around?"

Aah! And as the senior padre left on site, it was up to Nick to clear them all out before travel became impossible. Anna's thoughts went back Ambrose, hauled torn and bloody from the depths. She'd not known Ambrose well, but knew his clan would mourn him in the proper time. Meanwhile, Sponge had many ways of dealing out death, and could yet claim the last few hundred townsfolk if they didn't make tracks soon.

She'd felt the squalls in the air in recent weeks, a heaviness in the light. A sense of unease, as though the whole planet was taking a deep breath before shrugging its cloak into a more comfortable position. She'd never known the town work so late into the deepening nights. They were cutting it fine and Nick was looking to her to work things out. Her supper sat like lead in her stomach.

"We're lucky the last ones out are usually the shortest." Anna did the math. "They're, what, fifteen, sixteen cars each?"

Nick nodded. He was the planner and more on top of logistics. Anna just drove what she was given to drive.

"So that means splitting Seth's train up three ways, adding an extra five or six cars to each of the others." She sucked on her teeth. "That's manageable. We won't be able to push the speed on the road, but I don't see a big problem. There'll just be some futzing around to get them all hooked up. We'll have to bring them in one at a time alongside Seth's and shift the cars over. That's a long train to maneuver into the garage. Two days total, maybe three."

Nick frowned. "That's one helluva wait. And when we set off we can't lose much daylight or we'll never reach the first way station before dusk. So eating even a few hours into the next day it may as well be a full day."

Anna pondered. She'd started off with the simplest option just to give it a try. Surely the town planners had left some contingency in their calculations? Would a day or two really matter that much? But she knew the answer to that. The atmospheric violence to come was not predictable down to a day, or even a week. The only certainty was that it *would* come, and they had better be hunkered down in Laverne on the equator when it did.

She was too darned tired to give it much thought tonight. Since the rescue yesterday and a night out in the storms that marked the turning of the season, she'd had precious little rest. After docking her crawler, she'd gone over it with one of the maintenance crews. Her jaunt through that forest had been rough on the cab front and the leading drive wheels.

There had been questions to answer and reports to fill out. She might yet get reprimanded for risking her crawler going after Seth, but she *had* returned in one piece, with three people who would otherwise have been lost. The junior cleric writing up the incident report was from Ambrose's clan. His red-rimmed eyes spoke of loss and his demeanor showed gratitude that things hadn't been worse. Even so, right here and now, he was more worried about how to explain the loss of a crawler. The Company liked to assign blame and Seth was in the firing line. Anna gave her best surveyor's assessment of the unavoidable risks out in the field at this time of year. Subtext: don't be so karking greedy next season.

She didn't mention the forest to the cleric. That might have been a risk too far for him to swallow. She *had* mentioned it to the maintenance crew, but they wouldn't tell on her. She was paranoid about the state of her vehicle, especially with the trek ahead of her. Inspections and diagnostics took the rest of the afternoon before she was satisfied that no damage had been done.

A thought struck Anna. They were about to abandon the town to the long dark. This went against normal practice, but worth a shot ... "I guess we're not worried about a bit of atmosphere leakage now, are we? I can back a train just part of the way in. Leave it sticking out the lock while we tag on the extra cars. A lot easier than trying to wind a fifteen-car train all the way inside."

Nick shrugged. "Air's not a problem. Time is. Even if it's only a few hours I'll take it."

"And," Anna brightened at a sudden thought, "if we're not filling the whole garage we can use both locks and do two at a time."

"Talk to the other drivers and garage crews. Storms are bad enough already, we don't want to be out in the open when the weather shift hits for real."

Anna was about to heave herself out of her seat, but something in Nick's words held her back. She squinted at him, beating her fuddled brain to tease out something that didn't quite ring true. "I know we've been working late into the season this time. The ground's got dicey as kak and the winds whip up at night so crawlers can't stay out in the field, but surely the big shift must be weeks off yet. That's what the forecasters in the field office were saying last week. Is a day or two now really that big a deal?"

Nick looked shifty. "The forecasts aren't that precise on timing, but we know damned well what's coming. There's a shedload of heat being shunted around the globe. Two months while the surface air flows flip from summer to autumn patterns. We can't chance a crawler even in daytime in the middle of *that*. We've chewed up enough contingency already. Not a chance I want to take."

His tone was earnest. Too earnest.

"Don't play coy. There's something else on your mind." Anna's voice was stern, the same tone she'd used all too often with Mikey.

Nick puffed his cheeks and stared at the ceiling. "Okay. I don't expect you to understand, but here goes. The weather's serious, and it scares the kak out of me, but I'm also anxious to get to Laverne and tune in to the news from Jorvick."

Light glimmered. "Those Company suits? Really?" But then, Nick was one of the town's padres, quite high up in the planner/cleric guild. They were the ones who had to deal with the Company.

His face reddened. "The negotiations are well under way and could be over by the time we reach Laverne. The whole guild's talking about it. There are reps from all the cities and most of the town clans. Not all

taking part," he hastened to add, "but there in Jorvick to see the proceedings first hand."

Anna had never seen Nick so excited about something. It all seemed
remote and unreal to her. Talks about how the world would be run
for the next fifty or a hundred years. Whatever happened, whatever
was agreed between the planners and the suits, *they'd* still trek back
and forth across the equator every six-and-a-half Earth standard years.
Anna and her colleagues would survey the thawing surface, marking
safe routes and promising sites for the harvest crews. The most valuable
products from Sponge came from the depths and had to be sought out,
using clues from the surface features.

The worlds beyond still clamored for the drugs and medicines that
Sponge's unique biochemistry yielded. And the people here had shelter,
food, water, and power. None of that would change. What was there to
talk about?

She tried to fake an interest in Nick's words, but her half-hearted
efforts weren't fooling anyone.

"I said you wouldn't understand." He sighed. "I have to keep reminding myself that money is such a foreign idea to most of our people. I don't
think you get just how important these talks are."

Anna shrugged. "I can see they're important to you. I just don't get
what difference they'll make. But that's why we got clever bunnies like
you to do the worryin' for us." She gave Nick a playful punch on the
shoulder.

Nick winced. "Independence opens up a lot of doors. Other com-
panies would be able to compete for business. We'd hold on to our own
profits and not be trapped into a corporate monopoly."

"All this money talk, it just seems like a load of trouble. What good
is it? It never made any sense to me in school, and it sure as heck never
made any sense since."

"It's how things work off-world. Especially Earth." He chewed his
cheek. "Think about this, then. One of these days, we might be able to
get the equipment we need, when we need it, without getting stiffed at
every turn."

"Okay." Anna managed a weak grin as she hauled herself upright.
"Now *that* I can understand!"

Chapter 8

Anna hobbled through the cavernous South One vehicle garage alongside Sarah, and surveyed the driverless train that should have had Seth's vehicle attached to the front. Cargo pods and a few crew cars towered twelve or more meters high, alternating with massive pairs of drive wheels of the universal power units.

Stopping near the center of the garage, Anna turned slowly, assessing the logistics of the task ahead. Broad columns forty meters apart supported an upper deck where spare cars were stored. That would be empty now. Every serviceable unit would be needed in the southern hemisphere for the next season–another six long years of toil.

Rows of bright lights overhead dispelled shadows and picked out vibrant colors against the stark white of the ceiling. Pale blue crossbeams fanned out from the columns, and were eclipsed by neon red, green, and purple signs showing locations of exits, medical stations, and emergency kit lockers.

Dominating all were the vehicles themselves. Fluorescent yellow panels soared above her, stenciled in olive green with designations and serial numbers, directions to hatches and locks, ladders and emergency access points, and belay points. Silvery sprung mesh of the broad wheels counterpointed the yellow.

The functional setting felt cold and industrial to some. To Anna it was as much home as the solitude of her cab.

The headless train started some way back from the twin vehicle tunnels, intended to leave room for Seth's small train to reverse fully into the garage and hitch up. It wound between the columns and wrapped its tail end along the far wall of the garage over a hundred meters away.

Another complete train on the other side doubled back on itself and dominated the remaining space. "This is Gorge's, isn't it?"

Without waiting for an answer, Anna continued walking, studying the way the cars were positioned. "That's wound karking tight around that far column."

Sarah pursed her lips and nodded.

"I can see three ways of doing this. We can add on to Gorge's train right here, in situ."

"Not much room to maneuver," said Sarah with a glance over her shoulder towards the end of the garage. "We'll have to unhitch a car at a time and haul it around. Takes time."

Anna was already running the math in her head. Hitching and unhitching took about an hour each time, with all the futzing around with umbilical connections and safety checks. The less of that they had to do, the better.

"Plus, that gives Gorge one helluva long train to unwind through that tight turn and out through the lock."

Good point. "Better options are for him to drive most of the way out, and we'll have room to bring cars across in pairs at least, rather than singly."

"Or," said Sarah, "drive all the way out the right lock, then reverse through the left and marry up directly. Drop the hitch five or six cars back, and you're done."

"More driving, but less hitching." Anna gave Sarah an appraising stare. She'd already reached the same conclusion. Her thinking was sound, but Sarah's tone of voice told Anna her heart wasn't in it.

"Here we are talking about breaking up your train. It must be hard on you. Are you sure you want to be here?" Her stomach lurched. "You already moved your sanctum into that crew car, didn't you?"

Sarah nodded. "My personal estate was in there ready for the trek. Figured I'd get all my packing done before our final run, knowing we'd be on a tight schedule when we got back. All gone now. I can only thank the eternal skies the rest of my family hadn't yet moved anything in."

"What were you working on?"

"Tableware, mostly. I've spent the last eight years practicing my carving skills. Informal items, mostly ..."

The catch in her voice said there was more. Something more personal. Anna stopped and put her hand on Sarah's arm. Sarah shuddered and stood, facing away. For a moment, Anna wondered if she'd misjudged. When Sarah turned, her face was a mask of despondency. "Before she died, my Nana gifted me a table set. That's what got me interested in my own carving, but I'll never match her talent. That set was her life's work. A real family treasure."

Anna gave Sarah a deep hug. "Tell me about it."

"A full formal eighty piece set. Plates, bowls, mugs and goblets, serving platters ... all hand-carved from core knotwood."

Anna whistled. Of all the materials to come from Sponge's depths, core knotwood was the hardest and most durable. The finest of carved detail would withstand decades of hard wear. Handled with care, it could pass through countless generations. Core knotwood was notoriously a bitch to carve.

"You should have seen the grain patterns in the surface when it was polished up." Sarah grunted. "I was looking forward to handing it on to my own children one day."

"Look, I anchored a beacon on the hard ridge. That should survive the winter. We might be able to salvage the crawler next season."

"If Sponge doesn't take it in the meantime."

"The Deep gives and takes in equal measure," Anna muttered. Sarah's shoulders sagged. Anna chewed her lip, wondering what had brought that trite saying to mind. There had to be more comfort she could offer. "You are already welcome in my home, Sarah Miller. Please ride with me."

"I'd be an intrusion."

"No, honestly–"

"Anna, you drive solo. It's well known. You've been a loner since Luuk. Could you really put up with another sharing your cab?"

Good question. Could she? Never mind the hundreds of other people she'd be carrying, they'd be spread out over the train's half-kilometer length, but the drive cab up front was her domain, her sanctuary. And there would be several cargo cars between her and the nearest crew car. She'd planned on being undisturbed for most of the trip, just her and Mikey.

Anna caught an appraising look in Sarah's eyes, and realized Sarah had misinterpreted her hesitation. The question hadn't come up yet, but did Sarah think Anna had already asked Seth to join her?

Her stomach lurched. Yes, she did enjoy Seth's company. Maybe too much, that was the trouble. But since Luuk's death she'd been wary of getting too close to anyone, especially not to another field worker. And what if Seth asked to accompany her? She could hardly turn him down. Maybe more company, not less, would keep her safe from temptation.

The three thousand kilometer trek to Laverne on the equator would take fifteen days. There would be a few weeks of traditional celebrations in the big city as clans from several towns converged, swapped news, swapped brides and bridegrooms. That would be enough breathing room before the onward trek deep into the south. Yes, she could do this.

Before Anna could phrase a convincing reply, Sarah stiffened and pulled away. Under her breath she said, "Here comes Gorge and Gerard. Tread careful, Anna, Ambrose was Gorge's brother."

Oh kak! Ambrose *Mandel*? Anna had barely known Ambrose, hadn't made the connection, but she knew Gorge. He was a surly bugger. Touchy. Unpredictable. Although drivers on the whole formed something of an elite club in Elysium society, as a matter of choice Anna had had little to do with Gorge.

Gerard van Leuven, the remaining lead driver looked like he could have been Gorge's son, with a similar lanky frame and long dark hair, but as far as Anna knew there was no close family connection. Thankfully, his manner was day to Gorge's night.

She smiled a greeting to Gerard, then bobbed her head to Gorge and pressed her palms together in a sign of solidarity. "I didn't know Ambrose well, but my tears go with him to the Deep."

Gorge grunted and scowled. He turned away as a skeleton crew of garage mechanics gathered around them. Anna thought back to the day she'd lost Luuk, remembering how she'd felt back then, trying to imagine what would have helped her through that time. There was nothing, but her words seemed so empty. She struggled to bring some words of comfort, but Sarah placed a hand on her arm with a small shake of her head.

Anna let Sarah outline their thoughts to Gorge and the garage crew. After a few questions and nods of assent, Gorge strode off towards his cab. "Let's get this done then."

Anna and Sarah took themselves out of the way, leaning against one of the pillars supporting the upper deck. A working garage with heavy vehicles on the move was no place for stray onlookers. A series of muffled clunks punctuated a chorus of soft whines as vehicle segments came alive. The garage boss stood in the center, muttering into a microphone and flashing hand signals to his crews. One crew stood ready at the head of Sarah's cableless train, while another busied themselves a few cars back.

"I meant what I said, Sarah. I'd be honored if you'd ride with me." Anna shifted her weight to ease the throbbing in her injured foot. "This is going to be a tough drive, and I'd feel a lot happier knowing I have a first class relief driver. Someone I know will take good care of my rig."

Sarah stared into the distance. She seemed not to have heard Anna.

A low rumble filled the air, reverberating off the garage walls. "Skies above," Anna murmured, "that was quick."

"Gorge probably did most of his startup checks last night."

They exchanged glances. No matter what you checked previously, you always went through the full procedure before setting a rig in motion. At least Anna did. From the twist of Sarah's lips she reckoned she was in like-minded company.

Starting with a barely perceptible motion, the crawler picked up to a slow walking pace. Anna glanced over her shoulder, watching the stately procession of cars around the far column. Whoever had hitched up those last few cars had left precious little room for error.

"Relax," Sarah said. "He may skimp a little on the paranoid belt-and-braces stuff, but he's a careful driver."

Even so, it was only once the back of the train cleared the column that Anna felt the tension ease out of her shoulders. "I guess I'd better go start on my own checks."

When Sarah didn't answer, Anna heaved herself upright and placed her hands on Sarah's shoulders. "You coming or not?"

A few seconds' pause, then Sarah nodded. "Sure. And ... thanks."

A thin transparent face mask dangled around Simon Galloway's neck, the flexible edge seal and straps worn and dulled with use. Its unadorned, workaday appearance clashed with Galloway's midnight blue overcoat, lavishly embroidered, and silk collar peeping above the lapels. And yet, he seemed perfectly at ease with the workman's accessory, somehow turning it into a fashion statement. His long bleached hair was tied back in a severe ponytail. Pale eyes regarded Jennifer Steel with faint amusement.

Jennifer turned and paced the narrow catwalk. Her footsteps clacked on the textured floor. Galloway followed, a silent shadow.

Floor-to-ceiling polyglass separated the observation gallery from the bright-lit hangar stretching to gaping doors in the distance. Harsh metallic light streamed through the opening. Masked maintenance workers bustled around the small fleet of scramjets crowding the expanse of floor, unhitching pipes, slamming hatches, all very industrious.

When she judged they were far enough from their small retinue of Company staff and local guides to guarantee privacy, Jennifer leaned on the handrail running the length of the catwalk. She studied the activity below for a few moments. Figures clad in grease-stained overalls, many open to the waist in the oppressive heat to reveal bright-patterned civilian clothing, danced a mesmerizing kaleidoscope of color against the grey floor. The scene could have been a work site on any of the habitable worlds. Only the ubiquitous face masks hinted at the poisons lacing the air the other side of the polyglass.

Goosebumps pricked Jennifer's forearms, despite the heat. "You'd hardly think those people were all part-timers, pulled in here from the factories to service our fleet."

"Inefficient to keep a permanent airfield staff," Galloway murmured at her side. "It'll be over a year before the next longship passes by this way. Of course, the midsummer months would see this place heaving, supplies dropped, harvest carried away. Then, I understand, they practically shut down the factories to man the airfields." He sniffed. "Feast and famine. What a way to live."

"The locals would call it seasonal variation. They adapt."

"I'm happy to call it an advantage we can exploit."

His smug tone grated on Jennifer. She waited, but it seemed Galloway was in no hurry to explain. Or maybe he was teasing her, testing her. In the labyrinthine Company politics, knowledge was power. Admitting ignorance was a weakness. She resisted the urge to show her irritation and turned her attention back to the hangar floor.

Among the retreating ground crews, a growing trickle of Company people made their way out to the waiting aircraft. They were marked out by their Company green jackets and overalls as much as by the varied skin hues peeping through their masks, a familiar palette of tones next to the anemic pallor of the locals. A mix of flight technicians, pilots, and desk jockeys. A crew of administrators to audit the Company's assets while the negotiations played out.

More pieces of Galloway's puzzle clicked into place. An audit right now had made no sense to Jennifer when she was preparing her team for their own delicate work. She'd argued long and hard with the President about the optics of it, and the risks of antagonizing the locals when they needed to lull them with sweet talk. No wonder her opposition had fallen on deaf ears. A large-scale audit across eighteen equatorial cities would mean a lot of air movement. The dozen craft hopping from city to city would provide essential cover for Galloway's own movements.

"Clever," Jennifer muttered. "With no regular air traffic, and no local control facilities, all flights on this planet are the responsibility of the visiting longships. Your own flight plans would never be seen by the local authorities, but vapor trails in the sky might be noticed."

"A near certainty with the seasonal trek under way, and cause for comment, unless they're expected."

Was that a hint of disappointment in his voice? "I see your personal jet down there. That's hardly going to be suitable for your mission."

"I have a couple of specialized craft waiting on the longship. They and most of my technicians will join us directly from orbit."

"So, the colonists have tabled their deal that would set them free, the one we can work with to gain clear and sole title to any new discoveries." Jennifer sniffed. She'd already sent Nikolai to make discreet inquiries into that. Why hadn't Kyari told her about this alternative deal? "I'll make sure the terms are broad enough to cover your findings, no matter how they try to categorize them."

"Likely pharmaceuticals, but they might try to class the discovery as technology."

Jennifer raised an eyebrow. "It's a drug."

"It's specific to space travel. A radical advance in buffering the mind against prolonged wormhole travel."

"Fair point. Broad it is. And if you fail—"

"If the results prove negative," Galloway interrupted.

Jennifer allowed herself a small smile. "We steer them down the traditional path with the most favorable terms I can wring out of them."
She teased out a thought that had been at the back of her mind. "In
your best estimation, what's the likelihood of finding what you're looking for?"

"We have strong evidence already, but those results could have been
faked, or mistaken."

"For something this big, we need certainty."

Galloway nodded. "I need to see the chemical signatures for myself,
from samples my own crew has collected from the plant mass. Then I'll
send you the arranged message to guide your course."

Multicolored lights glinted off Sarah's eyes in the cozy haven of
Anna's cab. She habitually kept the interior lights dimmed while driving. Beyond the cab windows, the garage was a blaze of light but eerily
quiet. All the activity was going on next door in South One.

To Anna's left, Gerard's cab was fully lit. Through the windows she
could see Gerard and his crew readying their vehicle. They were all
waiting for Gorge to finish hitching up, then Anna and finally Gerard
would pick up their extra cars.

Minutes ticked by. She wondered which of the three trains Seth
would be on. Maybe he had a bunk assigned in one of the crew cars,
but it was anyone's guess which train that had been added to. She'd
meant to ask him last night, but somewhere in all yesterday's frenetic
activity, he must have left to rejoin his own clan. And she'd been too
busy with her own preparations to notice. And he hadn't broached the
subject with her, either. She swallowed against an unexpected pang at
the thought. Seth was his own man, he didn't owe her anything.

Surely Gorge must be in position by now. Anna had completed her
own vehicle checks and had been ready to move for twenty minutes.
Sarah's half-hearted attempts at conversation faltered into awkward
silence and the tension grew.

Finally, Anna thumbed the radio to life and hailed the field control
office. "Hey, Control, don't want to bug South One ground crew, but any
idea what's up? I'm ready to roll but the silence over there is deafening."

"Hold tight, Anna, they're working through a teensy tech snafu." A few seconds' pause. "Will see what I can find out."

More minutes passed. Anna exchanged a flicker of a smile with Sarah. The radio spluttered to life again. "So, they burned out two power couplings trying to hitch up. Something in the rear hitch is futzed. It was already on the snag list, that's why they put that car at the tail end originally ... wasn't meant to have anything else attached. The techs are tracing the fault and they sent the crew scavenging for a spare coupling."

"Skies above, Control, can't they cut that car off the end and tag it onto the back of the next train? We're burning daylight here."

The radio went silent. A minute stretched out to ten, then, "Good suggestion, Anna. Gorge says thanks, they'd pretty much reached the same conclusion, but it will take another coupla hours to shuffle cars around."

"Understood, Control, would appreciate a fifteen minute warning when they're ready to move so I can get into position as soon as they clear the lock. And I have a spare coupling down in the equipment bay if they still need one."

"Acknowledged, Anna. They'll send over a gopher to pick it up."

Anna glanced at Sarah again. "Two couplings burnt. Kak! I think I'm down to my last spare, too."

"Let's pray for a clean time of it driving, then."

"May as well grab some lunch. Larder upstairs is stocked up for the trip."

Sarah stood and ran her fingers through her hair. "At this rate, we're not going to all be ready before nightfall."

Anna counted in her head. Sarah was right. This had eaten up too much of the day and they still had two massive trains to reverse into place, hitch, then bring back into shelter. She picked up the microphone again. "Control, what's the forecast looking like tonight?"

After anxious and intense discussions with engineers and planners, they agreed to leave the fronts of the two trains out on the surface, battened down for the night. The town was sheltered from the brunt of the storms, and this would leave enough elbow room inside the garage to maneuver the remaining cars into position during the long hours of darkness. Then the last inhabitants of Elysium could begin boarding.

They'd still be able to set off at first light.

Chapter 9

The world around Mikel seemed to be dying. Their family quarters were bare. So few people around now, though that had been a slower realization. The noise of others usually washed over him as long as no-one got in his way or moved things around. But now the normally crowded tables in the common room were almost empty.

Anna hadn't been around last night. That was disturbing, too. Mikel knew she wasn't out in the field, she was down in one of the garages, but when she was home she *always* came to the family quarters to see him.

Not last night.

He'd lain awake for hours, wondering what he'd done wrong.

And why had Georgina roused him for breakfast so early? It was still the middle of the night! At least Anna had been there, but she seemed distracted. She barely spoke to him before hurrying off again.

He remembered to pick up his carry bag on his way out of the family quarters. He never usually carried a bag around like that, but Anna had lectured him endlessly the day before on the importance of taking his bag with him today.

There was a load of other stuff too, that seemed to have slid off the fringes of his mind, too strange and frightening to properly absorb, but taking the bag seemed to have stuck. He hadn't noticed before, but with his bag in his hands, his sleeping cubby was suddenly bare of any signs of life. Dead and empty. While he'd been at breakfast, someone had stripped the bedding away, leaving nothing but a bare bench against the wall.

He clutched his bag like a lifeline against the turbulent change surrounding him. There was something else he was supposed to remember. Anna said it was important, but what was it? He screwed his eyes shut and concentrated. It was all a muddle. Give him a problem to solve in biochemistry or structural mechanics and he was fine. Facts, equations, interconnections all made sense. But when it came to people ...

That's it! He was supposed to stay with Georgina.

He looked around, heart thudding. There was no-one to be seen. The dining area was bare, table cleared from breakfast. Urgent voices from the kitchen, a couple of the caterers cleaning up, but no sign of Georgina. He hadn't notice her leave, but then he hadn't been paying attention.

Kak! He was in trouble. He had his bag, good, Anna would be pleased with that, but he'd lost Georgina. Anna would be disappointed. Georgina would be furious.

He had to find her. To make things right.

He tried to think things through. Where could she be?

Desperate and miserable, he hurried from the family dome through strangely silent halls to the community dome where school was held. Georgina would be there, like normal ... wouldn't she? He needed her to be there, needed to know things were all right, but the consuming emptiness in his stomach told him things weren't all right. Nothing was as it should be.

The school rooms were as empty as the family quarters.

He sat, distraught, wondering what to make of it all, seeking some familiarity in the strangeness.

The senior field controller lounged in her chair, keeping one eye on the array of status screens as she wound up her final drivers' briefing. "Laverne forecasts intense electromags over the next ten days at least. Big Red has been flaring like there's no tomorrow for the last week. Shortwave will be line of sight only, so stick together. Air storm patterns consistent for this time of season. Take no chances."

Anna glanced at the other drivers. Nothing unexpected. The surface of Sponge and electrical activity may be treacherous as kak, but the atmosphere itself stayed relatively predictable. That part was pure thermal equilibrium.

"Field crews were out two hours ago loosening off the ties," the controller continued, "and folks started boarding soon after midnight. It was a long day yesterday. Hope you drivers got some decent shuteye."

Anna gave a wry smile, thinking back to the few hours of sleep after they finally closed the last hitch and checked all the connections. That had been a scary end to the day, sitting exposed in her cab out on the surface while winds shrieked around her, and the aurora competed with sheets of lightning to illuminate the valley and domes of Serendipity.

For once, checks completed, she'd been glad to leave the homeliness of her cab and take refuge in the town. She'd looked in on Mikey. Georgie met her with dark circles under her eyes, but assured her all was well.

"Party time in Laverne," the controller said. "Luck!"

"Luck," they echoed.

As she and the other drivers turned to rejoin their vehicles, Anna looked around the field operations office one last time. Until next season.

The largest display alongside the controller showed a map of Serendipity. The square kilometer of domes and tunnels usually glowed a constellation of green status lights. Apart from this admin center and the routes to the garages, most of the habitat domes had now turned ice blue as the shut-down crews ran through their checklists. All the warehouses and workshops on the outskirts already glowed the white of temporary death. Even as she watched, the ragged circle of white edged inwards like a spreading sickness, claiming another row of domes. Anna's scalp prickled.

She clutched a carry bag with her last few remaining possessions and hurried after the other drivers through echoing corridors to the southern garage complex. Like Sarah, she had already loaded most of her belongings into the cab before her last run out into the field. The extensive family support network had dealt with all the other logistics of packing and loading for the six-thousand-kilometer road trip.

As she entered the rear of South One, limping still despite the pain meds, the garage seemed curiously empty now since yesterday. Her and Gerard's trains began over half-way down, and headed straight through the hanging curtains of the vehicle exits.

A handful of people milled around the airlocks of the last few cars, checking in with tablet-wielding trek wardens as they boarded.

Instead of heading for the vehicles, Anna stayed along the left-hand wall and slipped through a surface lock near the far end. The cramped passageways of the crawlers would be heaving with people chatting and bickering—hopefully good naturedly at this point—as they found and settled into their assigned cars. That was the downside to leaving most of the train out in the open. Everyone would have been embarking from the rear through most of the night, and working their way forwards up and down steps and through narrow corridors.

Out on the surface, she reveled for a moment in the freedom, the openness, before setting off for her cab. A clear sky spanned the steep ridges that sheltered Serendipity, deep chocolate pricked with stars. A glorious calm after the hours of violence last night. To the east, the sky lightened to amber, Big Red not yet visible above the hills.

Quite possibly half the town's population had never set foot on the surface, spending their whole lives in the domed admin and community halls, warehouses, and workshops. Many were happy with the constant press of humanity in confined spaces. The next weeks in even closer proximity wouldn't trouble them.

She hauled herself up the ladder to the footplate, and on through the airlock to find Sarah propping her elbows on the back of the co-driver's seat. A glance at the control board showed they were still waiting for a few wardens to report in.

"Is Mikey here? My son," she added, at Sarah's questioning look. "I promised him he could ride in the drive cab with me."

"Perks of the position, huh? Sorry, just me up front."

Anna checked the chrono on the back wall. A subliminal rumble through the soles of her feet. Over to their right, Gorge's crawler eased forwards. Car after car slid into view through the vehicle lock until the whole train was clear.

Another glance at the chrono, then back to the control board.

"Go fetch him, Anna." Sarah slapped her shoulder and pushed her towards the steps at the back of the cab. "I've got this covered until you get back."

Anna hesitated.

"Go!"

"Okay. You know the warm-up drill. But double-check the status reports from the wardens, and bug them to double-check inventories. Everyone accounted for. My guess it's a bear pit back there with every-one pushing their way through from the rear, and we don't want anyone left behind in the scrum."

Anna left the cab and made her way back through the train. The first few cars she'd been towing were all cargo, so the stairs and corridors this far forward were empty.

She reached the foremost crew car, where the last few of her own clan was billeted. The four levels of a crew car's sleeping and living accommodation could house fifty people. With storage and provisions to last for weeks, it was a self-contained world. Enough for a harvesting crew out in the field, or for several family units on the trek. A sudden din met Anna as she opened the lock door into the car.

A quick glance down the steps to the lowest level showed it was empty. She headed up, where the excited chatter rose to a fever pitch. She acknowledged greetings, but her gaze scanned the room, seeking out hidden corners between sets of bunks. No Mikey.

She climbed the next set of steps. More bunks and storage. People hanging a few belongings in the sleeping nooks. From deeply ingrained habit, Anna's gaze skimmed over corners where couples and family units had staked their claim with clan and family emblems. In their enclosed world, so much of their living space was shared that those few square meters of privacy were precious and guarded by cultural taboos stronger than life itself. In the town domes there were doors and curtains, but the symbols of personal space were enough to bring on a willful blindness. A couple could make love in plain view, and they'd be as effectively invisible as behind closed doors.

A young family in the corner caught her eye, the father playing hide-and-seek around the corner with a young boy of maybe three or four years. She turned to the last upward steps with a sharp twinge in her chest. That could have been her, Mikey, and Luuk a decade ago. This was why she traveled alone.

Tears blinded her and she almost ran headlong into Georgie on the steps.

"Anna! Thank the skies! Do you have Mikey with you?" Georgie's face lit with comical relief, dashed a moment later when she caught Anna's expression.

A cold pit opened up in Anna's stomach. "No, he was coming with you."

"That was the plan. He knew that. I could see by the way he listened yesterday when you explained it all. We finished breakfast. I went to fetch my travel bag. Anna, I swear I was only out of the common room a couple of minutes, but when I came back he was gone."

Anna realized that Georgie was babbling, panic-stricken.

"I searched the dome from top to bottom. One of the engineers said he thought he saw Mikey following you, but he couldn't be certain when that was."

"The school room! Did you look there?"

Georgie's face crumpled. "Of course I did. The obvious place to try. Nothing. By the time I got back to our dome it was all powered down. I tried to call you but the town network's shut down now."

Nick had joined them, scanning his tablet with a worried frown. "He's not checked off on the roster."

"Could he have come in with someone else?" Anna tried to keep the desperation out of her voice.

"Not from our clan. He's the only one missing."

"And you know Mikey," Georgie added. "There's no karking way he'd hitch up with a stranger from another clan."

Anna raised her voice to cut above the chatter. "Has anyone seen Mikey since breakfast?"

Muttered negatives and shakes of heads.

Anna was down two decks and pulling on her mask before Nick caught up with her.

"Anna!"

She shook his hand off her arm. "I'm not leaving without Mikey, and you can't leave without me."

"There are three hundred people on this crawler. I will not endanger them. I *cannot!*" He wrung his hands together, imploring. "Anna, you *know* the rules here. *Everyone* knows. No exceptions."

She knew. That was the trouble. She *knew* that Nick was serious. You didn't miss the last train on the trek.

Now the lengthening nights pressed in, and the dusk storms threatened more violence. Weather cycles held themselves for months at a time in stable patterns, but as the frozen side of the planet thawed and the summer pole plunged into an expanding circle of dark, the world-girdling air movements flipped from one state to the next with cataclysmic fury. The next tipping point would arrive at any day now. They couldn't afford another day's delay. As the senior planner and padre on board, Nick wouldn't risk the lives in his care for one boy.

Not even for her.

"One hour. Please. The first leg is short. We'll still easily make the first way station before nightfall."

Nick paced the few meters of the lower deck, face contorted in indecision.

"Nick, I can't lose Mikey too." Anna's voice broke. "I'm going to find him, no matter what you do."

"An hour then, Anna. That's all I can give you. Then I tell Sarah to take your seat."

She slipped her mask over her face without a word and stepped into the lock. A rough shove surprised her. She turned to protest, but Georgie had already slammed the inner lock door. "Two of us can cover twice as much ground." Her mask muffled her words. She reached past and threw open the outer door.

Without a word, Anna swung herself down the ladder to the springy ground below. Together they hobbled and stumbled to the nearest garage lock and let themselves in. Beyond the garage, tunnels and domes were eerily dark and silent.

A dim glow from the dawn outside permeated the habitats through their translucent weather skin, but only a pale reflection penetrated the cross tunnels through the centers of the domes. In this unaccustomed twilight everything looked the same, ghostly and unfamiliar. Anna had spent her whole life navigating by subtle cues in her surroundings–not just the codes stenciled on walls and kit lockers, but differences in the styling of handrails at stairwells, clan symbols hanging over doors, a tapestry here, a communications panel there, a section of wall that had been replaced and stood out with a rougher texture than its surroundings–all these signposts gave her a subliminal sense of place. All now were gone or hidden in the shadows.

She stood in a darkened intersection, momentarily lost. Georgie grabbed her arm and led the way into the space that they had known as home all the long season. Up stairs, through empty living spaces, all was silent.

In one of the echoing clan meeting spaces, Anna forlornly clicked at a communications panel. If only she could have talked to Mikey, pleaded with him over the public address to come meet her, but all systems were dead, powered down for the winter.

They were about to head down the stairs when Georgie smacked her forehead. "Should have thought of it right away! He has a few bolt holes where he hides out when he's upset, but only one makes sense right now."

Galvanized, she raced up more stairs to the uppermost level, then up again to the roof of the habitat.

They were panting hoarse breaths by the time they emerged on top of the habitat. The circular roof, thirty meters across, was cluttered with boxes and domes sheltering ventilation machinery and the silvery caps of light wells that drew daylight filtering through the weather skin down into the core of the building.

Only a few meters above their heads, the structural ribs of the dome met in the middle, with the translucent skin a few meters beyond. The whole weather shield was designed to flex in the wind, always held a safe distance apart from the piled ziggurat of buildings it sheltered. Even in the dawn calm, the structure above and around them creaked and sighed like the breathing of a slumbering giant.

Funny, Anna thought, she'd never noticed how much the domes moved. Down at ground level the base was rigid and buried meters deep into the ground. The flexible weather shield seemed still at that height, married to the bowl of the base. It was only when you climbed a few stories high that any movement would be noticeable.

But people inside the dome never looked out. When you were home, eyes and thoughts turned inwards. Inside was safety. There were walkways around the lower levels, where the building stepped in to follow the arch of the dome and occupy as much as possible of the inside volume, but people rarely ventured onto those promenades.

Anna never did. When she needed escape, she had her crawler and the wide expanse of the surface.

The constant hubbub of people crammed into close proximity drowned out the sounds of the structure, until the storms hit and people huddled deep in the safety of the community halls, listening to the winds shriek like a thousand clawed demons.

Here, on top of their safe little world, the outside world always made itself felt, an ever present threat.

No wonder people did their best to ignore forces they could do nothing about.

Georgie squinted up, and pointed. Anna followed the line of sight to where a network of narrow catwalks threaded between the arching ribs. There, in the angle between catwalk and rib, a small shadow lurked.

How did he get up there? Anna cast around and saw several flexible ladders dangling from the catwalk. For a moment she wondered why the designers couldn't have stretched to proper stairs, then the answer became obvious. She hurried to the bottom of the nearest ladder and grabbed hold. It swayed gently above her with the movement of the dome. Given the clearance between buildings and dome, she guessed the foot of the ladder might be expected to drag itself five meters or more in any direction.

She wondered what kind of force could stretch the structure that far.

She shook herself and started climbing.

Up here, in the natural glow of dawn, it was hard to tell that the dome had been abandoned. That must be what had attracted him up here ... the sense of normality.

"Mikey!"

No response. He seemed to be staring into the distance, except there was nothing to see.

She closed the gap and reached out to touch his shoulder. He turned and gave her a tearful smile.

"Mikey, we need to go."

His eyes widened and he shook his head.

"I know this is unsettling, but when we reach the other side there'll be another dome just like this. Our clan will settle in and everything will carry on as before."

He frowned and shook his head again.

Kak! She needed to get through to him somehow. "You've heard of modular design?" She tried to keep rising panic out of her voice. He had to come willingly. He'd grown into a strapping teenager, not someone she could throw over her shoulders and carry down, much as she'd have liked to right now.

Mikey scrunched up his face and nodded.

"Everything's built that way. Modular. The domes of Serendipity South are exactly the same as here." Okay, maybe that was stretching the truth a bit, but it was close enough. "The living quarters are laid out the same. You've seen other family rooms in our clan and elsewhere."

Georgie had puffed and panted her way up the ladder to join them. "Mikel, sometimes it's hard to see just how alike all these places are until you see them empty. When people are living here, all the personal touches, the rugs and hangings, the pictures, the ornaments, make each room unique. It's not the town, the dome, that makes this a home. It's the people in it, and all the life and beauty they fill the place with."

Mikey looked thoughtful.

Seeing an opening, Anna pressed the thought. "All of that's now on the crawler. All our friends, our books and games ... your bed quilt."

His eyes widened a fraction.

"And," said Anna, "it's one big party all the way south. All your favorite food."

He'd let go his grasp on the stanchion supporting the catwalk.

"We have apple fritters tonight."

Mikey smiled.

———— • • ————

Nick screwed his eyes shut, trying to swallow past the constriction in his throat. He'd done what he could. Spread the word quietly to the other trek wardens down the length of the train.

There were strict rules around missing persons, protocols in place to safeguard the majority. He'd already gone against those rules allowing Anna and Georgie to return to town. Not that he could have stopped them. Sometimes, especially with Anna, even the most logical of rules had to bend in the face of human nature.

But each warden he'd spoken to told the same story. They all knew Mikey. None of them had seen him.

"Nick." He jumped at Sarah's voice on the intercom. "You're the last warden to report in. What's the hold-up?"

He gazed at the closed airlock door, mind suddenly blank.

"Nick?"

He gulped. "Just chasing down stragglers. With our crew car so far forward, someone might have boarded from the surface to bypass the crush at the back. They could have missed the wardens taking names back in the garage."

"Anna was going to bring her son up to the driver cab. Any idea where she is?"

Cold sweat trickled down Nick's back. "I think she's got some family business to sort out. You know this rig, can you get the start-up checks done and be ready to roll? I don't know how long she's going to be tied up."

He squeezed his eyes shut and counted the seconds of silence on the other end.

"Start-up checks, aye."

Nick strained to detect any hint of suspicion in the brusque reply. He checked the chrono on his tablet. It was coming up on the hour. But Anna was right, the first leg was an easy drive. He could give her a few minutes longer.

The ladder swayed as the dome creaked around them. Why was it so much more difficult to climb down than up? That made no sense. Georgie had backed her way along the catwalk and gone first. Anna took Mikey's hand and helped him past her on the narrow ledge so he could descend next. No way in hell was she leaving him up here to follow her down.

She edged her way down the topmost rungs, clinging on as the dome around them shifted again.

Anna looked down. Georgie had nearly reached the floor. Anna gripped the rung, overcome by a wash of vertigo. The floor was moving. No! It was an illusion. Suspended from the structural ribs, *they* were moving. The floor was still. She gritted her teeth and tried to convince her mind to deny the evidence of her eyes.

Kak, but that floor swept by fast when it wanted to. From the corner of her eye, Anna saw the vent housing too late to cry a warning. It slammed into the back of Georgie's calves. Georgie yelled and tumbled over the housing, landing in a heap on the floor.

Mikey gave a cry of alarm and scurried down the last few rungs to land lightly on his feet. Anna squeezed her eyes shut for a moment, then willed herself to descend. As she reached the last two meters she gauged her landing, waiting for a lull after another gust.

She hurried over to where Georgie lay. "Nothing broken," she gasped, "but definitely something twisted."

They tried to heave Georgie to her feet. She winced and leaned heavily on Mikey for support. How the kak were they going to get her down ten flights of stairs then all the way across town?

"Leave me." She must have been having the same thoughts.

"Not a chance in hell," Anna snarled.

"At least you run on ahead. Hold them up."

Anna turned the thought over in her mind while they maneuvered Georgie down the first flight. It took both her and Mikey together to stop her falling in a heap. If Anna went ahead, could she stop the crawler from leaving? Only if she knew they were nothing more than a few minutes behind.

And, her stomach churned, Mikey would have to stay behind to help Georgie. "That's not happening," she muttered.

The clumsy stumble back through dark domes and tunnels was even more unsettling. In her panic, rushing from the crawler, Anna hadn't noticed, but now the pervading sense of wrongness hit hard.

Airlocks guarded the passageways between domes, but the panels alongside each were lifeless. Moving from one place to another, safety habits were ingrained as soon as children could walk. Check the tell-tales. Watch for danger on the other side. The ritual was automatic, and now thwarted by the dead readouts.

She shuddered and hurried on with Georgie hanging between her and Mikey. With growing dread, Anna saw that even the lock leading into South One was dead. Maybe the shut-down crew had finished their work knowing the waiting crawler had no more need of powered services. She clung to the thought so hard, it took long seconds for the evidence of her own eyes to percolate through.

Still mercifully alone in the depths of the crew car, Nick de Jong slumped to the floor. Tears streamed freely down his face. "Forgive me. Forgive me," he repeated over and over to himself.

He'd fielded increasingly tense calls from Sarah, growing anxious at the lengthening delay. But the decision was his and his alone to make. This was his burden as the trek warden for his clan, and another of the cruel rules of the trek. Nick knew the reasoning. Consigning a friend or family member to the long dark was the hardest decision anyone could make, and some people would be tempted into heroics.

So, the loss would only be shared with the rest of the train, and most especially the driver, once they were well under way. Drivers in particular had to keep their sanity and their focus. There was no question of them sharing the guilt at driving off leaving someone behind.

His tablet sat in his lap, its screen an accusation. The checklist of personnel in his care showed 'all clear'. His words over the intercom to Sarah in the driver's seat would haunt him for the rest of his life. "Everyone is accounted for. Take us out."

Chapter 10

Anna's mind rebelled, grasping for the smallest glimmer of hope. Orange day filtered through the weather skin far above and limned the perimeter of the vast space in ghostly twilight. But the upper vehicle deck cast most of the floor in inky blackness. She was used to seeing this space bright lit at all hours, and unfamiliar shadows played tricks with perspective. The trains had been most of the way out of the vehicle locks at the far end and would be hard to see from so far away.

She squinted, looking for signs of running lights.

The pain in her foot was a distant grumble as she sprinted, heedless of hidden obstacles.

They had to be here. Nick wouldn't have left.

Would he?

Reason battled with mounting hysteria. She reached the far end. There were the twin tunnels. Empty.

An acrid catch at the back of her throat, and Anna retched. More by instinct than conscious thought, she pulled her mask over her face against the native air drifting in through the curtains, and steadied her breathing.

A thought struck her, rekindling forlorn hope. She was in the wrong garage!

That was it. She'd already got turned around in the eerily vacated town. She'd taken a wrong turn and hit the wrong garage. Which one was this? She must have hit South Two. She scurried to her left where an open airlock door beckoned. With the town's power shut down, the locks had no cycling mechanism. The far door simply opened ... to reveal the outdoor surface of Sponge. She'd been in the right garage after all.

She backed up in horror, unwilling still to admit the truth.

Left behind.

A hand on her sleeve brought a new wave of irrational panic. She turned to find Mikey and Georgie gazing at her with wide eyes through their masks. Mikey gripped her sleeve and tried to haul her away, back into the depths of the garage.

She stumbled back into the gloom, numb with shock. A distant voice sounded a note of urgency. The here and now came back with a rush as Georgie's words came into focus.

"The shut-down crew! They're always the last ones out. Where are they?"

Anna rasped, voice raw from brief exposure to the planet's air. "North One."

"Then go! Don't wait for me. Just get there and get them to wait a few minutes."

Anna caught Mikey's gaze. His eyes filled with tears, but he managed a weak smile and took Georgie's weight on one shoulder. With his free arm he made a shooing motion. Despite herself, she could see the logic. She'd move faster if she didn't have to keep checking behind her. With a last backward glance she staggered the length of the garage, legs and lungs afire, willing her body to make the kilometer dash through the place that was no longer home.

Near the far end she paused again, her eye caught by a pair of vehicles parked by the side wall. The hitching trucks! She slipped into a cab and muttered a brief prayer to the Deep as she punched the power button. The truck whispered to life.

A moment's indecision as Anna glanced back to where Georgie and Mikey, invisible in the shadows, were making their own halting progress.

No. Speed was of the essence and there was only room for one in the cab. They'd have to cling to the outside, and Anna had no intention of taking things gently. She pushed the throttle and the powerful little truck leapt forwards with an eager whine.

Designed to support the weight of a cargo or crew car and drag it around the garage, the truck seemed to dance in its unencumbered freedom as it rattled over the garage floor. Even jumping out to open airlocks, Anna made better progress through the long corridors of the empty domes than she could have managed on foot.

Adrenaline lent her speed and precision at every closed lock she encountered, and she rejoiced at each one she found open, threading the truck through the opening with reckless abandon.

Anxiety mounted as she neared the last dome before North One.

A rumble in the distance. They were still here! But they were starting up. Anna sped through the final lock and pushed the throttle to its max, teeth chattering as the truck bounced between unlit pillars.

A set of lights in the distance.

Then they were gone.

Anna sobbed in frustration. She aimed the truck at the still-swaying hangings guarding the vehicle lock. She eased up at the last moment and nosed the truck forward. The drapes were woven from fine Sponge flax, flexible and soft on the panels and fittings of moving crawlers, but heavy. Not something you hit at speed.

A burst on the throttle, then a push through the second set. Another burst, another set, and she was out on the surface.

Within seconds, the truck floundered to a halt in the soft terrain.

The crawler was already rounding the far dome to her left, too far away for them to see her, and moving too fast to catch.

———•◆•———

Mikel found Anna slumped over the controls of a tiny vehicle a few meters out on the surface. He stared a moment. Many times he'd come outside to watch Anna's crawler lumber out the garage and over the surface. Sometimes she'd be gone for many days, and he always came to wave her off.

Crawlers were huge. Yellow sides made them glow in the green and brown landscape, visible from miles away. Fat wheels raised them up far enough to walk right under without ducking. Sometimes, when Anna was in a playful mood, she'd let him stand out on the spongy surface and she'd drive right over him. He'd stand, transfixed, as one set of wheels after another rolled by on either side.

Sometimes, the planet seemed to call out to him as the crawler's wheels pressed into the surface. He'd feel wistful, a little sad, but maybe that was simply Mikel's own sadness that Anna was leaving, sometimes a twinge of pain, but most often an intense curiosity. The feelings seeped from the ground through his feet, then they were gone.

Once, he'd knelt and pressed his hands against the ground. "It's all right," he thought to himself. He was rewarded with a glow of warmth that lifted his spirits that whole day.

It was just plain weird, though, to see this tiny truck outdoors. What had Anna been thinking? Mikel could see right away that its little wheels were useless out here.

Then the wonder gave way to panic as his attention returned to Anna, weeping bitterly. He rushed forward and tried to hug her, but she didn't seem to notice him. Wrong! Wrong! Wrong! Anna didn't cry. She was grown up. How could the world get so broken that grown ups like Anna cried?

He had to get her back inside. Inside was safe. Things would be all right again.

He shook her shoulder.

No reaction.

Maybe he could carry her. Mikel thought about it for a moment. He was as big as many adults he knew, stronger than anyone his age. He could manage it. Those strips hanging in the tunnel would make it hard, though. They were heavy to shove aside. Come to think of it, Mikel couldn't explain what had drawn him to this particular lock in the first place. He'd helped Georgina, and found the garage empty. An overwhelming sensation of loss had tugged at him, bringing him through the curtains rather than out through the normal airlock.

Anna lifted her head. It was going to be okay! Then Mikel caught the look in her eyes and the last shreds of normality, of stability, evaporated. The world was broken. The world he'd always known really was gone.

———•◆•———

The emergency radio in the field control office hissed and spat at Anna. This secondary communications desk, tucked into one corner of the office, had an independent power supply. A layer of dust on top of the casing showed how often it was used. While the town was occupied, the habitat mechanics kept vital systems like power and air filters working with ruthless efficiency. Backup systems like this got called on once every few seasons. It was entirely possible this set hadn't been used for real in Anna's lifetime. It was probably last cleaned and tested when the startup crew opened up the town over six standard years ago.

But it still worked just fine.

The problem was the atmosphere outside.

The briefing only a couple of hours earlier had mentioned electrical activity. Big Red was pumping out flares, and even if it wasn't, electrical activity within Sponge itself was notoriously bad this time of the season.

Delicately, Anna tweaked tuners and sliders on the screen, coaxing the decoding software to the limits of its sensitivity. At the extreme end of the spectrum, it could make best guesses from the most random of noise, but that's all you'd get … random gibberish.

The difficulty, as she was all too painfully aware, was that she'd only receive something sensible if someone out there was trying to say something sensible to her. But her desperate pleas, mangled by the electromagnetic maelstrom outside, needed to be received and understood first. With their line of sight connections, the crawlers wouldn't be trying to coax meaning out of the prevailing static from further afield.

Georgie strolled over, painfully obvious in her attempts to appear casual. "Any other communications we can try?"

Anna bit back a snarky retort. Facing the reality of a slow and cold death, tempers were fraying, and Georgie was visibly scared yet trying her best not to antagonize Anna. She was probably feeling a shedload of guilt, too. Mikey had been in her care. That was how clans worked.

"This is the only desk with power. It's a kinda last resort backup system." Anna's shoulders slumped as she voiced truths she'd been keeping out of the forefront of her mind. "The main desks are wired into dome power. We'd need to bring the main unit back online and I don't know the startup procedures."

She gave the other consoles, and the pair of deeply cushioned swivel chairs, worn and patched but irresistibly comfortable, a sour look. Everything they needed was over there, but dead and useless. "If we could power up the landline to Laverne we'd be free of atmospherics, but then the question is would they send a vehicle out for us? Pretty doubtful. They'd be chancing the weather window closing up on them during the round trip."

Anna's fingers drummed the desktop. "I'd been hoping to raise one of the crawlers before they got too far, but they're already out of the valley and out of line of sight." She sighed. "I'll keep trying. You never know, we might get a clear window, or a lucky bounce off the ionosphere."

Georgie frowned. "Don't want to sound defeatist, but seems to me we need to be prepared in case we're still here tonight. With power down, it's going to get chilly. We'll need to find provisions, warmer clothing, and from what I recall, the warmest spot is down by the power core in the basement."

The desktop blurred through sudden tears. Was it really coming to this? Anna pulled herself together and wiped her eyes on her sleeve. She nodded. "Sounds like a good idea. Do you know how to get to the power room? I've never been down there before."

Georgie's scowl deepened, but Mikey's face lit up and he raised his hand with a cheeky grin.

Anna glared once more at the crackling radio, then stood abruptly. "Let's all go, see where we need to camp. Mikey, lead the way. I'll come back here every hour or so for another try, but meanwhile we'll all help make ourselves comfortable."

The ground ahead of Sarah's vantage point rose steeply. While most of the navigation beacons were gathered in for the winter, the safe route out of Serendipity followed the line of a structural rib and was marked by a series of large and permanent pylons. Built to withstand the oncoming deep freeze and the violent winds, some of these markers had been here ten seasons or more. Unlike so much of Sponge's surface, the ground around the complex network of ribs never shifted. At least, not in the span of human years.

The most dangerous part of the journey was already behind her. The series of unmarked crossings between town and the iron hard surface she now rode. Serendipity itself, set between ridges that broke the worst of the night storms' fury, was quickly lost from sight. Now there was just her, the tan-grey slope, and the occasional distant flash of yellow from Gerard's crawler up ahead.

A patchwork of vivid greens to her right and far below marked photosynthetic forests, struck through with glittering stretches of surface water. Deeper shadows surrounded a series of surface pores marching to the horizon.

They toiled on. This part was not to be hurried, angling across the steepest part of the slope. Readouts alongside her, segment by segment, showed the vehicle was well within its stable zone, but the ground here was deeply rutted. An awkward bounce on their huge, springy wheels had been known to tip a crawler trying to rush too recklessly.

Sarah was not reckless. She'd driven this route twice before, hauling loads to and from Laverne, and ridden as passenger on the treks. The details were lost with the passing years but somehow this climb stayed vivid. Another hour and they'd start to level off, finally emerging onto the broad uplands tens of klicks wide that would take them all the way to Laverne.

The top of the world.

The air was noticeably thinner up there. Somehow cleaner than the pits and valleys around town, laden with dust and microscopic detritus exhaled from Sponge's depths.

The solitude up there scared and exhilarated Sarah in equal measure. She was used to company and conversation up in the cab, and the tranquility around her was disconcerting. At the same time, it brought a novel perspective. The sky above was unblemished polished copper, brightening to straw to the south-east where Big Red peered above the uplands and cast her orange light.

The power at her fingertips brought a tingle across Sarah's scalp. The lightest touch on a joystick, and half a kilometer of rumbling machinery obeyed. She shook herself. Such solitude was dangerous. Could lead to delusions.

Where the kak was Anna? Sarah buried a twinge of guilt at taking Anna's drive seat, but that's what you had extra drivers for. Anna was busy, back there somewhere. Must be something important to keep her away from her beloved cab. Sarah had thought she'd be sitting this trip out, a useless passenger. It was good to feel useful after all.

Family business, Nick had said. Something involving her son, Sarah guessed. It had taken her a few moments to put two and two together when Anna mentioned his name, but the pieces clicked into place quickly enough. Another wash of buried guilt. Sarah was secretly relieved that Mikey wasn't up here with her. She'd never met him– Serendipity may not be large on the cosmic scale of things, but you only ever knew a fraction of twelve thousand people in a sprawling warren of domes and tunnels–but she'd certainly heard of him. Strange child. Mute. Retarded, some people said, but some of the stories suggested otherwise. Epic meltdowns when he didn't get what he wanted, that part was verified by some of the caterers and educators Sarah knew. Maybe that's what had happened today.

The ever-present hiss of static from the radio seemed to modulate into the ghost of a voice. Goosebumps raised themselves and Sarah shivered. She blinked and scanned the consoles around her, reassured herself that all status indicators were in the green. Hitches, hulls, locks, power, drive, all good. Had she drifted off briefly? She'd been thinking of Anna and for a moment she thought she'd heard Anna's voice.

She shivered. Enough of this *debeel* solitude! Sarah switched channels and hailed Gerard in the cab up ahead.

Chapter 11

Anna surveyed the meager collection of supplies she'd managed to assemble. She shivered, despite the trickle of heat from the thermal pile that dominated the circular room. It powered the dome during the long Elysium seasons of occupation. In shutdown mode it was designed to keep the frigid Sponge night at bay through the long dark, but that was only relative. Out near the skin of the dome that meant minus eighty. Bliss in comparison to conditions outside, where the air would turn to nitrogen rain in the dead of winter, but not human habitable. Even here near the dome's core, the few degrees warmer would hardly matter. They would never live to see midwinter, three standard years away yet.

Food. A few unopened bottles of water. Nothing more than scraps she'd salvaged from communal kitchens, too little to be worth packing away into the trains.

Anna shivered again, not from cold this time but from the memory of what she'd just done. *She'd invaded another clan's space!*

She had first cleaned out her own clan quarters, feeling grubby enough rummaging through unfamiliar kitchen areas belonging to other family groups. That hadn't turned up much. Her clan elders always instilled a devotion to tidiness that became instinctive.

So she'd gone to the next living dome, heart fluttering like a trapped bird, and stopped at the nearest doorway. She actually turned back, sick to her stomach at the thought of trespassing without an invitation, before steeling herself.

She reminded herself how bare her own quarters were now. Stripped of all personal items, these were no longer sanctums. The space was returned to the communal pool. She had as much right to be there as anyone. Heck, it might not even be the same clan billeted here when spring brought the harvesters back.

The thought helped, but not much. There was just too much taboo to overcome.

As she pushed the door open, uninvited, Anna imagined a thousand disapproving stares from behind blank walls and empty family quarters, whispered conversations, her reputation sunk beyond redemption. *Stiig*, they whispered. *Unclean, not to be trusted.*

A death sentence on Sponge.

Echoing emptiness welcomed her. She hurried through vacant quarters finding an odd water bottle here, a carton of dried food there. Nothing substantial to reward her efforts. Still, she felt haunted by unseen ghosts.

Finally, a splash of color glimpsed through a half-open door caught her eye. Fearfully she pushed the door wider. Her hand flew to her mouth and she doubled over and dry-retched.

It was a small suite, for a couple, maybe young and yet childless, or maybe in their later years whose children had started families of their own. Belongings lay partly packed, and an exquisitely-worked marquetry panel still hung on the wall.

What sudden tragedy had caused a person's memories to be left behind like this? Was there no family left to clear the room, to take in their treasures to hand on to their children? The sense of unforgivable intrusion on private grief overwhelmed Anna. Her heartbeat hammered in her ears, and she fled through the tunnel and through her own dome.

She clattered down stairs and along the service corridor to the power room lying under the heart of the admin dome. Anna slumped to the floor, aware of a growing chill at her back seeping through the walls. She frowned and wracked her brain for ideas. They had to do better than this.

The clean-up engineers had been through and locked all the dome's systems into winter mode. Anna was a driver. She didn't know the rituals needed to bring systems, power, light, sanitation, back online. If only Seth were here. He knew far more than she did about general engineering. But would it even matter? These habitats weren't meant to keep people safe through the glacial dark. Everything was drained and sealed off to protect it from cold damage. Bringing electrics and plumbing back to life through winter might cause irreparable harm.

Muffled footsteps and scraping noises outside, then Georgie gasped and spluttered her way into the room with four stuffed carry bags weighing her down.

Anna gaped, and smacked her forehead in shamefaced realization. The emergency lockers! She'd put herself to all that angst for nothing. Another taboo had blinded her. You never interfered with those lockers. They were there for emergencies, lives might depend on them if the shell got breached or if the power failed. They were untouchable.

The thought was so ingrained, the lockers had become invisible, a part of the walls. But this *was* an emergency. Their lives *were* at stake. That was an unwanted truth that Anna was still struggling to accept, and that unwillingness to face the gravity of their situation had blinded her to the obvious.

Proper field rations and water pouches, designed to last through deep freeze and be useable next season. More flashlights. Good thinking. A little light crept through the dome's skin and reflected into the lower corridors, but hours of daylight were limited now.

Georgie glanced at the pitiful pile Anna had gathered. "With all your experience out in the field, I thought you'd be better versed in emergency procedures."

A hot flush crept up Anna's cheeks. "Always the karking teacher, even now?"

"Your mind always was miles away. This isn't a class assignment now. This is *real*, Anna."

Fortunately, before Anna could dredge up a snarky reply, Mikey staggered in with an armful of outdoor gear: overalls, fleece-lined boots, gloves, hooded coats. Anna stared for a moment. It was going to get cold down here in the depths but not that bad for a few days at least. Then she caught Mikey's level gaze. No words were needed. He already understood what she'd agonized over all day. Their salvation lay out there. They had to find a way to leave this dome, this town, before the night killed them.

———— • • ————

Gusts of wind buffeted the flimsy covering of the dome, causing arched ribs to creak and sway. A rising banshee wail cut through the air and set Jennifer Steel's teeth on edge. Much the same as everything else on this miserable little world.

The team of technicians bowed their heads and backed away to the far side of the habitat's roof. They'd secured a direct microwave link to the longship *Pride of Cumbria*, and their job for the moment was done.

She reminded herself of her reason for being here: the disproportionate income stream from drug products extracted from the native plant's tissues. The one instance of non-terrestrial life yet encountered in explored space, and it had to choose such an ugly home to live on. And yet its non-terrestrial chemistry yielded unbelievably valuable bioactive compounds. Oh, the irony!

She stepped up to the communications set and donned the fishbowl-like helmet. She could see clearly through the polymer, but her face was obscured to onlookers and sound-cancelling technology ensured complete privacy, as well as providing relief from the unearthly din outside. Her own cadre of security goons ensured no interruptions or observation.

Her delegation had commandeered an entire habitat dome to accommodate them, and promptly sealed off the entrances from casual traffic. The planet's leading cleric had looked aghast at this desecration, but had voiced no objections. The city–Jennifer snorted to herself at the overblown appellation–was a dense warren of interconnecting tunnels linking domes together. Traffic could go around.

The communications link chimed. The encrypted connection was live.

"Captain Rose."

"Executive Steel." That was as far as either of them had ever gone with pleasantries. "The Ringmaster reports that the circus is in town."

Jennifer let the silence draw out, though she knew there couldn't possibly be anything further to report this early. She just had to let Galloway do his job.

When it became clear that the captain was going to add nothing more, Jennifer said, "My chief technician will make contact to our pre-arranged schedule."

"If the Ringmaster has anything to report in the next two weeks he'll need to deliver it in person. Flare activity is ramping up and we're going to get fried up here. I'll soon be forced to break orbit and move to Lagrange two to shelter behind the planet."

Which will put her out of range of the microwave transmitter. Jennifer fumed, then calmed herself. There was no arguing with physics. "The Company commends you for your care of its assets."

Negotiations would probably outlast the solar activity, but a visceral dread washed through Jennifer at the thought of being stuck here and out of contact. She reminded herself that the longship's safety was important to her personally, not just to the Company. If anything happened to that ship, it would be another year before the next visit was scheduled. The inconvenience of being out of touch paled against the thought of a full year on this rock.

She eyed the directional indicator on the screen, which showed the longship would soon dip below the horizon. "Regardless, we will attempt contact on schedule. Bear that in mind when you resume orbit."

She cut the contact, knowing her last words would irk the captain. The captain knew her job, but she also needed occasional reminders of who was in charge here. Minor power plays like this usually energized Jennifer. Today, she just felt hollow.

◦•━•◦

Their footsteps were lost in the echoing twilight of the abandoned North One garage. All usable drive cabs, cars, and wheel units were now trekking south, leaving behind an empty shell. The sense of loss lent an even bleaker air to surroundings that once felt homely and comforting.

Anna was still shaken after her humiliation over the emergency supplies. How could she have been so stupid? Georgie was right. That was the trouble. Her cheeks flushed at the memories of miserable lessons under the stern and intimidating gaze of Miss van Buren. How often had Anna struggled with a question that she *knew* the answer to? An answer that refused to show itself under Georgie's harsh impatience. How often had she heard the words, 'Come on, Anna, you *know* this,' while her mind stubbornly blanked itself?

She gritted her teeth and reminded herself that this garage, even bare and empty, was home territory when she wasn't roaming the surface guiding the harvest crews to safety.

Anna's flashlight picked out the nearest two pillars soaring fifteen meters overhead, supporting the upper storage deck. The remainder were lost in the inky gloom, marching away to the far end of the garage. There was always a remote chance there might be a usable vehicle up there, but she'd already discarded that idea. Without power to operate the hoists there was no way to bring anything down to floor level.

She roamed the perimeter, studying and inventorying the few pieces of machinery left behind. Her breath steamed and her foot ached, mirroring the feeling in the pit of her stomach as she catalogued the meager pickings. Mikey and Georgie trailed behind like ghosts.

Every garage had its own vehicle graveyard tucked away in one corner, where futzed-up cars and power units were stashed and cannibalized to keep their brethren running. Anna recognized many of them from her years out in the field, directing repair crews with the latest snag lists on each return to base, until the unit had creaked its last and was consigned to the graveyard.

Each vehicle segment acquired its own idiosyncrasies during its lifetime. Parts broken, parts patched up, non-critical functions abandoned as lost causes and added to communal lore, warnings shared between field crews.

There had been *Matilda*, chassis weakened and welded once too often. Still good for light loads but watch the weight. *L'il Gimpy*, the cargo pod whose top crane jammed at any angle past forty-five. *The Dump*, crew car with the dodgy plumbing. Used for short hauls only. *Versailles The Second*, dingy cousin to *The Dump*. Someone had a fine-tuned sense of irony.

Even far from their prime, those old characters were still essentially functional and had all been taken. Even partly-working equipment was too valuable to leave behind. Here, in the darkened garage, there were stripped carcasses, skeletons picked clean by the repair crews. Who knows, once they got down to a bare chassis of the right dimensions, maybe *Matilda's* body would be transplanted and given a new lease of life?

That was how you survived on Sponge—eternal inventiveness and makeshift solutions in a world starved of engineering resources.

That's what they'd depend on to save themselves. Anna kept her emotions in tight check, aware of the conflicting tugs between dark despair and the slenderest hope. Even if there was anything remotely salvageable here, their survival hung as much on clear thinking as on makeshift engineering.

Half way down the three-hundred-meter length of the garage, Anna's nose twitched and her eyes watered. "Masks on, folks." With power down, the air of Sponge was starting to seep through the heavy drapes covering the openings at the far end. Vehicle-sized airlocks simply weren't practical, so the early colonists didn't bother. Garages relied on a triple set of curtains and a slight overpressure to keep the toxins out. No power, no outflow. Eventually, physics did the rest.

As the cavernous end of the garage emerged, ghost-like, from the gloom, Anna let out a small cry of delight. Up to now, she'd not dared to express this glimmer of hope, not wanting to give Mikey and Georgie any false sense of optimism. Heck, not wanting to risk disappointing herself!

As well as the ubiquitous graveyard, vehicle garages often had one or two units not quite drive-worthy, needing more serious care than simple patching, but nevertheless worth repairing. Her flashlight beam triumphantly speared the ailing cab and drive unit, *Chance O'Glory*. As far as she knew, the yoop itself was operable, but the attached driver's cab's electronics were seriously futzed. It was a tough call whether to try for a repair, or to abandon the cab and attach the wheels to something else. Thinking had tilted in favor of repairs because they badly needed drive cabs, and because right now they had no other serviceable car in need of drive wheels.

The seasons had overtaken the service crew and any repairs were now a task for another year. Unless Anna got there first.

Georgie looked askance at the cab unit. "I know this isn't my department, but you've only got one pair of wheels here. You need to attach another unit to make a usable vehicle." She gestured behind them to the far end of the garage, lost in darkness. "Did you see anything workable back there?"

Anna quelled the surge of panic at Georgie's skeptical questioning. "First things first," she muttered. It was still too soon to raise their hopes. She clambered up the ladder to the lower lock. The telltales were dark and the inner door opened on manual without attempting a flush. This close to the vehicle exit the air was laden with Sponge toxins. Detectors would normally sniff them and clean the air before letting her through.

No power. Not a good sign.

But, Anna reasoned, the garage crew would surely have shut things down for the long winter ahead. No need to panic yet.

Up in the cab, her misgivings returned full force. The consoles were also dead, and not even a wake-me-up signal from the yoop.

A deep throbbing pain pounded in Anna's temples. She longed to take her mask off and breathe freely, but poisons from outside were leaching through the air. The sealed cab might be safe still, but a lifetime of drummed-in learning barred her from putting that guesswork to the test. She needed to power up the cab somehow, then the ubiquitous sensors would keep them safe from leaks, and the vehicle's filters would keep the air clean.

She ran weary fingers through a straggly tangle of hair. Skies above! She'd kill for a shower, too.

Angry, she kicked the console base, grimacing at the stab of pain through her damaged foot. The pain brought a new determination. She opened up the electrical closet and checked the wiring. All looked in order. Working systematically, she traced connections back to where the cab hooked on to the forward hitch of the yoop.

Climbing out onto the catwalk that straddled the massive axle, Anna leaned precariously out four meters above the garage floor and examined the hitch itself. Kak! The power connectors were missing and there wasn't a *nutloos* hope in hell of finding spares handy. That's why they scavenged pieces of machinery from condemned units. If they'd cannibalized this cab, one which they'd been planning to resurrect, things must have been desperate this season.

Thoughtful, Anna rubbed a finger around the lip of the coupling. It came away with a sooty residue. She rubbed her fingers together, studying the dry smear with a sudden burst of excitement. Maybe they hadn't scavenged the connector after all. It looked like it had simply burned out. Maybe it had been removed ready to be replaced when repairs resumed.

She became aware of two pairs of eyes gazing up at her. "What's the verdict, captain?" Georgie was at least trying to keep the tone light, but dark rings stood stark under her eyes even through the mask.

"Can't say yet. We're missing some wiring here. Without at least trickle power to the cab I can't fire up systems for a proper test." Anna sat on the edge of the catwalk, wishing she could wipe sweat from her forehead. "There's a local control panel up here. If I can at least see the power units are dormant, not dead, it'll be worth trawling the hulks back there for a spare coupling. I'm no mechanic. It'll take me a while to figure this out."

Hope and despair battled for the upper hand. It belatedly occurred to Anna that if she was having a hard time coping, how were the others doing? They were looking to her for salvation. Anna was used to working alone. Not used to others depending on her like this.

Okay, that wasn't true. The harvest crews depended utterly on her skills to find safe paths across the maze of surface hazards, but that was professional dependence. She knew her job. This was personal. Different. She was out of her depth.

They needed to keep busy, not just standing around watching her, helpless.

She gazed at Mikey's upturned face and eager eyes, then turned back to Georgie. "Tell you what, problems always seem less scary on a full stomach. Any chance you could plunder another emergency locker while I see what we've got here? Mikey can help me with the mechanics, if you're okay on your own."

"Sure." Georgie didn't look happy, but at least she didn't complain. She stretched her back and rolled her shoulders. "And I guess it would make sense to set up camp a bit closer than the admin dome, if this is going to be our base of operations."

"Good thinking!" Anna strained to add warmth to her voice, despite the chill settling down her back.

Mikey had already hauled down a retractable ladder on the wheel unit and clambered up alongside Anna.

She pointed to the umbilical couplings on the cab and the yoop. "The hitches are all standard. There'll be power connection points like this on every unit and every yoop. Same place. You're looking for one with a cable joining them. It's the cable we need. Should be white or red, doesn't matter, and about this thick." She made an 'O' with thumb and forefinger. "If you find one, come back and let me know. There are tools in the cab to undo it."

Mikey nodded.

"Work your way around the garage. Check every unit. These things are scarce. They burn out and we're always looking for replacements, so be methodical. Don't miss a unit, no matter how beat up it looks. You just never know."

Mikey gave her a thumbs-up.

"And, Mikey"—she squeezed his shoulders—"be careful."

By the time Mikey returned, grinning like a loon, Anna had levered the cover off a service panel and run a diagnostic on the pair of miniature fusion cores sitting atop the axle. Despite a layer of dust, everything looked good, which fit with her theory that they really had meant to save this battered old cab.

"You found me one?" Mikey nodded. Her heart leapt. "Well done."

Anna wiped grimy hands on her pants—yes, a shower *would* be good— and rummaged around in the cab's storage deck for tools. Standard equipment, should be here, but this cab was not in service, not being cared for by a safety-conscious driver. Where was the karking toolbox? Anna swallowed past a tightness in her throat. Panic wouldn't help. The beam of her flashlight picked out a jumble of misplaced parts—she would *never* let her cab get so untidy—before lighting on a flat red toolbox, dulled by dust and oil.

Her relief was as intense as her anxiety only moments before. Their plight was getting to her. These flip-flopping emotions. She was close to losing it.

She took a few moments to calm her breathing and compose herself. They needed answers, needed to know they weren't going to die cold and lonely in this abandoned shell. She had to hold it together.

As she emerged from the lower lock with the tools, Georgie appeared around the back of the yoop. "Hungry?" she asked.

Perplexed, Anna stared at Georgie. She'd come empty handed.

Georgie gestured behind her. "We need masks this close to the exits. I left everything back there. Should be more comfortable."

A manic laugh bubbled up the back of Anna's throat. She bit it back and nodded. "Give us a few. We're on a roll here and the suspense is killing me."

Mikey led them across the garage to one of the sad hulks in the vehicle graveyard. He clambered over a heap of sawn-off floor joists and ducked behind a stack of panels leaning against the near wheel. Anna squeezed into the gap with him and he pointed triumphantly up. The side panels had been peeled back, hiding the hitch, which explained why this treasure had gone unnoticed. A power connector, and it looked undamaged.

Toolbox open at her feet, Anna selected what looked like an odd-shaped spanner. Mikey had already boosted himself up to the yoop's catwalk and was examining his prize. Anna pointed to the U-shaped prongs at one end of the short handle. "This fits around the collar, where the cable plugs into the connector. Twist it half a turn thataway." She gestured a circle to her left and handed the tool up to Mikey.

"Good. Now the same at the other end. Then you use the smaller end of the spanner to pry the connector loose."

Mikey passed the precious cable down, followed by the spanner, then lowered himself to the floor. Barely able to contain her excitement, Anna draped the heavy, two-meter-long cable over her shoulders. "Now let's see if we're in business!"

Half an hour later, Anna let out a whoop of delight as the drive cab came slowly to life. Cabin lights ... main drive console ... most of the electronics were dead or missing, cabinets emptied of their burned-out circuits, but the critical connections to the yoop and the drive motors showed green. And, she listened hard, air filtration was coming back online. It would take a while yet to flush through the cabin's air but they'd be more comfortable tonight.

The final confirmation came when she exited the vehicle with a broad grin and two thumbs up, the airlock telltales were glowing again and flushing against the encroaching poisons from outside.

They perched on upturned tote boxes, far enough down the garage for the air to still be untainted. Anna sighed with relief as she stripped off her mask, and puzzled over her reaction. She'd worked in outdoor gear for hours at a time out in the field. A face mask and filtered air had never caused her discomfort before. But that was in the wide outdoors. There seemed to be something wrong and oppressive about gearing up indoors.

Through a mouthful of dried rations, Georgie said, "So, you reckon the drive cab's useable. I still don't see what we can hitch it to."

Anna was too dizzy with hope and relief to let Georgie's carping get to her. Suddenly ravenous, she swallowed a few spoonfuls of reconstituted root vegetable stew before replying. "It's easier to show you than try to explain. Eat! Then we have work to do."

———————

"The circus is in town." Jennifer Steel rolled the words around in her mind, the message she'd just received.

Nikolai Shevchenko looked up from the table he was setting for dinner. Veal Marsala Con i Funghi, if she'd heard correctly. Their Elysium hosts had shown how creative they could be in the kitchen department, feeding their population with the fruits of their extensive hydroponic farms, but however creative, it was still exclusively vegetarian. Jennifer demanded meat. A private luxury brought with her down from the longship. She wondered how long those precious stocks would last after the ship took refuge from the red giant's flares. There would be no more flights until it was safe to return to orbit.

Even the thought of Nikolai's cuisine, exquisite luxury beyond the imaginings of her hosts, barely cheered her. The message brought home the reality. Galloway's plan was in motion. Unstoppable.

She still hadn't come to terms with the depths of the betrayal she felt at the secrecy. The more she thought about it, the more it became clear this had been a carefully-orchestrated mission, months, maybe even years in the making. A whole web of intrigue within the Company that her own network of spies hadn't detected.

Regardless, Jennifer believed in picking her battles and not wasting energy fretting about things beyond her control. She had to focus on her own survival. Chance was for the weak-minded. Situations could always be engineered to favor those who prepared more carefully.

The contents of that damnable letter were known only to her senior officials on the mission, the Company president ... and Nikolai. Of course she'd shared her predicament with Nikolai. There were times when she needed things done, discreetly, and Nikolai's skills went far beyond the culinary.

"The suite is clean," he said. "If you need to speak freely, you can do so."

If Nikolai said the suite was clean, it meant not even the talented Jayne Kildare could be eavesdropping. "What did your inquiries find?"

"Kyari was tight-lipped about the details, but *someone*, it seems, planted the notion that the Company might be receptive to a departure from the normal style of agreement." He paused. "Although the source of this notion remains obscure, I got the feeling that this has been on the colonists' minds for some time."

Jennifer scowled. "And he didn't feel this departure worth mentioning earlier?"

"He had good reason. He couldn't mention this in any earlier contact because it would have meant nothing to you until now."

Jennifer mulled that over. Nikolai was right. "So Galloway's, or the President's, network laid the groundwork here ahead of time."

"Obviously." He pulled the chair from the table for Jennifer. "We already guessed they will have had some local help accessing the town."

She sat. "The town is empty. As soon as they shut down the landline to the nearest city–Laverne, I believe?–Galloway took off. He figured that, optimistically, he might have an answer in a matter of days. But we might need to stall the talks for weeks if things don't go so smoothly."

"And if you run out of time?"

"The president's letter wasn't specific." Jennifer allowed herself a small and sour smile at the thought. The one ray of brightness on her horizon. "I'll have to judge how long to draw things out so there can be no suggestion I jumped ship too hastily, but if he doesn't deliver in time then I go back to plan 'A'. Screw them for all they're worth."

Chapter 12

Anna grinned at Georgie's expression.

"I don't get it," Georgie spluttered at last. "This freight car is just an empty shell, and you say the drive wheels aren't even functional?"

"And yet, this is just what we need." Anna gazed up in satisfaction at the gutted shell towering above her near the back of the graveyard.

Georgie folded her arms and frowned. "I always did have my doubts about your sanity. As a student, you veered between dunce and genius. This had better be one of your latter moments."

Anna's grin widened. "Think about it. The drive cab has all we need to live. It has sleeping and living quarters up top, and we can stock it up with supplies. The yoop it's attached to is fully functional so we have drive. The only thing wrong with the cab is its electronics. The computer's fritzed, so all control will be fully manual. Joysticks hard-wired to wheel motors. There's a standard circuit that bypasses the computer. Not a problem."

"Okaaay." Georgie pursed her lips, still clearly waiting for the genius to show itself.

"We don't need another car or yoop, except to act as a counterbalance. We just need four wheels to have a stable vehicle."

Georgie's frown turned more pensive.

"You look at this cannibalized cargo pod and you notice what's missing. I care more about what's still there! A chassis, a serviceable hitch at one end, and a pair of *freewheeling* wheels at the other end." Anna pointed up to the empty mountings where the yoop's power and drive motors had been removed. "This is a *good* thing. Without a computer in the cab to co-ordinate things, I can't handle a second powered yoop. But I can manage the front wheels, and this just tags along behind keeping us upright."

For the first time, a small smile cracked Georgie's stern face. "End of term assignment, 'A' for ingenuity. But"—she wagged her finger at Anna—"I'll reserve my overall score until I see it working."

"I'm going to need your help to marry up the hitch, though." Anna eyed Georgie and Mikey. "Have either of you ever driven a hitching truck?"

<hr />

Hitching trucks, Mikel thought. So that was the funny little vehicle he'd seen Anna with outside. Now it made sense. They were meant for indoor work, useless on the surface. It had taken them half an hour to shift that bogged-down vehicle back into shelter, but Anna had insisted.

Odd. In all the times he'd come through a garage to meet Anna or to see her off, surely he must have seen them being used? Or maybe he'd just not paid attention. He knew to stay away from wherever garage crews were working. There was always a grumpy adult to yell at him if he strayed too close.

"So we do leave *some* useful kit behind, then." Georgina pouted at the handful of squat vehicles parked in a neat row against one wall of the garage.

Now he thought about it, Mikel was sure he *had* seen them, tucked under the front of a lumbering train. They'd always looked like a tiny part of the much larger crawlers, not separate vehicles.

"It's a trade-off," said Anna. "Space on the trek is at a premium. Sponge is hard on outdoor equipment, so that's always scarce and we cart our harvesting rigs with us. But these things live indoors, they hardly ever break down and we have no shortage of them. Why take up precious space hauling something we don't need to? And," Anna chewed her cheek, "for some reason, we've never had trouble shipping in new trucks when we need them."

Huh. There it was again. That strange inconsistency Mikel had wondered about the other night, when the adults had been grumbling about quotas. Quotas that the Company wanted them to fill. Or did they? It sounded like they went out of their way to make it difficult.

Anna spent a few minutes explaining the controls. Not that there was much to explain. Power button, and a joystick for maneuvering. The rest of the console had to do with linking into a train's power and drive systems, not something they'd be needing here.

"Normally," she said, "hauling a few cars around is a one-truck job. It takes the weight of the forward car, and manages the yoop's drive like we do from a driver's cab."

Yoop. Yoop. Mikel fought to look serious. Funny word. Short for Universal Power Unit. He tried to concentrate on Anna's words, to at least *look* like he was listening.

"The train moves around the garage under its own power, guided by the driver in the truck. But here, I'm going to be dragging around dead weight, so I'll need an assist. You two go trundle around a bit and get used to the handling while I get my truck into position."

After a few halting starts, both Mikel and Georgina backed their trucks out of the row.

It took only a few minutes for Mikel to get the feel for the simple controls. He stopped, started, reversed, did a few circuits and figures-of-eight. There was only so much variation you could explore with two degrees of freedom.

Freedom. As Mikel pushed the joystick forward to see just how fast this vehicle could go, he realized he was freer than he'd ever known. He'd scouted up and down a stretch of garage to confirm there were no obstacles in the center section, then opened up the throttle to an exhilarating rush of speed, faster than he could run. The truck's hum rose to a whine and the wheels grumbled across the floor. Frigid air whipped at his mask through the open cage of the cab. Deep gloom yawned ahead of him. Anything in the way would only appear in the gleam of his flashlight at the last moment, too close to avoid, but he'd checked out this space and there was no-one else around to get in the way.

For as long as he could think, Mikel had been hemmed in by the rules of other people. Seemingly arbitrary rules that everyone else seemed to know, but which he struggled to decipher. Familiarity, routine, and repetitive certainty became his refuge against mis-steps.

That world had started to come apart with talk of leaving, of the trek. Mikel had freaked out at the thought of coping with a whole new set of impossible rules, but here they were alone. Just him, Anna, and Georgina. That was a bad thing, Mikel understood, but Anna would fix it. Meanwhile, they were here, free to make up their own rules.

He let out a yip of delight and killed his speed, taking the truck in a lazy circle past Georgina, who still stopped and started in fitful bursts rather than a smooth glide. Seemed like educators were great on the brain stuff, not so much on the hands-on.

Mikel noticed that Anna had positioned her own truck under the cannibalized cargo car, where the front end was propped up on two legs. A hydraulic ram now extended from the roof of the truck to support the car.

Anna was up in the empty shell of the cargo car, slowly cranking one of the legs up. Her mask was off, and sweat gleamed on her face. She leaned on the crank handle and waved Mikel over. He abandoned his truck and clambered through the doorless airlock into the car's bare frame.

"Give that one a go." Anna pointed to the crank on the other leg. "I need a breather." She rolled her shoulders and stretched her back, then climbed down to the garage floor.

Mikel set to with a will. Surely the garage crews didn't have to do this all the time? But of course the cars normally had their own power. This one didn't.

From down below he heard Anna talking to Georgina. "Steering's okay, but you need to practice your fine drive control."

Mikel smiled to himself. That's what he'd thought, too.

Georgina muttered, "Never done anything like this before. Can't blame me if I'm not as smooth as you'd like."

The crank mechanism was stiff with age and disuse. Soon, Mikel's arms and shoulders ached. He paused to mop his face, and leaned over the side of the car to see how much further he had to go.

Anna was squatting on the sill of Georgina's truck. "You ease the stick forward. It's not a push. Start the pressure from your pinkie and roll up through your fingers to your thumb."

Yeah, Mikel had already figured that out.

"Practice that. Control the pressure until you can inch forwards at a crawl and ramp up and down at will."

Mikel returned to his task. Only another meter to go.

A loud screech of metal startled him and set his teeth on edge. He rushed to the airlock door. Anna was in Georgina's truck. She'd found an oil drum and stood it on end. She was pushing it upright, scraping along the floor.

"Your turn." She hopped out of the truck. "Keep practicing until you can move the drum without knocking it over."

Georgina nosed the truck forward and knocked the drum over. Anna grabbed it as it rumbled away and stood it in front of the truck. "Again."

Georgina gave her a glare. Anna shrugged. "You know you'll never live it down if there's something I can do that you can't. Prove me wrong."

At last Mikel finished winding the support leg up. He breathed a deep sigh and sat in the airlock, legs dangling over the drop to the garage floor. It looked like Georgina was finally getting the hang of it.

Anna turned and looked up at him. "Don't know what you're grinning about. Your turn next." She rolled out a second drum, then pointed in turn at Mikel, his truck, and the drum. He swung down to the floor, still grinning.

Georgina had managed to push her drum a whole ten meters without knocking it over. She stopped and called out, "Okay, you made your point, but why the need for such precision?"

"You're hot on theory, so get your mind around this scenario." Anna pointed to her truck now taking the weight of the cargo car. "My truck alone won't have the traction to drag that thing around. When we move a dead car around we need a shunt. A lead car, and one or two trucks nosed up against it. The movement has to be coordinated and smooth."

Georgina wrinkled her nose, gazing up at the towering skeleton of the cargo car.

"Now picture this. All three of us will be under that car. You kangaroo-hop me like you've been doing to that drum and you could push my ram off the lifting plate. Guess where that car will land?"

Georgina blanched. Mikel felt queasy.

Anna returned to the cargo car and gazed up at the lifting plate, where her truck supported the car's weight. She stood on the sill to get a closer look at the plate. Her earlier words to Georgie haunted her. Normally, the plates locked together, but without power up above the coupling wasn't as tight as it should be. Too hasty a move, and there was a real danger she'd slip out from underneath. The trucks' overhead rams should afford them some protection if that happened, as long as they connected with something structural, but that wasn't a chance she wanted to take.

She swallowed her unease and checked on her students' progress. As she suspected, Mikey had mastered the art quickly and was literally running rings around Georgie. For a moment, Anna relished the reversal of roles. School had not been the happiest of times, especially the stern teachings of Miss van Buren. Even so, Georgie had enough of the hang of it now. Good enough for one day.

She clapped her hands and called them over. "We'll bring some provisions over to the cab and have a proper meal. Tomorrow we put all this practice to the test."

Georgie looked pale, and she staggered as she climbed out of the truck. All this concentration on unfamiliar skills must be taking its toll.

Anna sent Mikey off in his truck to fetch supplies from the nearest emergency locker. Once he was out of earshot, she turned to Georgie. "Hard going, isn't it?" There was no sympathy in Anna's tone. Her long childhood of academic mediocrity spilled over. "I should have remembered the emergency lockers, I know that, but I was karking freaked out by all this. I may never have been a bright student, but *this* is my home turf and I'm good at what I do. Don't forget it."

Chapter 13

A smudge on the horizon heralded the end of a long day for Sarah. The last two hours had been spent in solitude. Electrical interference intensified as the afternoon wore on, until even line of sight communication was too much effort.

From then on it was just her, the crawler, and the wide outdoors. The bare ribs of Sponge rolled to the horizon in kilometer-wide undulations, shot through here and there with cracks and deep crevices. Driving up here on Sponge's highlands was a combination of intense concentration and crushing monotony. The nearest human company sat maybe a hundred meters away, five cars or more back.

The sky had been clear all day, but now thunderheads massed to her left, lit by the ruddy glow of Big Red's setting rays.

Rear cameras showed Tania's crawler carrying the last of the clean-up crew closing in behind. The much shorter vehicle could make better speed, and Tania could easily have overtaken Sarah some time ago, but she kept to her traditional position at the rear of the caravan. You didn't mess with solemn traditions like the trek.

Playful gusts whipped across the exposed highlands, rocking the cab from time to time, a prelude to the oncoming nightly fury. Whatever the holdup this morning, they'd cut it fine today. Sarah shuddered.

The thin shadow up ahead resolved into a parallel row of kilometer-long curved windbreaks anchored deep into the ground. Splashes of yellow showed two of the lanes already occupied. Gorge and Gerard were in position, and a glance through binocs confirmed the flurry of activity alongside as crews secured the crawlers for the night.

Sarah steered her own crawler to one side, then slowed and angled it to match the curve of the shelter. She was dimly aware of Tania dropping back and mirroring her movements to take up station in the next lane over. A series of taps on the drive computer's console switched to a program for fine control. The half-kilometer of cars behind her would now follow her cab's line precisely, denied the slight independence of movement they were normally allowed in the open country. She slowed to a crawl and piloted the leading cars into the lee of her chosen windbreak, keeping a steady two-meter gap as she brought the whole train into shelter.

At last, the rear car was safely tucked in. Sarah exhaled a deep sigh and started the shut down procedure. Each yoop in turn signaled it was switched over to standing power, with its pair of wheels firmly locked in place.

Only then did she pick up a microphone and switch on the internal PA. "Vehicle is stationary, safe to disembark. Trek wardens, duty crews outside to secure the vehicle."

A gratifying bustle of activity erupted down the length of the crawler. Within minutes, rooftop cameras showed a cats-cradle of lines tightening between crawler and the walls of the windbreak on either side. Her mind went back to their night in the lee of that guide vane. The night had been violent, but at least the ridges and valleys of the lowlands broke the teeth of the gale. Up here, so much closer to the planet-ringing jet streams, the storm front would sweep unchecked and hit like a hypersonic battering ram. Even in shelter, the stray turbulence spilling over the windbreaks would wreck an unsecured train.

She slumped in her seat and massaged her temples. The earlier exhilaration at being alone in the cab had long ago dissipated. Now she was just karking tired. She normally drove harvest crews from site to site around Serendipity. A couple of days' drive at the most, and in terrain that demanded close attention. She had something to focus on in those fertile but treacherous valleys, something to keep her mind occupied. Not like up here, on the planet's bleak highways.

Skies above. Another fourteen days of this monotony. She'd forgotten just how grueling the seasonal trek was. There would be some hard partying when they reached Laverne.

Then they'd have to do it all again before they finally reached their southern homes for the next harvesting season.

And where the kak *was* Anna? A couple of times during the day, Sarah had tried paging Nick. As the nearest trek warden, the human cargo this end of the train was his responsibility, but he'd been too busy all day to deal with casual inquiries.

By rights this drive was Anna's job, but then, Sarah knew how seriously Anna took her duties. If she wasn't here, she must be having real problems with her kid.

Sarah sighed and pulled over a hand-held tablet. One by one, she worked down the train's segments studying status indicators. Bearings on three starboard running a bit hot. Fuel cells on twelve will need replacing soon, but not yet. Check lube levels in nineteen's forward hitch. And so it went on. Sarah was utterly absorbed making up the snag list and assigning it to wardens to pass on to the maintenance crews.

Footsteps behind broke her concentration. "About time," she called over her shoulder. "Nearly done with the day log ... oh!"

"And nice to see you, too, Sarah." Seth dropped into the starboard navigation seat and grinned. "Hard day?"

Tension eased out of her shoulders at the welcome company. She managed a weak smile, then jumped when John spoke at her other shoulder. "Thought we'd bring up some tucker. Those dried rations stick in the throat after a while."

Sarah spared a guilty glance at the empty packaging littering the floor around her, then noticed the insulated tote bag over John's shoulder. An aroma of gravy and steamed vegetables set her mouth watering. "Just let me just finish off here. I need to wait for the outdoor crews to check in. I'll join you upstairs in a while."

Final checks complete, and after clearing up her mess from the day, Sarah wearily climbed to the upper accommodation deck. John had set out places at the dinette, and Seth was busy in the compact galley adding finishing touches to the evening meal.

Her stomach gave a loud gurgle as the smell of cooking hit her. "Proper food," she growled. "I can't thank you guys enough. And then that shower room had better have hot water."

"I checked," said John. "Everything up here is working just fine. But first, sit! Eat!"

Sarah gave him a grateful smile. "You've got no idea how good it is to see you guys. You could have popped up before now to say hello."

"Didn't want to intrude." Seth wore a puzzled frown as he ferried dishes to the table. "And I thought you were just riding shotgun on this trek."

"That was the plan, but something came up," Sarah mumbled through a mouthful of stew. "Company would have been welcome. I know Anna likes to keep her own company, but my mind was getting well futzed spending all day on my own."

John and Seth exchanged glances. "You could have paged us."

"Didn't know you were on board."

Sarah shoveled another spoonful into her mouth, heedless of manners. "Skies! That's good shit." She slowed and swallowed. "You know, when we split up our train Anna picked up the cargo cars that were left at the end. None of the crew cars. I just assumed you'd be riding one of the other trains with some of our own clan."

"Nah," said John. "We couldn't leave you all on your lonesome with these de Vries families."

Seth nodded. "Everyone slated for the crew car we lost split up to spread the load. Everyone's just looking for spare billets here and there. The planners have been doing their best to keep families together."

"But us single types," said John with a sly grin, "we can bunk down anywhere there's a horizontal surface."

Sarah looked around the cramped accommodation deck. "Then I guess you can bunk up here with me. I don't know what's happened to Anna ... either of you see her?"

Shrugs and shakes of the head. But Sarah noticed Seth's casual expression was a little strained. Anyone with half a brain would guess why he'd elected to ride *this* train.

"Whatever. I know this is her cab, but there's room here, and after today I think I've earned a bit of latitude."

———————

Nick de Jong mopped his forehead and unzipped his jacket in the cramped alleyway of the cargo car's lower deck. This was the closest to privacy you could get on the trek. Without a word, he settled himself against a tool rack to one side. Most of the floor space was taken up by shelves of equipment, leaving a narrow strip leading to the loading ramp at the far end.

"Flaming skies, Nick, you had us all worried today."

Nick acknowledged the stocky woman's complaint with a nod and a grimace, and waited for the other four wardens to make themselves as comfortable as they could.

He didn't trust himself to speak just yet. They'd been so late getting into shelter today they'd barely had time to lash down the vehicle properly and get everyone back indoors. It was a scramble, and there'd been a few bruises where stray gusts had blown people into wheels, dangling ladders, or the walls of the windbreaks. With emotions rubbed raw, Nick had personally checked everyone back on board. No more losses this trip.

There were things to be said and questions to be answered, but first they would pay their nightly respects to the elemental forces outside.

And here it comes!

As if in answer to a summons, all pairs of eyes turned skywards.

A low moan had been building up, like a giant playing kilometer-long pan pipes, but this was nothing more than an overture to the night's performance. The floor was already quivering when an ear-splitting shriek announced the arrival of the storm front. Despite the cradle of ties securing the car, the floor bucked and almost toppled Nick. He staggered and recovered, leaning back against the tool rack and clutching a shelf for support.

Nick glanced at the other wardens, each braced against the spasmodic shudders of the car around them. Each praying in their own fashion for safe passage through the night.

But Nick was praying for nothing more than the ground to open and swallow him. How could he break the news? The thing every warden dreaded.

He'd carefully avoided speaking to Sarah, alone up in the drive cab. Keeping her in the dark, at least, was protocol. For now. But he had to talk to her sooner or later.

Meanwhile he'd clung to a faint and ridiculous hope. Anna might have had time to cross town and join Tania's train, so it was too soon to alarm anyone. But that had been a long shot. As soon as they'd stopped and plugged the crawler into the primitive network spanning the way station's parking lanes, he'd made guarded inquiries with the neighboring crew.

No, they hadn't picked up any last-minute stragglers.

Anna and the others were still trapped there.

Kak, but he *had* cut it close. He really couldn't have given Anna any more time. His legs weakened as he realized how close he'd come to endangering the other three hundred people on this crawler. The alternative, to delay departure another day, brought its own risks of finding themselves caught out on the road when the big weather shift battered the globe. A week away, maybe two, this latitude would soon be a death trap.

He *knew* all that, but nothing took away from his shame and guilt at giving the order to leave. Even though nobody would blame him. Nobody could fault him. Heartbreaking decisions like this came with his role in the community, and everyone knew the rules of the trek.

The initial onslaught passed in a few minutes, and settled down to a manageable level of violence. Movement around the rocking cars would need care, and conversation would be almost impossible for the next few hours, but they all breathed more easily now the first front had passed and the vehicle was still intact.

He'd chosen a cargo car half-way down the train to hold this evening's trek wardens' debriefing. Normally, they'd commandeer a corner of a crew car's living deck and bring the wardens together from the other trains for a joint review of the day. There was no way for people to move safely between vehicles now, so the normal procedures would have to wait.

"Sorry, folks," Nick called above the hurricane trying to tear them loose. "Today was slow going, and we burned up all our contingency. That's on me."

"Madness being out here so late." That was the woman who'd spoken earlier.

Nick wasn't sure if she was referring to their late departure today, or being so late on in the season. He didn't have the heart to question her. "Noted. We had some people to account for, with so many people boarding from the few cars inside the garage."

"So, anything we should know about?" That was one of the other wardens, a bushy-bearded man in his sixties.

Anna, Nick thought, *and Mikey and Georgie*. But he couldn't bring himself to speak. He swallowed hard past a lump in his throat. Thankful for the banshee howls outside masking the catch in his voice he said,

"We'll hold a proper debrief tomorrow, when we can bring all the wardens together."

And put off the moment a while longer. He clung to the reasoning, that revealing friends left behind should be done with all the wardens present, and with due ceremony. A flimsy pretext, he knew, and he hated himself for his cowardice. But, a small unvoiced thought formed at the back of his mind, there was still one last hope. One that he dreaded and hardly dared consider.

Nick pushed the thought aside for now, and waited while each warden gave a short report on conditions in their crew cars. He brought the meeting to a close. "You and your ground crews get some sleep. We'll set off at daybreak tomorrow and not be so rushed on the next leg."

Chapter 14

Even after a week of this daily hike between her quarters and the negotiation room, Jennifer Steel couldn't get used to the crush of people here.

Closed environment colonies, like some of the mining outposts on airless worlds, were always cramped. In small machinery-filled rooms, it only took a handful of people to be on top of each other, to need patience and planning simply to make your way from one side of the room to the other. Jennifer had patience, and she prided herself on never suffering from claustrophobia. Those worlds she'd visited were cramped, but small in scale. A few hundred, maybe a thousand people. The environment was manageable.

Jorvick was anything but manageable. Outside the haven of her quarters, the place heaved and bustled. Through dome after dome people of all ages filled the hallways, rushing around or stopping to gossip. Conversations and laughter assaulted Jennifer's hearing, and her eyes hurt from the dizzying colors and geometric shapes decorating their clothing. It seemed as if the population here needed stimulation of all the senses at all times.

And then there was the constant oppressive heat of this equatorial base. Hadn't these people heard of air conditioning? The combination was overwhelming, even before you added in the sensation of permanent jet lag from the planet's thirty-hour day.

Jennifer squeezed through a knot of people at one of the dome's airlocks and entered the relative tranquility of a connecting tunnel. Thirty meters later, through another lock and into another hall throbbing with energy. Her retinue of guards and local guides followed at a respectful distance. Although she couldn't ditch her escort entirely, Jennifer had been at pains to keep them at arm's length today.

The reason she gave was to see if she could find her way unaided. Only a few domes separated her contingent's quarters from the community hall where the negotiations were held, but it was easy to become disoriented both through sensory overload and through the lack of a simple street grid. Even the modular construction was little help. Each dome was built on identical foundations with airlocks spaced evenly around the perimeter, but that resulted in a confusing hexagonal grid rather than the Earthly norm of right angles.

So Jennifer's pretext was credible, but the real reason was to get more of a feel for the community, some perspective on how they thought. As the negotiations got under way in earnest, Jennifer had an uneasy sense that the talks were drifting off course. Nothing overt, but there was an undercurrent like a boat being dragged past its safe berth on an unseen tide.

That was a problem.

When their shuttle dropped from the longship, Jennifer's own mission had seemed clear and simple. Keep the gravy train running. Dangle the carrot of eventual independence, but snare the colonists with legalese. Now, with Galloway's scheming, she had to keep the talks balanced on a knife edge until she received word of which way to go. That task was challenging enough without the nagging feeling that she was missing something important about Elysium.

As she crossed the intersection of passages at the heart of a dome, Jennifer paused to get her bearings. Somewhere in the distance, a flute struck up a lively reel and was soon joined by a chorus of voices. A door next to her burst open and a group of chattering children streamed out, parting around her like a river. She wrinkled her nose at a sudden wash of garlic.

Jennifer staggered through a fit of dizziness. The six halls radiating off this hub seemed to whirl around her. She regained her balance and glanced back to where her escort had started towards her. She waved them off with an impatient gesture, and took stock.

She'd recognized the passage she needed to take, but the sickening sensation had nothing to do with the physical environment. Jennifer had come to a startling realization. How the heck had she not seen the this before? If Galloway had his way, Jennifer would need to engineer a dramatic concession of terms in order to wring the necessary conditions as a trade off for the Company. Those seemingly innocuous conditions would eventually lead to untold wealth, but she'd been so focused on the benefit to the Company she'd not seen the implications to her personally.

In all her career, surviving decades of brutal politics, that was unheard of. Now, as she thought things through, she felt ill.

Signing that alternative agreement would be seen publicly as a calamitous climb down, an utter failure on her part. Only her senior staff and the President would know the truth. When the discovery broke, with all the proceeds reverting to the Company rather than the colonists, none of the credit would fall her way. There could be no suspicion of any foreknowledge. It would simply be good fortune reversing a negotiating setback that she'd been responsible for.

A bitter laugh forced its way past her lips. If this plan had been discussed with her while she was still on Earth, she could have bargained with the President for a soft landing in return for falling on her sword. Now, two hundred and fifty light years away, they were effectively cut off.

Oh, sure, on its way in, the longship had deployed a small fleet of unmanned drones in the gravity plain of one of the system's Lagrange points. Such fleets formed the backbone of interstellar communications. Drones with wormhole capability could shuttle from one system to another ferrying messages, but it would take days for a message to reach Earth. No use for the kind of delicate bargaining Jennifer would need.

No, she was on her own. She simply had to get on with the job in hand and plead for some scraps after the fact as back door consolation for her sacrifice.

Plead, not bargain. She had no position to speak of. No leverage.

She squared her shoulders and set off again through the last tunnel leading to the community dome, trying not to show any signs of her roiling emotions. Was this a plan to oust her altogether? Had she become too ambitious for the President's comfort? Had Galloway engineered this to create a vacancy in the upper ranks of the Company? If those kinds of plots had been cooking for as long as she thought, without her getting wind of it, she was sunk.

"Executive Steel!"

Distracted, Jennifer turned to the sound of her name. A rookie mistake. As long as she refused to acknowledge the calls of the media throng outside the doors to the conference hall they couldn't pester her with questions. But she'd turned in response. All of a sudden it was open season.

"Thank you for you time this morning, Executive Steel." A jolly, rotund woman had stationed herself between Jennifer and the safety of the conference hall. "How do you respond to the Auditor General's report that Elysium has repaid its colonial debt many times over?"

The stock Company answers froze on Jennifer's lips.

"Doesn't this amount to corporate slavery?" That was from a young, hawk-faced man wearing the logo of News Extra, a network known to promote colonial independence.

The words a few days ago of that engineer at the reception still haunted Jennifer. She gazed blankly at the reporter.

Jayne Kildare took her elbow and steered her through the doors. "No questions at this time. Executive Steel has a lot on her mind, including the future welfare of this colony."

Damn it all! The networks would all have their own swarms of drones waiting, eager to pick up microwave packets of gossip and carry them Earthwards. The President, the whole world in fact, would see her dithering before she could possibly set the record straight.

The moment of truth. Anna had drilled Mikey and Georgie in the few hand signals she'd need to co-ordinate their efforts. Little more than slow ahead, ramp up and ease off, and—most importantly—stop. She decided not to bother with turn signals. It took months of practice to get a three-truck team working in concert through the full range of maneuvers hauling a dead weight around. They would have to turn, but she'd just get them to back off and nudge in again at the right angle. Slower, but less chance of landing that dead weight in their laps.

Now they nosed in gently under Anna's guidance, until her own truck creaked under the pressure.

Hold there.

Good.

With her left fist raised, her right hand eased her own stick back. The truck strained against the cargo car's mass. One finger raised. The other two trucks joined in the push.

Gently. Ramp up the pressure.

With a deep groan of neglected bearings, the car shifted.

Anna glanced up to confirm the lifting plates were still engaged.

Her heart pounded. She had to project confidence, but it had been years since she'd actually done anything like this herself. The garage crews usually handled all the grunt work.

They were definitely rolling. Nothing more than a crawl, but they were moving. Her hand trembled on the joystick as she fought back her elation. There would be time for celebration when they were finally on the road.

Okay, stop.

Anna breathed deep, and got out of the truck to check their progress. She was working blind, reversing the car out into the umber twilight of the garage.

She got the others to back off and adjust their angle slightly. No rush. They were walking a vehicle the size of a house. This had to be done right. A few meters at a time, a few degrees of turn. Ease the car back and around so its front pointed down the garage, to where their drive cab waited.

———————

Nick tried to look casual as he climbed down stairs to the connecting tunnel at the rear of the clan's crew car, and entered the lock into the tunnel.

Some of his colleagues, the more senior and experienced planners, would have had an easier time of it, especially those in Jorvick who handled most off-world affairs. Dealing with the *vreemde* required a special skillset. But that was why *they* were in Jorvick leading the negotiations with the Company, and he was out here ministering to a small harvesting town. Deliberate deception was not in the make-up of most people on Sponge. Life was too precarious, and survival depended on absolute trust in each other. Loss of trust–*stiig*–was a death sentence.

How in all the wide skies did he get into this mess?

Airlock telltales shed a comforting green light as he reached the far end. Rhythmic tremors through the soles of his feet were the only hint of motion now they were out of the valleys and driving on the smooth, hard ribs that straddled the equatorial regions of the planet. Next along was one of many cargo cars making up this train. Pulling his mask into place, he climbed to the upper level and out onto the roof.

He nodded a greeting to two others, anonymous figures swaddled against the chill wind up here, and settled cross-legged on one of the tote boxes snugged in the honeycomb of recesses that made up the upper level of the car.

Nick stole a glance left and right while he wound a scarf around his face, leaving nothing more than a slit for his eyes. The crawler snaked a hundred meters ahead and hundreds behind, one car after another gliding across the landscape. Every rooftop sported a handful of figures sitting or lying, staring into the distance. "Taking the view," they called it. A traditional escape from the confines of the cramped indoors.

Normally Nick was an indoor person. He was a planner, an administrator, and a spiritual mentor to the town's population. He rarely had a need to leave the safety of the town's domes. He was born to the indoors, and the crush of humanity comforted rather than troubled him.

The open vista up here disturbed him. It sucked at his senses, enticing him towards the edge of the roof. He closed his eyes and braced gloved hands against the reassuring solidity of the storage box beneath him. His breathing steadied, and he cautiously cracked his eyelids open again to the bleakness of the outdoors.

On top of the world, the gargantuan rib of Sponge looked like bleached bone. It was hard to believe they were riding on the back of a giant plant.

A more urgent thrumming through his calves and buttocks told him the vast serpentine vehicle was still toiling uphill, despite the apparent flatness of the ground for kilometers around. Somewhere up ahead, out of sight, lay tonight's way station.

Grey overcast obscured the sky, with only brief slashes of copper glimpsed through the clouds. Not everyone shared his love of enclosed spaces. The wide outdoors drew many people.

People like Anna.

Nick's gut wrenched at the thought of her, left behind to the long dark. And Mikey and Georgie.

He'd made the right decision, he told himself over and over. Any of the other wardens would have done the same in his position. But nothing dimmed the pain of abandoning a childhood friend. And imagining what *she'd* be going through was unbearable. She'd be frantic when she found they'd left. Wandering those darkened hallways without hope. Waiting day after day for the bitter deepening nights to sap the last heat from the town.

If yesterday had been one long torment for Nick, the sleepless hours of darkness had sharpened his indecision to new heights of agony.

There was one last hope he could offer her, though the thought of it chilled him to the core. Offering this chance would entangle her in events that were outside his control. This path would have entirely unpredictable consequences for her. For all of them.

There were bigger issues at stake than three lives. The future of the entire planet hung on the conspiracy he was embroiled in, and depended on utmost secrecy. To an Elysium native, his choice was obvious. But conspiracy and secrecy were foreign concepts on Elysium. Company policy placed little value on lives, but to a member of Elysium society—*his* society—Company policy was taking more of a back seat these days. Faced with lives at stake, the simplistic imperative for survival took over.

However, Nick was aware, in ways few on Elysium could understand, that the *vreemde* didn't think like they did. When people's lives clashed with their infernal conspiracies, the outcome was impossible to predict.

The lifeline he was about to throw was dangerously weak, but the alternative was a slow and certain death.

He had no choice here. Not really.

He steeled himself with that thought, and fingered a hand-held remote control hidden in his jacket pocket.

The remote slaved to a short range radio nestled in a breast pocket, and to an automated microwave transceiver stashed in one of the storage boxes alongside him. A muted commentary in his ear told him that he still had fifty seconds before the longship appeared above the horizon. The gyro navigation and sensors in the compact unit would be lining up ready to make a direct connection as soon as it had line of sight.

Sweat beaded his forehead and trickled down the side of his nose. He quelled the urge to wipe it away. There was no such relief under a mask in the wide outdoors.

The transceiver warbled a warning note in his ear. All it needed was the signal from the remote to wake up, everything else was automatic.

There was only one destination it was programmed to call, and it was making contact.

"Identify yourself." The voice was faint and sounded angry.

There should also be no need to identify himself. The unit at his end sent a recognition code and he was the only person here who knew it existed, let alone how to use it. They knew perfectly well who was calling. But Nick played along with their off-world games, not that he had a choice in the matter. "This is the padre." He followed up with a prearranged recognition code.

"Lieutenant Harding. Is there a problem, padre? We were advised the caravan had left town."

He was referring to the last crew out of town. But with radio communications ineffective over anything more than a kilometer they were relying on the closing-down of the landline being one of the final acts of the shut-down crew, and confirmation that the town was empty. "Nothing like that. The caravan was behind schedule, but has left. I need to speak with Captain Rose."

"The captain is not available."

"Please, this is important."

"Of course it is," the lieutenant snapped. "This is an emergency communications link, so it had damned well better be a matter of *vital* importance, or there'll be consequences."

Nick swallowed and reminded himself how small a player he was in this game. In previous dealings throughout the long and complex prelude to these concluding negotiations, he'd been painfully aware that Company officials and employees looked on him as nothing more than an errand boy. To the lieutenant in the longship passing overhead, he was of no importance, and could hardly have anything important to say.

He also reminded himself that, regardless of his own wish to save Anna from the cruel nights to come, this was something the Company needed to know. He could defend that stance to the hilt if it came to it.

"I need to pass a message to the Ringmaster."

"Then you're talking to the right person." Even at the end of a faint and crackly voice link, Nick could hear the sneer in the lieutenant's voice. "Do you think the captain in person has time to run messages for you?"

"Then can you pass on this information when the circus arrives?"

"That may be outside my control." The sneering voice now sounded doubtful.

"What do you mean?"

"We're about to break orbit. We'll be out of range within the next few hours."

Nick's heart sank. But there was nothing he could do about this. He took a deep breath. "Nevertheless. Tell him the circus has some unexpected visitors. Please look after them."

There was a long pause.

"Acknowledged."

The connection broke.

Sweat streamed down Anna's back by the time they closed in on the drive cab. She was trembling with the sustained effort of keeping the car on course. Only two hundred meters of travel, but it had taken most of the day with frequent breaks for Mikey and Georgie to massage feeling back into strained fingers.

Anna was used to spending hours at a time clutching a joystick, but she still remembered the cramps from those early days. The last thing she needed was a slip nudging her too hard at the wrong moment.

Skies above, she would kill for a shower. But all they had was bottled water. Once they were under way, she'd seek out a catchpool and fill the cab's header tank. But right now, it was time to call it a day.

She signaled Mikey and Georgie. Their faces were pale and sweat pooled in the bottom of their masks.

"We eat and get some rest. Tomorrow we hitch up, then load up with supplies for our own private trek."

They both unfolded themselves from their seats and staggered as their feet met the garage floor. Anna turned and stretched.

Georgie eyed the few meters' gap between the salvaged car and the working yoop. "You really want to stop now?" Her tone was incredulous.

Anna saw rekindled disgust in Georgie's eyes. Sharp memories surfaced once more. As a teacher, Georgie often browbeat Anna about quitting too early when problems seemed too hard to solve. Anger surfaced along with the memories. *Is that what this is about?* She swallowed her ire with some difficulty and took a few deep breaths.

"Hold your hand out in front of you. Like this." Anna held her arm out, palm down, fingers splayed. Georgie tried to follow suit, but where Anna's hand was steady, Georgie's jittered violently in front of her. After a few seconds, she pulled her arm in and nursed her forearm against her chest.

"Guiding that hitch into place is going to take precision like we've not needed up to now. It's been a long day and neither of you are fit to tackle the next stage, no matter how eager you are to finish the job. Out in the field, far too many people die of impatience."

Georgie tried to meet Anna's eyes, but her gaze faltered. Anna leaned close and hissed, "Don't *ever* tell me my karking job again!"

Chapter 15

Orange dawn caressed the rim of the windbreak above Sarah's head by the time the outside crews finished untethering the crawler. She checked the status board as each warden confirmed everyone from the ground crew was back on board.

She wrinkled her nose in thought. That's right. Camera visuals all the way down the train. Nothing out of place and nothing still attached. The safety of the vehicle was ultimately the driver's responsibility. No matter how many wardens said they were clear–the chief curate himself might say so–the driver always checked.

The unfamiliar rituals of the trek felt strange, so different from being out in the field with a harvest crew. All drivers knew the drill but she was out of practice. Others usually handled the long, tedious runs between Serendipity and Laverne.

After another grueling day in the seat, she'd passed out in her bunk as soon as she'd eaten the meal Seth and John had prepared. They'd brought extra provisions up to the drive cab from somewhere back in the train, and John was an amazing cook. At least she'd had company yesterday to fill the tedium, and with the two of them riding the cab with her she didn't have to worry about cooking and cleaning.

All systems powered up, she was about to ease the crawler forward when she remembered just in time. On with the PA. "Vehicle is ready to roll. Secure for travel." Dammit. The formalities were so different when you had hundreds of passengers to worry about.

Sarah heaved a long sigh. Anna owed her big time for handling the rig while she was off dealing with family matters somewhere back there. Once again, she toyed with the thought of putting out a general page on the PA. Once again, she dismissed it. Anna must have some shit to deal with and Sarah wasn't going to embarrass her like that.

For now alone in the cab, with her boys still busy upstairs, a deep emptiness settled in her mind as the vehicle crept between the windbreaks.

She'd let Seth down. The loss of their crawler was on her head, and the memory of Ambrose's death would haunt her to her own dying days. They'd all been in a hurry to return to town, but *she* had been at the controls. She should have known better, should have spotted the subtle shift in terrain.

She blinked back a tear and concentrated on the path ahead. The narrow gap between windbreaks curved into the distance, finally opening to a sliver of burnished copper topped by towering clouds.

The nose of the cab peered out from shelter. Sarah glanced left and right, and acknowledged waves from the neighboring cabs already waiting. She thumbed the radio at her turn in the roll call from the lead vehicle, barely audible through a wash of static. "Charlie Tango seven niner, ready to roll." Kak! The unfamiliar call sign only emphasized her own failure. She should have been at the controls of her own rig, not riding someone else's cab.

She was barely aware of the vibration through her seat as first Gerard's then Gorge's crawlers lumbered forwards. She checked the drive controls and eased forwards, accelerating to cruising speed once the whole length was clear.

Big Red glowered at her, half showing above the horizon and lighting the underside of lowering clouds. The season was closing in.

<hr />

"Get your fingers limbered up," Anna said, "this is going to need a delicate touch."

Without power for two days now, the chill from outdoors seeped into the garage and settled deep in her bones. Breath steamed in their masks. That was the trouble with a cozy cab ... leaving it was a shock to the system. Anna flexed her fingers and frowned. She hadn't realized just how quickly this vast space would lose what little residual heat it held. This wouldn't do.

"Hold up," she called. "Walk around a bit. Get used to the cold but keep your bodies warmed up. I'll be back out in a minute."

She climbed back through the airlock into the equipment bay, and rummaged through the lockers praying they hadn't been stripped bare. A few minutes' search yielded a pair of flat gel packs the size of hand towels, emergency equipment to bring reviving warmth to anyone unfortunate enough to spend too long outside after dark. She plugged them into a power outlet. It only took a few minutes to absorb enough charge, and a gentle warmth spread through the material.

Anna strode over to the cargo car, eyeing the small distance to be covered. "Saddle up, folks. Right gloves off, and wrap this around your hand on the joystick. You need to be able to control your movements like we did yesterday, without your hand going numb."

Satisfied that Georgie and Mikey were settled in and ready to go, Anna took her own seat. "Remember the hand signals from yesterday. It'll be a slow approach and tiny movements."

They edged closer, with frequent stops for Anna to check their line. If they'd been moving a powered-up car this would have been so much easier. A video feed down to the truck's cab would give a clear view of the mating hitches overhead. As it was, slow and patient was the order of the day.

At last, a final push, Anna was rewarded with a bump, a scrape of metal on metal, and a satisfying click.

Satisfaction soon turned to frustration as Anna, sweating and swearing on the yoop's catwalk, wrestled with the locking clamps. She gave the stubborn lever one last frustrated kick, and sat on the edge of the catwalk to think things through.

A rush of despair and tears welled up. A hand on her shoulder. A squeeze. She sniffed and looked up into Mikey's wide eyes. She managed a weak smile. Anything out of the ordinary was hard on him, she knew. This must be torture. His whole world had been upended. The thought of the trek was bad enough, leaving home and safe routine behind, but *this* was a step into the unknown, the unimaginable.

She groaned to herself when Georgie joined them on the catwalk. Anna braced herself for some scathing remark at this latest setback, but Georgie's tone was surprisingly conciliatory. "I know I don't have anything useful to offer here, but sometimes it helps to talk these things out loud."

Anna sniffed again, and cleared her throat. She struggled to speak, forcing the words past a lump the size of an apple. "The hitch has a universal joint this side, on the yoop. The car has a matching socket." She pointed to the fastenings alongside her feet. "That side needs to clamp down to hold the hitch together. You can see it's a karking big mechanism."

"I guess it has to take quite a load."

"It's not like it has to pull the train along. Each segment drives itself along–"

"But it takes the weight of the car slung between the yoops."

"Exactly." Anna nodded. "So the clamps have to be solid. Fastening and letting go is normally motorized, like raising and lowering the support legs, no need to work up a sweat. But that car's yoop is dead. No power. So we do things by hand." She kicked the hitch again. "But this one's seized up."

Georgie leaned against the outer wall of the connecting tunnel that ran across the axle. "Any way to unstick it? I'm no engineer, but there must be lubricants and things that might loosen it up. Or some way to apply more brute force."

A tap on her shoulder. Anna looked up and realized Mikey was pointing at something. The power coupling? She puzzled for a moment, then understood what he was trying to say. "You know, that might just work!" She thought it through. "If we feed power from *this* yoop to the car, the motors on the hitch might be able to overcome the seized gears. They'll sure as heck be able to apply more force than I can manage."

"So, we need to find another power cable?"

Anna's mind raced. She talked excitedly, words starting to trip up over themselves in her haste. "We've searched this garage and only come up with one. We'll split up. Ride a truck each. You both have yours, and I'll find another one. I can't take mine out from under here until we secure this hitch."

They climbed down, eager to be doing something useful. At the bottom of the ladder, Georgie murmured, "Thought about apprenticing Mikey to a garage crew?"

Anna gaped at Georgie. "Really? Now?"

"We're getting out of this, Anna, and when we do, Mikey has to have a future. I know it's been troubling you. He needs an apprenticeship somewhere." She gestured to where Mikey had started up his truck and was driving in figures-of-eight. "He learns quickly, and he's clearly got a knack for this kind of thing."

Anna chewed the inside of her cheek. "Trouble is, communication is crucial to garage operations. Besides, he's not going to be a dome dweller. The crowds drive him mad, and he's always longed to travel the surface."

"Communication's even more life-and-death out there."

"Yeah, well unless we can get this rig mobile, it's all a pointless discussion." Anna waved and called out, "Mikey, you know the way to West One. I'll take East One. We'll meet up back at Admin Central, middle passage. Georgie, you head straight down to South One and work your way across. Mikey and I will join you and let you know sooner if we've found something."

They set off together, with a bit of scraping through the far airlock. Georgie still needed practice judging the width of her vehicle. Where the tunnel branched off to the administration dome, they split up. Mikey headed right to the western garage. Georgie carried on straight towards the main garage complex to the south. Anna branched off and through the admin dome.

As she pulled into the garage, an empty and echoing twin to the one she'd left behind with its cozy cab and almost-hitched car, she had an unsettling feeling she was missing something.

She stopped alongside this garage's cluster of cannibalized vehicles and got out. A few minutes' search turned up nothing of value. It was easy to scan the hitches at each end to see if there was a power coupling in place. She wasn't hopeful. It had been a miracle finding that one cable, hidden away. There were stacks of parts heaped up alongside. Anna toyed with the thought of rummaging through on the off-chance, but it was only a half-hearted thought. Power cables were one of those items, always in demand, always the first to be stripped from any condemned hulk. They were always being swapped out and moved around.

Swapped out! Anna smacked her forehead and ran for her truck. They were wasting their time.

She barreled a kilometer through darkened domes across town to the western garage, where she found Mikey scanning systematically down the far side.

"Mikey, we need to fetch Georgie back. We don't *need* another cable. We just swap over the one we've got. Close up the hitch and lock it in place, then put it back to power the driver's cab."

His mouth formed an 'O', and even under the mask his exaggerated roll of the eyes was comical.

With a whoop of joy they set off for the southern end of town. They reached the last habitat dome before South Two and Anna stopped in front of the closed airlock. Her mind was already running through the well-worn ritual of checking the airlock telltales, along with her mask and air filter, when her heart thudded.

The telltales were lit!

The garage had power. *What?* The sheer impossibility of it froze her to the spot, then her legs weakened under her and she stumbled to lean against the wall. There was someone there. *They were saved.*

Trembling fingers reached for the lock controls. Mikey's hand wrapped around hers and stilled the movement. He frowned and cocked his head to one side, regarding the lit controls. He gave his head a tiny shake.

As much to humor him as anything, Anna said, "You're right. Something's very odd about this. But maybe the clean-up crew forgot something and came back?" She didn't sound convincing even to herself. If there were rescuers here, surely Georgie would have raced back to tell them. And the glowing telltale was now starting to give her the shivers. There was something unnatural about it.

Mikey tugged her to the right, around the dome's perimeter. They left the trucks behind. The perimeter walk was little used and too narrow for vehicles. The next airlock led through to a smaller dome and then into South Three. The airlocks along the way were dark. Only when they reached a side tunnel linking South Three to South Two did they see another lit telltale. Cautiously, Anna and Mikey entered the lock.

Despite the hope in her heart, gnawing anxiety threatened to overwhelm her. They both winced at the soft hiss as the lock flushed clean air through. Windows in the far pair of doors let in a shaft of light from the garage beyond, giving the inside of the lock a ghostly air. After two days in subterranean gloom, the light was dazzling even though, when Anna peered through the window, it seemed to be nothing more than low level emergency lighting. She dropped her mask and took a deep breath of air that tasted sweet compared with the chemical taint now pervading the town.

She glanced at Mikey, then eased the door open.

Voices in the distance. There really were people here. They didn't sound friendly, though.

"There's only me." Georgie's voice carried clearly. "I was so relieved to see you. I thought I was stranded."

What? Was Georgie planning to escape and leave her and Mikey behind? Anna knew Georgie had a low opinion of her, and maybe she shouldn't have shown her up with the hitching trucks, but on Sponge you looked out for each other. Always.

Nearby, a pair of trucks stood silent guard alongside the dismembered skeleton of a crew car. Anna crept along the near wall and crouched behind a neatly-stacked pile of dismantled bunks and kit lockers from the crew car. She edged forward under cover of the salvaged materials, and froze.

Georgie knelt on the floor in the center of the garage, facing a dark-skinned stranger. The two of them were surrounded by half a dozen others.

All had offworlder skin tones and most of them wore drab green overalls. The one facing Georgie held her attention, though. His face was the color of dusk, framed by long braids that looked like raw, untreated flax. He wore a long overcoat embroidered with flowers and starbursts in a bewildering geometric pattern. Vivid reds and golds glowed against deep blue. His pale eyes held no promise of rescue.

Anna shivered.

"So, you say you're all alone here? Nobody with you?" If his eyes were cold, his voice promised unending night.

Georgie raised one hand, imploring. Anna noticed her other arm hung limp at her side. "I got left behind. There's no-one else here."

"And why," he whispered, "would they leave behind such a fine specimen?"

"Company policy."

"Remind me."

"When you miss the last train of the trek, nobody comes back for you. I was already making my peace before death took me."

"So be it." The tone was off-hand. Bored. He raised his hand and a sharp crack echoed through the garage, reverberating a second later from the curved wall at the far end.

Georgie slumped to the floor.

Anna jammed a fist in her mouth to stifle a cry. Her stomach heaved.

"Clean this mess up." The leader gave a dismissive wave of his hand. "And look for more vermin. Whatever this *retired employee* would have us believe, the padre said 'visitors'. Plural."

Chapter 16

Anna pulled her head back behind a concealing kit locker and pushed Mikey behind her. She crouched on her haunches and blinked back tears. She strained to listen above the hammering of her heart. Footsteps. Nearby. She shooed Mikey ahead of her and slipped behind one of the hitching trucks.

Trembling, her stomach performing somersaults inside her, she glanced above the frame of the truck's cab. These were indoor working vehicles with just a safety cradle to support the roof. No polyglass to obscure vision. She stared straight into the eyes of one of the overalled *vreemde*.

They both froze for a second. The man seemed as shocked as Anna, then the spell broke. Mikey let out a small yelp of panic and dashed for the airlock, just meters away. The stranger called out and ran past the far side of the truck to cut him off. He lunged for Mikey, ignoring Anna for the moment. She tripped him as he rounded the end of the truck. He sprawled to the floor with an enraged bellow, cut short as Anna's boot slammed into his face.

They scrambled into the airlock and hit the 'exit' sequence. The telltale at the other end glowed amber to signal trace toxins present beyond. The far door opened, allowing clean air to vent out.

Angry pounding on the door behind her spurred Anna on. She gave silent thanks for the few seconds' delay they'd gain while the lock flushed before allowing the inner door to open again.

Grabbing Mikey's hand, Anna sprinted to the end of the garage, back the way they'd come. Their clattering footsteps echoed from the far wall. If they could reach their abandoned trucks they'd make better time than on foot.

They entered the habitat dome around the wall from where they'd left the trucks. The rounded outer walls of the lower level apartments loomed in the morning light filtering through the dome's skin. The slam of a door and angry voices echoed from the right, around the curve of the walls. *Kak!* Someone had got there ahead of them. And boots clacked in the emptiness behind.

Mikey's shaking hand on her shoulder urged Anna in the opposite direction from the voices. They had to keep moving.

Trying to run quietly in work boots was impossible, but their pursuers were making enough noise of their own. Shouts and bangs echoed back and forth across the skin of the dome. It sounded like an army on the move. A high whine cut through the clamor. Someone was making use of the trucks.

As they neared the next exit and slowed, Anna peered around the corner into the cross corridor running through the center of the dome. A shadow in the distance crossed her line of sight, then backed up and turned towards her. Had she been seen? Or were they simply choosing the most obvious path to head off their quarry?

With the truck approaching from her right, and running footsteps behind, Anna yanked Mikey's arm and hurried through to the next dome. Out of sight for a few seconds, they raced down the hall feeling perilously exposed, and slipped into the nearest living quarters. Even pumped with adrenalin, Anna found herself muttering the ritual of greeting on entering someone else's space. She shook off momentary paralysis and crossed to the nearest stairs. Up two flights, and the small wedge-shaped suites of family quarters cut through by cross corridors gave way to a floor of communal spaces that spanned the width of the dome. From here, she could choose any of the stairwells to escape.

She stopped and strained her hearing for sounds of pursuit. Would the intruders just pass through this dome, or start searching the living quarters? They needed to find their way back to North One, but without leading the *vreemde* there. If they could only complete their work on the crawler, they could escape this nightmare. But first, they had to avoid capture.

Or worse.

Anna froze and fought down the image of Georgie, blood spraying the deck.

Focus!

She looked around, suddenly panicked. She was alone. "Mikey," she hissed. Where the kak was he? "Mikey." Louder this time. She winced as the sound echoed through a deserted dining hall.

He crept, ghost-like, down the stairs from the next level, holding a finger to his lips. Anna puzzled at the pair of bed sheets draped over his shoulders, then caught a glimmer of his intent when he gestured to the servery and the kitchens behind.

At the back of the kitchen, tucked into a corner beside a pantry, an unmarked door led outside. The levels of the living quarters stepped in every two or three floors forming an irregular circular pyramid following the curving arc of the outer skin. They stood on a deep ledge four meters wide that overlooked the ground-level perimeter walk. A railing separated them from the five meter drop, but they kept their backs pressed to the wall behind them. Away from the edge, they couldn't be seen from the walkway below.

But they could hear what was going on. "Good move," Anna breathed in Mikey's ear. She'd been worried about descending a stairwell and stumbling into a stealthy searcher. From up here, they could listen and observe with little chance of detection, and climb down when the coast was clear.

Mikey knotted the sheets together in readiness. Together they crept along until they were almost opposite the exit Anna wanted to take. The habitat domes were dangerous, she reasoned. Long, unbroken corridors left them too exposed, and those trucks could get up a turn of speed when they had a clear run. And she didn't want to risk heading too directly towards their destination. A diversion into the storage and processing plants on the western edge of town seemed a better bet.

Mikey slithered forward, keeping low to the floor, and tied one end of the sheets to the bottom of one of the railing posts. Everything remained out of sight from below. Two women passed below on foot, entering the dome and heading into its depths beneath their feet. From the brief snatch of overheard conversation, they seemed convinced their quarry was in here somewhere, and a systematic search was being planned. Anna gave Mikey a mental cheer for this idea. On the other hand, how long before someone discovered the little-used doorway out onto this ledge?

With no more sound from below, Anna risked a peek over the edge.

All clear.

She lowered the rope and scrambled down, dropping the last meter to the floor. Mikey followed. Her heart missed a beat when she realized they had no choice but to leave the sheets dangling for any passer-by to see. It would be obvious where they'd gone.

Nothing they could do about that. They crossed the hall and slipped through the nearest airlock doors. A short passage led to a long and narrow corridor that curved into the distance on either side. After the clamor of the pursuit, all was deathly quiet. Ghostly light filtered through the outer skin arching a few meters overhead.

The corridor ran past the ends of several warehouses and garages. If they could reach the accommodation dome at the far end, a hundred meters away, they could probably avoid detection in the maze beyond. It would take weeks for the handful of people she saw back there to make a complete search of the town.

A rumble behind them, and Anna cursed her luck. The truck was still out of sight, but only for a few seconds.

They ran.

An intersection.

Safety lay ahead, but too far to reach before they were seen. Another clatter and rumble to their right. The nearest cover lay a few meters away to the left, but this cross-corridor was dead straight. They'd be seen, whichever way they went.

Mikey pulled Anna into the intersection and to the left. Ignoring the frenzied whine as the truck, still forty or fifty meters away, sped up, they pounded through the airlock and into a vast, echoing warehouse. The place had been emptied out in readiness for the trek.

No cover.

Another lock lay over to their right, an impossible distance away. Anna prayed that the deep gloom at the heart of the warehouse would make them hard to see when the pursuit burst through the door. Every second counted.

Her breath rasped in her throat as they sprinted across the floor. The air in here had picked up a sour taint of Sponge's poison. Not enough yet to do harm, but enough to feel like her lungs were burning. She considered then discarded the notion of pulling on her mask. The filters simply couldn't keep up with the ragged gasps of air she was dragging in.

A flashlight beam picked them out just as they reached the door. They scurried through and emerged into an anteroom in the next dome. Warning signs on the next doors screamed danger. Anna paused and took two deep breaths to steady herself. "Masks," she rasped as she pushed through the door. They were in a processing factory, one of the rooms where husks harvested from the depths were stripped of their fibrous coatings. The process produced a toxic, choking dust. A thin layer still coated the floor.

They crossed the factory floor. As they went, Anna scuffed the floor, kicking up as much dust as she could. The door banged behind them. She risked a glance behind and saw faces peering through the window, flashlights painting ghostly fingers through the clouds. Snatches of fury and shouted orders echoed through the door as someone risked cracking it open again, but only briefly.

It sounded like the pursuers had read the signs on the door, and no cajoling or threats were getting them into the dust-choked air. Shame. Flax residue wasn't like the native air, it wouldn't kill them right away, but a deep breath and they'd be too ill to do any more hunting.

They'd bought a few moments, just the seconds it would take to find another way around. They left that dome and crossed the next, another steaming room. Sadly not hazardous.

Already, the whine of motors sounded from the corridor behind them. The *vreemde* were closing in, and a shout of jubilation said that the nearest had spotted them. Anna yanked Mikey into the airlock and pulled the door shut. There was no air cycle to delay their pursuers, but they'd have to get out of the truck to open the door. They'd either continue on foot, or waste time getting the truck through the lock. Either choice was a win for Anna. Through a short tunnel and another lock, and another pair of closed doors, and they were in another one of the town's warehouses.

Much of it had also been emptied out, but there were still towering stacks of building materials–girders and trusses, panels, boxes, and doors–all fashioned from Sponge's durable core materials. All ready for use in some future season, extending the town one dome at a time.

They dodged down an aisle and around the end of a stack, out of sight from the central thoroughfare. Out of sight of pursuers. For now.

A low growl and metallic clatter. In the broad aisles and wide open spaces of the depleted warehouse, vehicles would have the advantage of speed. Anna should have stuck to the narrower halls and maze of compartments of the domes.

She pulled Mikey along with her, deeper into the rows of stacked materials. A second vehicle had joined the first, and running footsteps behind that signaled the approach of reinforcements. From the shouted orders, they were organizing themselves to carry out a systematic search. She strained her ears for sounds of movement, all the while edging deeper into the warehouse.

They were now half-way down the two-hundred-meter length and running out of cover. The far end was mostly empty space. She thought furiously. Like the larger vehicle garages, the main warehouses had an upper deck set on rows of tall pillars. Could she lose them up there? With no power for the hoists the vehicles would be unable to follow. She quickly discarded that thought. The upper level was no better than down here, and they'd have no means of escape. There were enough people chasing them to cover the few stairwells. These people seemed determined, and it was only a matter of time.

It occurred to Anna that evading the search wasn't enough. She had to do something to reduce their numbers. An idea formed, reluctantly, going against every fiber of her upbringing. But, she steeled herself, they'd proved themselves *stüg* by killing Georgie so callously. She owed them no second thought.

Anna glanced at Mikey, pointed to the airlock behind them then to their masks. He pursed his lips, then his eyes gleamed and he nodded.

The next move had to be timed right. Anna hoped the pursuers were too pumped with adrenaline to think much beyond giving chase. She listened for the rattle of a truck down the center aisle, then dashed from cover, stopped as if realizing her mistake, and darted back along the side aisle. She dragged Mikey with her, aware of the screech of wheels on rough flooring. Damn! They were quicker off the mark than she expected.

A few moments of cursing and whining of motors, and the rumble grew to a steady murderous roar close behind.

She yanked open the nearer of the double doors. Mikey pulled the other, giving the truck free passage. They pounded the few meters and spilled out the far end.

Onto the surface of Sponge.

Anna and Mikey pulled their masks on as they ran, and Anna angled to the left, out towards open ground.

Two trucks slammed through the outer door in quick succession and were ten meters out before the drivers could react to their mistake.

The lead driver gave an agonized rasping cough, and scrabbled weakly at the controls, trying to turn the truck around.

The one behind him leaped from her truck and staggered back towards the warehouse. It seemed she was trying to hold her breath, but she heaved an involuntary breath and collapsed to her knees, retching thin acid. Two more figures emerged on foot and hastily retreated.

The memory of Georgie's body slumped to the floor haunted her. Anna had heard of guns, and watched the occasional vid from off-world, but nothing had prepared her for that raw violence. The crack of the gunshot would never be erased from her memory, but what made her sick was the *intent* behind it.

Everyone on Sponge was hardened to violent death. The choking agony of a leaking mask, the swift plunge into a bottomless chasm, sprung traps of thorns that grew around some of the more sensitive organs in the depths. Then there was the fury of wind and electrical storms. Supersonic gusts could fling unprepared crawlers like toys. Sponge was a deadly host, but that was simply the environment they lived in. Careful preparation and observance of procedures kept them as safe as they could be.

But Anna had just witnessed deliberate violence of one person against another. That was unheard of. Sponge was a fearsome enough foe without fighting among themselves.

Anna felt no remorse for the two truck drivers, now well beyond help. They'd done that to themselves. But there were others behind them.

"Come on. It won't take them long to find masks." At least they won't be so keen to chase blindly another time. Anna wracked her brain for options. They'd emerged into an open space between the warehouse, and garage West One a hundred meters away. There were any number of external airlocks where they could try to re-enter the town, but isn't that what these interlopers would expect?

Yet out here on the surface, they were more exposed than anywhere indoors.

Banks of clouds obscured the low-hanging sun, bringing a sudden chill. Urgent squalls tugged at Anna's jacket. The flapping of her collar against her mask brought her back to the here and now.

Over to their left, there was at least some cover. Every town stockpiled building materials to be used for repairs and expansion. Sponge might be brutal, but it also yielded much of what they needed to thrive here. Harvest crews were always on the lookout for rib veins of the right length and thickness to fashion the strong but flexible ribs for domes and tunnels. The raw material cut from the depths spent years in drying and curing, tempered by at least two full Sponge winters out in the open. Heaps of seasoning boughs and neater stacks of trimmed spars marched into the distance.

She looked into Mikey's eyes and jerked her head towards the stockpiles. He nodded.

They ran.

Chapter 17

Jennifer Steel smiled–although her skin felt so stretched surely the tension in her jaw must be plainly visible from across the room–and called a recess for her team. The entire contingent filed out of their seats and into the warren of offices and conference rooms that ringed the hall. Without pause, she stalked through their suite and into a smaller office followed by her senior advisors, leaving the more junior staff behind in the large common room.

She could smell the fear, the consternation, behind her. Fuck 'em. She'd deal with them later, but this discussion had to start at the top. As soon as the last of her senior team filed past, she pushed the door closed while keeping her gaze fixed on the tapestry adorning the far wall.

The click sounded like a gunshot in the silence. She let the tension build for a few seconds, daring anyone to speak out. She remained standing, forcing the handful of others in the room to do likewise.

"That was a shambles." Her tone remained level, but it held all the warmth of liquid helium. "What happened?"

Her gaze into space never wavered. From the corner of her eyes she was sharply aware of the glances from person to person as they did silent battle over who would speak first.

Samuel Wong, chief trade analyst, drew the short straw. He cleared his throat. "Our demand for a seven percent increase on rates for sheet metals was a feint. They should never have agreed to it, allowing us to 'relax' our stance and counter-offer what we really wanted." His tone was calm, reasonable, admirably free of the nervousness he must be feeling. To Jennifer it screamed deflection ... *not my fault.*

"Instead," she snapped, "they banked our offer of a reduction for machine parts, which they clearly wanted more than we thought, and gave up nothing of value in return."

"I don't understand it. With their planned rate of expansion, they need raw materials. Refusing should have been a no-brainer."

Okay, that was a fair point, but Jennifer was not about to let him off the hook. It was not up to her to provide answers. Let her staff earn their keep.

"Samuel's right," said Raisa Garina, one of Don Kozyr's deputies, promoted in his unlamented absence. Jennifer quirked an eyebrow. Raisa was remarkably self-assured for a young and newly-promoted staffer, raising her voice in such high-level company. She was stepping into her new role with confidence. Good.

Unfazed, Raisa continued, "But there were warning signs. Their import of raw materials has declined steadily over the last seventy years. My predecessor believed they've simply slowed their expansion, but other signals suggest otherwise."

"Such as?"

"Power plants of all sizes. There's a steady demand that nobody's properly accounted for. And other specialized machined parts, finished products that need high tech to manufacture."

"All the same," Timothy Finch, Jennifer's most experienced negotiation strategist said, "colonists on sealed-environment worlds *never* jeopardize raw supplies. Especially when their world is so metal poor. No matter the demand, or temporary lack of it, there's an innate aversion. *Always.*" He gulped and seemed to shrivel in on himself at making such a definitive pronouncement. His perpetually nervous demeanor irked Jennifer, but over the years she'd learned to curb her reactions. This was a fragile flower who needed nurturing. Jennifer was not the nurturing kind, but she made rare exceptions when she felt the payback was worth it.

But only *while* it was worth it. She gritted her teeth. "This is the third miss in two days. You are the Company's Alpha team, but these backwoods colonials are running rings around you. This. Does. Not. Happen."

"Someone's shafting us." Jasmine Golightly, Jennifer's acid-tongued legal counsel settled herself into a chair and glared at Jennifer, defying her to say something. "They've spent the past three days preaching about their aspirations for expansion. Railing at the Company for holding them back. Clearly playing to the media gallery but it's also as if they were baiting a trap. Why did we get no hint of this turnaround from Kyari? Are you sure he's reliable? He could be feeding us bull."

Momentarily distracted by Jasmine's insolence, Jennifer took a few seconds to home in on her meaning. She reviewed everything the Company held on Maximillian Kyari, together with Nikolai's more recent covert inquiries. "I'm sure. He's firmly in our pocket. Besides, he *did* warn us they might buy that offer. *You* assured me this move was safe." That last was directed back to Timothy Finch, master strategist.

"It should have been," he quavered. "We've crunched the numbers through the most sophisticated game theory models we have. This is how we run rings around everyone else."

"Usually." The one word dripped venom.

The energy that sustained her suddenly seemed to evaporate. Inwardly, Jennifer struggled for control, struggled not to let her shoulders droop. She allowed herself the luxury of closing her eyes for a second while she marshaled her thoughts. When she opened them again and glared around the room, it was her trademark gigawatt laser stare once more.

"I don't need to remind you, we need to keep this process on course, which means we need *control*. When I make a proposal I need to *know* how they'll respond. It was always going to be a tough balance with Galloway's little venture in the wind, but right now I feel like I'm shooting rapids in a rudderless boat."

She scanned the circle of faces once more, before settling on her strategist. His face paled, but he rallied gamely. "Most small colonies are nothing more than offshoots of Earth cultures. Placed under extreme environmental stress, but the motivational patterns are highly predictable. Something's different here. Entirely novel psychology."

At last. Some glimmer of analysis happening. A fraction of the tension eased out of Jennifer's shoulders.

Jasmine Golightly settled herself deeper in her seat. "Remember, it's been nearly a century since the agreement was last substantially revised. Since anyone from Earth has really studied them."

"We're normally treating with colonies in much earlier stages of development." Samuel Wong took up the theme. "The Company has kept Elysium in its control far longer than any other colony. They are on a unique evolutionary trajectory."

They may have a point, but Jennifer was not placated. "Regardless, you've had nine years now to prepare for this. Eight years of legal and commercial analysis, diplomatic hedging, political pressuring, opinion-shaping, before the Company and Elysium kicked off the formal rounds of preliminary positioning. What happened to all those years of research?"

"Thrown under the bus," Jasmine snarled, "the moment that second agreement hit the table."

Jennifer hesitated at the sudden anger in the lawyer's tone. This was a direction she hadn't expected. "Explain."

"Don't you see? You're all looking at these as two independent negotiations."

"And they're not." Light dawned.

"You got it. We came prepared to play hardball and wring as much as we could out of them."

"Oh ... God." Timothy Finch paled and slumped into the nearest chair. "The original agreement we prepared for was the traditional tie-in until colony debts repaid. The negotiation was going to be a straight arm-wrestle over the terms."

Jasmine nodded. "But put an alternative on the table, holding out the promise of an early escape, and the *whole* dynamic changes."

Timothy's fingers twined together on the table top. "We've been having to rein in the pressure on the first agreement, to keep it in play as a credible option. We've looked on it as nothing more than a linear shift, but in reality we're not playing it anything like how we planned."

"How far off are we?" Jennifer asked.

"Every strategy is being reassessed on the fly. Just small adjustments at first, but the deeper we go the further we're departing from the original plan."

Jennifer leaned back against the wall. "So, we're making it up as we go along?"

Timothy nodded miserably. "And half the time, these colonists aren't responding how we'd normally expect."

"Okay, so how do we bring things back on track? And why are our assumptions leading us astray?"

"Because they're assumptions we have no way of validating."

Jennifer glanced in surprise at Jayne Kildare, her chief of security. Jayne usually stayed aloof from strategy discussions.

"You've seen the skin pallor the locals have acquired," Jayne continued.

Jennifer sniffed. "Endemic peripheral cyanosis. How is this relevant?"

"Except it's not true cyanosis. Multi-generational exposure to traces of native toxins. Their chemistry is adapting."

"Still looking for relevance, Jayne."

"It makes it impossible for anyone off-world to blend in. Normal sources of intelligence are dry on this world. We can't insert spies directly into the population, and the agents we place into freight hauling teams report that the locals are impossible to turn."

"Deep-rooted loyalty?"

"They've turned their views inwards to an unprecedented degree. It's like they're barely aware that the universe outside exists." Jayne paused. "We, and anything we have to offer to any given individual, are essentially irrelevant to them."

"What about Galloway? He must have had help."

"Even *you* were kept in the dark about that. We don't *know* what interaction he had with these people. We can only assume he managed to convince local contacts that he was actually working in their interests."

"That's another thing, people." Jennifer placed her tablet on the conference table, a careful and precise movement. "Before the longship broke orbit, Galloway reported delays getting into the town, so he's behind schedule. This makes it all the more important that we regain control of this process. We need the ability to slow things down and keep the necessary balance. I need fine control, like landing a scramjet. And not simply over *what's* happening, but *when*."

She speared Timothy Finch with an icy glare. He bobbed his head, long fingers twining nervously in front of him. "We need more data points." Bob. Fidget. "The usual motivation matrices aren't giving us a good enough fit."

"In plain English," Jennifer gritted out, "we need to understand what makes these people tick."

Kak! Kak! Kak! They should have made a run for an airlock after all, and taken their chances in the town's labyrinth of passages.

Peering through gaps in the nearest heap of raw limbs of inner rim-wood, Anna watched the activity around the nearest warehouse with cold dread in the pit of her stomach. They had barely managed to gain their meager sanctuary before a half dozen masked men and women appeared.

One of the *vreemde* heaved their dead colleague from the idling truck and dumped his body unceremoniously on the ground. Skies above! What was going through these people's minds? At least Anna had the satisfaction of seeing the truck bog down on the soft surface. Any pursuit would be on foot. Not that it would matter much. These people were clearly organized and it wouldn't be hard to scour the stockpile aisle by aisle.

With a thud of her heart, Anna saw two more figures emerge from the garage opposite. Well, maybe that wouldn't have been such a good choice after all.

Someone in the middle of the group shouted instructions with determined hand gestures–too muffled to make out words at this distance, but the intent was sickeningly clear. The group split into pairs and marched purposefully towards the stockpile where Anna and Mikey hid.

Anna glanced around and led Mikey another row deeper in. Desperation started to creep into her thinking. The stockpile was cut through by broad avenues to allow lifting machinery in, wide open and exposed. The searchers would surely station people at the ends to spot any attempt to cross.

Their best bet seemed to be among the jumbled heaps of newly-harvested materials. Bulbous nodes of corewood loomed overhead, two or three meters thick, some with their long tails of tangled branches still attached. At first glance they might seem to offer a hiding place, but their dark, thick coating of raw fibers would snag clothing and rip exposed flesh with tiny but vicious barbs. An untreated corewood welt would bring on septic shock within a day. Anna felt a twinge of shame at the hope that at least one of the *vreemde* might explore these thickets.

The smooth and milky lengths of rimwood offered fewer hiding places, but at least didn't come cloaked in painful death.

While Anna strained for sounds of pursuit, Mikey stalked down the edge of the stack, pausing now and again to examine the angle where it met the surface. He waved Anna over, and pointed.

She stared at him. "Are you serious?" she hissed. She ducked, heart hammering, at the sound of voices from the other side of the stack, and gazed wildly around for somewhere to hide.

Somehow, Mikey had found an opening, little more than a meter-long tear in the surface fabric. It looked nothing more than a shallow depression, but Mikey crouched down and thrust his arm in up to the shoulder, feeling his way around below. He gesticulated urgently, and slipped his legs into the cut.

Debilitating numbness spread up her back and over her shoulders and neck. She shuddered and almost vomited into her mask. She must have misunderstood. He was going down below. Into Sponge. Into the nightmare world that had claimed Luuk and so many others.

A rushing roar sounded overhead. The noise pounded Anna's ears and she pressed back into the stacked trunks, trying to blend in. A jet swooped low from behind her and disappeared past the next heap of seasoning timbers. The hot wash of its exhaust tossed her hair. Had they seen her? She listened for the sound of it turning back, but the voices nearby presented a more immediate threat.

Mikey's eyes widened in alarm. Only his face was showing now and for an instant Anna thought he'd been snared by one of Sponge's many deadly traps. Trying to calm her ragged breathing, she belatedly realized his fear was for her, still out in the open.

Fear of the strangers, with their callous brand of violence, dueled with a visceral dread of the depths of Sponge. The planet, and the life cloaking it, was her home both familiar and threatening. The threats she understood well enough, at least on the surface. Down below was another world, one that haunted her nightmares in the years following Luuk's death. But she'd seen what they did to Georgie. To be caught up here meant certain death, and she couldn't abandon Mikey.

That last thought galvanized her. Whatever dangers lay below, they'd face them together. She closed her eyes for an instant and muttered a prayer to the clouded skies above, then slid into the hollow alongside Mikey.

He pulled her close and concealed the opening as best he could. She hoped the damage wasn't noticeable from above.

They huddled, half buried under a bough of rimwood, half covered by flimsy surface matting.

The roar returned and passed overhead again. With that jet still circling above, there was no chance they could reach town without being seen. Footsteps squelching nearby were a bigger problem.

"They must have come this way." A woman's voice. High and cold.

"Search this heap of crap, then. They can't be far." Male. Gruff.

The voices were whipped away on gusts of wind whistling through the stack. Another sound intruded—a sharp drumming from above.

"Oh, just fucking magic," the man grumbled.

A trickle of icy water worked around the edge of Anna's mask and down her neck. The trickle grew to a rivulet. The spongy mass under her soaked up the rain flooding into their hollow and soon saturated the front of her jacket.

Icicles seemed to pierce Anna's body. If the *vreemde* didn't get them, hypothermia would do the job quite nicely. In fact, Anna wondered how deep this narrow cleft ran. If it was shallow, they might drown before they froze to death.

Without warning, the ground under her softened. Anna let out an involuntary shriek as she slid backwards down a slick slope. Elbows jarred against smooth unyielding walls that formed a narrow chute. She landed in a heap alongside Mikey, with frigid water pooling around them.

Shouts from far above echoed off the iron-hard walls of the crevice.

Mikel splashed to his feet and helped Anna sit up. Her face had gone white, shining luminous through her mask in the shadows. It looked like she might be sick.

With a hint of reflected daylight up above, he studied the trunks around him and pictured the formation. Pictured its purpose and how it fitted into the surrounding plant mass. Images of the giant plant's inner structure danced through his mind, an intricate jigsaw of specialized organs.

A fractal network of criss-crossing trunks and branches gave form to Sponge, from the kilometers-thick ribs resting on bedrock, to the spongy filigree of the surface itself. This structure was shot through with a dense mass of organs—growth bodies, photosynthesis, storage, chemical factories—and circulation systems, catchpools, deep aquifers, and vast cathedral spaces of airways and surface vents.

The elements connected together in predictable ways, in patterns repeating over and over across the planet's surface.

Voices above told Mikel their presence wasn't much of a secret. They'd made noise as they fell, and the greenjackets up there must have noticed, even with the sound of rain that now lashed the timbers above.

Light brightened. Fresh cascades of icy water washed down the chute to join the growing pool.

Mikel squinted up to see movement and the spongy matting being torn aside. Their hiding place was discovered, although he was sure they were too far down in the darkness to be spotted. All the same, this was not a place to linger.

After a few seconds' gazing around, Mikel found what he was looking for. The water-filled hollow was cupped by smooth trunks and ribs twisting their way up to support the surface layers. Gaps between them led into a labyrinth of hard trunks, but one in particular caught Mikel's eye. There was always a wider path deeper into the under layers.

He grabbed Anna's arm and hauled her in that direction. He scrambled over the lip of the hollow, struggling to find purchase on the slick trunks, then turned to help Anna up.

They stood. Mikel tugged Anna's sleeve to draw her deeper, away from the light, and into safety. But she held her ground. Her eyes widened, panicked.

Pink light glared behind them, dazzling in the darkness. A flare, thrown from above, which hissed as it floated in the pool and drifted to the side.

Anna gasped. "Are they mad? Even with all this water, Sponge is flammable as hell."

Mikel shook his head. She should know her plant structures better. Given the chance, some organs would burn with vicious intensity, but this wasn't one of them.

And stupid greenjackets! The heat of the flare lifted a fog from the water that clouded the shaft above them.

"See anything?" That woman's voice chilled Mikel.

"Can't see a fuckin' thing now, but I got a good look as the flare dropped. No-one in sight."

"But they're down there."

Any further words were lost as a sharp tingling at Mikel's neck and shoulders suddenly overwhelmed him, growing to a deep throbbing pain. It felt like he was on fire. He gasped and his knees buckled. The pain subsided, and he opened his eyes to find Anna gazing at him, searching his face for clues as to what he was feeling.

He shuddered, then pushed himself back to his feet. Again, he yanked at her sleeve, his free arm jabbing in the direction he knew they had to go. He could feel her tremble through the thick lining of her jacket.

She placed her hands on his shoulders and looked him in the eye. Her breath fogged the lower part of her mask. She needed to calm her breathing or she'd overwhelm the tiny filters at her cheeks.

"If we go deeper in, can you find your way out again?"

He smiled encouragement, and nodded.

She chewed her lip. "You've never been down below though, have you?"

He shrugged, and pointed at his eyes then at his upturned palm, mimicking reading.

"You learned about it." Her voice was flat.

He nodded, then tilted his head to one side and raised a single eyebrow in an obvious 'and your point is?' expression.

A splash nearby startled them both.

In the guttering remains of the flare, the end of a rope was visible, trailing into the water.

"I don't give a sewer rat's ass, get down there after them!"

Mikel didn't know what a sewer rat was, or why anyone would want its ass, but the voice wasn't friendly and the intention was clear enough. Once again he tugged on Anna's jacket and this time she followed.

In deepening gloom they stumbled down a treacherous slope which leveled off after a few meters. This was part of a network of water collection systems, channeling rainwater to deeper storage pools. Rivulets were already forming, rushing past their feet, soaking into their boots.

Mikel dug out a small flashlight from his pocket once they were far enough from the catchpool to be hidden from sight.

They hastened on, fighting to keep their balance in the growing flood.

Muffled voices echoed from behind.

Mikel paused. The way ahead narrowed. He knelt and took off a glove, pressing his hand to the wall. The smoothness gave way to a surface with a slight roughness to it, and the barest perceptible yielding to his touch. The plant tissue here was not the same as the hard passageway they'd been in. He squeezed his eyes shut and felt *past* the superficial senses, picturing the veins around him.

His eyes snapped open. A twinge of fear shot up his spine. He recognized this formation.

He shone his flashlight, inching forward, then paused. Beckoning Anna over, he held the flashlight close and pointed out rows of delicate hairs protruding from the tunnel walls. The walls themselves glistened a sickly yellow, contrasting with the bleached tan elsewhere. He pointed at the hairs, and waggled his forefinger at them.

Anna swallowed and nodded.

Mikel swiveled edge-on and sidled down the passage, keeping well clear of the wall. Anna linked hands and followed, facing the opposite wall. A glow of gratification warmed Mikel, despite the cold sweat tickling his back. She'd understood, and was watching his back to make sure he didn't stray too close in that direction. He glanced back to check she was also staying out of danger.

Steadying each other, they shuffled sideways one step after another while water gushed around their feet, until the walls returned to their dry bleached look.

Shouts from behind. Mikel shut off his flashlight, but guessed the glow had already given them away.

Pounding feet. Lights shone in the distance, jerking side to side as the *vreemde* ran.

Anna glanced at Mikel, wide-eyed. "We need to hide," she hissed.

He shook his head, and turned to watch.

Bulky figures silhouetted in the glare of more flashlights seemed to fill the tunnel twenty meters away.

The leader's shoulder brushed the tunnel wall.

A wet snap, and a shriek that seemed to last forever.

This time Anna *was* sick. She ripped off her mask and tigered all over the tunnel floor, keeping enough presence of mind to replace her mask before heaving a breath.

Again.

And a third time.

Mikel was impressed. He'd not been sick often, but he remembered the urge to draw breath between retches. He knew it was possible to eat and drink in the outdoors, holding your breath while you lifted your mask. She must have developed amazing control out in the field for those instincts to kick in now.

They'd just passed through a valve, one of Sponge's defenses against debris washing down the rain channel clogging up the catchpools lower down. The valve would hold and digest any large organic lumps before opening again and releasing the harmless remains into the flow.

Mikel wasn't sure whether Sponge was up to digesting alien tissue, but now didn't seem the right time for curiosity. Checking that Anna was on her feet once more, albeit unsteady, he switched his flashlight back on and led them deeper into the labyrinth.

After half an hour worming their way through a series of narrow paths, Anna was sure there was no way they'd be found. She wasn't sure they'd be able to find their way out, either, but Mikey seemed to know where he was heading.

She was still reeling from the shock of seeing a man crushed to death. Well, seeing, not so much, but his cries echoed again and again through her mind.

At first, nerves on a hair trigger, she cringed with every step they took wondering what more lethal traps Sponge had to spring. But her reserves of nervous energy were long since exhausted. Her feet moved mechanically, her mind numb to the possibilities. Again, Mikey seemed to know the innards of Sponge, and know where it was safe to move.

And, a pragmatic corner of her mind understood that they were *here*, they were committed, and the only way out was forward.

She tried to remind herself that this was the world the harvest crews worked in. It held its hazards, but they were well known and taught to all youngsters from an early age. Anna's own schooling seemed distant and her mind blocked all recollection of below surface. She knew the surface above, and knew how to read its structures, its moods, and she understood what they'd find beneath. That was her skill as a surveyor.

But ever since Luuk's death in the deep, her mind had blotted out all thoughts of actually being down here herself.

Eventually, Anna realized the tremors wracking her body no longer had anything to do with paralyzing terror. Most of her body was numb. She took off a glove and touched her jaw at the edge of her mask. A sliver of ice broke away in her fingers. Her jacket crackled as she moved.

Night was falling, somewhere out of sight. They must still be near the surface, and temperatures were plunging.

"M-m-mikey," she forced out through chattering teeth. "We n-need to get into w-warmth." Skies above, the effort those few words had taken.

He turned, lips pressed thin and tinged with blue. He made a fist, opened out splaying his fingers. A fist, splayed fingers again, then he mimed walking with fore- and middle fingers.

Ten minutes more. Anna nodded, relieved. They would soon be out of here.

Ten bone-chilling minutes later, and relief turned to puzzlement. They seemed no nearer the surface, and the plant mass around them had changed in nature. No longer sloshing through a rain-filled channel, they found themselves in a broad but low-ceilinged cavern filled with meter-thick columns. She couldn't discern the far side.

Mikey seemed to be searching for something. He knelt, hands caressing the spongy floor near the base of a column. His faced screwed up in concentration, then his eyes flicked open and he favored her with a broad smile. He beckoned her over and patted the ground by his side.

Too numb to argue, Anna sat beside him. "Is this really a good time for a rest, Mikey?" she grumbled. But her protests were only half-hearted. A rest would be good. Sleep would be good, but she wondered if she'd ever be able to get up again. "We need to find a way back into town without being seen." The ground was soft, and warm. Inviting.

"We can't be caught out here all night." Huh! For all she knew, night had already fallen and they'd be swept away the moment they stuck their heads above ground. They were probably already too late.

Warm? Reality caught up with her as circulation returned to her thighs and buttocks. The ground was warm! She snuggled down into a slight hollow, luxuriating in the sensation of tingling skin.

"Mikey, you little beauty! You found a warm patch for the night."

He settled alongside her. Blessed relief for now overcame Anna's lingering terror at being below ground. In the bowels of a giant plant. A plant that ate people. Yeah, that really did sound silly. And people worked in these depths all the time without coming to harm.

Mostly.

While Anna wrestled one worry into submission, more questions surfaced in its place. Who were those intruders in town? What the kak were they doing there? Why were they hunting Anna and Mikey?

Georgie was dead. Anna's mouth stretched wide in a silent howl of grief. But through the anguish, something nagged at her. She thought back to the moments before Georgie's death, to her final words. And to her appearance. Belatedly, Anna recognized the look of a dislocated shoulder, and although Georgie's face had been mostly turned away, she was sure there had been signs of bruising.

What had first sounded like a betrayal suddenly became clear. Georgie had been trying to protect Anna and Mikey from discovery.

That made more sense. For all their disagreements, Anna had known Georgie all her life and knew her to be sound. Not exactly a friend, but someone to be relied on.

Fresh grief overcame Anna, then anger. Whoever these *vreemde* were, they were not going to take Anna and Mikey. She owed it to Georgie to survive, get the kak out of here, and tell people what had happened.

As exhaustion finally crept over her, the leader's words back in the garage hovered on the edge of awareness. What did he mean by 'the padre'?

————◆————

Nick climbed up to the car's lower airlock and hauled himself on board with a weary sigh.

He'd been a trek warden before, but this was the first time he'd been the senior warden, and not just for his train, but for the whole caravan.

Not much of a caravan, granted, but just these four crawlers at the tail end of the exodus were taxing his patience. How did people manage the migrations of a dozen or more at a time? Or was it just his bad luck to land a troublesome journey? Maybe it was karma plaguing him, or maybe people were on edge in the rapidly shortening days.

Last evening he'd been called over to Gorge's train to calm heated emotions over the settling of Ambrose's estate. They'd not had time to handle his death properly before leaving town. His clan was still griev-ing, yet arguments were breaking out over coveted belongings, promises made, promises imagined.

More seriously, tonight Nick had visited Gerard's train to hear about a broken freezer and a whole car left with spoiled supplies. Hasty calls between trains ensured no-one would go hungry. Not unless there were more mishaps.

It still preyed on Nick's mind that he hadn't yet called the traditional wardens' briefing, where they would have to announce the three missing from his own clan. He knew he couldn't put it off much longer, but he was grateful that other demands were claiming his time.

And he still had no idea how to approach the subject. Sarah, a safe distance away up in the drive cab, was still trying to pin him down. There was only so long he could plead busyness. He'd fobbed her off with saying that Anna was occupied. How long would that flimsy excuse hold up? It was cold comfort that he was technically correct, lying only by omission.

Sarah would be distraught. Drivers formed a tight-knit elite within the extended clan structure. And then there was Seth. The more he thought about it, the more Nick realized that was where his main dread now lay. How could he ever look Seth in the eye again, knowing what he'd done?

On top of all of that, Nick refused to believe that all was lost. He'd alerted the visiting team at Serendipity. They'd find the stragglers and bring them home. Though that would take some explaining, which Nick also hadn't figured out. The Company's mission was of the utmost secrecy.

Gods! But this was a mess.

He couldn't reveal this glimmer of hope to the crew here, and how in all the wide skies would he later explain the reappearance of three people who'd been left behind?

The only slim prospect Nick could see was to keep their fate a secret and hope they could somehow reappear in Laverne, as if they'd been on the train the whole time. Maybe the 'occupied' fallacy could be developed into something to explain why she'd been out of sight. Yes, maybe that could work, as long as they were found and delivered as he hoped.

Anna woke to darkness and biting cold once more. Her heart gave a loud thud that seemed to echo through the surrounding air as panic seized her. She swallowed hard and fought to bring her breathing under control. The previous day's memories surfaced in fragments, her mind still unwilling to accept what had happened.

Shivering violently, she felt cautiously beneath her. Despite her numbed hands, the matted floor confirmed her fears. Yesterday had been real. They were still down beneath the surface of Sponge. And the warmth that had lured her to sleep was gone, leaving a deep ache in her bones.

A broken memory came to the fore, from years ago. Educator Georgina van Buren—a young woman, but still seeming old in the eyes of an even younger Anna—talking about Sponge's heat management. Pockets of warm water drawn from the depths to protect upper layers from the ravages of the night. The flow slowed as night progressed.

Anna guessed it must be near dawn. The storms would be past. If they wanted to re-enter the town unseen, now would be the time to do it.

She groped around in the dark. No Mikey.

Anna jerked upright. A parched moan rasped from her throat at the splitting pain in her head brought on by her sudden movement. She fumbled in her pocket for a flashlight. The beam was dazzling after the dark. It illuminated a forest of thick pillars receding into shadows, but nobody nearby.

"Mikey," she croaked. She worked up a miserly dribble of saliva to wet her throat and tried again. "Mikey!"

A shadow flitted through the pillars, startling Anna. She stifled a gasp, and blinked away tears. Her throat felt on fire. She squinted and picked out Mikey's jacket in the distance. His own flashlight beam dazzled her, then flicked away again, back the way he'd come. He beckoned.

Okay. We were back to this game again. He seemed to know how to find his way beneath the surface. Accustomed to being in control of her surroundings, Anna felt small and useless.

Breathing through the pain of her pounding head and seized joints, Anna staggered to her feet and limped after Mikey. Stale sweat and fresh fear infused her mask. Her injured foot seemed to have regained a phantom memory of her last brief foray under the surface. The wound shrieked at her with each stumbling contact.

A glimmer in the distance gave her direction.

She stretched a hand to the nearest pillar to steady herself, and snatched it away in horror. Hair-thin needles pricked her palm. She stood, rooted to the spot in terror, wondering what trap she'd just triggered. Her breath came in short pants. Her mask fogged. She remained frozen, squeezing her eyes shut and replaying the *vreemde's* agonized screams before the plant crushed the life from him.

Sudden weight on her shoulders sent a spasm through her body, and a warm trickle down her leg. She trembled violently, but the death she braced for kept its distance. Instead, she became aware of a familiar warmth of comfort. She cracked her eyes open. Past the fogged mask, Mikey peered into her eyes. His hands kneaded her shoulders.

She whimpered, then swallowed back her fright. A few calmer breaths and she managed a weak smile. "Can you get us out of here?"

The roll of his eyes restored a small sense of normalcy.

"Just don't go running off too far ahead." Mom service also restored.

Mikey flashed a brief grin, and led the way. After a few minutes, the measured ranks of columns closed in around them. The soft and level floor gave way to a tangle of roots. The going got harder, and Anna realized they were climbing. Her muscles ached, but her spirit soared at the thought of regaining the surface. Soon they were forced to clamber up into narrow gaps as the network of trunks became a three-dimensional labyrinth. This had been Luuk's world. *Was* Seth's world. She shuddered.

Eventually, a new surface appeared overhead in the beams of their flashlights. Hard, and silver grey. Shiny. Anna puzzled, then her eyes widened in recognition. "Mikey," she croaked, "we must be *under* one of the domes."

He glanced down at her and nodded. Through the reflections off his mask, Anna could see him frown and cast his gaze around. Anxiety gripped her. He looked lost.

After a minute, he set off again, pausing now and then to gaze up at the barrier.

Eventually, Anna saw they were climbing again. The polished surface, glimpsed here and there through gnarled plant growth, sloped up ever steeper. They were close.

Now, the hard and twisted limbs, all beige and grey, were joined by knots and tangles of matting plugging the gaps. Somehow Mikey found a way through. The spongy mass seemed to part in front of him. A few more meters, and Anna's head emerged into clear air. She groaned and hauled herself out. She rolled over onto her back, heaving a deep sigh of relief. The sky arched above them, lit by flickering streamers of the aurora.

Another sigh, and Anna sat up. Mikey squatted nearby, gazing at her patiently. They couldn't stay out here. They had a crawler to fix. Anna rolled onto her knees.

Puzzled, she patted the ground around her. It was the normal, slightly soft terrain around town.

There was no sign of the hole they'd just crawled out of.

By the dancing light of the aurora, Anna studied the nearby domes and the overlooking hills to get her bearings. "We crossed right under the town," she whispered. They'd emerged alongside the eastern garage. Just five hundred meters of open ground skirting the northeastern cluster of domes separated them from North One, where their salvaged crawler sat.

Mikey's eyes gleamed in the blue-green glow. He gave a thumbs-up.

"Keep close to the domes. Eyes and ears open. It's still night but I don't trust this lot. They seemed determined to find us and I think we ticked them off a bit."

As they slunk from dome to dome, shadows within shadows, Mikey tugged on her jacket. They both froze. Out to their right, less than a hundred meters away, someone was strolling past, silhouetted against washed-out grey hills in the ghostly lightshow.

Anna signaled to Mikey, and they lowered themselves to the ground, flattening themselves into the pliable surface. A flashlight flicked on.

The beam swept the side of the dome above their heads and moved on. It switched suddenly to somewhere behind them.

"Huh! It's you." Male voice. One of the ones who'd searched for them in the stockpile.

"It's just me. You're sounding jumpy, Colin. Don't flake out on us now."

"Thought I saw something, but I'm going stir crazy on this creepy planet. What a waste of fucking time this is."

"Just Galloway's idea of making a point. You lost them. You pay the price."

"They must have got eaten by this fucking plant. Look what happened to Joseph."

Anna decided they must be circling the town, on the lookout for anyone trying to re-enter. She also wondered how many more of them were out here.

More to the point, what were they doing here in the first place?

"Look on the bright side. We get to stroll around up here–"

"Freezing our bollocks off."

"–while everyone else is doing the heavy work, unloading machinery from the shuttle."

"Point," Colin grunted. The two shadows moved on.

Anna and Mikey stayed still for minutes after that, braving the icy chill, watching the two intruders patrol in opposite directions. Machinery? What was all that about? And who ever used an aircraft for that kind of work on Sponge? Most times of the year flying was a risky business, and the further you got from the equator the bigger the risks.

Craning her neck, she could see the one called Colin disappear around the end of East One. Ahead of them, the other was heading towards North One. Anna prayed he kept walking.

At last, satisfied that they were alone, they eased their aching limbs into motion again.

"We'll go in through the vehicle lock. Don't want to risk the airlock. The doors make too much noise." They inched around the top end of the garage and slipped between the outer set of hanging drapes. All quiet. Through the middle set, then Anna gently made a gap in the inner curtains to peer through. The garage lay in darkness. No flashlights pierced the gloom. She hesitated, weighing up the chances of someone lying in wait. How many of them were there? She had only seen a handful. Surely they didn't have bodies to spare to stake out all the garages on the off chance?

A faint glow through the weather shield signaled dawn. They had to get moving if they were to have a chance of reaching the first way station by nightfall. Now they were so close, Anna felt misgivings surface … anxieties she'd kept under strict control the whole time they'd been assembling this minimalist train. The unit was functional, she was sure she could get it moving, but under stick control she had no idea how the rig would handle. Or what kind of time they'd be able to make. Shorter trains were faster and more maneuverable than longer ones, that was received wisdom, but that also assumed working yoops and active drive and hitch management. She'd be pulling a dead weight, without computer assistance, through a locked hitch frozen in place without power.

And, with these *vreemde* wandering about outdoors could they get away unseen?

Anna shook herself. There was only one way to find out, and this was their only path out of here. She slid between two of the drapes and stepped cautiously out onto the darkened garage floor. Mikey slipped a hand around her arm and pressed close behind, peering over her shoulder.

"Keep a look out, Mikey. If anyone comes, we'll need to slip through the nearest lock and out onto the surface." And, she thought to herself, they'd come equipped with masks this time. They weren't stupid.

Anna retrieved her toolbox from the storage compartment–out of habit, she'd stowed it neatly in its proper place–and began unclipping the salvaged power cable between the yoop and the driver's cab. Even in deep shadows in the angle between the rear of the cab and the tunnel running from the cab to the cargo car, it was only the work of a few minutes. Then she hauled the heavy cable along the catwalk to the rear of the yoop, and connected it to the empty cargo car. She paused and stretched in the chill air of the garage.

A movement out the corner of her eye. Anna glanced up, but it was only Mikey peering out through gaps in the car's paneling, patrolling one side then the other. She climbed along the hitch and into the gaping hole of the car's forward lock. Mikey gave her a questioning look.

"Okay," she said, "let's see if we're in business." She flipped open a maintenance box and studied the handful of status lights. That was a good sign. Power was getting through and the hitch unit appeared functional. Still she hesitated, hardly daring to put her hopes to the test. A rap of knuckles on her shoulder. She turned in alarm, scanning the darkness for danger. But Mikey was frowning at her, and looking pointedly first at her then at the hitch.

"Yeah, okay, no more avoidance." She pushed the 'Lock' button and jumped at the metallic 'clunk' that echoed through the garage.

They both froze, listening hard for any signs that they'd been heard. Maybe it hadn't been as loud as she'd imagined, but to Anna it sounded like someone had dropped a toolbox from the upper level.

She breathed again, and studied the status lights. The panic gave way to elation. The hitch was locked. They could drive out of here.

"Hey, Mikey," she hissed, "you're supposed to be on guard duty, remember?"

He pouted, then nodded.

His eyes widened.

Voices.

Anna peered through the nearest gap then jerked her head back. At least three people were out there, approaching their car. There was nothing else of interest down this end of the garage. They were still searching. Looking for hiding places. If they realized this vehicle was operational, they'd surely do something about it.

So close to freedom, it was more than Anna could stand. She gripped her wrench tightly. It was the only weapon she had to hand.

"They sure keep a load of crap in here." That was karking *Colin* again. What was he doing? Following her by karking *scent?*

Had they heard the clunk of the hitch locking? It had sounded so loud to Anna, but they seemed in no hurry. Maybe the sound hadn't carried as far as she thought.

"Poor colony. Can't even afford to throw out the garbage. They keep everything and pick it clean for spares."

"Well, the front of this one looks useable. Why isn't this one motoring south with the rest of the blueskins?"

With dread weighing her stomach like yesterday's stew, Anna realized they were talking about this cab. They sounded curious. Maybe suspicious. If they decided to search it, Anna and Mikey were trapped. Footsteps echoed around the rear of the cargo car. More sounded on the far side heading towards the cab.

Anna prayed briefly, then led Mikey deeper into concealing darkness in one corner of the car.

Boots clanged on the ladder leading up to the drive cab's lower air-lock. A pause. "Nah. This one's dead after all. There's a panel here by the airlock. Should be lights on, but it's dead as a dodo."

Another voice, surly and impatient. "We're wasting our time here. Come on. We've all got real work to do. Galloway wants samples and results. Yesterday."

"Then why send us poncing off after a harmless bitch and her pup?"

"Loose ends." The chill threat in his tone raised goose bumps up Anna's neck. She squeezed her eyes shut, trying to block out the memory of Georgie's body on the floor.

A snort. "Once we're done here, the planet will deal with them soon enough. You seen the nights now. Just wait 'till it gets *really* dark."

The voices receded.

Anna stood, frozen in terror, straining to hear the diminishing sound of footsteps long after they'd dwindled to nothing. Then her legs collapsed under her and she sank to the floor.

She waited a few minutes more, willing the hammering in her chest to subside. Would they return? Was their parting conversation a trick to persuade her to come out from hiding? Surely not. If they'd honestly suspected there was anyone in hiding here they'd have simply searched the vehicle. Her heartbeat calmed a bit further.

Next to her, Mikey was propped against the adjacent wall, eyes fixed on a spot across from him. When she stirred, his gaze swiveled her way and he managed a weak smile under his mask.

"Now you see why we need to keep watch?"

He swallowed, and grimaced. He stood and helped Anna to her feet. She felt unsteady, like the crawler sat on soggy ground. "Let's get this thing connected up and get out of here."

It took Anna only a few minutes more to reconnect the yoop to the drive cab. If those *vreemde* returned now, the lights on the outer lock would give them away. This was their chance to escape.

All the same, Anna wasn't prepared to rush matters. Methodical checks saved lives. She confirmed the yoop's power unit was still showing green status lights on the maintenance board, then she closed up the cabinet.

Already, a barely audible hum and sigh of air told Anna that the filters were running again. She stifled a brief shudder as she realized how close they'd come to discovery. If she'd had those few minutes to connect the power before the searchers arrived, their presence would have been obvious.

Through the connecting tunnel and into the cab, she willed the hiss of the airlock to silence itself, imagining unfriendly ears pricking at the sound that must surely be audible the length of the garage.

Oh, kak! In her haste, she'd forgotten about the hitching truck still sitting under the cargo car.

"Be right back," she murmured. Mask on again, and out through the lower lock, Anna climbed into the truck and lowered the hydraulic jack. She maneuvered the truck out from under the car and parked it well out of her way.

A shout in the distance froze her to the spot. A powerful flashlight beam scanned the end of the garage, crossed over her, painting a ghostly shadow across the near wall. It returned, spearing her in its beam.

Kak! Kak! Kak!

She ran for the cab and sprang up the ladder, waiting an agonizing eternity before the lock would admit her.

She flung herself into the seat, and abandoned any thought of start-up checks. She fired up the yoop and, with little more than a cursory confirmation that the controls were patched straight through to the drive wheels, she gripped the joysticks on either side of her.

Careful now. She had to back up the rig before she could line it up with the vehicle lock. It was like pushing noodles across a plate. Impossible to steer. More power to the left drive wheel corrected her line enough. She must be karking close to the nearest garage pillar, but she was driving blind. And she had no idea how far away those *vreemde* were. A couple of hundred meters, maybe, when they first spotted her? They must be close now.

Something hard clacked off the window to her right, frosting the polyglass. Mikey yelped in fright.

She eyed the lock ahead of her. A meter clearance either side. She aimed and shoved the joysticks forward. The vehicle yawed wildly. Kak!

Anna slammed it into reverse, but without power and steering in the rear yoop it was just leading her around in a circle, facing away from the lock. She pushed the sticks forward again, more carefully this time, and was rewarded with a more balanced movement. She took off for the back of the garage, aware of a pair of figures running to keep up on her left.

Nutloos barfbrains! Should've stayed by the lock if you wanted to catch me! She counted the passing columns, judging the gaps, then tapped the left joystick back. The crawler jammed left, straining the hitch to its limit. Taken by surprise, the two now directly ahead of her flung themselves out of her path as she headed once more for the vehicle lock.

Better line this time. At the last moment, Anna eased up on the power and nosed the crawler through the first set of curtains. A metallic shriek and she glanced off one wall. Corrected. Over-corrected and scraped the opposite wall. Sweating, she slowed to a crawl.

The shriek continued.

Mikey!

" 'S okay, love, I've got this!" She had to line up better for the next curtain or she'd catch on the rib up the side wall framing the exit.

Through the middle curtain. She didn't know where the two *vreemde* were, and didn't much care. With the cargo car rattling from one wall to the other they'd get themselves squished if they tried to climb aboard.

One last curtain to freedom. She took a deep breath and focused on threading her rig through the gap. Then they were through.

A few moments' indecision. They'd been spotted. They would raise the alarm. How long did she have before they got that jet into the air?

They would expect her to head south, to join the rest of the trek. She eased the sticks forward and headed north. The ground was tricky up there, but if she could stay out of reach for the next hour or two there were other routes up out of this valley. They would eventually take them back to the main Laverne highway a hundred klicks to the west.

She squinted through the cab windows, trying to make out the shape of the ground ahead in the gathering dawn, not wanting to chance putting on her running lights. She was taking a huge risk, but she knew the land around here well ... as long as Sponge hadn't been busy rearranging the furniture.

Chapter 19

As the minutes ticked by and the shadows outside rolled past, Anna started to relax. They were on their way at last.

It would be a long road to Laverne. There wasn't a hope of catching up to the last train so they'd be on their own the whole way. But some of the way stations had communications sheds hooked into the permanent land line. A few days' travel, as long as this cobbled-together rig held out that long, and they could make contact. Report what had happened back in Serendipity. Report what had happened to Georgie. Maybe someone at Laverne would send a crawler out to meet them half way.

Now she could make plans beyond immediate survival, another worry surfaced. "Mikey, do you know how to work a pickup hose and filter?" She glanced sidelong to see him waggle a hand. *Maybe.* "Okay. It's easy enough. We have to take on water before we reach the high ground. Our tanks have been drained for the winter."

They'd go hungry, they'd only hauled over a limited stock of emergency rations, but they could cope with that. Water was another matter.

Anna reached for the computer at her side. She cursed. Everything had been stripped out, including the navigation system. She had to rely on her memory.

A line of orange, blinding against gunmetal sky, lit the horizon ahead and to their left. Soon their valley would be in full daylight. Anna thought furiously, matching half-seen landmarks against her memory of the terrain. There would be a forest to her right, dying off for winter. A place to avoid, especially with such a light and futzed vehicle. Level ground to the left. Dangerously soft. But a few klicks past, there were shallow aquifers and surface catchpools. They would be draining out now, water reserves moving deep down where the slow metabolism of Sponge kept the winter deep freeze at bay. That was their best chance.

Rhythmic vibrations through her seat measured the passing kilometers. Grey sky slowly turned copper.

"Do you know how to recognize a water pickup hose?" she asked Mikey. He scrunched up his face and gave a cautious nod. "You're looking for a coil of blue hose, coupla centimeters thick. See what you can find down in the storage deck."

And, Anna thought, pray we find some surface water. Bet this stripped-out rig isn't carrying a booster pump if we have to go deep.

Half an hour later Anna breathed a deep sigh. Orange glints ahead reflected brightening sky, and Mikey had scavenged two coils of hose along with connectors and an intake strainer from the junk pile down below.

As she parked the crawler near the surface pool, Anna said, "Okay, we'll have to be quick. Here's how it works. I'll take one coil up to the roof and throw one end down to you. Attach it to the other coil, and fit that strainer basket to the other end." She checked Mikey's expression. Technical instructions rarely needed repeating. "Throw the end into the pool. Don't get too close, ground's likely to be soft."

On the roof of the cab, Anna attached her hose to the main inlet. Like the air, the water on Sponge was laced with poisons but easy to filter. People had masks to wear, and carried water bottles with filters built in. Domes and vehicles had the same technology on a larger scale. Air and water were plentiful resources here. All Sponge demanded in return was eternal vigilance.

While Mikey connected the hoses down on the ground, Anna gazed anxiously around, feeling painfully exposed. Her stomach clenched. Mikey was leaving visible footprints in the surface.

Frost! Skies above, it had been so long she'd forgotten what frost looked like. She craned over the roof guard rail to peer past the skeleton of the cargo car. Kak! They'd left a clear trail behind. If the *vreemde* took to the air, they couldn't help but spot it. She wondered if their track was visible all the way back to town.

"Snap it up, Mikey! We're leaving tracks. We need to hit the high ground asap."

He waved, and unrolled the coil of hose down to the water's edge. He swung the end with the strainer basket and let fly.

Not too hard! Anna bit her lip, but Mikey sensibly kept hold of the last loop of the coil. It unreeled, jerked taut and plopped into deep water.

A thin skim of ice crackled on the ripples. The tension in her shoulders eased a bit. That was actually neatly done.

She checked the filter system and switched on the pump. While water sloshed reassuringly into the holding tank at her feet, she strained eyes and ears southwards for signs of a search.

Anna paced the cab roof, fretting at each passing minute. Her attention flicked from the holding tank, to the southern horizon, and away to the north. *Focus!* She should be using the time to plot their course out of here, but the skies to the south, bearing unseen threats, kept drawing her back.

In the end, she heard it before she saw it. A faint rumble echoed off the hills in the distance. Unlike any thunder she'd ever heard, the sound had a metallic taint, utterly foreign to Sponge. It rolled over them, a blight, an alien intruder in this plant-wrapped land.

Without looking to see if they'd been spotted yet, Anna ran to the edge of the roof. With those tracks they were leaving it was only a matter of time. "Mikey," she called, "we got company."

He waved and hauled the hose to shore.

"Leave the hose, no time to coil it up."

He didn't seem to hear. He twirled the end with the heavy strainer basket and let fly. It sailed up towards Anna, the trailing hose whipping after it. She ducked, and snagged the hose flying past her face. The strainer clanged to the roof. Damaged or not, it hardly mattered. There was nowhere up on the highlands to use it. "Good work! Now get the kak inside!" She reached over the side of the cab and hauled the dangling loop of hose over the railing. She'd stow it properly later.

If there was a 'later'.

She gnawed her lip in frustration as the upper airlock cycled, then bolted down the ladder and hurdled into her seat. Mikey was already there, panting hard as he stripped his mask off to let it dangle around his neck.

"It's okay. As long as we're moving they can't stop us." She directed the crawler away from soft ground around the network of catchpools, but tried to keep higher ground between them and the approaching aircraft. "They'd have to land and come at us on foot, and there's no way they can outrun us."

By now, after an hour's driving, Anna reckoned she had the feel for her unconventional vehicle's handling. She toyed with the idea of seeking cover, then hastily discarded it. As the last shadows melted from the valleys the ground frost sparkled white. Their trail down here was too obvious. She'd be better off on the harder high ground. They'd be more exposed but their wheels would create less disturbance, and the frost would evaporate sooner on the sunlit uplands. If they could make enough distance, it was just possible their trail would be lost. She angled higher and eased the sticks forward. Let's see how fast a one-car train can go!

A deep whoosh overhead blew away any hope of evasion. Mikey cried out. With her hands on the sticks Anna almost rolled the crawler. She quickly corrected, veering back downhill to stabilize their yawing, rocking motion. "Kak! That was close."

She swallowed her terror and concentrated on keeping the vehicle moving. "Can you see where they are?"

Mikey ran from one side of the cab to the other, peering out the wraparound windows. He grunted and pointed. Anna glanced his way and caught the barest glimpse of a tiny black speck growing at an alarming rate. She jerked the sticks back and jammed the crawler to one side.

The slope ahead lit up like an arc welder. The concussion hit them a second later, followed by a rain of burning fragments.

Anna jinked the crawler again to avoid the blackened scar. "Guess I was wrong about them needing to land."

The crawler bounced dangerously as Anna threw full power into the drive, but even that, she knew, was hopeless. The people on Sponge had no weapons. Who'd have thought the offworlders would bring armed fighters with them?

There was nowhere to hide, nowhere to run. The only kind of cover on Sponge was underground, or in one of the sprawling patches of forests. She couldn't take the crawler in there. This rig was too light to force its way through like she'd done only a few days before, and it would still be plainly visible from above.

But she couldn't outrun a jet.

She wracked her memory and swerved for the nearest forest. A few klicks, she reckoned. Could she stay out of trouble for the next few minutes?

The jet screamed close. Anna waited until the last moment and swerved again, then immediately back to her original course.

The shot missed. The pilot had anticipated her swerve, but not the correction. How long could she stay lucky?

A dark smudge in the distance. Still too far.

The jet, little more than a dot against lowering orange-lit clouds, wheeled around ahead of them.

Anna had precious little knowledge of aircraft. Jets, she was fairly sure, needed to keep moving. Fast. That's how they operated. She also knew that some of them could slow and hover for take-off and landing. What could this one do? And weapons. How good was their aim? Proper military would surely have hit them the first time around. Was this some civilian modification? From the fact they were still in one piece, Anna realized she might have some advantage to play with. It couldn't be easy hitting a moving target from a craft hurtling across the landscape at that speed.

And here they came again. She yanked the sticks one way and the other, trying not to settle into a predictable pattern. The next shot was way off.

Another minute's breathing space.

"Mikey, keep an eye aft. I need to know when they're closing for another shot."

The withering boughs of the forest loomed close now. Trunks bowing, feathered fronds waving in gusting winds just above the height of the cab. She brought the crawler around, running along the edge of the forest. A few outlying fronds whipped at the windows, but Anna kept out of the thick of it.

Mikey whined from the far side of the cab, the sounds almost on the verge of forming words.

Anna jammed the crawler into reverse.

The sky ahead of them split like lightning. Kak, that was close!

The crawler inched ahead again, slowly, while Anna surveyed the results of that last shot. It pained her to see the destruction, but as she'd hoped, flames engulfed the nearby fronds, leaping from trunk to trunk. Above them, grey smoke roiled into the air, already forming a spreading pall over the landscape.

She veered away from the burning forest and headed north again. The smoke would hide them for many kilometers. The fire would burn all day, until darkness brought storms and rains. If they were still here by then, they were dead. In fact, Anna now wondered if they'd still have time to reach the first way station by nightfall. With this game of hide-and-seek holding them back they might be dead regardless.

Lightning stabbed through the blanket, again and again, stitching the ground with blackened scars. They must be firing at random through the smoke, hoping for a lucky strike, or simply keeping them penned in.

Behind her, Mikey screamed. She frantically scanned the windows either side to see what had alarmed him, but he wasn't looking outside. He was slumped in the angle between the floor and the back of the cab, eyes screwed shut, hands pressed to his temples.

The ground in front of the windows opened up. Before Anna could react, the crawler dropped into the chasm. Smoke-laden daylight vanished overhead. She pitched from her seat and slammed into the panoramic cab windows.

———•—•———

"I think you've already seen we're a very informal society." Josiah Handel guided Jennifer Steel to a front row seat. Many of her entourage followed and took seats nearby. "Most of the time, when we make music it's spontaneous and joyous."

For a fleeting moment, Jennifer pictured a hillbilly hoedown. She squashed the image. Belittling the opposition was a mistake. It led to underestimation, which led to disastrous miscalculations.

All the same, she'd heard evidence to support Josiah's description. Walking from her team's quarters through neighboring domes, distant music always seemed to form a backdrop to the ever-present hubbub of the crowded halls. Whatever the time of day or night, there seemed to be a party somewhere, distance and direction impossible to determine in the confusion of echoes. And as the reception a week had progressed, impromptu jam sessions had broken out. Musical instruments appeared as if by magic, and people rushed to join in. There hadn't seemed to be any order to it. As one group tired, another struck up across the room.

Spontaneous and joyous seemed apt. What did this tell her about the psyche of her negotiation foes?

"That doesn't mean we don't appreciate more mathematical beauty." Josiah's voice battled with the discord of last-minute tuning. "The program this morning is formal. We've several orchestras in Jorvick with more-or-less stable membership."

Jennifer gave a non-committal grunt. "I thank you for arranging this welcome break from the negotiating table." Where was this leading?

Josiah leaned in to whisper, "I know a person of your standing is used to a more cultured environment. It must be hard on you to be trapped on such a backward world."

"Trapped?"

"Big Red is flaring. Your ship can't take up orbit again until things calm down, which could be weeks yet."

Jennifer's heart sank. How the heck did he pinpoint her fears so precisely?

But Josiah gave his broadest, most welcoming smile. "So, I thought we'd do our best to bring you a bit of culture."

Before Jennifer could frame a response, the leader of the orchestra strode to the center of the stage. An expectant hush fell.

Much of the concert was clearly of local compositions. The instruments gave an unearthly sound, unsettling at first until Jennifer's ears became attuned to the alien harmonics and rhythms.

There were strings, both plucked and struck but, Jennifer noted, no bowed instruments. Strange. Breathy arrays of pipes—though no brass— and a wide range of percussion. Banks of drums drove an infectious beat while hard knotwood bars produced rich and complex bell-like tones.

On a hunch, in the quiet of an interlude, Jennifer leaned close and murmured, "Am I right in guessing all these instruments are of Elysium design and manufacture?"

"Of course." Josiah gave her a puzzled look, as if the answer was so obvious the question didn't merit the effort of asking.

The finale, a six-part fugue, wove magic in the air. For the first time, Jennifer sat entranced as themes danced through and around each other in a delicate tracery of sound.

As the last chords died away, Jennifer barely remembered who and where she was. She was still on display, and cursed herself for forgetting it for the past fifteen minutes of rapt attention. Had anyone noticed? She joined in the applause with measured restraint.

As they stood to leave, she murmured to Josiah, "I believe I understand why you brought us to this recital."

"Oh, I very much doubt that."

Jennifer swore she saw a hint of calculation behind his air of mischief. "You're trying to impress me with the level of sophistication present here. To allay my very public concerns for the future of this colony."

"Executive Steel, if you seek to be impressed, all you need do is open your eyes as you walk the halls of this city. No, I am merely showing the concern of a host for the comfort of his guests."

Jennifer gritted her teeth. "I hate to sound like a looped recording, but there is still the matter of viewing some of your manufacturing facilities, as requested—"

"During the opening of the negotiations," Josiah continued smoothly. "Of course. I appreciate your patience."

"Please remember that this was a precondition for my goodwill in the matter of considering a move to full independence."

"And please be assured I am not procrastinating." His trademark jolly smile beamed. "We simply wanted time to prepare suitable keepsakes of your visit."

Chapter 20

Mikel felt as if his hair was on fire. The burning, crushing pain receded slowly and other pains came to the fore. Arms and thighs ached. Something sharp stuck in his ribs. He tasted blood on his tongue.

Blearily, he cracked his eyes open.

Dark.

Shouldn't be dark, it was still morning, wasn't it? Memories of bright light and smoke, but no amount of smoke would blot out the sun like that.

The dark was relieved by a few pinpoint glows of red and orange and green. The cab. There was something terribly wrong with it. The rough floor covering scratched at his cheek as he tried to look around, and the floor was on a slope.

The pressure across his chest clamored for attention. Mikel looked down. He was wedged under a seat, wrapped around the seat's supports. It must be Anna's, he decided, looking at the gunmetal columns of the empty computer console by his head, and the distance to the side window.

This was all wrong, but things had been wrong for days. Emptiness ached inside him, drowning out the physical aches. The floor, seat, windows whirled around him in a kaleidoscope of shadows. He wanted to tiger, but the constriction across his chest wouldn't let him heave. Besides, he'd had nothing to eat since yesterday. So wrong. His world was gone. He needed to reclaim the familiar, somehow. Home, routine, people ... yes, even those maddening people crowding his mind with their *debeel* unfathomable social rules. He drowned in the depths of his loss.

He squeezed his eyes shut to stop the spinning. It was all in his mind. The cab was still there.

Cautiously, he opened his eyes again. A glimmer of hope beckoned him, enticing in its simplicity. The familiar, rule-bound world was gone.

Maybe it was still out there, somewhere. Maybe Anna and Georgina were right. There was another town, somewhere else, that would be just like the one they'd left. He couldn't picture himself there, that was too much of a leap of imagination, but he could, even provisionally, trust the grown-ups.

They'd done this before, they said. So, even though he couldn't see it, he could accept that his familiar world would be resumed at the end of the trek. But right here and now, he was living in a world without people rules. The only rule was ... do what you need to. The *vreemde* had proved that. Georgina's mangled body on the floor of the garage proved that. *They* acknowledged no rules. So, for now, Mikel felt the same free- dom. All that mattered was getting him and Anna out of their reach and back to the rest of their clan. No rules. Just do what must be done.

A flash of panic squeezed his mind, not from within, it came from outside. Mikel gritted his teeth and worked his arms under him to grasp the seat support struts. The inside of the cab came into sharp focus at last. A subtle movement through the floor at his cheek, as if they were still driving, but that made no sense. He levered himself up, bracing against the canted floor and the seat. Yes, there was a definite sway, and a low rumbling creak from somewhere back there. That couldn't be good.

The view through the cab windows beneath his feet was not quite dark. A ghostly luminescence silhouetted the network of struts at floor level and the frames of the windows. Something else was down there, slumped across the polyglass. That something shifted and groaned. Anna!

Anxiety ripped through him once more. They had to get out of here.

Gingerly, he lowered himself around the console and down the slope, using the console supports as handholds. Anna stirred again. "Mikey?" She started to sit up.

The cab swayed.

Mikel had never so keenly felt the need to form words, to warn Anna of their danger. But although words were clear enough in his mind, there was no connection to his mouth and throat. Sometimes, alone in the dark, he used to experiment. Sounds came. Sounds were easy, but shap- ing them with the finesse and dexterity needed for speech eluded him.

So he gave a low 'Hnnnhh', a sound he used to attract Anna's atten-tion. Over the years he'd developed many shades of inflection, which she seemed to understand. In one brief sound, he conveyed the need for attention, a level of urgency, but also a warning and that he himself was okay. Who needed words?

She looked up, then froze as the cab shifted again.

He beckoned, then signaled the need to move slowly.

Anna nodded, and carefully slid herself up the slope of the floor, to where she could grasp the seat supports. A few anxious moments later and she was alongside him, peering around at the tilted cab.

Ahead and below, through the downturned windows, the world out-side became more distinct. Skeins of dim blue-green and yellow radi-ance etched a dizzying vista of columns lining a narrow chasm, marching into the distance and plunging out of sight.

"We need to get out of here," she whispered, as if even the sound of her voice could topple them.

Mikel felt around to his right, where the wall at his back ended. Around the corner, steps led down to the maintenance deck and the lower airlock. Gripping the edge of the partition, he hauled himself around in one smooth motion. He held out his hand and helped Anna to follow. With a wall to support them on the downhill side it was easy going to reach the lower level. There, they were able to brace them-selves in the confines of the narrow alley to the airlock.

All the while, the vehicle creaked and groaned, setting Mikel's teeth on edge.

He couldn't shake the image of them hanging out over that impos-sible drop. His muscles wanted to freeze him in place. But then the thought of that jet, somewhere still overhead surely seeking them out through the pall of smoke, gave him fresh urgency.

Outside the lower airlock was a narrow ledge, then the ladder. Then nothing. Mikel propped himself up along the doorframe and peered around. Anna wedged herself in the doorway beside him, one arm pro-tectively around his waist. Out here, free of the reflections from the cab's lights off the windows, it was easier to survey the dimly-lit space around them. Above their heads, too far to reach, smoke-filled daylight filtered through a web of torn strands. The whole crawler had fallen through the surface, several meters down.

To his left, towards the front of the cab, and below his feet biolu-minescence revealed the chasm more clearly. Trunks and branches on either side twisted towards them to support the surface layers, and vanished into unguessable depths. Broad limbs twined through the maze, criss-crossing the chasm and lining the sides like a series of uneven balconies.

The nose of the crawler dangled in space, swaying slightly with each movement they made. It must be hanging on by the hitch, with the cargo car caught somewhere behind them.

Anna seemed to be studying the rip they'd fallen through. Did she really think they'd make it back up there? Mikel couldn't see a way, although the view was obscured by the bulk of the car behind them. The surface layers seemed to have collapsed behind and around them.

A rumble and whoosh somewhere overhead told them the jet was still circling, hunting. Even if they made it to the surface, could they escape those eyes in the sky? Two people on foot would be harder to spot than a bright yellow twenty-five-meter crawler, but there was nowhere to hide, nowhere to shelter.

Light above brightened, then dimmed again. Through drifts of smoke, clearer skies shone. The wind must be shifting direction. They couldn't even count on the obscuring smoke for much longer.

Safer to head down than up. Mikel nudged Anna with his elbow and pointed. One of the broader boughs passed just fifteen meters below, threading a path into the distance. Something the harvesters called a 'way'.

Too far to jump, but if they could reach it, Mikel was sure they'd be able to find a path to safety.

Anna blanched behind her mask, and returned her gaze upwards before finally nodding. "You could be right. They're going to find us before long."

She touched a control on the pad by her shoulder. Below Mikel's feet, a narrow catwalk pivoted out from under the cab and clicked into place. "Thank the skies that still works, at least." Anna braced herself against the uphill side of the door and pointed. "You know where the cable drums are? Around the front?"

Mikel nodded.

"See if you can shimmy along the running board and around the front. If you can grab the end of a line, clip yourself onto it. I can control the drum from here and lower you down."

She pursed her lips, judging the gap. "You'll need to signal me when you're level with that ledge. You'll need to swing across."

Mikel lowered himself onto the catwalk, holding on to the low railing at his side. He worked his way forwards and inched around the corner. Another catwalk dangled a meter away, running along the front of the cab. The windows bulged above his head, reflecting pale green light from the depths. He studied the gap, working out how to hold on. There were handholds at intervals along the walls, and belay points for lines, but the front of the cab was a looming overhang. The narrow ledge sloped away with only the thigh-high railing between him and an unknown drop into darkness.

Mikel's gaze traveled along the front to the cable drums.

To where the cable drums should be.

His heart sank. They'd been stripped off. Salvaged.

He glanced back at Anna and shook his head.

"What's wrong? Can you make the gap?"

He nodded, then jerked his head towards where the drums would be and shook his head again with a frown.

"Something wrong with the drums?" The despair in her voice was clear, even to Mikel.

The crawler lurched, then jerked to a halt. His grip broken, Mikel slid off the end of his catwalk and crashed into the railing of the next. He felt himself slipping and clawed desperately for a handhold. Somewhere, in the distance, Anna screamed. Mikel dangled, clinging to the precarious railing, over the dark depths.

———◦—◦—◦———

Sarah glanced between the navigation screen beside her, and the barren landscape ahead. Mid-morning sun slanted through a gap in lowering clouds and highlighted the texture of the uplands: Sponge's hard shell dry, cracked and crazed with flowing patterns of fissures from hairline fractures to meter-wide chasms. These vast plateaus, meandering north and south across half the planet, were ancient and unmoving. Not like the volatile plant mass that filled the valleys in between.

At times like this, perched high above ground in the prow of the vehicle, she could imagine she was flying. There was just an occasional vibration through the seat cushion to hint at movement. Warmth and cinnamon wafted from the vent above her head.

John, sprawled in the seat to her left, plucked a soothing ballad on a mandolin. Seth lounged in the starboard navigation chair.

Sarah shook herself, close to dozing off. "Seth, I need a stretch. Can you spell me a while?"

Seth looked squint-eyed at the collection of Anna's personal items marking her territory around the center seat. "Can I steer from here?"

"Turning control over to your stick." Sarah waited until Seth had control before relinquishing her hold. "You got the nav plot showing? We keep to this heading for the next fifty klicks. Just watch for bumps and dips. Easy enough to see and avoid in this light. I won't be long."

When Sarah returned from the cramped washroom, Seth said, "You need a relief driver. You can't do too many full days like this on your own."

Sarah glanced at Anna's photos and her careworn dreamcatcher, and murmured a brief acceptance of hospitality before taking her ... Anna's ... seat. The ritual came unbidden, instincts so deep only Anna's formal welcome last week allowed her to sit here at the main controls. She caught the looks of understanding that passed between John and Seth, and caught the unspoken thought on all their minds.

John strummed a few jarring chords, and shook his head with a wry smile. "Why do you need an excuse to go see how she is?"

"I don't ..." Seth spluttered.

"Sure you do."

"Ahh, skies above!" Seth glared at John. "You a shrink as well as a quack now? You're right. Seems I can only talk to her about work. Any hint of getting personal and she clams up. So, yes, I need a karking excuse, okay?"

"Well, Nick was pretty clear that Anna wasn't to be disturbed." Sarah's voice betrayed her uncertainty. And anxiety. "I told him I was okay, but someone needs to spell me properly soon."

John set his mandolin to one side. "Then, purely for the safety of the train of course, we'll head aft and see what's up."

Sarah glanced at Seth, who was already out of his seat.

"If she needs to be elsewhere, I don't need much of her time. There are other drivers on board, but no-one will take the seat while it's marked as a sanctum. I just need her to depersonalize it."

"We're on it."

Mikel's hands clenched the railing, knuckles turning white with desperation. Anna's face, pale and worried, appeared around the corner of the catwalk, impossibly far away. "Can you climb up?"

He shook his head. His arms burned with the effort of holding on.

Something heavy clattered above his head, swinging and banging against the windows of the cab. Startled, Mikel almost lost his grip.

Anna had heard it too. A wild look crossed her face. "Wait! Just hold on for a minute. Mikey"–her voice was pleading–"don't you dare let go. I can't lose you too."

She disappeared from view.

Mikel clung to the railing, wondering how long he could hold on for, wondering if he had the strength to lift himself up. Surely if he could swing a leg up, catch that railing with his ankle, he could lever himself back to safety.

Something banged against the window again, then scraped. Bang. Scrape. A movement from the corner of his eye, hard to make out, his mask was so fogged up with the effort.

The movement came closer. Away again. Closer.

He yelped and almost lost his grip when the water hose with its heavy strainer basket appeared from the gloom. It swung away again, then back towards him.

With a frantic effort, Mikel opened his legs and hooked the hose between his ankles. He released one hand and grabbed the hose. The other hand, fingers numbed, lost its hold and he wrapped his arms around the hose trying to hold himself in position. He couldn't stop himself slipping down, down ...

With a bump, the strainer basket stopped him.

A cry from above. The hose slipped a meter before stopping again, almost unseating him.

He swung, spinning wildly, catching his breath.

He didn't fall.

Anna called out from above, "Hang on there, I'm going to lower you."

On one of his wayward gyrations, Mikel glimpsed Anna peering over her shoulder over the top railing of the cab. She looked to be braced in the lower angle between sloping roof and the railing. The hose jerked down a few centimeters at a time. The spinning slowed, stopped, then reversed as the twisted hose untwisted itself.

Before it got too fast, Mikel took the opportunity to extend and draw in his legs in time with the swing, in the direction of the ledge below him.

He was close. How strong was the hose? It seemed to take his weight easily enough but what about Anna?

Another couple of meters and his feet barely cleared the rounded slope of the bough. The basket grated beneath him and he rolled off, still hanging on to the hose.

Mikel took a few deep breaths and made sure he was on a solid surface before rising to his knees, then his feet.

He gazed, wild-eyed, up at Anna.

"Good man!" she called. "Can you secure that end so I can climb down?"

Mikel held up one finger—wait first—and pointed to the hose then beckoned. He glanced behind him and pulled gently. Anna got the message and fed him some slack. He backed to the far side of the ledge. The rounded branch started to slope away, giving him a bit more purchase.

He wrapped the hose behind him then twisted a turn around his forearm. The other hand gripped the basket dangling at his side and tightened the hose across his back. Anna waved and ducked from sight.

"Secured here. Take the strain."

Mikel leaned back and let it take his weight.

Anna wasted no more time. Without hesitation she climbed over the railing and started clambering down, hand over hand, with a few slips and jerks.

No! That last jerk wasn't Anna slipping. Mikel stumbled back a pace as the tension slackened slightly. He gave an urgent cry.

Anna was already picking up the pace. She let out a long and piercing scream as the hose slipped between her fists. She slid the last few meters and hit the sloping ground hard, scrabbling for purchase. Mikel released his grip on the strainer basket and rushed to help. He desperately untwisted himself from the hose, flung himself forward arms outstretched, and clung to Anna's hands.

A metallic rending sound from beyond them marked the fall of the crawler. Mikel ducked as the hose and strainer rattled across the ledge. He counted the seconds before a long drawn-out rumble sounded from the depths.

———·•·———

Anna lay on her back, gasping. Sunlight silhouetted the tangle of branches and surface matting edging the gash the crawler had torn in the ground above. A part of her registered the clear and smokeless sky. Most of her wrestled with the fact that she was still alive, despite the odds.

Still too winded to speak, she flopped her raw and bloody hand sideways until she found Mikey lying beside her. She turned her head and gave what she hoped was a reassuring smile. He pantomimed mopping his brow with the back of his hand. Relief.

A distant recollection beckoned, crystallizing into coherent thought. "C'mon," she wheezed. "Can't stay here. They might still come looking for us." She tried to sit, but slumped back, too feeble to move. She heaved an arm up and held her hand out in front of her eyes. Her fingers fluttered, the shaking impossible to quell. "Kak! KakkakkakkakKAK!" Anna snarled in frustration and rolled onto her side. Leaving a bloody smear on the ledge, she pressed herself onto her knees and crawled a meter farther away from the sickening drop behind.

Mikey nodded wearily and hauled himself to his feet.

"Careful," Anna called as he swayed in place. He collected himself and staggered towards her. He held out a hand and grasped Anna's elbow, helping her up. Together they shuffled onto the center of the bough.

Anna looked both ways, wondering which way to go. Their ledge wound a perilous course between vertical columns, branching and twining its way into the distance. Over to their right, denser tangles seemed to mark one edge of this chasm. Anna was fearful of switching on their flashlights just yet, in case anyone up above was watching for signs of life. But stumbling around in dim light at the edge of unknown drops didn't appeal either.

Mikey frowned in concentration, peering into the distance. He knelt. His hands caressed the curved smoothness of the floor.

At least there were no thorns here. Anna shuddered. Venturing into the depths was something the harvesters did, not surveyors. But folklore was ingrained in everyone on the planet from a young age. Sponge had many tricks to deal grisly death to intruders. Her treasures were not gleaned without cost.

Anna surveyed the edges of the gash maybe forty meters above their heads. There seemed to be no path, nothing they could climb, to reach the surface from here. Harvesters plumbed the depths with ropes and winches, grapples and climbing gear. And still they died with appalling regularity. She shuddered, trying to push aside thoughts of their hopeless situation. They'd just lost their vehicle, the only remotely salvageable rig in town. They had no food, no water. Maybe tonight they could make their way back to town. Maybe they could steal that jet. Maybe ... maybe ... For now, they just had to survive and hide out long enough for the hunters to give up the chase.

Mikey stood and beckoned. Yes, they had to move. There was no way out here. They'd have to find another way back to the surface. Mikey had done it before. And, though she decided not to voice the thought, she wanted to put some distance between them and the fallen crawler. Those *vreemde* wanted them dead, and for all Anna knew they might land and explore below ground to make sure.

Chapter 21

Their walk through halls and airlocks seemed endless, but Jennifer had refused the offer of cars to cross the city for this long-promised visit this afternoon.

The conveyance from the landing field on the edge of the city–it felt so long ago, had it really been just three weeks?–had left her with nothing more than subliminal and woefully incomplete impressions of Jorvick. They'd all crammed into a series of open-sided wagons that lurched and rattled over hard floors through long echoing tunnels. The lasting impression was of endlessly sprawling *sameness*, one kilometer after another.

As she kept reminding her staff, they needed deeper understanding of the unique psychology at play here if they were to get these talks back on track.

At last, Josiah Handel was making good on his promise to show them something of the industrial side of Jorvick. A chance, maybe, to learn something of value.

A cadre of security staff and senior negotiators accompanied Jennifer as they marched through dome after dome with their local guides. Jennifer's calves burned and the pace was taking its toll on soft, desk-bound bodies, but they knew better than to whisper a word of complaint.

Josiah led the way, providing occasional commentary and answering questions. "This whole quarter is mostly habitat." He gave an expansive wave as they filed past a boisterous crush of people cheering on something that Jennifer couldn't make out through the press of bodies.

He seemed oblivious to the team's discomfort. In fact, everyone around them walked at a furious pace. People didn't appear to be consciously in a hurry, and they had no aversion to stopping and idling time away in small talk, but when they moved, they *moved*. Perhaps not surprising, with so many kilometers of sprawl to traverse, and almost all movement of people was on foot. The major arteries running through the heart of the city were designed for vehicles, but they almost exclusively conveyed materials. Few of the powerful little trucks were equipped for passengers. Without exception, Jennifer noted, this was a hard and fit population. She filed the observation away for now.

They skirted one segment of an administration section. Mostly planning offices and healthcare, Josiah explained. Community domes sprinkled through the neighborhood: school rooms, meeting places, social and fitness centers.

With all this modular sameness, Jennifer realized with a sudden chill that they would be utterly lost without their guides. Even backtracking would be problematic, because there was no simple straight path through this maze. They cut through the center of some domes, but sometimes veered off left or right where the hallways met, and sometimes skirted the perimeter rather than cutting through. She'd lost all sense of direction, and with hundreds of domes covering many square kilometers they could wander at random for days without finding anywhere familiar. For a surreal moment, she pictured their hosts abandoning them in some remote quarter if the negotiations went badly.

"This city is quite the maze. How do you find your way around?" She barely managed to keep her tone casual.

Josiah looked puzzled for a moment. "I can't say I've ever thought about it. We just know which way to go."

"Earth cities are laid out in blocks and streets. Everything is named and signposted." She gestured around. "Unless I'm missing something, I don't see any signposts."

"Well, each hallway is unique. I always know where I am and which way to turn."

"Are you referring to the decorations on the walls?" Jennifer frowned, taking more careful note of the hangings and decorative panels lining the hall.

Josiah glanced around. "Yes, absolutely. People get to know their neighborhood at a young age. Each clan leaves its own unique mark on its space."

Jennifer caught just a hint of evasiveness in his tone. There had to be more to it, but maybe it really was an unconscious skill, one which a native would be hard-pressed to articulate.

"You say each dome has its own power, filtration and waste management?" Raisa Garina asked. "Wouldn't it be more efficient to centralize some of that infrastructure?"

Young, financially very astute, hence her promotion, but naive in many ways. All the same, it would be interesting to see how Josiah answered.

"We are growing and expanding." His eyes twinkled. "A lot easier when it's just a simple matter of adding a few more domes. No worries about central capacity. And if you happen to live out near the edge and there's a major shield breach on the city side, you'll be thankful for your own life-preserving machinery."

So, emphasize the people aspect. No mention of the fact that centralized infrastructure would mean heavier machinery in smaller quantities, and fewer but more critical replacement parts when things went wrong. More dependence on outside—read Company—help in an emergency. Decentralization spread and lessened the risk. And with hundreds of identical plants across this city alone, a defective dome could be abandoned and its machinery cannibalized to keep others running. The duplication seemed wasteful on the surface, but it greatly increased their independence. And that was a line of thinking jovial Josiah seemed keen to steer away from.

They entered one of the vehicle tunnels, similar to the one they'd ridden along on the journey to their quarters. Every few hundred meters, the tunnel widened out to provide pedestrian access and to allow vehicles to turn. They paused by the airlock while a truck, towing three covered wagons, swung wide and eased its way through doors on the far side. They followed.

On the other side of the vehicle highway the neighborhood changed from residential to industrial. This was what Jennifer had asked to see. Once again, she'd left it up to Josiah to guide them, and once again Jennifer looked for clues in his choice of destinations to tour.

After a series of curving passages that skirted the edges of domes, resonating with the hum of machinery behind partition walls, they climbed a flight of stairs and emerged on a balcony. Windows separated them from the floor below.

Jennifer took in the scene below. "Why so much protective gear?"

Josiah pointed to a row of tables on the far side of the dome, where workers, clad anonymously in full-cover overalls and masks, manhandled fibrous masses from a cart. "The raw flax you see there is highly toxic. The fibers are coated in barbs, and the dust raised by the handling is deadly."

A team of workers teased a mass out onto the table, and used shears to separate it into manageable lengths. A second team hauled the fibers into a series of large wheeled vats.

"What you see there is the outer coating of some kinds of tubers found deep in the plant mass. The tubers are part of Sponge's network of chemical factories. The right ones yield the raw materials for our drug exports."

"I understand some of the work is done in the towns."

Josiah nodded enthusiastically. "It's a logistical balance. The tubers are large and yield relatively small quantities of useful chemicals. It would be wasteful to transport them whole to the equator, so a lot of the initial processing is done at source. But the coatings are shipped whole. Today we're following the fibers to the softening and spinning rooms."

Textiles. Interesting. Jennifer had wondered if Josiah would bring them to the pharmaceutical refineries—a reminder of the Company's source of profits from this world. Or maybe he'd want to show off the colonists' heavy machine shops where many of the building components for new domes were made. But he'd settled on the fabric and clothing workshops. Safe. Innocuous. It may just be coincidence, but was Josiah leery of revealing too much of Elysium's heavier industrial capability?

By the time they'd followed the process through a series of connected workshops, and reached the cutting and sewing rooms, something in the atmosphere felt different. Jennifer suppressed a frown, not wishing to give away her puzzlement, but behind her serene expression her mind raced, backtracking through the sections they'd visited.

Raisa Garina had noticed it too. "Are we between shifts, or on a break or something?"

Trust the accountant to notice, but she'd pinpointed what was bugging Jennifer too. The earlier workshops, where raw materials got processed into useable yarn, were industrious hives of activity, people bustling purposefully and efficiently. Here, tables were laid out with half-finished garments, but many of them were unattended. Some people worked, others sat in small groups talking. There was a relaxed feel to the place at odds with its factory furnishings.

Josiah gave Raisa an appraising look. He pursed his lips. "This is how Elysium works, lass. Everyone finds their niche in life, to bring in the essentials. Harvesters, and drivers to haul in our finds. People skilled in stripping and processing. Engineers to run the machinery. Medics, teachers, planners. All the basics."

"And, as I understand it, this is all on a ... a *collective* basis." Raisa's hesitant interruption, her questioning tone, said she was struggling to wrap her mind around the idea of a society without money.

"Aye. Everyone plays a part in providing the raw materials for life: shelter, power, air, water, food. Things beyond that, beyond the basics, are in people's hands to make for themselves. Furniture, rugs, clothes. Everyone nurtures their own skills to use in their spare time, to add to the richness of life."

"Hobbies?"

He frowned, an expression at odds with his usual relentless cheeriness. "Not sure I'd care to use that word. It sounds frivolous to our ears. Our crafts are undertaken with joy and passion, but they are always with a mind to enriching ourselves and our society. Not mere *pastimes*."

"So ..."

He waved his hand back the way they'd come. "Everything you've seen up to this point was in the former camp. Essentials, for the common good. Dedicated workers concoct dyes, spin yarn and weave cloth to keep our warehouses stocked. But turning these materials into clothing is an individual labor. In this workshop, people are here in their off-duty hours, making the things they need."

"And ... you just give them materials? There is no payment involved?"

Again, Josiah frowned as if wrestling with unpalatable thoughts. "Most people here wouldn't even understand your question. I do only because I deal with you outsiders. They are free to take the materials they need. All we ask is they use them well."

Raisa bowed her head. "An admirable sentiment." Jennifer caught just the hint of a smile on her lips, and had to hide a smile herself. Raisa had played her ignorance to perfection, drawing out new insights into Elysium culture. Company dealings with the colony only ever revealed its outward face. Its inner workings remained largely secret.

Josiah led them away from the workshop to a comfortably furnished lounge area. A counter down one side held mugs and a steaming urn. From the bitter odor wafting across the room, Jennifer suspected it held char, their universally-favored brew. Tables and chairs had been neatly lined up across from the counter.

"Meet Jorgen, our weaving and textiles supervisor."

A cadaverous man approached and bobbed his head. His bald head shone in the yellow ceiling light. Jennifer had to crane her neck to look him in the eye, an unusual situation for her.

Two young girls behind him laid wrapped bundles on a table at Jennifer's side. She glanced at Josiah, then turned her attention to the bundles. One of the girls rummaged through the packages and handed one to Jennifer.

Josiah smiled and jutted his chin towards the table. "There is a gift here for every member of your contingent."

She loosened the ties, and unwrapped a hooded jacket.

Homespun. Quite literally. There was no way in hell she'd be caught dead wearing it, but as a gift she realized this was an item of extreme value in this culture. Most clothing and personal items, she'd learned, were hand-crafted either by the owner or by someone close in the community. Often handed down within families, items were not for sale, though they were occasionally gifted in ceremony or thanks for some service.

There was no concept of monetary trade here, a bizarre notion reinforced by their recent conversation. In fact, in the hurried glimpses of the administration and community domes she'd passed through, there was a startling absence of commerce. No shops, no malls.

The jacket was decorated in the flowing, organic designs favored by the locals, in the disconcertingly alien color palette of locally-derived dyes. This was a deep almost-burgundy, with writhing vines trailing up the front in a bronzy-pewter that shifted in the light like oil on water.

As Jennifer held it up, the feel of it startled her. She'd seen the coarse mats of fibers teased from limbs and tubers. She'd gazed through windows at masked and overalled workers steeping the pulpy mass in steaming chemical vats. She'd watched the dance of looms and cutting and sewing machinery. But nothing prepared her for the exquisite, luxurious feel of the finished product. Cashmere was the closest she could come to describing it.

She turned it around in her hands, admiring–despite her inbred cynicism–the craftmanship. She fingered the cloth. Tight-woven, it felt like it would keep cold winds at bay and the wearer cozy in a harsh winter. Yet it was so lightweight. She'd not felt the like in any of her high-end couturiers.

A part of her recognized the potential here. What a good marketing department could do with a product like this. Well, with a more refined styling for the discerning customer anyway.

But, Jennifer also recognized with a deep chill, this was exactly why the Company kept such tight rein on Elysium's access to machinery. The real profits lay in the pharmaceutical output which the Company had tied unbreakable claims to over the centuries, for as long as the colony was bound to them in debt. Couldn't have the industrious and inventive little beggars finding a new export market and making enough profit to buy their way out of their colonial agreement.

They walked for hours through a subterranean miracle. Mikel had studied the mechanics of Sponge and knew the structures intimately ... how they linked together to hold shape against the relentless tug of gravity, how they caught and filtered water in an endless cycle, how the movement of air and water shunted heat, waste, and nutrients through its vast depths.

But to see it close up, rather than in diagrams and models, the staggering whole thrummed with life and energy around him.

Anna followed silently. She'd barely said a word since leaving the place where the crawler fell. Once out of sight of that canyon, out of sight of any greenjackets who might dare venture below, she'd paused to rummage through the pockets of her bulky outdoor jacket. Mikel noticed her hands tremble as she opened up a tiny pouch and struggled with the lid of a tube. He'd put his hands on her shoulders, horrified to see the tears in her eyes. He'd helped her open the tube and gently rubbed a smear of salve into the raw flesh of her palms, praying that the relief would bring back the Anna he knew.

No such luck. Since then, she trailed Mikel like a shadow, seeming less alive than the vast and complex web of tissue surrounding them, out of place in the shimmering ethereal glow.

Mikel knelt, pressing both hands to the floor. No longer hard and smooth, it was wrinkled like old skin and had a slight give to it. Sounds whispered from near and far as the giant organism stretched and breathed, warmed in the lowering sun and squeezed columns of water to the upper reaches to soak in the last rays of the season. He closed his eyes, but still felt the plant around him, etched in his mind, guiding him to where they needed to go. Sharp tingles of electricity buzzed through his palms and filled him with peace and certainty.

He tried to swallow. His parched tongue clung to his palate. But they were close, he could tell. The texture of the tissue around him had been changing as they walked. Now, there was need of caution. The gutters down from the surface contained choke points like the one those stupid *vreemde* had stumbled into, intended to catch and digest large debris that might otherwise clog the system. The trick was to find ways past those gullets and arrive at one of the aquifers from above.

Surely even Anna, stumbling along in a zombified state, could hear it now. Water trickling. Yes, her eyes gained a spark of life.

Another ten minutes, now picking up the pace, they emerged high up on the edge of a cavern whose far side was lost in darkness. A network of pools glistened in the beams of their flashlights.

"Surface catchpools are draining out for winter," Anna noted. Mikel nodded, relieved to hear her talk once more. This cavern would normally be filled, but Sponge was preparing for the coming deep freeze.

They clambered down the slick and glistening slope to the nearest pool.

"Careful," Anna said. "Footing's treacherous and those pools could be deep."

Mikel's heart leapt. That was more like it.

They both pulled out their hip flasks and uncoiled the thin pickup tubes. A few quick pumps on the siphon bulb drew water up through the tube and forced it through the filter set into the cap.

Following Anna's lead, Mikel took a deep breath and pulled off his mask. Taking a swallow without breathing was trickier than he imagined. He almost choked as a tendril of native air leaked past his tongue.

Anna helped him replace and flush out his mask before he coughed and gulped deep breaths. Another couple of tries and he had the hang of it enough to slake his thirst one mouthful at a time.

Anna grinned and drained her own flask with practiced ease. They refilled and drank again, then filled once more. Anna sat and gazed around. "Well, we won't die of thirst just yet, but I still haven't figured out what to do. I guess we need to find our way back up top at some point and get back to town. Hope we can sneak in without being seen, and raid another emergency locker."

Mikel gave her a hug. He'd missed the old Anna. Her silence these past hours wasn't natural, and it was starting to panic him. It was a profound relief that she was back, maybe not quite her usual self but close enough.

"Not much of a plan, but it's the best we've got right now." She shrugged. "Any idea which way we're heading? Can't get my bearings down here, but for some reason it feels like we've been moving north, away from town."

It was Mikel's turn to shrug. He hadn't been heading any particular direction, simply *away* from immediate danger and towards something that should lead them back up ... eventually.

That was a problem, though. This stretch for kilometers around was mostly structural, shot through with vast caverns and canyons like the one they'd left behind, some even bigger. Ways to climb up would be few and far between. They had some walking yet to do.

Chapter 22

Towards the end of the afternoon, Sarah realized she was still alone in the cab. She'd had to battle growing weariness to keep her focus through the tedium, but at last the inertial navigation screen showed their destination was close.

Had either Seth or John come back in the last few hours? She couldn't remember. Would she have noticed? Maybe they were upstairs preparing an evening meal. Her stomach grumbled at the thought. Food. And a hot shower.

And sleep.

She needed a relief driver tomorrow.

She was absorbed in the unfamiliar approach to the next way station, a tricky one as the normally featureless uplands wrinkled at a meeting point of Sponge's vast ribs. At nightfall, the supersonic airflows gusted across the undulations in giant eddies–turbulence on scales of tens of kilometers. Extra rings of outlying baffles surrounded the way station like giant fairy circles, shielding them from all points of the compass. Concentrating in equal measure on the landscape outside, and the computer at her side, Sarah threaded a path through the obstacle course.

A commotion at the back of the cab broke her concentration. A glance over her shoulder revealed Seth and John with a flustered-looking Nick.

"Take the party upstairs, guys. Got a rig to dock."

"*Meneer* de Jong has some explaining to do."

An uncharacteristic edge in John's voice, and the unusual formality, sent a shiver of alarm through Sarah, but she brushed it aside. "What, now? Bit busy, John."

"He needs to tell us where Anna is."

"Seems a bit reticent." Seth's voice was calmer on the surface, but Sarah saw with a shock that he was barely controlling himself. His fists clenched and unclenched at his side, and he held his body like a coiled spring.

"I don't know what you mean," Nick squeaked. His breath whuffed through his lips as John shoved him into the seat to Sarah's left.

Sarah returned her attention to her steering, and cursed when she saw how far off her planned line she'd drifted. She slowed the crawler and eased it perilously close to the last row of baffles, doing her best to calm her thudding heart. That could have been nasty.

The ends of the windbreaks lay up ahead, combing the clouds. Sarah picked an empty lane and tried to plot a course to bring the crawler in at the right angle, but those confounded baffles complicated matters.

And there were John's words nagging at her, dividing her attention.

"Thing is, Nick, I've been talking to people back there."

He had news of Anna, and something sounded off.

"Kak!" Sarah couldn't concentrate properly until she'd heard what they had to say. "Will you *nutloos* boys get to the karking point?" She brought the crawler to a stop, and swiveled around in her chair.

"Last anyone remembers," John said, in a tone that mirrored the Elysium winter, "Anna was looking for her son. Several people remember she called out in the crew car but nobody'd seen him."

"Hey, Sarah, what's up?" the radio squawked through a hiss of static. "You're blocking my entrance."

"Not now, Tania." Sarah chewed her lip, guilty at her unusual sharpness. Normally she'd happily rise to the innuendo. "Got a wetware problem to deal with here."

"Most folks I talked to didn't miss her," John continued as if the interruption hadn't happened. "They just assumed she was driving. That's her job. Didn't even occur to anyone that anything might be amiss." He stationed himself in front of Nick and planted balled fists on the armrests either side. "Several people were very clear on one thing, though. You were the last one seen talking to her, just before we left."

The communications board at Sarah's shoulder pinged, then again. A growing constellation of status lights showed people up and down the train trying to call her.

Nick gazed with wide eyes up at John towering over him. He looked like he was trying to crawl through the back of the seat.

"And, apparently, all this time you've been telling folks back there she was up here in the drive cab." Seth spoke from the far side of the cab, facing the window, arms hugging his body. "You didn't just *assume* it, you stated it as fact. Now why would you say *that* when you knew it wasn't true?"

Skies above, he's about to blow.

More pings. Sarah jerked the microphone off its hook and snapped into the PA, "Back off, folks. Slight technical delay. We'll be rolling again soon."

She whirled back in her seat.

Nick's voice came out as little more than a whisper. "I didn't know how to break it to the clan. To you."

Realization dawned for Sarah with a deepening sense of unreality. "You *left* her?" Astonishment gave way to anger as another thought struck her. "And a young boy?"

"There's more," John growled.

Nick buried his face in his hands and nodded. "Mikey's teacher went with Anna to look for him."

Sarah gaped at him. It took a few moments to find her voice, and then her words came out as little more than a squeak. "You cleared me to *leave*."

"I gave them as much time as I could. They had a deadline. Even when time was up, I gave them a little longer, praying they'd make it back."

"You said they were accounted for."

"Yes, *accounted for*." A flash of anger, of defiance. "I knew where they were! I knew they were not on board."

"Everyone knows the rules. You don't miss the last train out of town." Seth spoke through a quiet sob, and his words sent a shock through Sarah. *She* knew the rules, too. Both Seth and Nick were right. It was rare but there were precedents, others left behind. It happened once every few seasons. One sacrificed for the safety of the many.

When it happened, the name was recorded on the trek warden's log marked 'MLT'. Missed Last Train. The family would grieve, would hold a funeral ceremony when they reached the equatorial city, and life would go on.

Nobody blamed the trek wardens. Their duty lay with the train and the people on board. Everyone knew the rules.

"So why keep it quiet?" Seth collapsed into the starboard seat, tears running freely down his cheeks.

"I knew how close you guys were. I knew I couldn't put it off much longer, but I *have* been putting it off." Nick buried his face in his hands. "I used the rules as an excuse."

"Rules?" John looked confused.

Sarah could barely speak through the lump in her throat. "You don't tell the driver."

John gaped, then his face reddened. "What? In case you do something reckless? Like turn back?"

"The driver needs a clear head." Sarah's voice seemed to be coming from far away. "The whole train depends on it. Last thing you need is a driver distracted by guilt at driving off leaving someone to die."

She squeezed her eyes shut. The next season, the first maintenance crews into town would do a search. Sometimes they found a body huddled pitifully in one of the basement power rooms surrounded by heaps of bottles and containers from the emergency lockers, frozen corpse perfectly preserved in the long dark. From the amount of trash, they estimated that people lasted days, sometimes weeks, before succumbing to the creeping cold.

More often, there would be no body. People left behind knew what they faced. Knew there would be no rescue. Once they were sure they were alone, they took one last walk onto the surface and took off their masks.

They would never have gone far from town, but Sponge left no trace of them.

Another hour of walking. Anna was numb with exhaustion. She was slowly coming to the realization that they had no chance of regaining shelter before darkness fell. She'd lost track of time, but her body told her it was missing at least a couple of meals.

She stopped and called to Mikey. "Is there any way up from here?"

He pointed up, then wrapped his arms around himself and shivered.

"Yes, it's going to get cold up there on the surface. I get that." She frowned. "You're saying we shouldn't try to climb up yet."

He pointed forward, held up three fingers, then five with a shrug, then placed his hands by his head indicating sleep.

Anna frowned. "You might be right." She gazed upwards. "There's some thickness of plant life above us. I guess that might be insulation enough. We can probably survive the night."

In fact, she realized, it was unusually cozy in this network. They'd been walking along a broad avenue, clambering occasionally over rounded ridges that made the tunnel look disturbingly like a giant throat. One that could comfortably swallow a crawler. She squinted sharply at Mikey. "Do you recognize these formations?"

He rolled his eyes. Okay, maybe she deserved that.

"This is an air artery, isn't it?"

Mikey nodded again. Anna wracked her mind. She usually focused on surface formations, seeking safe paths for heavy vehicles. But surface features went hand in hand with subsurface detail. She should *know* this stuff. He studied her, arms crossed, face twisted in a pantomime of patience. "You're probably already ahead of me, aren't you? Let me guess. This is a warm air flow, which is why you think we can bed down and stay cozy."

At last, his expression said.

"Question is, can we reach the surface again?"

A frown, the fingers walked again. A hand wobble. Uncertainty.

"Well, I guess we can't be any worse off than we already are, and there's no obvious path back up from here."

"You realize, of course, that a world like this can never be truly self-sufficient?"

Wordlessly, Josiah sipped his char, his eyes crinkling in amusement over the rim of his cup. Nikolai hovered discreetly in the background, ready to serve, but more importantly ready to listen.

"I mean ..." Jennifer realized too late that she'd been goaded by Josiah's silence into speaking on. She chided herself for her lapse, but she had no choice but to complete the thought. "The workshops were impressive. You can obviously manufacture ninety percent of your needs from native materials, but you're lacking in things like metals, machining, electronics."

"Oh, we would never be able to support the sophistication of advanced technology, but the need for that is correspondingly limited. And"–he wagged a plump finger at Jennifer–"that comprises a miniscule proportion by weight and volume of our import manifests."

Another sip and an infuriating twinkle of the eyes. This time Jennifer held her silence. Josiah had a purpose in this conversation. Clearly to gain some leverage in the negotiations, that was a given, but what specifically? Maybe to hint that Elysium didn't intend to be held in thrall to one company's shipping monopoly. To hint that they were actively exploring other avenues. But how far would they go in pursuit of that aim? And, more importantly, how far might they have already gone?

"Sponge provides a remarkable wealth of basic materials, aye, but if we could source our own metals that would fill a substantial gap."

Oh! So that's their goal. "Out of curiosity, how would you imagine conducting a mining operation with the planet covered by a thick layer of plant life? To my knowledge, nobody's ever plumbed the depths to reach the mineral surface."

"You're quite right, of course. But beyond the plant line, nearer the poles, almost half the planet's surface remains unexplored. Mostly."

Jennifer's stomach lurched. Have they seriously been prospecting on the open surface? "There's a good reason for that. Above latitude forty the surface is pretty much uninhabitable. Scorching in summer, and deep freeze in winter."

"True enough," Josiah laughed. "True enough. Sponge has always thrown up its challenges."

A veiled reminder that the colonists had proved adept and determined in meeting those challenges.

Heedless of the damp trailing down her cheeks, Sarah lay awake listening to the sounds from outside. At other times of the year, winds shrieked and whistled around the cars of a crawler, playing on edges and angles of the many pieces of equipment protruding from the cars, or singing through the open mesh of the wheels. But out on the exposed backbone of Sponge, so close to the late summer change, the jet stream dipped across the nighttime terminator to hug the ground. At ground level some of its energy was broken by outlying baffles set to protect the way station, but it still hit the windbreak with supersonic force.

Fingers clutched the sides of the bunk as turbulent spillage from that sheet of air, a mere fraction of a percent of its fury, rocked the car against its restraints. The rest passed above their heads drawing a deep, penetrating moan as it crossed the curving vanes of the way station. The note was so deep as to be almost inaudible, but it filled the cab with a solid presence.

And yet it wasn't the oppressive hum keeping Sarah awake, nor even the cab's restless motion. Once you got used to it, that was easy to ignore. No, it was the conversations that followed the evening's revelations that played again and again through her mind.

She'd had to take a walk, on the pretext of checking the train before the winds hit, to settle her roiling emotions. In part, she felt some sympathy for Nick. He'd acted in accordance with Company dictates, and had only done what others before him had done. Nobody held it against them.

On reflection, he'd actually cut it dangerously fine. There had been little leeway once they'd reached that first way station. Another hour and they'd have struggled to properly secure the train. It had been slower going than usual with those extra cars. They were late in the season and the days were shortening. Nick knew that, which was why he'd been so anxious to leave. He had more than just three missing people to worry about.

Heck, if he'd waited any longer to clear the train for departure, Sarah would have had to override him. And she would have. Wouldn't she? In the driving seat, the whole train was in her care.

But it was his evasion since then that infuriated her. Why not simply come clean and announce the missing people? Didn't he trust her? Kak! He'd let her believe Anna was on board. *Occupied?* What a *debeel* excuse. How did she not see through that nonsense? Never mind that he was still playing by the rules, the sense of betrayal ached inside her.

What had he expected her to do? But she couldn't silence a niggling doubt. *Maybe Nick was right.*

She ground her teeth to blot out that treacherous thought. Her knuckles cracked on the side of the bunk.

Again, Sarah's mind replayed the emotional evening. Once she'd returned to the cab, intense discussions went around in circles, seeking some solace, some solution.

"Could they have got onto the shut-down crew's train? They were a while behind us, finishing off." That was Seth, clutching at straws.

"I already checked." The despair on Nick's face washed away some of Sarah's anger. "First night we stopped. That was my last hope. Another reason not to say anything until I was sure."

Then John had roused himself with another false hope. "The Company has jets on the planet. For the negotiations. It would only be a matter of hours from Jorvick to Serendipity. They could be back within a day, with no danger to anyone."

Nick shook his head. "Those jets will stay grounded. The Company won't sanction a flight just for three people."

John muttered under his breath in the background, but it was Seth that Sarah watched intently. He was holding himself back from most of the talks. Sarah got the impression he was barely controlling himself. After all, this was *Anna* they were talking about. Maybe another reason for Nick to keep quiet as long as possible. She could just imagine Seth wrestling the controls of the crawler and turning them back.

She shivered. There must be a dozen ways impatient hands at the helm could wreck a train and leave them all stranded.

"More importantly," Nick continued, "you're forgetting there *is* a karking shedload of danger. The atmosphere is crazy enough during quiet months, but why do you think all the freight runs are jammed into a standard year or so before midsummer? Outside that quiet window, like right now, *any* flight is a big risk. Wind shear, electrical storms ..."

"I'm not forgetting *anything*," John gritted out. "Pilot training, remember? I *know* the dangers, I just believe some things are worth risking."

Sarah's anger boiled again. "If it's so bad, why'd they pick *right now* to bring a posse of suits in for negotiations?"

Nick shrugged, but he avoided her eyes. "Simple fact is, their jets are more precious to them than three colonists' lives."

"Karking *vreemde!*" John had expressed the disgust on all their minds.

Now in the small hours, Sarah gazed up at the shadowed ceiling, lit only by a faint crimson wash from the exits and emergency medical locker. The sound that filled the air eased, only slightly, but enough to signal an end to this night's gale. Up and down the train, she knew veterans of many treks would rouse from restless slumber before settling to deeper sleep, secure in the knowledge that Sponge had spared them to ride another day.

But sleep still escaped her. Restless thoughts plagued her. She'd let Seth down, had driven his crew into danger, technically as lost as Anna was now. Anna had broken off contact with the field controller to rescue them. Sarah, Seth, and John owed Anna their lives.

And now she'd abandoned Anna. She'd failed again.

That left one course of action that Sarah was certain had been on their minds, but which had not been voiced.

She slid off the bunk and stood, hugging her arms around herself. This was madness. As close to treason as it was possible to come around here. She paced the couple of meters clear space, and back again, trying to think things through.

It was technically doable, she was sure of that. But could she manage it alone? Anna would have, there was no question of that. She spent weeks alone in the field, but this was different. A trickier thought: how was she going to persuade Seth and John to return to a crew car without arousing suspicion?

Pace. Pace. Kak! This was getting her nowhere. If she was going to act, she had to get on with it.

"Something troubling you?" Seth's voice was a low rumble across the compartment. Sarah leapt and whirled around.

"N-nothing."

"Ahh, nonsense." Eyes glinted in the nightlight from the next bunk. "You're going back, aren't you?"

Sarah fumbled in her mind for a denial.

"Was wondering how long it would take for you to decide."

"What do you mean?"

"I can't drive a train. And I couldn't *ask* you to, no matter how much I needed to. Had to be you made up your own mind."

It took a few moments for Sarah to process his words, her shock, and the implications.

"You know you'll never boss a harvest crew again after this."

"And you'll never take a driver's seat again. But we're not leaving Anna behind, and we've a better chance with two of us."

"Three."
They both turned to see John sitting up on his bunk.

Chapter 23

The howling gale had subsided, even though it was still the middle of the night. The three of them worked quietly to cast off the lines holding the drive cab and the first three cargo cars. Sarah didn't want to take any more cars than she had to. She could have made do with just one to stabilize the cab, but she was conscious of the extra length she'd be adding to Tania's train. On the other hand, they were taking a big risk and she didn't want to endanger any more equipment than necessary. Three seemed like a reasonable compromise. Not that it mattered much. They'd spend the rest of their lives swabbing out steaming vats for such a serious breach of rules, even if they did return in one piece.

They chose not to risk lighting the external spots, but the overcast above them glowed, lit from above by Elysium's intense planet-wide aurora.

Butterflies fluttered through Sarah's stomach at the enormity of what they were doing. While there were precedents for leaving stragglers behind, nobody had ever dared go back for them.

As she reached up to unclip a line from the cab, her skin crawled. There was someone up there gazing through the window down at her. She could swear it. But she blinked and looked again and the apparition was gone. With her pulse thudding in her throat she climbed onto the front running board and hauled herself up level with the drive cabin's floor. Through the overhanging windows she scanned the floor past chair legs and console pedestals. There was no-one there.

Trembling, she returned to work.

Finally, with the front of the train free, Sarah climbed up to the fourth yoop and flipped open an access panel next to the trailing car's hitch. She lowered the pair of front legs to support the weight of the car. She carefully studied the strain gauges to confirm that the legs held the weight, and there was no pressure left on the hitch.

With long years of practice, Sarah and John ran through the rest of the undocking procedure. The airlocks on either side of the yoop sealed, the rear tunnel connecting it to the next car unsealed and retracted. Power couplings took a few minutes to unfasten.

One final check, and she hit the hitch release. After a few seconds, when the car behind showed no signs of settling, she also released the breath she'd been holding. Her mask fogged, and she shook off the small-hours chill that invaded her layers of outdoor clothing.

They were free. All she had left to do was reconfigure the drive computer for the shorter train and they could drive away. As soon as they were clear of the windbreak she'd alert Tania. Tania would have no trouble reversing between the windbreaks to pick up the stranded cars.

Sarah sent Seth and John on ahead while she conducted one last visual check on the crawler. At last, she gritted her teeth in determination and hauled herself up into the cab's airlock.

As she stripped off her mask and emerged from the steps into the cabin, she found John and Seth standing with their arms folded, looking grim. "Seems we got company," John growled.

Sarah's heart missed a beat. She peered around the corner to see Nick facing off her two boys. A cold sensation crept up her neck when she saw three stern figures behind him, blocking the way to the driver's seat.

She swallowed. She recognized Ben de Vries, patriarch of Anna's clan. Reputation for discipline and no nonsense.

And those must be his twin daughters, toying meaningfully with belay pitons in their meaty hands. Sarah had never met them, but nobody in Serendipity would ever mistake them. Reputation for humorless loyalty to the clan, and for never losing an argument.

"Meneer de Jong informed me of your little escapade." Ben's voice was like the grinding of a stripped drive clutch.

Sarah glanced sidelong at Seth, but he was gazing steadily at the floor. The twins, on the other hand, were staring at her with disconcerting intensity. Skies! Did those girls ever blink?

"Talk of you stealing the head of our train." He scrunched up his face. "Stealing. Not a word I'm used to hearing on Sponge. Not a word we use in polite society. Sponge is a harsh place to live. People live and die by the trust others place in them."

Silence begged to be filled, but Sarah had nothing to say. Nothing seemed adequate. Ben was right. Trust was everything. And yet ... trust went many different ways.

Ben seemed to pick up on her thoughts. "Nick explained why, of course. Very noble thoughts, I must say."

Sarah's anger boiled over. "Did he explain that he left Anna and her son and his teacher to die?" No response from the twin gargoyles, which was a relief. She'd just talked back at a senior member of the community.

"So, the three of you were going back on your own to mount a rescue." Ben shook his head, eyes downcast. "I can't let you do that."

Sarah slumped against the wall, utterly deflated. Seth and John were each maybe a match for any one of the three heavies, but Sarah couldn't handle anyone other than Nick. Sure, she'd kick that slimeball's ass all the way to Laverne but that still left one free agent to tip the balance. And those three had their reputation on their side. This wasn't a fight they could even start, let alone win.

"It could take you days to search the town. More than fifty domes, top to bottom. I figured a few more pairs of eyes would halve the time."

Sarah straightened, frowning, trying to catch onto Ben's meaning.

Ben inspected his fingernails. "Anna saved both my girls last season. I've lost count of how many rules she's broken, but the town is always the richer for it, in the ways that matter."

Nick's eyes widened, mirroring Sarah's own disbelief. Disbelief turned to panic when a brawny fist clamped around each of his arms.

"I believe we're all slackened off and unhitched," Ben said. "Time is of the essence, Sarah Miller, you have some driving to do."

"Wait. What about him?" She jerked her head towards Nick, who looked like Sponge had just opened up and swallowed him.

"My girls will make sure he's comfortable upstairs."

Sarah grimaced. "Sorry, but he can't stay on this train. I won't be responsible for his safety."

Ben pondered this for a moment. "If we let him go, how do you think he'll explain all this to the other padres on the train? What story will he tell to the curate in Laverne?"

Sarah chewed her lip. "He's already shown he's not above sneakery. And we know how karking scared he is of what he did."

That was too much for Nick, despite the two beside him who'd just turned from associates to jailers. "I had no choice! We *had* to leave."

"I'm not talking about *giving the order*," Sarah snarled, "I'm talking about your *debeel* attempt at hiding it."

"Exactly so," Ben said. "Do you really think he's going to be straight and tell it like it is? Or do you think he'll look to cover his ass? At your expense?"

With an exasperated shake of her head, Sarah took her seat. Still trying to rein in her emotions, she busied herself with the drive computer and startup checks. Cabin lights dimmed and the curving lane ahead lit up through the windows under the crawler's running lights. Minutes passed without another word as the walls crept past, until they emerged onto open ground.

Sarah halted the vehicle and twisted around in her seat. "I still don't like it."

"Let him go and he gets to write his own story of our perfidy." Ben grinned. "But take him with us, and he becomes an accomplice."

Beside him, Nick blanched.

"Enough people were roused by his bleating, and saw him fetch us from the car. What do you suppose they'll assume when we're all found gone?"

Sarah pursed her lips. They were already in deep. A little bit of abduction and unwilling confinement could hardly make things worse. "Just keep the karking little worm quiet, is all I ask." She eased the stick and the crawler surged into the blushing dawn.

"Mikey, you little beauty!" Anna stared at the shaft of light in the distance. Wind whistled past her, swirling up the tunnel and whipping at her coat. Their tunnel joined others, merging into a vast cavern opening into a shaft and a sunlit lip far above. "You found an outflow."

Mikey looked sidelong at her with just the hint of a smile. One of his 'did you ever doubt me' looks. She punched his shoulder. "Come on, let's get out of here. I don't know where we'll come out, but I bet it's a long hike back to town."

She sobered at the thought. They'd slept well enough in the warm depths, but fatigue and hunger still dragged at Anna. Those, she could deal with for now, but they had to find another source of water before long. She wondered how Mikey was coping. She almost asked, then thought better of it. While his mind seemed occupied with navigating, there was no point reminding him of things outside their immediate control. They'd surely find a catchpool somewhere out there.

Her tongue felt swollen enough to fill her mouth. Her head pounded. Anna pushed aside the discomfort and looked for a route up. Mikey huffed for attention and pointed to one side. She squinted and followed the line he'd spotted.

The floor of the cavern sloped up ever steeper into a near-vertical funnel fifty meters across, opening to the sky. Meter-wide ridges and ribs criss-crossed the sides, offering a broken ladder.

She tested her footing on the nearest rib. It was hard, rounded, but rough enough to give good traction. Not for the first time, Anna wished they had some climbing equipment with them. They needed to trace a spiral path around the inner surface, trying to stick with the gentlest slope. But at some point, they'd have to traverse a vertical section. They'd have to be careful.

This was unknown territory. Anna hesitated. Harvest crews never ventured into the rash of pores pockmarking Sponge's surface. Sponge had a complex but well-defined structure. Airflows, water flows, regions of synthesis and temperature management. Patterns repeating endlessly across the planet's surface. Pores might provide an easy route into the depths, but the valuable tubers they sought had simply never been found nearby. More profitable to camp out where the patchwork quilt of the surface indicated hidden treasures and break through directly. So here, there was no folklore to draw on, no talk of traps or other dangers to watch out for.

"Do you know anything about these upflows? Anything we should watch out for?"

Mikey pouted in thought, then shook his head. But the slight frown he wore didn't inspire confidence.

"Okay. Here goes." Anna eased herself along the ledge, resisting the temptation to rush, even though the going was easy here. "Any idea where we're coming out? We always seemed to be heading north, but my sense of direction may have gotten turned around down below."

Mikey pursed his lips and quirked an eyebrow.

"You're saying I'm right? We *will* have a trek then. Fifteen klicks? Maybe twenty?" Anna eyed the pattern of ridges ahead. "Climb up to that next level, I think. Looks like an easier route up to that wide rib up there."

She helped Mikey clamber up, then he turned and held out a hand for her.

They paused to catch their breath. "Try not to look down," she said, then immediately ignored her own advice. Her head swam. They were now maybe fifteen meters up from the floor, and the side was steep beneath them. She gulped. Yes. Don't look down.

"When we get topside I should be able to figure out where we are. Kak!" She noticed the ledge they were on petered out about thirty meters ahead.

Mikey nudged her and pointed behind them. Anna puzzled, then followed his finger up and around. "Yeah, good call." More clambering. Anna's breaths came in sharp gasps and her healing foot throbbed like the devil. Water, they could find on the hike back. Sadly, pain meds didn't grow out in the open.

"Question is," she panted, "what to do when we get there. Wonder if they'll still be patrolling. If we can get into town without being spotted, we can hide out in one of the domes for a while. There'll be food, water, shelter ..."

Another raised eyebrow.

"Yeah. I know. That just leaves us all the way back at square one, doesn't it?"

At last they emerged into sunlight, where the funnel mouth of the outflow widened and the ground leveled off to the point where they could finally stand and walk. Big Red peeped at them between towering guide vanes ringing the outflow. Wind keened through the vanes, channeled across the mouth of the vast pore in the surface drawing an infrasonic note that trembled Anna's gut and made her feel queasy.

They climbed higher, scrambling across ridges, and worked their way back and forth between the labyrinth of vanes. The guide vanes grew higher, the lanes between them wider. There was nothing they could do other than follow the valleys around and hope they emerged at some point.

Wind funneled through the narrow canyons shrieking and howling around them, at times making it hard to stand. Despair and frustration began to gnaw at Anna. This valley seemed to go on forever, winding around the outflow. At last, a gap to their left let them through into a wider path. This looked more hopeful.

Anna's foot dislodged something gleaming in the feathery surface. She bent to look closer. "A piton." She picked it up, then looked again at the valley they stood in, and the sharp ridges either side. "You know, this could be one of mine."

Excitement caught her. "This must be North Seventeen. This is where we sheltered the other day." More implications caught up with her. She strode out into the open, emerging onto a broad upland spine that curved away into the distance.

"Yes! Oh, kak, I wonder ..."

Below the surface, Mikey had taken charge, but up here was unmistakably Anna's domain. She took the lead, striding out onto the hard shell, following its line. The irresistible pull of hope and anxiety propelled her at a furious pace, overriding the hammering ache in her foot. From time to time she glanced back to Mikey, trailing behind, and waved him on.

Anna shaded her eyes and cursed the moisture fogging her mask. A slender pole stood lonely guard on the horizon. The beacon she'd planted ... how many days ago now? She tried to count back and got lost. A week, maybe. Whatever. Her thoughts were rambling. Not a good sign. She realized that if this remote hope failed them, they may no longer have the strength to hike all the way back to town.

Trembling legs responded sluggishly to Anna's urging. She was at the limits of her endurance. There was no longer any question in her mind, their survival depended on whatever lay tantalizingly out of sight the far side of that crest.

She forced herself, step after step, needing to know, yet not wanting to see what lay beyond.

A splash of yellow in the distance. Her heart leaped. Seth's crawler hadn't vanished into the depths. Not completely. Only the line of the roof was visible, but it was still reachable. Maybe ...

Mikel jumped and yipped his delight.

"Wait," Anna croaked, before he could race off towards the stranded vehicle. She hadn't forgotten the treachery of this stretch of ground ... her plunge into the depths, and Ambrose's torn and pierced body.

She knelt, caressing the matting. The parallels with Mikey's own actions below ground struck her, and she stifled a fit of laughter.

The ground swept up to meet her. Kak! She was seriously losing it. Mikey hauled her to her knees, concern creasing his forehead.

"Thanks," she gasped, swallowing another fit of giggles. "Need food and drink. We'll be okay when we reach that cab. There's a crew car too, should be well stocked."

Mikey nodded and jerked his head in the direction of the crawler. *What are we waiting for?*

"Yeah, just a minute ... what was I doing down here? Oh, yeah ..." Memory returned. The surface. The rotting surface, that opened up and swallowed them.

Anna puzzled. The texture here had transformed from the fragile matting of a week ago. It was now spiky, and rock hard. Bumps and knobs here on the edge of the lowlands grew in the distance to a wrinkled covering of hillocks. Sponge had rearranged itself, part of its metamorphosis into winter. The colonists rarely saw formations like this. It was a grim reminder of how late they'd stayed this season.

"Looks like the ground is solid again. Seth just had bad luck to cross right when it was shifting. Everything soft, moving around." She puzzled. "Wonder why it does that?" A short laugh burst out, once more on the verge of madness. "I guess even a giant plant has to winterize itself to cope with two hundred below."

She rose, and trod carefully. The ground held. She felt naked out here without at least a rope to save her if the worst happened, but there seemed to be no other option. They had to reach that crawler.

Chapter 24

Anna inspected the almost-buried vehicle with a mixture of relief and dismay. Relief that they'd safely traversed the kilometer that had claimed Ambrose and very nearly the rest of the crew. The surface had indeed hardened again, into tussocks of iron-hard spicules ranging from fine needles to lengths the size of ventilation pipes. They branched and twisted in tufts and fronds reaching for the sky. In between, the ground was a carpet of needles, thankfully too densely packed to pierce their boots.

She finally recognized the formations from studies years ago. Few people were ever around to see this, but Sponge swapped summertime photosynthesis for winter thermosynthesis, using the vast temperature drop to drive its chemical factories. This whole kilometers-wide valley was one immense heat sink in the making.

Relief too, that the crawler looked fairly intact. Lights gleamed in windows, so power was still active. They had shelter for now, warmth, food, water, medical supplies. They would be comfortable while they decided their next move.

But that relief battled with a dismay that betrayed an impossible, foolish hope she'd been clinging to all this while. As soon as she'd seen the yellow roof peering above ground level, Anna had pictured them somehow dragging the crawler out of the ground and striking out once more for the equator.

That hope seemed dashed. Almost flush with the surrounding surface, it had been spared the worst of the nighttime hurricanes that lashed the mid latitudes this time of year. But it still looked in sorry shape. The sides were battered and dented, and now Anna wondered about hull integrity. And when she peered down into the pit the crawler sat in, it looked like tendrils had grown through the mesh of the wheels, binding them into the fabric of the planet.

One problem at a time. They needed to care for themselves, then they could figure out the crawler.

They clambered down into the gash alongside the cab, tearing gloves and outer clothes to ribbons on the iron-hard spikes that made up the surface. The airlock showed they still had good atmosphere in there. It was a start. A million times better than their situation a few hours ago.

A shower and hot food restored a measure of optimism, despite the hurdles ahead. In the bunkroom above the cab, Anna found an old work shirt she recognized. She buried her face in the fabric and breathed deep. It still held a lingering trace of Seth's scent. A new determination burned deep inside.

Anna had little in the way of a plan to return to and then escape Serendipity. But, refreshed, she sorted through memories of all the town's garages, mentally itemizing the rigs she knew about. None came close to the state of readiness of poor, deceased *Chance O'Glory*. And that had been a desperately long shot.

They might have a better chance of sneaking out in that scramjet, as long as the *vreemde* weren't guarding it too closely.

Of course, it would help if Anna knew how to fly. But then, she decided she would rather die in a blaze of defiance than slowly freezing to death.

And before it reached that point, she still held out a spark of hope of getting Seth's rig up and running. That was where her attention lay now.

Anna settled into the driver's seat and brought the controls to life. For half an hour she studied readouts and status reports, checking every aspect of the entrenched vehicle. "It's in a lot better shape than it looks. Cab's good. Shame the crew car back there's been breached, but we can get in with masks and bring forward supplies if we need to."

Mikey uncurled from the port co-driver's seat, where he'd been watching over Anna's shoulder.

"Most systems are working. This is a well-maintained rig." Thank you, Seth! "I'm a bit worried about cars four onwards, though. Where the back end dropped through, the hitches back there are damaged. We might have to cut them loose."

She tried to keep her tone upbeat for Mikey's sake. It was true, the crawler was in better shape than it looked from outside, but that wasn't saying much. And most systems were working. Just. She glossed over the many damage warning signals, the leaking lubricants, the fused hitch hydraulics, the power cells hovering on the verge of failure. Mikey didn't need to know about that.

She cautiously brought the main drives online and gave the motors a tiny surge of power. She could feel the rig around her straining to be free, but it was locked down solid.

Well, it was worth a try. Sometimes a bogged-down crawler could break itself free from tangles of plant tissue, but that was in the springtime, when the new growth was still soft.

She bounced out of her seat. "Zip up and mask on. Internals look as good as we can expect, let's have a closer look outside."

They worked their way from front to back as methodically as her systems check.

"Two problems," Anna announced as they wormed their way back towards the front. "The obvious one is hauling ourselves out of this pit."

Mikey's eyes widened. Anna laughed. "Sounds a tall order, but we've got a whole train full of equipment to play with. Harvesting and hauling tackle, cargo cranes up top to help set things up. I bet there's cutting equipment too." Her heart leapt at the thought. "I've had to rescue mired crawlers before. You know, we might actually be able to do this."

His expression was a clear 'I'll believe it when I see it'.

"But this is what's really bugging me." She patted the nearest wheel, where a dense mat of roots entwined the open mesh. "Freeing us up from this crap without damaging the wheels. Wonder how tough those fibers are, and how much damage they've done. They've already started pulling this one out of shape."

The endless maze of narrow halls and windowless rooms pressed in around Jennifer. Alone in her suite—she'd instructed ever-attentive Nikolai to leave—she gripped the arms of her chair and tried to regain some balance.

The suite was large, and now it was empty, and yet the walls hemmed her in. The eternal heat, humidity, the ever-present tang of trace chemicals coating her tongue, and the unseen press of people beyond the walls felt like an assault.

This was crazy. Even the months enclosed in the longship hadn't preyed on her like this. Admittedly, she'd surrounded herself there with accustomed opulence to ease the trip, but the cabins were tiny in comparison, and the few decks given over to her and her entourage could be traversed and navigated in minutes.

She'd worked on at least a dozen planets, some terraformed and with breathable atmospheres, some vacuum-clad where the colonists lived in domes and habitats like Elysium, but confinement never assailed her like this. There was always, without exception, some access to the outside, some viewing gallery where vistas opened up to relieve the oppression.

It was, she concluded, the sheer *wrongness* of being on a planet, with an atmosphere, above ground, and yet without a window in sight. There must be vistas out there, bleak though they may be, but inaccessible from here, hidden from this sprawling mass of people.

How did they cope, cooped up like this with no sight of the wilderness outside? And yet they seemed to relish it, turned inwards, ignoring the outdoors, taking comfort in endless inescapable human company.

Inside is safe, they say, outside lies danger. That thinking was baked into their simplest most mundane activities. She'd watched them, the unconscious glances and twitching finger movements every time they went through a door, reciting procedures to themselves so ingrained from childhood they were no longer even aware of them. Am I moving away from or towards safety? Even with wide open doors they still checked the airlocks, and confirmed their compact emergency mask still sat in its pocket on their hip. Every ... damned ... doorway they passed through!

And so, they instinctively sought the deepest nests to call home, to relax in. In what passed for privilege in this infuriatingly egalitarian world, the innermost suites near ground level were the most sought-after. Bizarre behavior to an inveterate penthouse-dweller like Jennifer. Not that a penthouse here would offer any benefit, with no windows and anyway nothing to see beyond those non-existent windows than the opaque skin of the dome.

She'd known this, intellectually, and had made sure not only to commandeer an entire habitat dome for herself and her staff, but—against all her instincts—had co-opted a large space on one of the lower levels for herself. She expected the best, wherever she went, but was always careful to ensure that 'best' was best by whatever measure impressed the locals. It was they, after all, who most needed reminding of her importance.

Darling Nikolai had done his best to make this bare suite more homely, but the alienness of the environment drowned her. The bewildering kaleidoscope of the crowded labyrinth, the incomprehensible attitudes of the locals, the reek of chemicals tainting the air, the noise ...

It was no good. She couldn't think straight in here. She needed to get outdoors.

Breaking up the train was the first thing to deal with. Assuming they could get out of here, the rear cars were too damaged to haul along with them. As Anna had guessed, the cars and hitches back there were badly twisted.

Competing pressures warred in her mind. If they could rescue this vehicle, she'd like to salvage as much as possible. That was just Sponge thinking through and through, and too deeply entrenched to ignore. But that gave them more cars to free up and haul out. More work.

On the other hand, Anna knew from experience that very short trains were jittery to handle out in the open. They had a long drive ahead, and the more stable the ride, the better.

She settled for keeping three cars and ditching the rest.

"Next job," Anna puffed, climbing back into the connecting tunnel. "Go and detach all the power couplings back there. We're taking them with us."

Mikey gave her a wry look.

"Yep," she said. "Obsessive, I know, but after all the hassle we had back in town ..."

Mikey rolled his eyes and scurried off to comply.

Anna busied herself rooting through the equipment stowed in the mired train. By the time Mikey returned, bowed down under the weight of the final two power couplings, she'd unpacked a range of cutting and lifting equipment.

"Good work, Mikey. Now let's see how handy you are with a power saw."

His eyes lit up. Anna frowned at him and hefted the long-bladed tool. "You used these in basic handicraft, didn't you?" His excitement was infectious, but mildly alarming. She pointed to a pile of safety gear, gauntlets and armored greaves. "Get kitted up and show me what you remember about safe handling."

Satisfied that Mikey knew what to do, Anna climbed up through the nearest car and unshipped the cargo crane. Hours passed. Slowly, an A-frame took shape over the front of the cab.

Anchoring the running tackle a hundred meters out across the plain stumped Anna for a while. Usually, she drove pitons deep into the surface, but the ground here was too hard even for the pneumatic spike driver on maximum power. In the end, she passed loops behind one of the mounds pimpling the surface, snagging them under the protruding spikes.

Soon, a network of lines ran through a complex series of pulleys laid out across the surface and down to the cable drums mounted on the front of the cab. Anna double-checked the layout, and patched the remote control on her lapel into Seth's crawler. She fed power to a lightweight winch and hauled the A-frame upright.

More checks, despite the urgency of their situation. Check now or repent later … Sponge was an unforgiving teacher.

Power to the heavy duty winch, small increments, and the main lifting line grew taut. Anna paused and reviewed her arrangements one last time.

No, not true. She'd check it all over again in the morning, but that was enough for today. Big Red was casting long shadows and they needed an early start if they were to make the way station before nightfall. Anna slackened off the lines and brought the A-frame back down, then lashed everything down securely for the night.

Fatigue washed over her as she scrambled back into the ravine. She'd held it at bay all afternoon, but now the lifting arrangements were finished her overworked body clamored for relief.

"C'mon, Mikey." Anna peered down the train. It had been unusually quiet for half an hour, and she was starting to worry. Her heart gave a thump when she saw him slumped by the third yoop.

"Mikey!"

He looked up, his face pale. As she got closer, Anna saw sweat glistening on his cheeks behind his mask. His arms were outstretched, embracing the leading edge of the wheel. He must be exhausted, too.

"Come on, it's been a long day." She studied the tangled fibers that still enmeshed the wheel. "That cutter doesn't seem to be making much impression, does it."

She checked the eight wheels. Mikey had clearly been to work on each of them. Broken strands littered the space around and under the yoops, but the heart of the matting still looked intact.

Thoughtfully, she picked up the saw. It whirred to life, but the blade jarred and bounced off the iron-hard thicket. She could barely scratch it.

She sighed. "Another problem for another day." It was too much to hope that it would be that easy. These tools were designed for different kinds of tissues deep down. The surface around here was unlike anything the harvest crews ever had to deal with. "Maybe power snips might do better than a saw. Tomorrow, I'll see if there's any heavier-duty machinery in one of the cargo cars."

The tiny ground car clattered to a halt in the echoing garage, the largest enclosed space Jennifer had seen on Elysium. She unfolded herself from the hard bucket seat and stretched her spine, careful not to show any signs of discomfort, of weakness, to the small group of natives gathering around them.

Jayne Kildare, Jennifer's head of security, stepped around the car to her side. Another car disgorged the rest of her escort, and Josiah Handel.

Jennifer gazed up at the vehicle towering above them with a twinge of misgiving. She hadn't realized these centipedes were so damned huge.

Narrow windows higher up gave a sense of scale. That ugly yellow box must be three or four floors tall. No wonder their shipping costs were so astronomical.

Three large and surly men stood in the shadow of one vast wheel, dressed for the outdoors. Jennifer scowled. "My instructions were for a minimal crew. I understand these centipedes are fully computerized, even on this world. My own security contingent and a driver is all I need."

There were snorts of muffled laughter. One of the three, the driver, Jennifer guessed, stepped forward and straightened. "Mai *centipede*," he announced, with exaggerated diction, "is indeed fully equipped with the latest helectronic driving and safety haids hafforded by the boundless generosity of the Company."

More hacks of suppressed laughter surrounded her. Jennifer bristled at the outright insubordination. She turned a furious gaze to Josiah, but he studiously avoided meeting her eyes and held a hand to cover his mouth.

"Ye're looking at the minimal crew," the driver snarled, all pretense at gentility gone, "even for a short trip outside. You'se being the one *debeel* enough to want a night jaunt. Mayhap it squalls up and we need to lash down in a hurry. Not a job for one on 'is lonesome."

Jennifer smiled. The temperature in the garage dipped noticeably. "I have my own staff here." She nodded to the two security personnel on either side. "They can provide any assistance you need."

The driver looked her up and down, slow and measured. Then he snorted. "You'se offworlders don't count. Yer the cargo." He turned and climbed through the airlock to the cab.

———————•◦•———————

Mikel's head span. The crawler, the cab, felt insubstantial, see-through. Not simply transparent like the windows, but the walls and the floor misted into non-being.

He sensed the network of voids beneath him, and the fractal complexity of spines and spicules knitting together to form the surface. But the plain out there was not a surface by any kind of design—a barrier to separate plant from not-plant—it was simply a phase change where the warm heart of Sponge far below reached out to the cooling atmosphere above. The whole buzzed with energy, a charge that stood Mikel's hair on end.

Some of it was memory from hours of study, but the sensation right now was more compelling than mere memory. He was *experiencing* Sponge itself.

There were more changes to come, Mikel understood. He had no idea how he knew this. It was not in any textbook, any lesson that he could recall, but he *knew* that when the temperature dropped to true winter the spiked surface around him would turn into a giant superconductor, channeling the vast temperature drop through kilometer-deep thermocouples to drive Sponge's nighttime chemistry.

He could *feel* it.

The structure of Sponge baffled people. The textbooks spoke of the plainly visible structures on scales from millimeters to kilometers. They talked as if analyzing air and water flows, catchpools and peristaltic pumps, explained how Sponge worked.

Hubris! They knew *nothing*.

When it came to real understanding, the textbooks stopped at the fact that Sponge had no cellular structure, no DNA, no obvious means of replication. Nobody understood how this planet-wide plant organized itself, let alone how it reorganized its structure so regularly.

To people who worked the surface, the outdoors was always seen to be still, unmoving. And yet everyone took for granted that the surface you drove on today might be transformed when you next passed by. Nobody acknowledged the paradox in those conflicting views.

To Mikel the answer was clear. Sponge was capable of movement, rapid movement, and could marshal vast energies with precision. Had anyone stopped to calculate how many terawatts of power it would take to shift a hundred square kilometers of landscape overnight?

They hadn't. They ignored the obvious, because to acknowledge it was too freaking scary.

But Mikel knew. He understood. And he also understood that what was done could just as easily be undone. Those iron hard trunks and vines holding them back had grown into place over the last few days. What was stopping them from *ungrowing*?

Mikel poured his heart into the desperate need to escape, to ride free and rejoin his family. Somewhere, an echo answered him. From deep down and from all around, a warmth touched his mind.

At first it was hard for Jennifer to adjust to the mask. Her temple throbbed against the press of the edge seal, bringing on irrational panic.

She'd worn EVA suits before but this, like so much on this planet, was a disconcerting hybrid. Suits enclosed you completely. They fed air to the helmet and siphoned waste gases away. They controlled the inside climate … temperature, humidity, gas composition … a bubble against harsh vacuum.

On worlds with a breathable atmosphere, you dressed for the local weather but breathed the air freely.

This was neither one nor the other. She was well-wrapped against the night chill, with heavy jacket, scarf and cloak, insulated cargo pants and laced working boots. She could feel the wind working its way into seams and gaps where a corner of her cloak flapped free. That all seemed deceptively normal, but a flimsy mask covered her face, no climate control, just the filters screening her from deadly poisons. When she exhaled, her breath vented and steamed beyond the mask. The taint of alien chemicals still caught her throat, despite the filters.

"Just breath naturally, but through your nose," a native guide had told her when he'd helped fit her mask. Such simple, childlike advice, but so hard to follow when every instinct told her to gulp deeply against the soft suck of the filters at her cheeks. She'd fought to avoid hyper-ventilating on her first steps away from the crawler. Her rising panic, her rational self reminded her, could be fatal out here even with help close by. The feelings of suffocation tempted her to rip her mask off and breathe freely.

A few breaths was all it would take for Elysium to claim her.

She glanced sidelong to where one of her security detail, chest heaving and face turning purple beneath his mask, turned and bolted back to the airlock. Smirking local crew ushered him through the lock cycle. She exchanged looks with Jayne Kildare. An unmistakable 'we'll talk later'. Even Jayne, iron-willed, looked pale in the glare of the vehicle's spotlights.

With dizzying insight, Jennifer suddenly understood the colonists' obsession with procedure. The normality of gravity and air pressure was a beguiling lure, tempting the unwary.

Elysium weeded out the unwary with ruthless efficiency.

Inside is safe, outside lies danger. The code by which these people lived. But Jennifer had equated turning from danger with cowardice, with weakness. Now she understood what else her helper had told her. "Language evolves, and changes in meaning can easily lead to misunder-standing. On Sponge, the word 'danger' simply means 'caution needed'. Not something to be feared or avoided, but something to be respected. Safety is where we can relax, let down our guard. But we always need to remind ourselves to put our guard up again whenever we leave safety behind."

Jennifer stepped away from the pool of light. They'd left Jorvick and driven for nearly an hour, climbing steadily to one of the uplands surrounding the city. Jennifer had asked to be taken somewhere there was a clear view all round, no obstacles to hem her in. Those cramped and crowded halls would do anyone's head in.

A rough hand on her arm startled her. "What the kak are you doin', missy?"

"Taking a walk. That's why we're out here." She struggled to keep her tone level, despite the hammering of her heart. This world really was getting to her.

The driver shook his head. It felt like a teacher admonishing a dull-witted child. "Ye go nowhere wi'out me." He released her arm and fished out a flashlight. In his other hand he held a long pole. He strode ahead, scanning the ground and tapping it occasionally with his staff.

"Why?" Jennifer stared ahead in the sweep of his flashlight, but could see nothing to cause alarm. The ground ahead rose slightly then rolled away in a gentle slope. There were no predators out here, no cliffs to wander off.

"You're standing on the spines of a giant plant. A living, breathing thing. You take nothing for granted out here."

A cold shiver ran up her spine. Weird planet. No wonder the local population was all touched in the head.

Curious nevertheless, Jennifer knelt and switched on her own flashlight. The ground beneath her feet looked like moss-covered rock, not out of place on the bare slope of a rolling hill.

But it wasn't rock, it was a living thing. A single organism smothering half the planet.

She pulled off a glove and touched the plant. The mossy-looking surface felt springy, but hard like wire wool. She pressed. The 'rock' beneath had a slight give to it, and gave off a gentle warmth soothing away the bitter chill of the night air.

With shocking abruptness, Jennifer felt herself perched on an insubstantial eggshell over a vast drop. The shell bore the weight of her, her companions, and the crawler, but it was nothing more than an arched covering held up by a network of columns rising from the roots of the plant a kilometer or more beneath her feet. Even the columns were porous, shot through with air gaps between a fibrous network that was itself spongy. The whole a huge fractal structure. The human body, she knew, was mostly water. This deep plant mass, in comparison, was ninety-nine percent air.

And it tingled with electricity, humming in the depths with activity and a slow, brooding awareness.

It was watching her. Judging her.

She yanked her hand away and stood, trembling, fighting to regain her poise.

The driver stood patiently a few meters away, his lips curled in a sneer. "So, ye've done the cheap tourist thing then. Yes, it's a karking big plant. Happy now?"

Jennifer drew herself up. "Not quite. I want to get away from the floodlights, where I can see properly."

He sniffed. "Why did ye not say?" He touched a panel on the breast of his jacket, and the vehicle lights dimmed.

Looking up, Jennifer suppressed a tug of disappointment. No stars. Instead, curtains of radiance cloaked the sky. The Elysium aurora, product of their giant red primary's damnable stormy nature. The same nature that fucked with communications and caused the longship to flee orbit and leave her stranded here. Jennifer clutched her cloak more tightly around her in an unconscious and entirely pointless effort to shield her body from cascades of radiation she imagined raining down on her. An aurora all the way down to the equator. Company scientists had studied the phenomenon, and the planet's ferocious, turbulent magnetic field, and pronounced it safe for human occupation.

Turning her gaze from the sky, inky blackness spread like a deep lake to the horizon. In the distance a soft haze of light marked the city. Not like the hard-edged flaring neons of any Earthly city, this one cloaked the land for kilometers in luminous bubbles like sea foam.

A fine filigree of harder points of light spread out from the city covering yet more square kilometers. As Jennifer watched, she saw that some of the rows of tiny lights were on the move. Vehicles. Hundreds of them, parked out on the plains. One fucking city-sized trailer park. The trek! She'd read about it, but yet again the scale of the operation was hard to grasp from numbers on a page. Half the planet's population on the move, chasing the summer, sheltering on the equator while the planet's atmosphere roiled in a gargantuan transfer of heat from one hemisphere to the other.

No wonder the city was so crowded, with this influx of visitors.

As she began to relax and drink in the freedom of the outdoors, Jennifer came to another realization. That city really was huge. Not by Earthly standards, granted, but compared to any closed habitat she'd ever heard of. All those domes covering square kilometers. Their shipments could only account for a fraction of a percent of that mass of building material. That meant most—as close to all as made no difference—had to have been sourced locally. Their industrial capacity was orders of magnitude greater than anyone at headquarters thought. How could they have missed this?

The more she thought about it, the greater she felt the depths of the Company's failure on this planet. Seriously, how *could* they have missed something this fucking *huge?*

The answer was obvious. They *hadn't* missed it. It was worse than that. They'd never even been *looking* for it. Everyone dismissed them as just another primitive colony.

Chapter 25

It was an uneasy night. Dusk brought down a wind that hit like a battering ram. With the crawler mostly buried, only the top couple of meters were exposed but that was enough to shake the cars like toys. At least, Anna thought as another violent gust almost pitched her from her seat, the half-buried wheels locked them down more firmly than any nest of restraining ties.

Mikey had taken up his favorite station, stretched out at her feet where the floor sloped up to clear polyglass. He lay face down, gazing at the spiked wall and floor a few meters away outside.

The forest of spines and bristles stretching into the distance drew an unworldly chorus of moans from the relentless gale. Different notes spanned the octaves, and combined in warbling chords that verged on meaning as if Sponge itself was singing to the night.

As always, the storm slackened off and Anna relaxed into needed sleep. When she woke, curled in the driver's seat, console lights lit ghostly white on the wraparound windows.

She sat with a gasp. Snow. She'd never before been around to see it. She glanced around at the empty cab and stumbled to her feet.

A quick check upstairs. She was alone in the cab, and Mikey's outdoor gear was missing. She clambered through the lower airlock into a waist-high drift. His track was easy to follow. She found him clearing snow away from the wheel he'd last been working on.

Anna gazed at the bottom of the wheel in amazement. "I guess you must have made more of an impression than I thought." She kicked at the plant fibers, now brittle and shattered around the wheel. "Or did the cold last night do this? Or maybe you weakened it and the storm did the rest."

Mikey shrugged and fidgeted, but his mask couldn't conceal a faint smile playing on his lips.

She swept accumulated snow away from the next wheel to reveal the same story. "Well, who the kak cares? Mikey, follow me!" Energized, she leaped back into the cab and fired up the drive. Like yesterday, she experimented with a gentle back-and-forth rocking.

Unlike yesterday, there was a distinct give. She was able to roll the crawler forward a meter. The narrowing end of the gash in which the crawler sat loomed close. She gave Mikey a broad grin. "We're in business."

His shy smile broadened into a cheeky grin.

Together, they hurried up top to untie Anna's rigging. She raised the A-frame and checked over her lines once more. She had to force her racing thoughts to focus on the task at hand, excitement threatening to throw caution to the deep.

Back in the cab, the familiarity of her routine start-up checks brought back a measure of calm. Her fingers caressed the train's controls, locking the hitches ready for the lift.

Another reason to keep as much of the train intact as possible, Anna mused. Under normal conditions, the drive computer managed the orientation of the hitches to give a smooth ride across any terrain. It was all automatic, sensors constantly adjusting the hitch hydraulics. But there were times when you needed to stiffen things up. It was the same trick she'd used with the dead car back in the garage. Freeze the hitch in place.

But this was where the system came into its own. The hitches were strong enough to hold several cars at a time rigid and to take their full weight. Handy for crossing ravines ... or for levering yourself out of a pit.

Slowly, one meter at a time, the heavy-duty winch lifted the front of the cab clear. Anxiously, Anna studied the strain gauges as the rigid train angled upwards, suspended between its nose and the rearmost wheels.

With the front wheels finally resting on the surface, she switched to a second cable drum and winched the vehicle forward. She now had to reverse the procedure with the hitches, softening the first one to allow the cab to tilt forwards.

The next car cleared the lip. The next pair of wheels hit level ground. It was easy from here. With enough weight up front to counterbalance the tail of their small train the rear cars lifted clear.

They were free!

Anna forced back a pang of guilt as she unclipped the leading lines. She was going to abandon the A-frame here. It went so strongly against the grain, but they had no time to clear up properly. Big Red loomed high above the horizon. Half the morning had already been spent.

She dropped back into the drive seat with a sigh and an exhilaration she'd never expected to feel again. "Okay, Mikey, let's head for the hills."

An hour later, the crawler lurched like a drunkard up the skirts of the hill. Relieved at least to have a working navigation computer, Anna plotted a roundabout course away from town to meet the western uplands. From there, she knew she could rejoin the long road south.

Always assuming she could keep this wayward train going straight.

With the wheels bent out of shape, the damaged crew car throwing everything off balance, and the barely-working mechanics, it took all her skill and concentration to avoid driving around in circles.

This was going to be a *very* long drive home.

She didn't even have time or energy to fret about that scramjet finding them again. At least Mikey was keeping a lookout, roaming from one side of the cab to the other and scanning the horizons for signs of pursuit. That left Anna to focus on driving. Not that they could do anything about it. They were now climbing steadily onto one of the network of gargantuan ribs that wove a planetary girdle for thousands of klicks north and south across the equator. Out in the open, there was nowhere to hide.

Jennifer Steel slammed her fist on the conference table, shocking the senior negotiating executives who sat, bleary-eyed, in her hastily-convened war cabinet.

"The foundations for the traditional agreement are fucked," she snarled. "The last couple of days have shown me just how big their home-grown industrial base is."

This break from her usual icy calm was something this circle of people had never seen. This was a Jennifer Steel who was normally kept under lock and key, deep inside. Normally, the ice bitch version of Jennifer was her weapon of choice, but that persona took effort and tight control to maintain.

Effort and tight control had fled the bridge, leaving the raw and untamed Jennifer in charge.

And she didn't give a flying fuck any more.

"Your task in the next hour is to tell me how we dig ourselves out of this godawful stinking mess. Not only that, you will explain to me exactly how this happened in the first place. I need someone to *hurt* for this." Her gaze skewered negotiation strategist, Timothy Finch, like a bug on a pin.

She drew herself up and folded her arms, staring off into space. This was a pose her team understood. They were under the gun to deliver answers.

"As I said a week ago, we've been working off false assumptions." Timothy's voice quavered. "My models are only as good as they data they're fed. If what you say is true, then none of the traditional motivations for a tied colony hold true any more ..."

He tailed off in ashen-faced silence as Jennifer rounded on him with a face of pure thunder. "Then find the right goddamned numbers to stick in your fucking model. That's your *job*. If you're not up to it, you can leave my employment and find your own way home."

She drowned herself in her own black thoughts while Timothy Finch and Samuel Wong conferred, and Raisa Garina ferreted financial data from her archives. Had she been set up? How could the Company researchers not have briefed her team on the true state of affairs down here?

Her mind came back again and again to Galloway and his backroom maneuverings. He'd managed to plot—with the Company president, no less—to mount his own mission under her nose. The logistics alone were daunting. He'd managed to hide a ground-to-orbit lifter, aircraft, and a survey crew in the longship's manifest without her getting a whiff of anything untoward. What else might he have arranged along the way?

"The colonists have been steadily sneaking concessions out of us," Samuel said at last, "pretending to fight hard for things that really didn't matter to them. All the while, making their real gains while our attention was elsewhere."

"The pattern of behavior was consistent with a traditional colony," Timothy muttered. "We kept thinking we had them on the ropes."

"But it all makes sense in light of what we've learned," said Raisa.

"What *I* learned," Jennifer snarled.

A lavish breakfast lay untouched on the side table, set out at Jennifer's instructions. She caught the occasional longing glance in that direction, but she was too furious to think of eating. And if she didn't, nobody else would either. Fucking lightweights!

"We'll just have to salvage what we can in the traditional agreement, but honestly we're too far gone to make substantial changes. Our only real hope there lies in the poison pill clauses we've been working into the text. Meanwhile, pray to whatever deities you recognize that Galloway comes through."

She glanced at the chrono on the far wall. "It's time."

At the head of her delegation, Jennifer Steel entered the negotiation hall with her head held high, and the steady gait of a condemned prisoner marching to the gallows. Unlike a condemned prisoner, though, she had a long and hard day ahead of her.

With sighs of relief, Anna and Mikey stretched out on bunks in the living area above the driver's cab. They'd have to sort out a proper meal to keep up their strength, but for now neither had the energy to get up.

Big Red was slipping below the horizon when the welcome shadows of the first way station had come into view. Thank the skies for inertial navigation. Anna knew the lowlands for two hundred klicks around Serendipity like the back of her hand—barring the frequent rearrangements Sponge was fond of. But she was a surveyor. She didn't handle the freight runs to and from Laverne, so she didn't know the route. Once you climbed onto the bleak uplands, one ridge looked like every other with few landmarks to guide you. She shuddered at the thought of trying to find her way without a computer. If they *had* managed to escape in that stripped out rig they'd never have lasted the night.

As it was, they'd limped into shelter and strapped down just in time.

They were safe for tonight. But what about tomorrow? And the next day? The first station was normally a gentle ride from town. Granted, they'd left late this morning but it had still been a struggle to make the necessary speed. Tomorrow they'd have to set out before dawn, and pray the rig held itself together.

Skies above, though, with all the damage to wheels and hitches it was a devil to drive. Anna prayed *she'd* be able to hold it together for two long weeks. For Mikey's sake, she had to. Besides, Seth's rig had always been known as a lucky rig, and it was loved and cared for. She couldn't ask for anything more.

Oh, Seth! What was he thinking right now? Had he even realized she was missing? Anna felt hollow at the thought. Whether he knew yet or not, it didn't matter. Sooner or later he'd find out and she knew the loss would hurt him deeply.

They were close friends, but nothing more. Anna had always been careful of that. Their friendship held the promise of something so much more. That's what scared her. That's what made her so careful to hold him at arm's length.

Even after eleven years, she still nursed an empty ache where Luuk's warmth used to be. Seth was too much like Luuk. Took too many of the same risks down in the depths of Sponge. She couldn't survive another loss like that, so she kept things safe between them.

He cared for her. There was no question of that. Her deliberate distance caused him pain, but it was a steady ache of unfilled potential, a known part of their lives. It was a balance she dared not disturb.

Now, or sometime soon, he'd find her gone. She tried to convince herself that it was better they'd never gotten too involved. There wasn't too much to lose. Not like her and Luuk. But she was kidding herself. Seth would be distraught. No! You didn't put friends through that kind of pain. It wouldn't come to that. They were going to get home.

———•◆•———

Jennifer blinked at Jayne Kildare over the congealing dish of vegetable risotto she'd been toying with for the last half an hour. A mental daisy chain of legal clauses and logical connections evaporated. Jennifer was sure they could rescue the traditional agreement somehow. She'd been so close to a solution, or was that just wishful thinking? But Jayne's interruption, barging in on Jennifer's solitude in one corner of the common room, had scattered her thoughts.

Jennifer realized she'd completely missed whatever Jayne had just said. She forced herself back to the here-and-now with an effort.

"Two of the audit team's jets set off together from Giana to Fredericia," Jayne hissed, with a sidelong glance towards the nearest occupied table five meters away. The analysts there were in deep debate and paid Jennifer and Jayne no heed. "They failed to arrive."

Jennifer stared at her. "How the heck ..." She glared at the next table as startled faces turned their way, and hastily turned back. She lowered her voice to a panicked whisper. "How do you lose two aircraft?"

"No local air traffic control."

"Backward freaking planet." Jennifer's shoulders slumped. "Flight operations have to be directed from orbit ..."

"And the longship's pulled out."

"Wait a minute." Jennifer frowned "Tight beam directional microwave links are about the only thing able to punch through the atmospheric noise. With no radio communications, how can you be sure they're lost?"

Jayne perched on the edge of a chair across the corner of the table from Jennifer and leaned close. "Strictly speaking, we don't. But they're hours late, on a trip that should have taken them just an hour."

"So, if they came down between cities, surely someone will have seen something?"

"Again, how would they communicate it? It's two and a half thousand kilometers from one city to the next. Doesn't sound much, until you're out there in all that emptiness, and there is literally *nothing* in between."

A world of contrasts, Jennifer thought. It had taken her all this time to get a true sense of the size of these teeming centers of population. But outside these domes it went from crowded to zero in a hand-span. A short list of equatorial cities and mid-latitude harvesting towns, and that was it. No villages, hamlets, or homesteads filling the void.

Her mind raced, trying to fathom the implications. Craft lost. Heads would roll. What more could go wrong on this benighted world? "And I suppose there's no way of mounting a search."

"That's the question, isn't it? A ground search would take weeks, a waste of time. Do we chance diverting another craft to overfly the route? The local government warned the Company of air travel risks way back in the planning stage. The atmosphere's dangerous."

"An understatement." Jennifer felt a yawning emptiness inside. "Jayne, this is a disaster. Who authorized them to fly blind like that?"

"Galloway's standing instructions, according to the audit head here in Jorvick, were to keep up air movements regardless." Jayne's grimaced. "To mask his own comings and goings."

A tiny beam of clarity lit Jennifer's mind. "Of course. The audit team is under Galloway." She let out a long breath. This was someone else's fuck-up. "Galloway is out of contact, isn't he? Holed up in that northern town."

Jayne nodded. "With the longship out of reach, he'd have to physically come here, or at least reach one of the cities and contact us on the land line."

"Let Galloway's instructions stand, but we'll not risk any special flights until *Pride of Cumbria* is back on station."

"Acknowledged."

"And Jayne," Jennifer held her security chief's eye. "Not a word to the local authorities."

Let Galloway clean up his own mess. Maybe Jennifer could capitalize on this mishap in due course, but right now she still had bigger problems of her own to deal with.

Chapter 26

A speck of yellow on the horizon caught Sarah's eye. She grabbed the binocs and peered in disbelief. "Hey, guys," she called on the intercom, "you got to see *this*."

Seth and John clattered down the steps and squinted into the distance.

"What the kak *is* that?" John pulled more binocs from a rack behind him and passed a pair to Seth.

"It's a train," Seth breathed. He screwed his eyes in concentration, then widened them in shock. "That's got to be *our* train. Some of it, anyway."

"That has to be Anna," Ben rumbled from the back of the cab. "Isn't that the train you reported lost?"

John gave a low whistle. "How in the name of all heaven did she fish *that* out of its hole?"

"Regardless," said Ben, "unless you believe in ghosts, and the spirits of lost harvesters roaming the wilds in search of eternal rest, I'll take the evident fact that she managed, somehow." He rubbed his hands together. "Our job just got a whole lot easier, and we might yet retire to Laverne with our hides and our futures intact."

Sarah angled her vehicle up the slope towards the other crawler. When they got closer, it was clear Anna was struggling. Wheels sagged, sections of mesh missing. Sarah thumbed the radio to life and hailed the other cab. It took long frustrating minutes of fiddling with the decoder settings before any recognizable words emerged. Joyful squeals from the other cab, three klicks away and closing, made words hard to discern even without the waves of static.

When they got close enough for a halfway sane conversation, Sarah tried again. "Your rig looks a mess."

"Half the drives are seriously futzed from sitting axle deep in crap."

Okay, that's what it sounded like, and Sarah could believe it. "Hey, guys," she muttered, "what's the chance of saving that rig?"

"I know it goes against the grain to abandon a vehicle out in the open"–Seth frowned–"but the people are what we came for."

Ben fingered his chin. "Ye know, a bit of salvage might temper the wrath we're going to face in Laverne for turning back. Think they can make it to the way station?"

Sarah checked her navigation plot. "We're a lot closer to station One than Two. Even without a dodgy rig it'd be a close call to get back to Two today."

"That settles it then," Ben rumbled. "We make for One today, then make tracks for Laverne tomorrow."

Sarah picked up the radio again. "Anna, you have to turn around. We'll overnight back at the first way station. You'll never make it all the way to Two today." She repeated the message twice more before she was sure it had been received and understood.

She drove on past and checked the camera feeds to confirm Anna had also swung around to follow. She seemed to take an unusually wide turn, limping around as though her hitches were seized solid. The rig had taken a serious beating in Sponge's clutches.

Had Anna really hoped to reach Laverne in that wreck?

Turning back? No! The giddy euphoria washed away in a cold dose of reality. Anna slammed the microphone back into its cradle and swallowed past the lump in her throat.

When she'd seen a crawler heading her way she had to call Mikey to confirm she wasn't hallucinating. The halting conversation on the crackling, spitting radio buoyed her beyond belief after all they'd been through. She had yearned to simply stop and join Sarah's–no, her!– crawler and abandon this derelict to the long dark. But with a sinking heart she knew Sarah was right.

A cold clammy hand seemed to squeeze her gut. She realized how lucky she'd been to make it this far. They'd only just got into the first way station in time last night, and mechanics were showing the strain. Their progress today had been pitiful. She wondered if they'd have even made it to the second station, let alone all the way to Laverne. Now,

Sarah was doing what was prudent, heading for the nearest shelter and hoping to save this vehicle.

But Sarah didn't know about those *vreemde* and their jet. How far from Serendipity might they roam? No, she tried to reassure herself, they'd destroyed her old crawler. There'd be no reason for them to still be searching. Besides, this road served other towns too. A crawler here shouldn't arouse suspicions.

She clasped Mikey's hand that pressed reassuringly on her shoulder. One more day. They could still beat the coming storms, and they'd be able to make good time in that intact rig. They might even be able to catch the other trains. Most importantly, they were no longer alone in this mess.

Relief at not being alone! That was a sentiment Anna never expected to feel. Her spirits soared once more despite the backtracking. And who did Sarah have with her? Anna was sure there'd been other voices in the background, but she'd been concentrating so hard making out Sarah's words she hadn't thought to ask. She mentally kicked herself.

The crippled crawler responded sluggishly to her commands. Status lights flared red across the console as wheels sagged and hitches strained. Lubricants leaked, and power cells gasped their dying glow into frayed circuits. Anna nursed the vehicle in a wide arc across the face of the slope to follow Sarah.

They limped back across the barren uplands, retracing hard-won kilometers until at last the way station appeared in the distance.

Anna hung back, watching Sarah slide her crawler smoothly between two windbreaks. Her own line was good, for now, but even with the help of the drive computer, maneuvering was patchy at best. The uneven power to the wheels, seized and grinding hitches, and irregular deformities in the wheels themselves confused the computer. Sure, there were algorithms to compensate for irregularities. Damage occurred in the field, and the computers were designed to allow for that but they relied on some kind of stable baseline to work from. This rig had so much damage all the way along, it had no useable point of reference to calculate from. The computer was all but lost.

She ground her teeth as the crawler lurched off course and the computer over-corrected.

Tears blinded her, and she swept them angrily away. Slow down. This was no worse than nudging that wrecked car into line back in the garage, or steering that first makeshift train by hand. She could do this. She realized she was impatient for adult contact, after the days of solitude, being hunted, fighting for her and Mikey's lives. Up ahead, there were people from outside that nightmare world. A connection back to normality that she was desperate to embrace. Maybe one person in particular she thought she'd never see again.

The wayward crawler was a hindrance frustrating her. But it was just a dumb machine. She was better than this. She squinted hard to overcome fatigue from so many long hours of concentration. The sheltered lane lay ahead. This time she anticipated the sideways lurch from the mis-shaped portside wheels and kept the vehicle on course.

The walls of the lane enveloped her. Anna would normally have chosen a computer setting to help keep the rear cars faithfully following the cab, but she didn't trust the bamboozled software. Although there was little clearance on either side, as long as the head of the train ran true the rest would follow. Trailing cars might bounce and scrape from side to side—Anna winced as car three careened off the starboard wall—but the damage they'd suffer was nothing compared to the mess they were already in.

At last, the rear of Sarah's train came into view around the gentle curve. Anna heaved a sigh and cut the drive, locking the wheels in place. Already, masked figures worked their way down the narrow gap ahead, cranking lines taut between anchor points on Sarah's cars and the surrounding walls.

Would this train survive the turning season's storms and the coming standard years of deep freeze? Anna couldn't remember if anyone had over-wintered a crawler in a way station before. She made a mental note to drain the cab's header tank, and turned to Mikey. "Masks and outdoor gear. Let's get this rig secured."

Out on the ground, Anna squeezed past the front of the cab. Securing the train could wait a few minutes. First things first.

Sarah bounded forwards to meet her. Anna let out a strangled cry as they embraced, but words failed her. At last, her vision swam back into focus past the tears streaming down her cheeks. "I can't believe you ... anyone ... would come back for us." She squinted blearily at the crowd gathering around them, aware for the first time just how many people there were.

Seth pulled her into a crushing bear hug. Her arms ached as she returned the favor, then without fully releasing Seth she clasped hands with John.

Anna glanced around to check on Mikey. He hung back, but the relieved smile on his face told her he was okay. They exchanged glances. Okay at being found. Okay that they were finally heading for safety in a useable vehicle. A crowd of noisy people ... not so okay. She understood.

She turned back and her heart hammered when she recognized Ben de Vries. Skies above, the patriarch himself? Had he honestly sanctioned this rescue? It seemed impossible, yet here he was, with his twins.

Anna smothered her shock, straightened, and gave a formal nod. "It's a surprise to find you here, Ben. I owe you a deep debt of service for this act of kindness."

He shook his head. "Many a time you've taught me the value of kindness over protocols. The clan has found itself indebted to you more than once. So what's a man to do when he finds a rescue in progress and nigh unstoppable?" He glanced either side of Anna, at Sarah, Seth, and John. "Swept away on the current, we were." He grinned.

A movement behind him caught Anna's eye. One last figure held back behind the rest, hesitant, furtive. Nick de Jong. What the heck was *he* doing here? If she was amazed at Ben flouting the rules, she was doubly so at Nick. Straight-laced, serious Nick. It went so completely against his nature.

And yet here he was.

Holding back.

Again, not like him. He may always be serious and rule-bound, but he was always friendly, always ready to come forward and greet people ... especially her.

But he kept his gaze downturned, refusing to meet her eyes.

Suspicion formed in the back of her mind. Anna stared hard at Nick. She swallowed, then again, unable to speak past the lump in her throat.

She tried again, the words finally coming out in a hoarse rasp. "They killed Georgie."

From the corner of her eye she saw blank stares. Her words meant nothing to most of her audience, coming out of the blue like that. But her focus was on Nick, cringing and sweating under his mask. The shock and guilt on his face told her all she needed to know. "Their leader said something about a padre." Anger flared white hot through her mind and she pushed past Seth to launch herself at Nick. She struggled in vain against the clutches of the de Vries twins. "*You* told them we were there! They killed Georgie, and they knew there were more of us!" Her struggles were futile, and left her exhausted. "They chased us and tried to kill us, too," she gasped out. "And they came so close."

The anguish of the last few days swept through her, leaving her drained and empty. The reaction, the release at being found, hit her and her legs buckled. "You're the reason they hunted us down." The words came out as a whisper.

Nick shook his head. Tears streamed down his face. "I wanted you found. I knew it would lead to some awkward questions, but I never thought they'd harm you. Anna"–he stretched his hands out, pleading–"I could never wish you harm."

Ben de Vries swiveled his head from Anna to Nick, his mouth hanging open. At last he seemed to remember his rank and reputation. He closed his mouth and straightened up to his full height, barely up to Nick's chin, but his solidity looked set to stand unmoved in the face of the jet stream.

The twins lowered Anna to the ground with a gentleness so at odds with their brutish appearance. She hugged her knees to her chest, barely aware of Mikey wrapping his arms around her from behind. Kak! This must be hard on him. He hated seeing grownups distressed and arguing. She rubbed the backs of his hands reassuringly.

"I think there's some explaining to be done here." That was Ben's gravelly voice. Soft, but brooking no dissent. There would be a full accounting before he was satisfied. "But not right here and now. Meneer de Jong"–Anna shuddered at the unaccustomed and calculated formality–"make yourself useful up in the galley." Skies above, Ben wasn't showing it, but beneath that iron control he was incandescent with rage. "Clara, help Anna into the cab and settle her in the nav seat."

Anna croaked a protest, but Ben silenced her with a smoldering glance. "The rest of us will finish securing the crawlers."

As Mikey and Clara helped her to her feet, Anna turned to Mikey. He didn't meet her eyes, he was staring over her shoulder to where Nick had already disappeared down towards the head of the train. The look in Mikey's eyes chilled her. What had happened to her teenage son? His world had been turned upside down, and he looked ready to murder Nick.

Ben gripped his shoulder. "Mikel, lad, would you be aright to help us tie down? My girl will see your mam's well *behaaglijk*. No fretting now."

Reluctantly, he looked away and glanced at Anna, chewing his lip.

She nodded. " 'S okay, Mikey. Ben's a good teacher. He'll show you what to do."

The slow hobble to the front of the good train took all Anna's remaining strength. They walked beneath the three cars between pairs of silvery wheels, Anna leaning heavily on Clara's shoulder, but the climb up to the airlock almost defeated her.

Anna sat a while, miserably, on the bottom step of the ladder. "Gimme a minute. I'll make it." She flashed a grin at Clara's blank and unmoving expression. "Don't want you having to winch me up with the cargo crane."

A brief pause, then Clara cracked the most fleeting of smiles. It was enough. Spirits restored, Anna heaved herself up and into the airlock.

In the cab, she collapsed into the nav seat, following Ben's instructions to the letter. She lacked the energy to do anything else.

———— ♦ ————

Anna opened her eyes. She'd only shut them for a moment it seemed, but dusk was now falling outside the windows, and Mikey was curled up at her feet, snuggled in the angle between floor and the lower part of the wraparound window.

She stirred and struggled to her feet, body aching all over from the days of unfamiliar exertion. In the seat next to her, Sarah peered over the stack of drive consoles. "Do you want your seat back?"

With a start of guilt, Anna glanced at her photos, dreamcatcher and her personal insignia adorning the central driver's station. The rush of familiarity overwhelmed her, but also an awful realization. "I'm sorry, Sarah, I meant to take down all my personal stuff before we set off."

"Lucky you welcomed me into your space already, or I'd have had a karking hard time taking the lead seat in this rig." Sarah shrugged. "I looked after it for you. Wouldn't have wanted anyone else handling the controls anyhow."

Mikey sat and yawned, then unfolded himself from his perch overlooking the parking lane. In the far seat, Seth also stood and stretched.

Outside, the sky darkened with shocking speed and a wild shriek ripped through the air. Anna glanced out, momentarily startled, then relaxed. The cab rocked under her feet, tugging on the securing lines. Just another autumn night on the highlands of Sponge.

Sarah stood and beckoned. "Bet you're hungry. Ben told me to bring you two up when you woke."

Food! Anna couldn't believe she'd overlooked the ravenous hunger gnawing at her. Together they climbed to the living area at the top of the cab. The crush of people in the tiny space should have bothered her, but for once she found company reassuring. Familiar faces. Friendly faces. Mostly. She didn't know yet how she felt about Nick. His actions had landed her and Mikey in this mess, and yet his grief at the news seemed genuine enough.

Still, doubt nagged her. Loss of trust was a serious business, not something you gave in to lightly. You always looked for the best motive. Assumption of good intent was the rule on Sponge, another deeply ingrained habit, until the evidence made it impossible to ignore. Once lost, trust was never regained, and was usually a death sentence in a world where people depended utterly on each other for survival.

Nick didn't meet her eyes as he ladled food into bowls and handed them around.

Ben sat at the head of the dinette table, with Clara and Helga and Sarah crowded along the bench to one side. Narrow windows behind them looked ahead to the parking lane and the aurora strobing through fierce-driven clouds. Anna sat on one of the two bunks, along the front wall next to the dinette. Mikey snuggled in to her right side, furthest away from the dinette and galley, while Seth was a comforting presence to her left. John propped himself up on the end of the galley counter, while Nick stationed himself in the far corner.

They ate in silence for a while. The knots in Anna's shoulders slowly eased. Decade-old memories crept out of hiding. It had been years since Anna had last driven with a crew, not since Sponge claimed Luuk.

The sounds of the planet's rage, the buffeting of the bunk beneath her thighs and the wall at her back, these were familiar enough, but she was used to an empty cab. The crush of people in the confined space reawakened another world to her senses. The warmth of so many people threatened to overwhelm the living space's ventilation. A damp mugginess hung in the air, along with a cloying smell of hot oil and unwashed bodies.

Far from being repulsed, Anna for once drew comfort in the nearness of people, recalling the gruff conviviality of a crew out in the field. Except this company lacked the coarse banter she remembered. Unspoken questions weighed them down. The tension built, with covert glances from one person to another, eyes hastily averted. Who was going to break the spell?

Anna glanced over to Ben de Vries at the head of the table. He was the elder here, notwithstanding Nick's position as a padre. But he seemed in no hurry, wiping his bowl clean with a hunk of rice bread.

At last, he looked up. "My thanks, Meneer de Jong," he rumbled, "for this evening's repast. Now, I believe there's a little matter of some explanations owin' to us for recent events."

Nick grimaced and set his own bowl on the counter behind him. He straightened his shoulders and faced the company. His face was pale, but determined. "To put it simply, Elysium is carrying out winter explorations. Not deep winter, of course, but on the margins of livable conditions."

Ben grunted. "The combined councils are always exploring possibilities, pushing boundaries. I've heard nothing yet to be so concerned about." He waved Nick to continue.

"I know a similar exploration happened in the southern lands last trek, before I was recruited to the effort. It gave them enough results to convince them there was something of value there. This exploration is supposed to confirm the findings. I was supposed to ensure the town was clear for the survey team to enter."

"And who is 'they' in this case?"

Nick hesitated before answering. "Before, I thought this was all the Elysium council's work. But Anna says the team there was all off-worlders. That was news to me."

Anna grimaced and pressed herself closer to Seth.

"And why such covert scurrying around?"

"Sometimes, planners have to keep secrets. There are things we talk about that won't be popular, and many things that may never come to pass."

"Secrets!" Ben chewed his lip in thought. "Must be an almighty discomfort to ye."

"It's a part of my role that makes me feel ... unclean. At least I don't ... didn't ... have to deal directly with offworlders. The kinds of deceptions that go on beyond our world"–he shuddered–"that takes a special kind of mentality to deal with."

"So, this was one such secret?"

"In this case, I thought it was to hide the prospects from the Company. They have a way of sniffing out and taking the lion's share of any useful discoveries."

"And yet, it sounds like Company men back there."

"They have that ruthlessness about them. Now, I'm not sure who's keeping secrets from whom."

There it was again, the evasiveness. It seemed Nick knew far more than he was telling. Anna wondered if anyone else sensed it, or if she was simply being hard on Nick for all the traumas they'd gone through. For Georgie.

Ben glowered at Nick. "That's as maybe, but let me get one thing aright in my fuddled mind. You knew we were headed back to town to find Anna and the others." He held his hand up and checked off points one by one on his fingers. "You also knew there were uninvited visitors there. Hence, you must have known we would run into them ourselves."

Nick slumped to the floor, back against the galley counter, a picture of misery. "I hadn't figured out how to bring it up without revealing everything. Everything happened so fast. And there's a chance they'd be finished and gone by the time we got there."

"So, you figured on saying nowt, and at worst maybe feigning all surprised when we found what a busy little town it was all of a sudden?"

Nick shrugged. "The worst I expected was some red faces and a whole heap of recriminations. At best, everyone would have agreed to keep quiet. We went against policy, endangered lives and equipment, but officially *they* had no business there at all. They wouldn't have wanted us talking about that."

"Well, you got *that* right," Anna spat.

"I didn't know they'd kill to keep their secret. And from where I was standing there was no hope for you. Letting them know you were there offered a chance of rescue, the only one I thought you had. It was better than nothing."

He looked utterly deflated, and some of Anna's anger evaporated. He was right. As soon as that last train left, they were effectively dead. That was the way of it.

"Anyway," he muttered at last, "yes, Ben, I figured on keeping quiet. I thought we'd have the stronger negotiating hand with the prospectors. Our silence was likely more valuable to them than theirs was to us." He turned his gaze to Anna. "I thought I'd even enlist them in looking for you so we could be on our way back all the sooner."

Anna chewed her lip, not knowing how to feel. Her head swam with the effort of unraveling the tangle of plots and players and motivations. And she baulked at trying to figure out Nick's role in all of this. He'd alerted the *vreemde* expecting them to rescue her. She clung to that thought like a lifeline.

"Which brings us to the salient question," Ben grated out, "of what *are* they doing there?"

"They have some *debeel* idea of finding new marketable drugs when Sponge's biochemistry changes with the season."

Ben snorted. "What if they do? Who's going to harvest it?"

Nick shrugged again. "I figured that was their problem. My only job was to advise them how and where to enter the town, and when it was going to be empty so they could work without being seen."

"Your job ..." Ben frowned. "What job could ye possibly have beyond the looking after of our little town?"

Nick gazed at the floor, silent.

"I mean, what would persuade you to act for these *vreemde?*"

"I received instructions, sealed messages in the normal freight and supplies shipments, from someone high in the council of planners, all the right phrasing and under the council's seal."

"Did it not strike you as odd?"

"It seemed odd, but I trusted the instructions really were coming from the central council even though they never identified themselves by name. I still assumed the secrecy was to keep these explorations hidden from the Company. I wasn't expecting it to be Company men I was letting in."

Ben shook his head. "You knew they were offworlders when you spoke to them."

"I never spoke to them. When it came to the final instructions, those were all relayed through the longship, so then of course I knew there had to be offworlders involved somehow. All the same, I know we don't have the kind of equipment left on site for survey operations, so it had to be coming from *somewhere*." Nick grimaced. "Regardless, we've got Anna and Mikey. We can head for Laverne and leave them to their explorations. I want nothing more to do with any of it."

On that point, Anna had no argument whatsoever.

———————

Anna woke and stretched. A hot shower last night had done wonders for her sense of well-being. Okay, more a damp sponge-off under the slowest trickle she could manage—with nine of them in a cab supplied for two or three people, they had to husband their resources carefully—but even that felt like the height of luxury.

And sleep! Even the night's shrieking winds and bucking cab couldn't keep her awake.

And, best of all, they were under way. Anna felt the soothing rocking of a crawler at speed. She had slept in. They'd untied and started without bothering to rouse her. Only the tiniest twinge of guilt marred the sense of peace that enveloped her.

Something was off, though. Anna couldn't place it at first. She sat up gingerly and scanned the confines of the crew quarters. She did a double-take, momentarily disoriented, but her bearings were right. Windows opposite her bunk showed the backbone of Sponge rolling by, but morning sun should have been streaming in from somewhere ahead. Instead, this side of the crawler was in shadow.

They were heading back north.

She made a small, frightened animal sound, and jumped at the appearance of Clara around the end of the bunk. Clara pressed her gently but firmly back onto the bunk. "Da!" she called. " 'S awake."

A moment later, Ben's grizzled face appeared. "Why, good morrow, Anna. Now don't ye be fretting. We cleared out the rig you rescued. All comestibles from the crew car, and anything else we felt would be of use. The lovely Sarah was overjoyed to retrieve her family heirlooms. We drained and winterized the car and cab, as I'm sure you'd have had a mind to. So all is left in good order. I'm sure the rig will be salvageable come springtime."

Anna reeled at the onslaught of words. She'd never known the patriarch to be so talkative. Then her mind returned to her original panic. The shock seemed to have passed, and maybe that was Ben's intent, but her anxiety and confusion remained.

"Why are we heading back?" she blurted.

"Aah." Ben had the good grace to look sheepish. "Trust a driver to spot the obvious. I don't believe our Meneer de Jong has noticed yet, thank the Skies."

"He's a dome dweller. And you didn't answer my question."

Ben scowled. "You're right. It occurred to me last night that our young Nick has still been somewhat economical on the details." He speared Anna with a pitying look. "You made the connection yourself. He told the *vreemde* that you were left behind."

Anna stared at him. He didn't seem in any hurry to elaborate, just lounged back on the end of the bunk. She frowned, then it hit her. "How did he talk to them? For us to be left behind, the crawler had already left. He was on it. Radio's futzed, so how the kak did he *tell* them?"

"Exactly." Ben grinned. The expression didn't reach his eyes. "I put the same thought to Meneer de Jong last night. Happens he had a directional microwave kit stashed somewhere on the crawler."

Thoughts and confusion whirled through Anna's mind.

"Here's how I see it. Whatever the *vreemde* are up to, it's been long in the making. A lot of thought and organization gone into it. And a lot of high tech resources, far more than Elysium can stretch to alone. I sense the hand of the Company behind this, not the council. And"–the scowl returned–"with all the secrecy, I'll be betting it's good for the Company but not good for us."

"So, we're going back to have a look." The words came out flat and emotionless, revealing no hint of the raw terror that gripped her.

In all the years Anna had lived here, she'd never before looked down on Serendipity from this angle. This steep ridge sheltering the town wasn't on any of the usual routes to harvest sites.

The crawler sat out of sight behind them, a couple of klicks back, hidden as best they could manage in the fringes of a decaying forest. It probably wouldn't help against that jet, and anyway, Anna realized, the tracks it left in clinging snow would be a bit of a giveaway. She was jittery as all hell at the risk of losing yet another vehicle, and any meager attempts at concealment were better than nothing.

Worse, she'd barely had the chance to speak to Seth this morning. They had so much to catch up on, but he'd been mysteriously absent from the drive cab all morning. The thought of separation, even by such a short distance, racked up her anxiety level another notch. But Ben had instructed her to spy on the town with him and the twins, and when the patriarch spoke, nobody argued.

She shivered, and not just from the cold or the threat of being stranded again. They were losing time. The cataclysmic autumn weather shift could come any day now, and they needed to reach lower latitudes to have any chance of surviving it. What was Ben thinking?

While she lay, peering over the lip of the ridge, Mikey snuggled into her side for warmth. Where Anna went, Mikey followed. Alongside her, Ben and his twins wormed their way forward to get a better view. Glittering white frosted the fronts of their jackets.

From their vantage point, the domes in the valley were laid out like a map.

"Hey, Sarah, you hearing me?" Ben muttered into his line of sight radio. Anna couldn't make out the reply, but Ben nodded and crawled the last few meters to join Anna. "We've still got contact, and she's keeping the rig fired up and ready for a quick exit if we need it."

"Do you think they'll be keeping a lookout?"

Ben grunted. "Can't hurt to be careful."

"Not much we can do if they spot us from the air, though."

"That's a chance we'll have to take. Besides, there's no reason for them to suppose we're any kind of threat. My guess is they'd think we were just a lone crawler trekking from one of the more northern towns. Now, let's see what we can see."

Anna pressed binocs to her eyes and swept the town below. "Looks dead, doesn't it?"

"I'm guessing that's the point, though."

"True enough." Anna zoomed in and studied the periphery. "I see tracks. They must have been made today. They're still sending people out to patrol."

Ben barked a soft laugh. "Wonder if they'd ha' bothered if you hadna put the wind up them."

"I'll take that as a compliment," Anna said drily. "Now, what the kak is *that*?"

She directed Ben to the far side of town. A pair of unloading docks stretched in two-hundred-meter shallow arcs, designed to allow crawlers to pull up alongside. Nestled by the nearer dock, almost hidden, was a boxy-looking craft.

"Well I'll be ..." Ben muttered. "I've read about rigs like that. That's all workin' on the assumption that I'm seeing things aright. Used for mining and survey operations on some worlds, if I'm not mistaken. Not something we've ever had a mind to investin' in, what with the less than placid atmosphere we're blessed with."

"So, I guess that confirms what Nick says. They're prospecting for something."

"Huh. Switch yer 'nocs to thermal."

Anna did so. "Good thought." She scanned again. Most of her view was dark and cold, but ... "Yep. They're still on the lookout. I see a pair coming out behind the near stockpile. Hmm. Most of the town's dark, but South Two's lit up like midsummer, so's that craft, and there's another heat signature ..."

"If I'm not mistaken, that's the assay shed."

That made sense, again bolstering Nick's story. Why haul assay equipment with them when there's a whole laboratory already on site?

Anna's scalp crawled. She ached to be gone from here, riding the hills to Laverne. Anywhere but here.

"Seen enough?" She tried to keep the pleading out of her voice.

Ben grunted, eyes glued to his binocs. Beside him, Clara and Helga gazed down into the valley, faces devoid of expression. But Anna had worked with these two in the past. There was more going on behind those blank masks than people gave credit for. Right now, she sensed a deep anger brewing.

"Come on, Ben. We can see there are people here who shouldn't be here. They're digging for something and testing the results. Doesn't matter what they're looking for, they have no business here. We need to get in contact with the council in Laverne."

"An' say what?"

"Tell the Laverne curate—and our own town planners when we can— what we've seen!" Why was he being so *debeel* about this? It was obvious, and the longer they hung around here the greater the risk of being spotted. All it would take was one of those craft to take to the air.

Ben shook his head. "By the time we persuade someone to haul ass out here—and that's a hairy great 'if', not 'when'—they'll be long gone, their nefarious deeds done."

"We don't need to get all the way into Laverne. We just need to reach the nearest way station with a comms shed."

"It'll still take several days to make contact, and a coupla weeks for them to send a rig out here, even if they choose to take the risk. Meantime, they'll clear up after the'selves. If our Nick's to be believed they've done this afore. And no-one was owt the wiser. Even if we're believed, and someone chooses to look into it, my betting is there'll be nary a trace of evidence to be found."

"But surely they'll believe us? We've all seen it, and they'll have to believe Nick. Then they'll have to do *something*."

Another sad shake. "What makes you think Nick will say owt? Seems it's less problem to him if this all goes away quietly."

Anna gazed at him, dumbstruck. Surely Nick would back them up. Wouldn't he?

" 'Nother thing. It occurs to me that they must indeed have more local help than just our Nick, and higher up, too."

Anna squinted at Ben.

"Think, gal! They've fired up livin' and heatin' in a garage and a dome. Outsiders! Who told them how to do that? And who sent Nick his instructions? Who knows what help they might have here? And that help might be placed high enough to quash anything we might say."

Anna rolled onto her back and gave vent to a silent scream of frustration.

"Seems to me," Ben said, "these interlopers are on their way to achieving whatever it is they're after. Not unless we can take back some hard evidence."

Anger washed through her. Memories of Georgie, of their relentless pursuit through town and into the depths of Sponge. Those people had wanted her and her son dead, for what? For a secret? She'd seen them trespassing. So what? How could that possibly warrant their deaths?

It was incomprehensible. It was the thinking of *stiig vreemde*. Not something any decent-minded person could hope to understand.

It was abominable. Unacceptable.

Anger burned to a white heat, a simmering rage.

A need to *do* something.

At last, Anna turned to look at Ben. He narrowed his eyes at her. "I see new fire in yer eyes all of a sudden."

Anna took a deep breath. "You talk about evidence, but if there's high-placed power behind them I'm not sure what evidence would suffice. Who could we take it to, where it won't get quietly dropped to the Deep?"

Ben tilted his head. "You've a better idea?"

"Yes. Screw the evidence. Let's throw a karking wrench in their gears."

"What do ye have in mind?"

Beyond Ben, Clara and Helga sat up, expressions showing interest and anticipation.

"Not sure, yet. But whatever it is, it'll mean getting back into town ... without getting seen along the way."

A thought struck her. "Mikey, you led us under the surface to come up near town. Could you do it again? From farther away?"

Mikey scrunched up his face. He studied the two or three klicks of ground between them and the town. Then he lay face down and pressed his hands hard against the ground, squinting in concentration.

Ben looked on, open mouthed. "What's he about?"

Anna quickly recounted their forays underground. "The more I think about it," she concluded, "the more it seems he has a deeper understanding of Sponge than anyone I know."

"Understanding? *Communin'* wi't karking great plant, more like!" Ben frowned, but the twins both gave fleeting smiles and nods.

Mikey looked up at last and pointed down the slope and some way to their left.

"You think you can find a way in down there?"

He nodded.

"And bring us up somewhere near town?" If they could emerge close enough, they should be able to sneak into an airlock while the patrol was out of sight.

Mikey smiled and nodded again, an energetic and emphatic 'yes'.

"Huh." Ben chewed his lip, deep in thought. "Ye've some kind of sabotage in mind, then?"

"Could we mess with their samples, maybe? Reset the calibrations on the assay equipment? Cripple their aircraft somehow?"

"How many of them do ye reckon there are?"

Anna hesitated, replaying the scene in her mind, trying to blot out the memory of Georgie in the middle and picture instead the ring of onlookers. "I'm sure I saw maybe ten or a dozen. Couldn't tell if that was all. But at least three died chasing us, so they're down in numbers."

"Still leaves at least as many as us. And you say their leader has a weapon?"

Anna shuddered. Georgie's blood sprayed the floor in her mind's eye. She couldn't keep the memory at bay.

"Any other weapons?"

That was a good question. "They do have a jet kitted out as a fighter, but hand held weapons? If they had, surely they'd have used them when they were chasing me and Mikey."

Ben grunted. "Mayhap. Not sure how much of a chance we want to take on that count, though."

"What can we do about it?"

"Could use something to occupy their attention. Draw them away from the assay shed and give us a free hand."

Anna sat and pondered. This was getting complicated and she wondered what her impetuous outburst was getting them into.

"Could use some weapons of our own."

Anna gave Helga a startled look. The thought of any kind of combat–armed or otherwise–made her queasy, but it would be good to even up the odds a bit.

Clara's face lit up. "Take the depth guard off a spike driver and it'd throw a piton a good ways, wouldn't it?"

"Tha's right," Helga squealed. "I used to play with a spike gun. Could spear a rimwood bough at ten meters."

It took a few moments for her meaning to sink in, then Anna sank her head between her knees, feeling faint.

"Well," said Ben, patting her back. "I think we've seen enough here. There's nowt more to be done today, we need to get our rig back to the way station an' safety for the night. On the way we'll talk it all through with t'others."

"What about Nick?"

"What about him?"

"He's going to rage sky high when he finds out what's happening. He's a part of the plans we're putting a spike in."

Ben's eyes twinkled. "Ye don't get to lead a clan wi'out some sneaky dealin's with these planners. I had a quiet word with young Sarah last night. We're keeping him busy back in the cargo cars. And besides, he wouldn't know one end of the uplands from the other if he happens to mosey on up to the cab. Biggest risk is if he sees we've stopped right now and wonders why we're ass-buried in a forest."

Anna's curiosity was piqued. "Busy? How?"

Ben snorted with laughter. "Seth and John took him back to car two. We don't have a crew car and the drive cab's too cramped for all of us for the whole trek, so they're doin' some rearranging back there to make space for the boys to bunk."

Anna gaped. "You've got him doing manual work?"

"Better than that. We've put him *in charge* of the arrangements. From what I saw on the drive this morning, he's in his element, and utterly occupied."

———— • ————

Jennifer Steel closed the door to her suite, and fastened the latch that Company engineers had added. Her brow creased in a frown as she sought meaning in the strangeness of this place. She felt adrift, a symptom, she knew, of fatigue and the pressures of presenting a front at all times.

Most small colonies she visited had only rudimentary physical security, but it was always present somewhere. Burglary, theft, was rare to unheard-of in small populations, but by the time they grew beyond the thousands it always crept back in. Always. And with it, people rediscovered the need to lock doors.

The very concept of locks, of personal security, seemed to have been forgotten here. Her request, when she first examined her quarters, had been met with blank stares. Not 'we don't bother with that here', they literally had no concept of fastening a door against human intrusion. To them, a 'lock' was an enabling device, not a barrier. A means of safe passage from one environment to another.

But Jennifer's ingrained habits would not be placated. She couldn't feel safe without surrounding herself with a decent physical perimeter. Maybe the colonists themselves were too entrenched in their taboos to intrude in someone else's private space, but her own staff had no such qualms.

She pressed a palm to the cool surface of the door and closed her eyes briefly. She turned and loosened her collar.

Nikolai appeared at a respectful distance bearing a tray with a glass cup of scented tea. She took the tea without a word and sipped before acknowledging Nikolai.

"Tough day." It was a statement. He knew her habits too well.

She nodded and sighed, a sign of weakness she allowed herself in no-one else's presence. There were also secrets she shared that she would air in no-one else's presence.

"With all the mis-steps we've blundered into, the traditional agreement is far weaker than I would like."

"With all due respect"—Nikolai set the tray on a sideboard—"you excel at tilting agreements in the Company's favor."

Jennifer snorted. "We have plenty of legal traps and conditions in place, but it's all flimsy as hell. The President won't be happy if this is the best we can do. And remember, if we have to go down that path, it means Galloway's investigations failed. The President will be mad as hell and looking for blood. I doubt she'd be happy even if I handed her the planet on a silver platter for the next millennium."

"It would be a grave blow, indeed."

"It beggars belief, but I now find myself pinning my hopes on Galloway." Jennifer's mouth twisted at the admission. "The alternative terms that the colonists wanted are in place, along with the clauses Galloway needs. *That* agreement is exactly where we need it."

Nikolai looked somber. "A triumph for the Company, which will only emerge over time."

"And a public humiliation for me, in the meantime." Jennifer collapsed onto a couch and took another sip of tea. Nothing she did would protect her when the world crashed around her. She'd considered whether she could share these secrets with anyone for her own insurance, but she was sure the President, and doubtless Galloway, would have taken precautions against that before they'd left Earth. "Either way, you realize I am likely finished after this? What will you do without me?"

"I am ever in your debt. My children and grandchildren would not be where they are without your patronage."

His children and grandchildren. Their homes in safe neighborhoods, their education … their lives. That last had never been spoken aloud. It was implied and understood.

"You would stay by my side, even in my fall from grace?"

"It goes without saying." He bowed his head and retired from the room to prepare supper.

After so many decades in her service, she wondered these days if she even needed the leverage she held. But then, she wondered just how well you could really know a person, even after so many decades.

Jennifer rose and drifted through to an adjoining room where Nikolai was setting a table for her.

She gazed around the utilitarian space. Bare walls, no trace of ornament let alone luxury. She grudgingly admitted that the colonists themselves made their homes more homely, even if it was with barbaric carvings and primitive homespun tapestries. But, as she'd read in her research, items like that were intensely personal, almost religious. Not something you left to soften the walls of a stranger's chamber.

Once, centuries ago, these habitats would have been made of alloy and plastic shipped from off-planet. Now, this whole structure was crafted from native materials. Knotwood, corewood, rimwood, flax … The colonists had become inventive over the years, becoming less and less dependent on imported materials. That realization had come perilously late in the day.

Thankfully they were not geared up to export. Their processing facilities could barely fulfill local demand. At least, that's what they'd have her believe. They'd certainly made no moves to develop other export markets, and surely they would have if they'd been able? Unless their government was stunningly incompetent.

Their one revenue stream still depended on the drugs they processed from the host organism, which the Company kept a substantial stake in. But the colonial agreement only gave the Company a stake in the export of bioactive substances, an omission Jennifer would have to rectify if she could. It would be bad news if some inventive colonist figured out how to profit exclusively from the unique structural materials they harvested.

This sparse shell chilled her, despite the oppressive equatorial heat. She felt hemmed in. And to think that she and Nikolai occupied a space that would comfortably house twenty or more locals. Such an unhealthy crush of people. How did they get along without degenerating into anarchy?

Chapter 28

Once more in the drive seat of Seth's salvaged crawler, Anna wrestled with the controls through a tricky chicane between an outflow on one side, and treacherous flatlands on the other. Finally on hard and safe ground, she relaxed her grip for a moment, first one hand then the other, clenching and unclenching to loosen up her fingers. Steeped in morning shadows, a broad valley wound towards Serendipity, still out of sight in the distance.

To think she'd hoped to drive all the way to Laverne in this pitiful wreck. It had been hard enough returning to the way station after meeting Sarah, then back here this morning. She must have been mad.

No. Desperate. A position she didn't want to be in again, and yet here she was.

She hastily muttered a prayer of contrition under her breath. This battered rig had been abused more than any piece of machinery should be. Seth and Sarah had cared for it well and it had brought her and Mikey to safety. Drivers formed a special bond with their rigs and this one deserved more respect. And at the end of today's run, it would overwinter snug in a garage rather than exposed to the elements at a way station. Maybe next season it would be repaired and haul trains again.

With an easier few kilometers in front of her, she glanced sidelong at Ben, who was gazing intently ahead. "The more I think about it, the less sense it makes."

"Hmm?" He swiveled his seat to face her.

"I mean, we're sure the Company is doing the prospecting, not just the council, and we're sure they don't have our interests at heart. *You* seem pretty sure of that, anyway, and that's why we're on our way to spit in their soup."

Ben grunted.

"But then why the secrecy? I mean, if it really was only the council at work, I can understand our own folks keeping this from the Company, but it seems the Company is in on it anyway. Both sides are. So why the secrecy? What have they got to hide from each other?"

Ben huffed and swung back and forth in his seat a while. Anna was wondering if he'd chosen to ignore the question, when he faced her once more with a thoughtful frown. "So, what if our own leadership is not as clued in as Nick supposes?"

"You mean, his instructions didn't really come from the council?"

Ben shrugged. "Seems the only thing that fits. As you say, we *know* the Company is involved. But the council's involvement is ... what's the word? ... circumstantial. And I cannae see how they could hide it anyhow."

Anna snorted. "Who knows what the planners get up to in their secretive meetings. I don't see any difficulty in them hiding stuff from the rest of us."

"Now, that's a harsh judgment," Ben chided.

"Maybe. Sorry, that was uncalled for."

"Besides, us clan leaders talk to each other. A lot. And to the town padres. There's a whole lot gets discussed about our future on Sponge, and not all to do with harvesting quotas neither."

"So?"

"Maybe they could hide something like this. Maybe not. All the same this has to be summat to do with the talks goin' on in Jorvick, but durned if I can figure out what."

"The negotiations?"

"They all came on that one longship. Can't be coincidence. The Company is up to summat, and I reckon there's a bit of corporate swindlin' goin' on here."

"Doesn't change our plan, though, does it? In fact, seems all the more reason to spike their plans but good!"

The derelict crawler bumped and rattled to a stop. Anna breathed a deep sigh of relief that it had carried them this far.

The chrono told her they'd made it into position with a good half-hour in hand. Now they just needed to wait. And hope no aircraft chose to fly over.

Anna scanned the sky. "Wonder how the others are doing."

"Mikey seems to have some kind of talent, from what I've seen an' heard. We're placing a deal of trust in him."

With a jolt of guilt, Anna realized she'd actually been thinking about Seth, not Mikey. She considered Ben's words. "He's never been out in the field, and yet he was completely at home in the depths."

"I ken he's been a quick study."

"Unlike his useless mother?" Anna snorted. "I know you and Georgie used to talk about *my* future."

Ben started to protest, but Anna cut him short. "Book learning's one thing. Every dome dweller gets the same learning, but this was more. A deeper understanding than anything I've ever seen." She scanned the skies once more. "I know I've got my own hang-ups, but oddly I'm not worried about Mikey below the surface. It's those *vreemde* that scare the kak out of me."

Ben swiveled around in the nav seat and squinted at Anna through half-closed eyes. "Your son will be awright. Seth's a good man."

"True that," she answered cautiously.

"Just been wonderin' if there's the prospect of a marriage when we reach Laverne?"

Anna's cheeks flushed. Where the heck did *that* come from? She stumbled for a non-committal answer.

"Reason is that I need to be strategizin' if so," Ben mused. "Seth would be a good addition to our clan, ye see. But then again, I know for a fact the Fischer clan would welcome one such as yerself to their ranks."

"Well you can keep your karking hypothetical musings to yourself!"

Ben's lips curled in a wry grin. "Regardless, I'd expect some hard bargaining to be had in such a match."

Anxious to change the subject, Anna gestured to the spike gun propped up alongside Ben's seat. "You don't really expect me to carry one of those, do you?"

"Aye, and use it if ye have to."

Her stomach churned again at the thought. She'd used the hand-held spike drivers many times out in the field, sometimes to position anchoring pitons to haul out bogged crawlers or to tie down rigs for the night, but most often to steady the network of guiding beacons she laid out for harvesters to follow. The pneumatic guns had a fearsome kick to them, mostly absorbed when the head of the piton hit the depth guard and transferred its momentum back into the recoil springs. With that guard removed, there was nothing to stop the piton flying out.

Ten meters, Helga had said. Into rimwood. Not as tough as core knotwood, but still many times tougher than a person.

Silence fell as the chrono ticked towards the appointed hour. They'd left the way station hours before dawn, risking the drive in the dark, and arrived at their vantage point above Serendipity as Big Red cleared the horizon.

They'd still managed to keep Nick in the dark too, pretending that the way station they'd returned to last night was actually number two. He'd find out sooner or later, and he'd be furious. But he might also try to interfere with their interference, so later was better.

So far so good.

And Anna had driven the battered wreck as close behind Sarah as possible, so as to be mostly out of sight of the cab in case Nick decided to visit. To a casual glance from an inexpert eye, Anna's short train could easily be taken for the tail end of Sarah's. Thank the skies for the myopic ignorance of habitual dome dwellers. Nick was entirely lost out on the surface, and wouldn't even notice they were heading the wrong way.

Sarah hid her rig in the same spot as yesterday, behind the western ridge sheltering the town. This was the one aspect of the plan that Anna feared most–that crawler was their only ticket out of here. If anything happened to it ...

She found an unexpected determination to make good use of that spike gun if the need arose. Those karking *vreemde* were *not* stranding them here to die.

Two hours ago, with a lump in her throat, Anna had watched the boys and the twins–Mikey, Seth, John, Clara and Helga–dismount from Sarah's last car and head on foot towards the lip of the ridge, where they'd spied on Serendipity yesterday and hatched this madcap plan of sabotage.

Through the line of sight radio, and a smothering crackle of static, they'd told Anna that there'd been a tense moment when Nick appeared in the drive cab and asked why they'd stopped. Sarah spun him a tale of the need to tighten the hitches along the train, some status lights were bugging her, he didn't want the rig to fall apart in the middle of nowhere with no prospect of help arriving, did he now?

No, he did not!

That near miss actually gave them a good excuse to disembark with tools in their hands, but everyone knew Nick would not stay fooled for long.

Guided by Mikey, the ground team set off down the hill to look for a way to approach unseen. They checked their chronos, and Anna and Ben took a detour far to the north to approach Serendipity from the direction Anna had escaped to all those days ago.

They were the diversion, the bait.

Anna swallowed, and checked her own modified spike gun and bundle of pitons.

Mikel gnawed his lip in frustration, and surveyed their subterranean surroundings in the glint of multiple flashlights. He knew which way they needed to go, but the walls of a major rainwater channel blocked their path. He hadn't expected that. He thought he'd seen the lay of the land from above, and everything down below had just *felt* right. Up until now.

He rested his hands and forehead against the fluted mass of tissue barring the way. It stretched left and right into the distance. Maybe there was a way under or over. His mouth hung open in a silent howl of despair.

If only they could find a way through the wall they could cross the channel. It would be empty now. The air above was dry now, a turn-around from the deluges of previous weeks.

A cough and shuffling of feet startled him out of his misery. He glanced around, guilt burning his cheeks. He'd let them down. They'd have to turn back.

John rested a hand on his shoulder. "C'mon, Mikey. We just need to find a way round." He looked around, and back the way they'd come. "We can't be more than twenty meters down. Maybe we can push a way up to the surface and see what's what. Drop down again, or maybe we're close enough to get the rest of the way without being seen."

Seth gazed at the roof of their tunnel, as if he could see past the dense mass of fibers. "Surely we must be getting close to the western stockpile by now. If we could find a way up, would that give us enough cover from any patrols?"

"From the tracks we saw, they stuck close to town," Helga added. "Went between town and the stockpile so we'd be hidden. Maybe."

"Either way," said Seth, "we need to crack on. Need to be in position when Anna draws them away."

"Hey, Mikey," Clara called. "Wall seems a little soft right here. Do ya see?"

Mikel turned back to where he'd rested. Clara was right. Why hadn't he seen that before? He pushed. A fold of tissue eased back leaving a narrow cleft. He wriggled his way through.

Behind him, John muttered under his breath. "Could have sworn this wall was sound."

They clambered down into the vein, dark and empty except for a foot of sluggish flow in the bottom of the channel, and up the other side.

Once again, Mikel pressed his hand to the far wall, feeling his way along. In his mind's eye, he pictured the structure around him, the honeycomb of pillars reaching deep down, shot through with channels, drains, pumps, vast starchy stores of winter food, and invisible networks of electrical activity writhing throughout the whole mass.

This time, he felt the connection clearly. He *needed* a way through. A subtle, unseen and soundless *shifting* in the tissue under his palms, and he pushed.

Just like before, edges teased apart leaving an opening just wide enough to crawl through.

"Well I'll be ..." Seth murmured as he followed. "If this path keeps on in the same direction, we'll be there on time after all."

———— • ————

Anna smacked the console. A brief flicker and it went dead again.

Ben gazed at her, silent, but Anna could feel the tension between them.

"Console's futzed." Stating the karking obvious, but Anna felt the need to say *something*. "Kak!" Anger and frustration burned through her. They were on the clock, Seth and Mikey and the rest were depending on them to draw the *vreemde* away. But they were stuck with a dead drive computer.

No. Wait. Anna was so used to riding with a dimmed cab she hadn't noticed another possibility. She leapt out of her seat and flicked the cabin lights. "We've lost power. Bet it's that *nutloos* power coupling."

Ben's eyebrows beetled up into his hairline, but relief flooded through Anna. If it was as simple as the coupling, she could fix that. Mikey had salvaged spares from the cars they'd abandoned.

As she headed down to the storage compartment she yelled back up the stairs, "Mask on, Ben. There'll be some atmosphere leakage without power in the locks."

The coupling spanner was in its expected place–thank you, Seth!– and Anna quickly checked the connection at the back of the cab. The oily, sooty residue around the socket confirmed her suspicion. The yoop was still powered up fine. It was just the connection. Easy fix!

Fifteen minutes later, Anna stormed back into the cab. "This is unbelievable! We scavenged spare couplings when we rescued this train, but I can't find them anywhere."

Ben's face reddened. "Like I might have mentioned, lass, when we camped up at the way station we stripped this rig of any useful supplies. Last I knew, spare power couplings would have fallen into that category." He grimaced. "Sorry."

Anna gaped at him. The sinking in her stomach, the despair, battled with impotent fury. She closed her eyes. This was not Ben's fault. He was right. They'd have taken those couplings. It was the right thing to do. It was what Anna would have done.

But she had to get this crawler moving. She needed power in the cab. She didn't need power from that trailing yoop, though.

———

Morning sun peering above the hills blinded Mikel as he followed John up through the surface of Sponge.

"Looks quiet," John whispered, crouching and scanning their surroundings. "Hope Anna's managed to draw them off."

"Hope she doesn't get tangled with them, too," Seth muttered from behind, echoing Mikel's fervent wish. Mikel still remembered what they'd done to Georgina. He clambered out onto the surface after John.

"Question is," Seth continued, as he followed Mikel, "where have we come out?"

John peered around, eying the buildings and the skyline. "Looks like ... yes, right behind the western dock. That's South Three over there. Good work, Mikey."

They stepped back and surveyed the domes looming above them. A warehouse to their left, and the garage a hundred and fifty meters away to the right, formed a broad 'V' with the domes of Serendipity visible beyond the gap at the far end.

"Warehouse here," Seth muttered. "Probably a safer way in. Anna said they're using the southern garages."

Clara and Helga crawled out of the ground side by side. Their faces both hardened and as one they swung their spike guns up. The *whump-clack* of the guns sounded together, echoing off the back of the dock.

Mikel, Seth and John whirled around. Two overalled figures behind them staggered, their mouths open in disbelief.

The nearer, a burly man, dropped the long-handled flaying knife he'd raised overhead ready to strike, and clutched the head of the piton that had sprouted in his chest.

The woman behind him screamed as the pain hit. Clara's piton had blown clear through her shoulder. She doubled over and vomited, scrabbling the filled mask from her face.

Her next gulping breath was her last.

John sat back on the ground, looking stunned.

The impaled man had sunk to his knees, gasping for breath. Seth grimaced, then with a jerk ripped the man's mask off his face.

Seth looked like he might be sick, but he pulled himself together. In a shaky voice he said, "He wasn't going to last. Needed to be done."

Mikel trembled. Visions of Georgina on the garage floor haunted him. These greenjackets had tried to kill him and Anna, he reminded himself over and over. And they were about to butcher them just now. All the same, he felt lightheaded.

"They'd not have stopped," John said. "It's them or us. You know that. They crept up on us, thinking they'd take two of us out quickly and finish off the third. The twins popping up out the ground must have shocked them."

Mikel jumped when a hand clapped his shoulder. But it was only Helga. "Good to know these things work, eh?" She exchanged glances with Clara.

Mikel sidled over and picked up the wicked-looking combat knife the woman had dropped. Seth hadn't allowed him a spike gun, but Mikel didn't like the idea of being unarmed. Not given the murderous intent of these *vreemde*.

"Well," said Seth, "I'm wondering if the plan's already gone to the Deep. If these two were out here still, it means Anna hasn't caught their attention after all. That means, *we're* now the diversion."

The world, or at least best-laid plans, seemed to be falling apart around Anna. She'd finally coaxed the crawler into life, and limped the last few kilometers to town. She'd intended to take it slowly and fake the extent of the damage, in keeping with the rig's battered appearance, to make sure any patrols around town would have time to spot them and raise the alarm.

In the event, their halting progress needed no faking. The rig was already cranky at best with glaring red alarms firing up all over the console, but with a trailing car and freewheeling yoop without guidance, it took all Anna's skill to keep it within thirty degrees of a steady heading.

It was one thing, she realized, to steer a one-car vehicle by hand. A powered forward pair dragging one freewheeling rear was manageable. But throw two more cars into the middle, with wobbly wheels and jamming hitches, and the drive computer was worse than useless.

Eventually she snarled in frustration and threw everything bar the forward wheels into freewheel mode and hoped those forward wheels had enough traction to drag the rest of the train along.

They did.

Barely.

So they limped along marginally faster than a person could run. Anna had been banking on a turn of speed to draw pursuers out in a chase before entering a garage and losing them on foot in the labyrinth of domes and tunnels. But not only did they have no reserves of speed to draw on, they had no pursuers. Bad news on both counts.

"Any signs of life?" Anna fought down a rising sense of panic for Mikey, Seth and the others. She focused on her driving while Ben clamped binocs to his eyes and scanned back and forth.

"Not a soul," he rumbled. "Take a swing past the western edge, 'tween town and that stockpile, then around the south."

"Maybe they've given up patrolling."

"All the more reason to pass by the southern bounds and around the eastern dock. Seems to be their main work site. We might get lucky there."

"Skies above!" Anna spluttered as the town rolled by with no signs of alarm. "What do we have to do to be seen? Knock? Set off fireworks? Fly a hundred meter karking *banner* saying 'Come and get me'?"

"More vexin'," Ben muttered, "no signs of t'others neither."

A deep chill ran up Anna's spine. "I'm heading in when we reach East One. Something's gone wrong."

Chapter 29

Mikel shrank back as they neared the end lock of the warehouse. All had been quiet so far, but creeping through the eerily empty space brought back unwanted memories of deadly hide-and-seek.

Down below the surface, he'd been in his element, in tune with his surroundings. He felt Sponge all around him, a living comforting presence.

An *aware* presence, Mikel realized. Ever since he could remember, dreams and visions had haunted him. Fleeting at first, and soon lost in the light of day, a scant impression, nothing more than the ghost of a residue from the deepest slumber. With age they'd become more frequent and more intense, then waking visions impressing themselves on him. More sensory and emotional than true visions, but vivid nonetheless.

He'd always assumed there was something wrong with him. Something linked to his inability to speak, maybe, but a defect entirely within. Now he had cause to doubt. The connection he'd always felt whenever he was out on the surface, and more recently below the surface, couldn't be denied. Now he knew what to look for, he sensed massive life energy all around, cradling the town. More distant here, with layers of man-made structures in between, but still there.

And it was aware of *him*.

He shivered.

A hand on his shoulder steadied him. He turned his head and smiled at Clara. Hardly a muscle in her face moved, but he saw the smile beneath the mask as plain as midsummer. "We got yer back, Mikel, dinna fret."

Helga pressed in from the other side as they entered the lock, a solid, reassuring presence.

They followed Seth and John, scouting ahead and listening for sounds of life. Through a long tunnel and into the ghost of an admin dome. Then they were in the habitat dome that Mikel recognized. Off to their right, lock telltales glowed in the distance. The entrance to South Two where ... where ... Mikel pulled away from Clara and Helga and hurried to catch John's arm. He pointed to the pinpricks of light at the far end of the abandoned hall.

"Interesting," John whispered. "That where they've hangared that jet Anna told us about?"

Mikel nodded. *And where they killed Georgina.* He blinked back a tear.

"And from here on, we're on the main path between the south garages and the assay lab. Need to keep eyes peeled."

Seth pondered. "I guess if we *are* spotted then that's kinda the whole idea of being here now, isn't it?"

"Sure, but I'd rather be in control of how and when they spot us."

"Ideally, yes, but they could be anywhere. Ahead ... behind ..." Seth eyed Mikel. "We'll string out a bit. Me and John stay on point, Helga drop back and watch our rear. Clara, you're with Mikey. If we hit trouble from either front or rear it's your job to get him out of sight and keep him safe. Skies know, I'm not keen to tangle with armed *vreemde*, but that's nothing to the thought of facing Anna again if anything happened to Mikey."

"When we get in there, what's the plan?"

"Depends what we find when we get there. Another reason to scout things out first if we can. Mess up their readings, for sure. Maybe some-one can go sabotage that groundhopper outside so they can't do any more digging. I dunno! We improvise."

"Meantime," John said, "if you're spotted let out a yell–like surprise, not like it's a warning–and leg it. The rest of us will try not to be seen and hopefully you'll draw enough of them away. If we get split up, we'll meet back at the warehouse where we came in."

The five of them crept through dark and empty halls, until they came to a silent workshop next to the assay shed.

Compared with the darkened airlock panels all through town, the glowing lights at the far side of the workshop looked ominously out of place. Mikel trembled. The memory of being hunted was still too sharp in his mind. He seemed trapped in a nightmare, facing situations he found impossible to grasp. The world was not meant to work like this.

Seth and John whispered together, then John slid along the near wall and approached the lock. He slipped inside and was lost to view. The wait seemed endless.

While Mikel was alone with Anna, escaping the greenjackets, he'd coped by throwing out the rulebook he'd spent all his life learning. The town was no longer home, the intruders clearly had rules of their own that had nothing to do with Serendipity, so Mikel was able to suspend his own obedience. But now, he was back with familiar faces. Now the old world with all its rules collided with the lawless one he'd been thrust into. The conflict was driving him nuts.

And he felt a disconcerting echo of his feelings from the unseen glittering depths beneath his feet.

John finally reappeared and Seth drew a deep sigh of relief. They took shelter behind a tall stack of empty shelving. "I see five, maybe six," John said. "Hard to tell through that narrow window. They're all huddled around the big analyzer."

"Guess they got their samples, then," said Seth. "What can we do to mess them up?"

"Steal the samples?"

"They'd only go back to the sites they visited and dig up more."

"Not if their survey craft's unusable," said Clara.

Seth gave her a thoughtful nod. "So, a two-pronged approach, then? Spoil the samples and wreck the survey craft?"

"Or we could just kill them all."

Mikel gave Helga a thumbs-up at that. Seth and John just gaped at her. After long seconds of silence Seth sighed. "Tempting, to be sure, but we're not like that."

"*We* are," said Clara. But she gave Mikel a flicker of a wink and he knew this was just her idea of a joke.

"In self defense don't hesitate to pull the trigger, but we're not killing anyone in cold blood." Seth's voice, little more than a whisper, brooked no argument. "Let's deal with that craft first. If there are that many of them in the assay shed, there may not be anyone guarding it."

———•••———

Mikel shivered in the bitter wind scything across the open platform of the loading dock. John and Seth sidled up to the aircraft fifty meters further along the dock, spike drivers raised, looking for signs of life. Little more than a box hung with engines on swivel mountings, it stood square and solid next to the loading platform, tied down against the elements. A flurry of snow whipped at Mikel's mask.

A sudden unexpected warmth enveloped him. He looked up, startled, to meet Clara's gaze. "We'll look after ye, little'un." One hand cradled her spike gun. The other rested on Mikel's shoulder. He gave her a weak smile.

John popped the side cargo hatch, and a few moments later Seth waved them forwards. They clambered into the welcome shelter of the cargo bay and crowded into the doorway of the tiny cockpit.

"So," said Seth, "how do you go about disabling a heavy-duty ground lifter like this?"

John scratched his jaw at the edge of his mask seal. "Lots of ways come to mind. Lets see if we can find a toolbox back there. I might be able to undo a fuel nozzle or something." He thought some more. "I guess we want to do something that'll stop them lifting off, not something that'll bring them down mid-air."

Mikel caught a brief glimmer of disappointment in Clara's eyes. This was taking way too long. Frustration darkened his vision. He ached to be with Anna again, to see she was safe, and to put this nightmare behind him.

He reached around and lifted a piton from Clara's shoulder bag. It was about forty centimeters long, heavy at the head where it ended in a belay ring. It had a good heft to it. He swung it at the navigation computer, which splintered with a satisfying crunch. A couple more swings. More shattered displays.

Seth stared open mouthed as Mikel casually handed the piton to Clara and high-fived her on the way back to the hatch.

"Well, I guess there's always that. They'll never find their way back to wherever they took their samples from."

Back in the workshop, John checked through the window to the assay shed again. "They're still at it. Now someone needs to get in and futz up their samples and readings. Let's see what we can do to create a distraction."

"And make sure we can get away from them, too," added Seth.

Mikel eyed the nearby shelving. He tapped one of the supports. Hard rimwood. It made a faint ringing sound. He tugged on Seth's sleeve and pointed, miming pushing the shelves over.

Seth studied the bank of shelves. "Not fastened down. Should make a good noise ..."

"Especially if we stack a couple of those toolboxes on top," added John. "Most of us can hide out in the next dome around, ready to wreak havoc as soon as it's empty, but someone still needs to get seen here, draw them away, *and* escape."

Mikel rolled his eyes. It seemed so obvious. He pointed behind in the general direction of the nearest garage and sketched the outline of a hitching truck in the air in front of him. He ground his teeth in frustration at the blank looks. They didn't have time for this. Where was Anna when he needed her? She always understood what he was trying to say, with minimal prompting. It was as if she could read his thoughts. Everyone else was so slow in comparison, even the twins, who could normally clue in to his meaning better than most.

He clenched his fists, then beckoned them to follow. Without waiting for a reply, he took off at a jog through the adjacent empty warehouse and into the top of South One.

Clara's face lit up when he hopped into the nearest hitching truck and punched the starter button. It came to life with a soft whir.

"Nice one, Mikey! Use a truck to push the shelves over, then take off through the warehouse. They'll never catch you."

John chewed his cheek and held up his hand. "Let's plan a bit ahead here. Decide on an escape route and make sure the airlock doors are left open."

With a route mapped out and prepared, Mikel followed them in the truck back to the workshop, thankful he'd had so much practice already.

Seth pointed to the adjacent lock. "When you drop the shelves, they should come barreling out here. John and I'll head to the next workshop around and wait."

"I'll stick with Mikey," said Clara. "Make sure he don't get hi'self into bother."

John scratched his head. "Guess that's about the best we can do. Don't want to leave Mikey alone. Helga will come with us. We might need a second diversion to keep them busy. I'm betting they won't all go chasing after one or even two of you just like that."

Alone with Clara, Mikel maneuvered the truck around in the confines of the workshop.

"Ye goin' to reverse into it?" Clara asked. "Smart thinkin'. Facing the right way to the airlock wi'out all this futzting about."

Mikel gave her a questioning look and briefly wondered that she'd only just realized that. It had seemed so obvious to him from the outset.

"Yeah, the others should be in position by now. Let's do it!"

Mikel's heart pounded. His hand suddenly felt clammy on the truck's joystick. He'd been chased by these *vreemde* before. It wasn't an experience he wished to repeat, and yet here he was. And it had been *his* idea! What the kak had he been thinking?

Clara patted him on the shoulder. "I got yer back, Mikey. If it makes ye feel any better, take my gun. I'll need both hands to hang on to the truck anyway."

Mikel accepted the weapon, checked the trigger mechanism was in the 'off' position–didn't want any accidents–and stowed it down by the side of his seat. He gave Clara a brave smile and a nod, then motioned her to back off out of harm's way.

Without giving himself time for second thoughts, he rammed the truck into reverse.

After the initial collision, the shelf at first seemed to topple in slow and silent motion. Then all hell broke loose. The crash of the heavy toolboxes placed on top reverberated through the dome. The clatter of struts and crossbeams rang out. A heavy canister rumbled across the floor.

Mikel sat frozen in shock, ears ringing.

"Mikey! C'mon!" Clara's eyes widened and she waved him on.

He glanced over his shoulder and the world came back into focus. The airlock door behind him burst open.

Mikel jammed the joystick forward and the truck leapt to life with a rising whine. He remembered to slow and steer carefully through the airlock doors, giving Clara time to jump onto the back and cling to the cage of the open cab.

Through the tunnel and the open airlock, then they were in an echoing warehouse. Now Mikel was able to open up the throttle.

"Not too fast, Mikey," Clara hissed in his ear.

He wondered if she was in danger of being thrown off, then he caught her meaning. They had to make an escape, but not too quickly. They had first to stay just enough ahead to draw their pursuers on.

Feet clattered behind them.

"Those fucking blueskins again!"

"How'd they get back? Carmel said they were dead."

Clara let out a low groan. "Only two of 'em followin'. Was hoping for more."

A savage grin slowly made its way across Mikel's face as Clara's words sank home. This was a very different game from the one they'd played before. Yes, he was still the one on the run, but before it had been played out on the *vreemde's* terms. This time, his own clan was driving the agenda. He was not blindly fleeing death, his job was to lead them on for as long as possible.

The end of the warehouse came into sight. He slowed again, calculating how close he could let them approach.

"Nice work, Mikey," Clara whispered. "Take it easy through the next lock. I'll tell ye if they get too near."

The short tunnel led them into the end of another warehouse. Another two-hundred meter clear run to allow them to make distance if they needed it. John had planned their route well. Didn't look like they needed the vehicle's speed, though. The two pursuers staggered out into the open, gasping for breath.

Mikel set off for the far end at a moderate jogging pace and checked over his shoulder. *C'mon, you can't be that unfit, surely?*

"They're giving up," Clara hissed. "We need to lose the truck."

Mikel rolled his eyes. Okay, he could see her point. He was nearing the airlock. He allowed his line to drift a little off. The right hand side of the truck jammed against the side. He made a show of backing up and getting the truck even further wedged in place.

They were getting close. Clara tapped him on the shoulder and said, "Let's go."

He grabbed the spike gun and followed her down the tunnel. They paused at the end and took stock. They were now in the town's main admin dome. The two following them seemed to have taken heart at seeing their quarry on foot and were still after them. A few turns led them through a maze of habitats up near North One before they finally gave the *vreemde* the slip.

"We done our job good, Mikey," Clara whispered. "Let's go find t'others."

Mikel grinned as he followed her on a circuitous route back across town.

They approached the assay shed from the north, from the workshop where Helga and the others had planned to wait. There was no sign of life there, and the view into the assay shed was blocked by a partition wall. They backed up and tried the first workshop, where they'd dropped the shelving.

They waited a few minutes, listening to a deep silence.

Clara went first into the airlock, and immediately emerged accompanied by an outraged shout. Mikel didn't hesitate, and darted ahead of her into the tunnel and through the next lock back into the warehouse. Familiar territory from the last dash, but this time they were on foot and the unseen man behind them sounded angry. His heart pounded in fright.

Without breaking her stride, Clara shoved Mikel into the shadow of an emergency cabinet to one side of the airlock. She continued running, boots clacking on the hard floor, breath whuffing and echoing through the hall.

Mikel grinned to himself. She sounded like someone on her last legs, tempting the man now rushing past Mikel's hiding place into thinking he had an easy kill. He was in for a shock. Clara could run from one side of Serendipity to the other and back again without breaking a sweat.

A lonely realization dispelled his momentary delight. He was on his own. It was up to him to finish the job they'd come here to do.

Approaching the assay shed again, his heart sank. He knew Clara was leading one of them away, and there was still no sign of Helga, John or Seth. But peering through the airlock window, there were still two dark-skinned *vreemde* stubbornly in place.

One of them was the one who'd shot Georgina.

Chapter 30

Sweat beaded on Anna's brow as she nosed the crawler into East One, partly from the intense concentration of steering a rig with all the handling characteristics of a wet noodle, and partly from blinding anxiety. Why was it so quiet all of a sudden? When she'd last been here, on the run, the town seemed to be crawling with dark-skinned foreigners.

A flash of insight, tempting in its simplicity. They'd finished their job and left! All this skulking around was for nothing. The town was empty.

Maybe.

Then maybe not. That strange survey craft was still grounded alongside the eastern dock, surrounded by fresh tracks. The *vreemde* were still here. But where? Anna couldn't shake the feeling that things had gone awry.

Ben's brooding and silent presence alongside did nothing to reassure her. Even the stolid patriarch was worried sick.

She managed to keep the head of the crawler from snagging on obstructions in the vehicle tunnel. A half-dead rig like this would be impossible to back up for another try. At last, the echoing emptiness of the garage came into view.

"I'll bring us up to the far end and turn us around. If we need to run for it, at least we'll be pointing the right way."

"Make it quick," Ben muttered. Anna had no argument with that sentiment.

The lower lock hissed through its cycle. In just those few days Sponge's poisons had tainted the air all the way through the vast space of the garage.

Masks on, they dismounted and surveyed their surroundings. Anna's nerves were keyed like a lute string, straining for sounds of life–friendly or otherwise.

They both stared at the unlit airlock leading into the working quarter of town.

"There's a row of processing sheds, then the assay shed. No knowing where they'll be, but their main movements will probably be between assay, South Two, and the dock."

Ben grunted. "Seems to me the direct approach is as good as any, then. Let's go."

Anna's worry grew as they crept through darkened domes with their empty tool shops and bare stripping benches. At last, they neared the assay shed.

"Dome's got power," Anna whispered, pointing out the glowing telltale alongside the airlock. "They're still here." Dread settled in her stomach.

"Mikey'll be fine. He's in good company."

He meant well, but Anna's nerves would not be soothed. She checked her spike gun, making sure the piton was loaded properly, nothing to snag it. *If they've hurt Mikey ...*

They crept up to the airlock. Anna paused. "Problem," she hissed. "We're going into clean air, the lock will cycle. Anyone in there's going to hear it unless they're making a noise."

"Can ye sneak a peek inside first?"

Anna slid through the outer door and peered through the window of the inner door. "We're at the back of the offices. Shop floor's beyond them. Can't see if anyone's there." She pressed her ear to the door. "No noise either ... wait ... a bit of a hum. There's machinery running."

"This is always a quiet shop, though," Ben mused. "Unless someone's paring down a sample there's nowt to make much noise. Hang about ..." He studied the telltale panel behind him. "We're in luck. Air in the dome behind us is still clean. The lock won't cycle."

"Sure?"

Ben's falsely cheerful smile and shrug wasn't reassuring. Heart pounding, Anna eased the door open. She breathed a sigh when it opened without fuss or a revealing hiss of flushing air. They slipped through into a corridor that separated the dome canopy from the three narrow floors of offices ahead.

Sounds came more clearly from beyond. Anna had never spent much time in the assay room, but the soft whine of equipment was distinctive enough. It was background noise to a pair of voices.

"Some of those earlier samples were close, but the readings on this one are looking damned good."

"Let the machine do its job before we reach a conclusion."

Anna froze at that voice. Casual venom laced the words. She tried to blot out the memory of Georgie slumping to the floor.

"And I know *my* job, Galloway. This is it, I'm telling you."

Galloway. At last Anna had a name to focus her fury on.

"If we get a confirmed positive on this one, I'm taking my jet to Jorvick. I'll leave you in charge of tidying up."

"What about those blueskins?"

A soft laugh. "Once we have our answer, there's no point trying to track them down in this maze. They must have a vehicle somewhere. Check the garages and disable it. If there's nothing there it must be close by. Get Carmel to take the fighter up and circle the town. We know they can only run so fast. Take away their transport, the planet will do the rest."

"Fighter." The word sounded like a curse. "Call that civilian retrofit job a *fighter*? Improvised weapons, manual targeting ..."

"Fair point. Even *I* couldn't hide a military craft in the manifest. Not that high-tech targeting would be much good in this electromagnetic fog." A long pause. "Is that thing nearly finished yet?" A grunt of annoyance. "Of course, Carmel's no military pilot either, but I thought even *she* could manage a target the size of a house."

Anna ground her teeth, stifling the urge to leap out and put a piton through that smug face. She imagined him, standing only a few meters away around the corner, in that ornate frock coat, his pale eyes and hair around dark face like an old-fashioned photographic negative.

A sudden chime made her jump.

A long silence, then, "That's it. Told you."

For a moment, Anna's chest clenched at the thought they'd been discovered, but the voices resumed their conversation.

"No doubt this time. The cows have come home."

Anna had no idea what Galloway was talking about, but the triumph in his voice was unmistakable.

"The cows have come home," he repeated. "I need to get this information to the negotiators. Damn this planet's antiquated communications!"

She glanced at Ben. "We can't let him leave," she whispered.

"What's that?" the other voice snapped.

Kak! She *thought* she'd whispered.

Footsteps clattered towards them. To kak with this! Anna stepped into view. A burly man in dusty green overalls was almost on her. She jumped back, barely avoiding a roundhouse slash with a foot-long paring knife. The spike gun jerked in her hands. The man with the knife stared down in astonishment, then crumpled, bleeding, to the floor.

Galloway gaped, then his eyes narrowed. "Well. They advised me this colony had no weapons. But they also said you were inventive." He trained his pistol on Anna.

Ben stepped around from behind her with his spike driver pointed at Galloway. The pistol wavered away from Anna.

"But single shot weapons? Really?" The pistol barked at the same time Ben's gun thwacked the piton across the room. Both men leaped aside as they fired. The piton grazed Galloway's shoulder and shattered the dust extractor hood of the workbench behind him. Ben gasped and clutched his side.

Anna locked eyes with Galloway. There was no way in hell she'd be able to reload before he killed her, but her hands moved of their own volition smoothly sliding another piton from her pouch and fitting it into the barrel. She could do this in her sleep. Her gaze never wavered, locked, mesmerizing, on Galloway's.

Time slowed, measuring out the last second of her life in ever reducing fragments. Galloway's hand came up in slow motion. His eyes, ethereally pale and blue, widened.

A noise to her right broke the spell.

"Oh, for fucksake!" Galloway's urbane calm broke too. He dived aside. Another piton smacked into the workbench.

Anna jerked her head around. "Mikey!"

He ran to her.

No! Galloway! Unless there were others with Mikey they were all out of shots and he must have a nearly full magazine.

Her fingers fumbled with the half-loaded piton, nerveless. It clattered to the floor.

They were dead.

But Galloway was gone.

Anna's attention was torn between blessed relief at seeing Mikey safe, Ben groaning on the floor clearly *not* safe, and the receding drum of footsteps through the far airlock.

She settled for pulling Mikey into a sideways hug as she scurried to kneel by Ben.

"Leave me, gal!" he ground out between clenched teeth. "Get after that karking *stüg vreemde*."

Anna's mouth hardened into a thin line as she rose and raced through the workshop.

Mikey followed. A protest died on her lips. Chasing Galloway was dangerous. He was armed. But staying put was dangerous too. Other intruders were still loose in the town and they could return any moment. On balance, she preferred Mikey with her where she could do something to protect him, or die trying.

She fumbled another piton from her pouch as she ran and handed it to Mikey, then another for herself. She quickly realized she couldn't load it properly on the run. Another agonizing choice. She decided speed was preferable.

Through a warehouse, Anna traced the route she was sure Galloway would be taking to South Two. That had to be his destination. She wracked her memory for a faster route to cut him off, but there was no short cut without taking them out to the surface.

A thought popped unbidden. He'd talked about his jet, *and* a fighter. They had *two* scramjets down here? Might be worth disabling that fighter if she had a chance. The thought of losing another crawler brought her neck out in goose bumps. She was *not* dying in the winter dark.

Across another warehouse. A scurry of steps on the other side. They were gaining! Through a long tunnel glowing in midday light, and there he was nearing the habitat dome next to South Two.

That fleeting glimpse spurred Anna on. She pounded through the lock and into the perimeter hall of the habitat dome. Galloway vanished through the far side of the dome and slapped the lock control. Of course, this one had power from South Two, the lock that had given her and Mikey the first warning that they were not alone.

The door hissed shut behind him. Anna raced through the dome's ring corridor and danced in frustration as the lock cycled through its safety sequence. She scrambled through the gap the moment there was room, Mikey close behind her.

In the distance, Galloway had reached the far end of the link tunnel and the airlock leading into South Two where his jet was parked. He paused on the threshold and turned back to face them. He reached into his jacket with a scowl, and pulled out his pistol.

Anna barely had time to think as she grabbed Mikey and yanked him back behind the door frame. Two shots cracked like splintering knotwood in the confined space. With her back pressed against the wall of the lock, the impacts against the other side jarred through her shoulder blades. She heaved a sob of relief that the first few meters of the dome's perimeter wall was structural, especially around the airlocks. The weather shield above head height could withstand the dispersed pressure of seven-hundred-kilometer-per-hour winds, but a gunshot would rip right through.

More shots split the air. Her ears still rang from the discharges, but Galloway's snarl of anger carried clearly through the sixty meters of tunnel.

She peered cautiously around the corner, then yelped in fright as Mikey dashed across the open doorway and surveyed the tunnel from shelter on the other side.

Galloway seemed to have been caught napping by Mikey's reckless dash. His face like thunder, the pistol wavered in his hand from one side to the other.

Anna realized they were both exposed, staring at Galloway standing in the far lock. She had no idea how easy or hard it might be to hit a target at that distance, but if it was easy surely Galloway would have done it by now. Her hands had already moved on autopilot to reload the spike gun, but she was barely aware of the movement.

Her eyes widened. "You only have one shot left, don't you?"

His face hardened. He stiffened and aimed the pistol at Anna, but no shot came. His indecision was evident, replaced by a flicker of panic when Mikey stepped fully out from cover.

"Stay back! I'm warning you!"

Heedless, Anna also stepped out. Rage boiled through her veins and lent a depth and finality to her voice she didn't know she possessed. "Shoot one of us, and the other will rip you limb from limb." The words came unbidden and Anna, unused to thoughts of bodily violence, was surprised to realize she believed them.

From his expression, Galloway believed her, too. And, when she risked a sidelong glance at Mikey, she shuddered at the implacable set of his face and shoulders.

Then Galloway smiled, slow and predatory. He aimed at the ceiling half way down the tunnel. The crack of the discharge shook her.

The look of puzzlement on his face would be comical if the situation wasn't so desperate. Anna was no spacegoer, but she instantly recognized his mistake. An easy one to make for someone used to associating sealed environments with space. "Not a karking vacuum out there, you dumbass!"

But he was already gone, both doors of the far lock sliding shut behind him. He had been expecting explosive decompression, not the slow drift of mingling gases at equal pressure. Even so, the omnipresent sensors had already detected native toxins. The distant telltale on the control panel glowed red showing a breach, and the lock would take time to cycle.

Time they didn't have.

Anna wept in frustration as the lock went through its stately procedure. By the time they emerged into the vastness of the garage, the air thrummed with power as a sleek craft raised itself off the ground and slunk toward the far exit.

A tug at her sleeve. Mikey had already fastened his mask and was pulling her towards South One and the nearest exit onto the surface. She followed, pulling her own mask over her head, but her feet felt leaden with defeat.

Outside, they raced through the long shadow cast by the sloping garage walls. The machine whine, felt at first as a distant clamor through the walls, rose as the midnight black dart emerged.

What could she do? He'd escaped. What had Mikey dragged her out here for? He used to love coming out here to watch vehicles come and go. Was that it? She fought to smother a hysterical laugh. Maybe he had the right idea. It was about as useful as anything *she* could come up with.

Mikey was neither giving chase nor standing watching. He was kneeling and had removed his gloves, plunging his hands wrist deep into the spongy surface. His eyes were squeezed tight in concentration.

Despite herself, Anna watched with resigned curiosity. She slumped to the ground alongside Mikey. They had lost.

No. She tried to swallow the bitter defeat and look on the positive side. They already had a good life here, didn't they? They might struggle with mechanical supplies, but the eternal battle to keep machinery running also kept wits sharp. Who needed artificial games and entertainments when you could spend days figuring out how to jury-rig drive flux coils from spare refrigeration plant? And they were never short of food or water, air or shelter. From the newsvids she's seen of life elsewhere, not everyone could claim that luxury. None of that would go away. All they'd lost was an insubstantial dream. Self governance might matter to a few curates, but what difference would it really make to the rest of them?

Two hundred meters away, Galloway's jet lifted a few meters higher and pointed its nose lazily towards the west. The scramjet's whine rose to an earsplitting shriek. He would be gone in seconds. The Company would offer terms almost too good to be true, knowing they had a fortune to be made here. The Elysium negotiators would be only too eager to sign. By the time news of the Company's treachery reached them, it would be too late.

A new noise joined the machine shriek, felt through her feet and buttocks rather than truly heard. Anna feverishly pushed herself back up against the security of the garage and her foot throbbed in sympathy. Last time she heard this sound she'd fallen into the depths and Ambrose had screamed his last.

A subliminal rumble became a thunderous ripping, like a distant world being sundered by giants.

A spike a hundred meters long thrust up from the planet's surface, neatly spearing the jet.

The craft hung in mid air for a second, spinning slowly at first, then with increasing speed on its delicate-looking pivot, before erupting in a blaze of yellow-white flame.

The concussion hit half a second later, snapping Anna out of her stupor. She grabbed Mikey's collar and dragged him back alongside her.

A few seconds later, the rumbling echo of the explosion rolled back across the valley. Fluttering fragments cascaded along the slope of the garage and peppered the ground around them.

The rain of debris slowed. Mikel patted a scorch on his knee where a glowing ember landed. He wormed free of Anna's clutches and turned to face her.

His heart thudded in dread. Anna's eyes were wide. Her hands shook as she pressed herself back against the wall of the garage. Not good. He needed strong and decisive Anna back again.

He shook her shoulders, gently, then more forcefully, relieved when her eyes regained some focus and her cheeks reddened.

She pulled herself upright. "Did you do that?" Her voice was weak and shaky.

He shrugged. Maybe. He didn't know *what* he did. Just wished with all his might, and the depths beneath him responded. He suffered a brief moment of terror that, somehow, he'd done the wrong thing.

Anna gulped, glanced over his shoulder to where wreckage smoldered, then squinted back at him. "I don't know what just happened, but ... well done."

He gave a shy smile. That's more like it.

"C'mon," Anna muttered. "That noise must have been heard all across town. It'll bring everyone here. We need to be gone. We need to round up the others, wherever they've gone ... Kak! Ben!" She hauled Mikel towards the eastern loading dock. "There's a lock back there. Not far from the assay shed."

Mikel's breath was rasping, his sides ached, and his mask fogged up by the time they sprinted the two hundred meters past the back of the loading dock. Tunnels led from the curving dock to the labyrinth of workshops and warehouses behind. There were no sounds of pursuit and the assay shed was still quiet.

Ben had hauled himself across the floor and propped himself up against the long bulk of the spectral analyzer. He lowered his spike gun when he saw them. "Jeez, gal, you nearly got yersel' ventilated burstin' in like that."

"Galloway's gone," Anna blurted out. "I mean, dead. We ... Mikey ... Sponge ... stopped him."

Mikel pulled off his mask and let it dangle around his neck while he fought for breath. He looked up as Anna's frantic gabbling sputtered to a halt. Ben's gaze skewered him and he averted his eyes from the unwanted attention. He couldn't explain what had just happened, even to himself. Inwardly, he pleaded for the unasked questions, that he knew were plaguing all three of them, to go away.

Beside him, Anna gulped a few deep breaths and seemed to calm down. Her voice took on an urgent tone. "We need a med kit, patch you up so you can walk without leaking all over the place, then get the kak out of here."

Good. Change the subject.

"I'll manage. We still have a wrench to throw, remember?" Ben grinned weakly. "Well, for starters I bin and reset this machine an' wiped the logs. They're back to square one."

He coughed and grimaced.

Anna rushed to his side. "We can't move until we get a dressing on that wound. You lost blood just crawling that distance."

"Bullet went right through. Don't think it hit anything I can't live wi'out."

"All the same." Anna reached for an emergency medical locker. "Can we hide or destroy the samples?" she called over her shoulder as she rummaged in the locker.

Ben grunted. "Tha'll buy some time. But if the prize is rich enough, they'll be back somehow. Depend on it."

Mikel picked up one of the clear sample bags, neatly labeled with point of collection—map co-ordinates, depth, tissue type. He tipped out a twisted tangle of fibrous material onto the workbench and picked up a strand as thick as his finger. He turned it around, seeing how it caught the light, almost translucent.

Mikel's eyes met Anna's and a spark of understanding leapt between them.

"Mikey," she breathed. "This looks kinda familiar. You see it? Like the strands we cut Seth's crawler free from. Not exactly the same stuff, I can see that, but I wonder if *they'd* notice the difference?"

So, she saw it too. Mikel nodded.

"Ben, there was only Galloway and the dead guy here in the room when the results came up."

"Aye."

"So nobody knows what they found. If we replace the samples with some similar-looking crap, they'll get a negative result. They won't come back if they think there's nothing to find."

Ben wheezed a laugh that turned into a cry of pain. "Ne'er mind me, gal," he gasped as Anna lurched towards him. "Get moving before they come back."

Anna dropped a med kit on the bench and grabbed Mikel's hands. "Seth's crawler's in the top end of East One. I bet there are still some of those fibers lodged in the wheels. Make it quick. And be careful."

He gave her hands a squeeze, then turned and slipped his mask on.

He crept from airlock to tunnel to dome. Orange daylight in the tunnels and perimeter walks contrasted with the gloom of the workshops. Silhouettes of hulking machinery cast menacing shadows. Shelves loomed in the dark. He daren't use his flashlight, and he strained his ears for the slightest sound.

Dome weather shields creaked in fitful gusts, the only sounds beyond his own scuffling footsteps and ragged breathing.

Mikel hefted the spike gun, remembering how it felt to fire it. The noise they made scared him, and the kick of the recoil. He'd missed with his last shot, but he'd been lucky. Galloway had run off. Would he be so lucky again?

And, a cold wave ran through his gut, he only had the one piton. No spares.

Chapter 31

As Mikel scurried off, Anna handed the med kit to Ben. "Can you manage on your own for a moment?"

Without waiting for an answer, she opened up each sample bag and tipped the contents out onto the bench. She chewed her lip, casting around for ideas, finally settling on sweeping the samples into a garbage bag and stashing it in one of the upper offices.

By the time she'd finished cleaning up and helping Ben dress his wound, Mikey had returned, panting, with an armful of fragments. They quickly refilled the sample bags and left them on the workbench.

She studied the room, pursing her lips in satisfaction. "Would take an expert eye to spot the swap. Or a chemist with a shitload of analysis machines"–she gestured around the room–"who will soon realize that what he's looking for isn't to be found here. Now, we need to move."

Ben's face turned grey as they eased him to his feet. He groaned, but managed to wrap an arm around Anna and Mikey on either side.

Shuffling awkwardly across the assay room towards the airlock they'd first entered, Anna soon decided they were not going to be traveling far or fast.

Which sucked, because there were voices approaching from the next lock around.

"That was Galloway's jet. You saw the nose cone out there, and the rest of the wreckage."

"But where did that sodding great spear come from? It wasn't there this morning."

Anna and Mikey hauled Ben as quietly as possible behind the bank of offices. Heart pounding, she scanned the floor behind them, praying nobody had dragged their feet through the pools of blood spattering the floor.

"What the fuck ..." A man, voice quavering. A deathly hush. "It's run him right through. Told you those nail guns were something to watch out for."

"This place is giving me the creeps." High pitched. Nervous. How many of them were left? "Galloway's dead. There's nothing to keep us here."

"You want to face the Company going back empty handed?" That was another woman. Harsh and commanding.

A long silence.

"Galloway was a slimy fucker but I'll do him the credit of assuming he left because he'd got a result to report. But he's out of the picture, so it's up to us to finish the job. Heather, check the machines."

"Already on it. Freaking blueskins got here first. Wiped out the results. Whatever Galloway had, we'll have to rerun the assays."

"You can do that?"

Another pause. Anna gazed longingly at the airlock door, only a few meters away.

"They wiped the logs, but at least the fuckers were too stupid to screw with the settings, else we'd be royally in the shit. Only Galloway had the parameters for the signature we're looking for in this chemical soup, secretive bastard."

Anna exchanged glances with Ben. He gave a lopsided shrug. She gave him a thumbs up. This was a good thing.

The second woman snarled under her breath. "How long?"

"To rerun all these samples? A few hours."

"Then what are you standing around for? Jules, Kevin, do another trawl around the town, inside and outside. We're still missing Colin and Gail. Haven't seen them since they went out on patrol."

Anna held her breath, fingering the loaded spike gun hanging by her side. A couple of them were leaving, but out of the four exits ringing the assay dome, which would they choose? Ben's arm slipped from her shoulder. She glanced at him in sudden concern, but he was also readying his gun.

A glance confirmed Mikey had loaded his own gun at some point. Between them, they had three shots ready. But ... that woman was giving orders to three people. That meant four to deal with. At least.

"Wait!"

Anna jumped. That was the harsh woman, who seemed to be the leader now in Galloway's absence.

"We know these rats are armed, so don't get tangled with them. Just find Colin and Gail. Especially Colin. We need him to shut down these domes again. Remember, we still need to clean up so nobody's any the wiser when they come back to town next spring."

While she talked, Anna signaled the other two. Carefully, they eased their way back around the perimeter corridor and huddled behind an emergency cabinet. It wasn't perfect, but they were mostly out of sight from either of the two nearest exits.

Footsteps raised the hairs on Anna's neck. A pair of shadows crossed her line of sight not ten meters away, but the two weren't looking back. "Don't get tangled," one of them grumbled. "Too right. I'm a bloody biologist, not a fighter." The airlock clicked shut behind them.

Anna released her breath. Back in the workshop, cutting equipment whined into action, along with the rush of a dust extractor. Under cover of the noise, they edged back the way they'd come and through the lock.

"We'll never get Ben back to Sarah's crawler." Anna finally voiced the realization that had lurked in the back of her mind. "Don't argue with me," she hissed. Ben shut his mouth.

They limped through the next workshop. Anna peered through the airlock windows, wondering how fast the other two were moving. "We'll make for Seth's crawler in East One. I was hoping to leave it here, but we can drive up to meet Sarah and secure it back at the first station like we'd planned to originally."

"We could do wi' finding t'others first." Ben's face was dripping with sweat, despite the chill in the unheated dome. Anna cursed to herself.

"Masks on from here." She tried to keep her mind on practicalities. "Air gets bad somewhere along the way, and there'll be no warning from the telltales. When we reach the crawler we'll leave you there while Mikey and I try to find the others."

She hoped the two *vreemde* had moved on far enough by now to not be a problem. With her gun leveled, she pushed through the lock and scanned the next workshop.

They crept through town, lock by lock, dome by dome, in the orange glow through the weather skins.

At last, they reached the garage. Anna scouted ahead for signs of life before returning to help Mikey with Ben. The climb up into the lower lock almost defeated them, but step by step they eased Ben into the maintenance bay beneath the drive deck.

Anna stared down at Ben, with growing misgivings. "We need to get you better sorted out, and proper care. There's not a karking prayer of getting you up to the living area. We'll make you comfortable here for now. Mikey, go fetch some cushions and blankets."

Busying herself with the nearest med kit from the equipment rack, Anna looked up as Mikey clattered back down the steps. He was empty-handed, and the look in his eyes froze her to the core. He beckoned. Numb, she followed.

A glance told her all she needed to know. The *vreemde* had found the crawler. While Anna and Mikey were putting a wrench in their plans, they'd been returning the favor.

Putting a wrench in.

Literally.

Fragments from the drive computer and the consoles littered the floor.

Anna gazed at the wrecked cab, struggling to rise above the despair drowning her. A tug on her jacket pulled her out of her maelstrom of bleak thoughts. Mikey pointed to himself, then upstairs, then to Anna and downstairs.

After all these years she normally understood him like telepathy, but it took a few moments of blankness to take his meaning. "Oh, yes. Ben. Kak!"

He raced up to the living level. She headed down to where Ben lay, almost missing a step as she tried to fathom what to tell him.

"Cab's wrecked," she blurted. *Great bedside manner, Anna!* "Those *vreemde* got here ahead of us. Must have figured this is how we all arrived and decided to strand us here."

Ben stared at her, then astonished her with a sharp bark of laughter. "No frettin', lass. Look on the silver lining. 'T means they'll not be looking too hard for the *other* crawler, now, will it?"

Anna's heartbeat slowed to a mere gallop as she considered his words. "There is that, I guess. But we still have the problem of how to get you out of here."

"One problem at a time. Chances are, they won't be back soon, so see if ye can round up t'others. Sure a solution will present itself."

Mikey reappeared with an armful of bedding while Anna bound Ben's wound more firmly and administered a cocktail of drugs to combat pain, shock, infection, and whatever else she could think of for someone who's just had a hole punched through him. It was, she reflected, no different from treating an injury inflicted by Sponge.

Together, they made Ben comfortable at the back of the maintenance bay, facing the inner airlock door at his insistence.

"If they *do* come back," he said, "they're in for a shock."

Anna loaded his spike gun and handed him Mikey's too. "They seem to travel in pairs. I don't think you'll have time to reload."

Ben nodded.

"Mikey, you were with Seth and the others. I don't know how you got separated, but do you know where they might be?"

His face lit up. Anna watched a hurried series of hand signals, checking for confirmation as she translated. "Split up ... meet up ... warehouse ..." He pointed. "West. South-west? That's where you were told to meet?" She followed him into the airlock with only a brief glance back at Ben. "Stay safe!"

"Luck, Anna." He gave a shaky smile, eyes glazed with pain.

Mikey led her across the heart of town. They raced down long shadowed halls, pausing at each lock and intersection to slow their hearts and breathing enough to listen out for signs of life.

The hike seemed endless. Anna's breath rasped raw in her throat, but barely suppressed fears overcame the pain in chest and legs. As they neared the far row of warehouses, she pressed herself into the wall, hugging Mikey close. A silhouette flitted through the golden light at the end of the hall. Mikey shoved her restraining arm away and gave her a cross look.

She looked again, and belatedly recognized Seth in the distance. She heaved a long sigh of relief and stepped into the open on trembling legs. Seth waved her to follow.

Hidden near the end door of the warehouse, John joined them. "What happened?" he asked. "We came out near town and got jumped by a patrol. Figured you must've got caught or held up."

"The latter. You? Wait ... a patrol?"

Seth snorted. "The twins dealt with them. Stashed the bodies behind the western dock."

Anna's knees weakened. They'd all had too many lucky escapes today. "That's why we saw no-one on the way in. Where are the twins?"

"I sent them off to check the assay room. Come on." Seth draped an arm over Anna's shoulders and set off in that direction. "We all got split up, arranged to meet back here. We were still missing Mikey, and you, of course. But Clara left him near the assay room while she drew one of them away, so that was the obvious place to start."

"We heard an explosion," John said. "No idea what happened but figured Mikey had worked out some kind of sabotage."

"Ben and I found Mikey. We dealt with Galloway ... their leader. That was his jet. Ben's back in East One. Hurt." Anna's throat and chest burned. The words came out in chopped sentences as they hurried across town again. She stopped trying to talk at last and focused on drawing long ragged breaths, risking taking her mask off for a few minutes to make the going easier. The air in the heart of town was still clean.

They slowed as they neared the warehouses again, and finally spotted the twins approaching.

All together at last, they skirted the warehouse and workshop quarter, slinking silently from cover to cover, always on the lookout for the remaining intruders. For once, Anna felt they had the advantage. From her mental count their own party must now outnumber the surviving *vreemde*. And they still had spike guns, where it seemed only Galloway had been properly armed. The others had improvised with tools found in the workshops.

They regained the cover of the crawler and Anna rapped on the inner airlock door to alert Ben. Not a good time to get skewered accidentally.

She flashed Ben a quick smile as she passed. "All here! Now, let's see if we can get this show on the road."

Seth and John followed her up to the driver's cab and groaned in unison when they saw the damage.

"There's nothing we can do to repair this. Doubt if we'll find spares in the junkyard either."

"Not planning to." Anna brushed debris from the center seat, and checked the connections to the joysticks on either side with renewed hope. She traced the cables back to the wiring closet, and gave a slow smile of satisfaction. "Good job those *nutloos* Company creeps don't know a crawler from a char kettle. We can still move this thing."

John's face fell when Anna explained what she wanted them to do. "You must be going soft in the head. You can't be serious, surely?"

He wilted under Anna's stare. "Who's the karking driver here?"

"Aye," Seth grunted. "The *best* driver in town, by her own estimation of course." But she could sense in his tone that he was at least half convinced.

"And this won't be the first time I've done this."

"Sure. What have we got to lose?"

Half an hour later, with the rear cars unhitched and the one remaining crew car freewheeling behind them, driving on manual sticks seemed like a homecoming to Anna. She swallowed a lump in her throat as she threaded through the vehicle lock and out into the early afternoon sun. In all the rushing around, she'd forgotten her thought about sabotaging that other jet still hangared in South Two. "Eyes peeled, folks. There's still unfriendly people out here. Last thing we need is for them to chase us in that jet."

Her whole body trembled with anxiety as they rolled away from town. Only when they'd put a low ridge behind them, hiding them from direct sight of town, did she start to relax.

An hour later, after a circuitous path out of the valley, Sarah's rig showed flashes of yellow through shriveled trunks. Anna dared allow herself real hope. Transfer over to the intact train and they still had time to reach the way station before dusk.

This rig would have to be abandoned. It was too cranky and slow to drive. Only a fully working short train at full throttle would have a chance to make it. She felt a pang at the waste, but her spirits soared. They'd fucked the *vreemde's* plans. They'd still need to figure out what it was Galloway was searching for, but he'd found it and it promised riches. Simply knowing it was out there was enough. They'd retrace his steps somehow. They could freight in all the spare crawlers they needed after this.

And they were finally on their way home.

Nick staggered back and collapsed onto the dinette bench, his mouth hanging open. "You did what?" His face paled to an ashen grey.

The twins eased Ben into his accustomed seat at the head of the dinette and regarded Nick with blank stares.

With Sarah at the controls downstairs, the crawler rumbled into life, quivering in seeming eagerness to be gone. Anna wondered how Nick could have spent so long in ignorance, not realizing they were at a standstill. Dome dweller, she reminded herself. Rarely ventured onto the surface, and had no feel for the sounds and vibrations of a crawler on the move. And, to be fair, after a long day of travel, of subtle sensation underfoot, the memory of movement stayed with you fooling the senses for hours after.

"We spiked their plans," Anna said. "Those *vreemde* murdered Georgie and tried to kill me and Mikey. And you said yourself they're here to look for treasures in the winter mass."

"They're Company men," added Seth. "They're not doing it for our benefit."

"Aye," Ben growled. "Whate'er they dug up, they'd not a mind to share it with anyone. So we put them off the scent."

Nick's face crumpled. A damp trail down his cheek glistened. "I don't ..." he gasped. He tried again. "No. Not your fault. You can't possibly know what you've just done."

Ben frowned. "What gives me the overwhelming feeling ye've been keeping more back than we credited?"

Seth and John's faces hardened too. Anna looked from one to the other in confusion, certain that something had gone horribly wrong yet for the life of her she couldn't fathom *what*.

A whiff of cooking oil and the hum of strained ventilation gave the scene a surreal homely feel, but Anna felt like she was thrashing her way out of a dream, desperate to escape back to reality but unable to move, unable to scream for help.

"Methinks," Ben grated out at last, "it's time for the *full* story this time."

Nick gulped and nodded. Helga passed him a glass of water, which he slurped greedily. The glass rattled as he set it down on the table.

"Okay. Where to start?" He paused. "Some of it you know. Everything I told you is true enough. I was recruited to make sure the Company got access to the town and the sample site we'd identified."

"And ye still believe it was our own senior council?" asked Ben.

"Why would they betray us like this?" John blurted.

"Yes, and they didn't." Nick rubbed his eyes. His voice quavered. "It was our own people. They ... we ... fed information to the Company but it was vital they thought they were running a secret mission for *their* benefit."

"I'm curious," said Ben, "what is it ye all hoped to find out there?"

Nick rolled his eyes to the ceiling. "Oh, for kak's sake, not *hoping* to find. We found it years ago and we've been figuring out how to handle it." He licked his lips, a nervous flick of the tongue. "I can't impress on you enough the secrecy here." A pause. A gulp. "You know how dangerous wormhole travel is?"

A few shrugs, a few cautious nods. Anna shook her head, perplexed. Space flight brought them supplies and took away their harvests. Beyond that she'd long forgotten anything taught about its mechanics.

"You lot are karking hopeless cases," Nick blurted in frustration. "Trust me on this. Space travel is limited by how far we can jump without scrambling people's minds. They use powerful drugs to see them safely through the wormhole, drugs that support the body and especially the mind."

"This is textbook stuff." It was John's turn to roll his eyes. Anna remembered how he'd once started training as a ground-to-orbit pilot but flunked out in the end. Turned out he got chronically airsick. Not an endearing trait in a pilot. But trust him to follow Nick's ramblings. "Get to the point."

Nick took a deep breath. "Well, we found signs of drug precursors that would blow our existing drugs out the airlock. Some Jorvick noggins years back reckoned Sponge must have ways to protect itself from the depths of winter. The environmental stresses have some parallels with wormhole travel, so maybe something could be adapted for human use. They've been looking ever since. Finally found something."

"Why not just prospect ourselves? Why all the skulking around?"

"Think about it. What we found promises to extend our reach in space a hundredfold. That opens up a million times more volume of space than we can reach today. Imagine the possibilities."

"All the more reason, surely, to lay claim to it ourselves." John's eyes fairly gleamed.

Ben, however, sat back shaking his head sadly.

Nick glanced at him and nodded. "You see the problem too. I've seen too often how the Company works. If we'd come up with the discovery ourselves, there was no chance they'd let us keep a fair share. *Any* share, even. The colony agreement gives them too much stake as it is, and by the time their lawyers got finished we'd be no better off."

The dream of bettering the planet withered in Anna's mind.

"So, we figured we'd lure them in with the scent of riches impossible to ignore, and distract them from our real objective. The negotiations going on right now include a proposal to set us on a guaranteed timetable to independence. No ties to profits or performance or all the other factors the Company can manipulate in their favor. Not something they'd normally countenance, but with an eye on this discovery they'll agree, after working in some seemingly-innocent compensation for themselves–clauses to give them clear title to new discoveries. That's the bait."

John snorted in exasperation. "So, you high and mighty planners just gave up the chase?"

"We're not interested in the new drug. Yes, it would be nice, but it won't last. When this breaks, the Earth Nations will likely pounce and declare it a common good. The Company knows this, too, of course, but they can poise themselves to profit while the going's good, before the implications get too widely known. Something we could never do. Meanwhile, we'll cut the knot at last and be truly able to steer our own course."

Nick wiped his eyes once more and stared around the room. "But all that depended on them reporting back a *successful* find."

"Oh, kak!" It was Anna's turn to feel her legs collapsing under her. She stretched out a hand and guided herself to the nearest bunk while the cabin seemed to spin around her.

Dark despair clouded her vision. In the sudden silence, the weight of everyone's gazes pressed in on her. Anna lurched from the bunk and stumbled the few steps to the top of the stairs. She paused to regain her balance, then staggered down to the drive deck. Ignoring Sarah's questioning glance from the driver's seat as she rounded the corner, Anna hurried past the seats to the next flight down. She entered the tunnel leading back to the cargo cars and paused again to gather her breath.

Kak! Kak, kak, kak! What a mess.

She needed to be alone like never before in her life. How could she face them again? How could she face anyone, when news of this defeat spread? It was *her* idea to sabotage the survey. Her determination to kick back at the people who'd killed Georgie and tried to kill her and Mikey. The others had been happy to go along with it, despite the mounting danger of further delays, but *she* had been the driver behind this act of revenge.

She'd spend the rest of her life hearing real or imagined whisperings wherever she went. *That's Anna*, they'd say. *We could have been freed of Company control, but* she *futzed it all up.*

Maybe she could ride out the afternoon on top of one of the cars. On the trek, many people took refuge up there from the press of people. Even among dome dwellers, tempers frayed after days in such close confines. People respected each other's privacy up there.

Through the cramped mid-deck of the cargo car and into the next tunnel. In the next car, she found where Nick, Seth and John had made space to bed down.

This deck was half empty, she remembered, because the lower cargo hoist was futzed. Good for people looking for an empty shelf to turn into a sleeping rack. A shelf that should have been filled with valuable equipment with space on the trek being so precious. But—tears blurred her sight at the thought—the usefulness of this car was limited by yet more futzed-up machinery.

More machinery that they could easily repair if only the *stüg debeel karking* Company stopped playing futzed-up *money* games with their lives.

No!

Every day's delay increased their peril at these latitudes, but there were bigger things at stake for the whole planet. She was *not* going down in the town's chronicles as the one who let this happen.

Fired up once more, Anna stormed back through the train. She calmed her breathing down as she entered the drive cab.

"You okay?" Sarah asked, worry etched in her expression. Seth and John hovered in the far corner. Looked like they'd been talking.

"Hardly," Anna spat. "Turn this rig around. We have to go back. Again."

"So, what's the plan?" John asked yet again.

"Working on it," Anna gritted out for the tenth time. No, she had no idea what they were going to do. Somehow they needed to put the *vreemde* back on track again. Maybe they could swap the samples back. She'd only hidden them, not destroyed them. But how to do that without being discovered?

Well, as far as the *vreemde* were concerned, the locals were still in town. They hadn't been spotted leaving, or surely that jet would have come after them again. So a bit more sabotage wouldn't be suspicious. But tricky to engineer. They'd be on the lookout.

The cab was crowded. They'd left Ben and Sarah back on the ridge in the good crawler, but everyone else was standing over Anna's shoulders, expecting her to drive a manual rig *and* come up with a plan at the same time.

At last she spat out, "I'm kinda busy driving. We need to switch the samples back. You guys figure something out." She bit her lip. She hadn't meant to shout, but here they were, heading back into town when she longed for them to be on their way to safety. She had a right to be cranky.

The next ten minutes passed in strained silence as she wrestled the rig's steering against the slope. The town of Serendipity approached, nestled in the valley ahead.

The entrance to North One loomed large and Anna slowed to a crawl. Above the muted rumble of wheels, a distant whine rose in pitch.

Anna knew *that* sound. "Incoming!" she yelped. She jostled with the sticks, frantically lining up with the vehicle lock. She'd only get one shot at this before the jet circled around town. Why didn't she remember to disable it when she had the chance? Of course, she was trying to save Ben, but–

Kak!

The crawler nosed into the lock, too close to the left. The front wheels made it in, but the car behind ground against the side. Anna swore and backed up, knowing she had no effective way to steer.

Forward again. A bit farther this time, but the car still stuck against the side of the tunnel.

The jet must have spotted them by now. Would it fire on the garage? The intruders wanted to leave without trace. A blasted dome would be hard to explain. Would they land instead?

Either way, Anna felt trapped and helpless in here. Either way, their presence was hardly a secret now.

"Everyone out. Lower lock should be usable." Thank the skies there was still clearance down the right hand side of the narrow tunnel.

Into the garage, pushing through the two remaining sets of curtains. Further from harm if the jet fired on the crawler.

Anna paused and caught her breath. They still had their spike guns, and surely they outnumbered the intruders by now. She exchanged looks with Seth. "I'm done with running."

He gazed back, then glanced at John. They both nodded. The twins' eyes gleamed. Five of them. She wasn't counting Nick, and she wasn't risking Mikey in a fight.

"If they land, we're taking them. I don't think they'll shoot up the town. All this is still supposed to be secret."

They hurried back out to the surface through one of the side air-locks. Anna scanned the sky, eyes and ears straining. The jet was circling somewhere, but hidden behind the curve of the garage. It didn't seem to be approaching. It seemed to be over on the far side of town. The knot in her shoulders eased. They hadn't been spotted.

So what *was* the jet doing up there?

Oh, kak!

Anna sprinted away from the garage and looked behind her. As she ran, the ridge from where they'd spied on the town yesterday came into view above the domes. The ridge where they'd left Sarah and Ben ... and the other crawler.

A tiny black speck circled in the distance.

"No!" Anna screamed. Others rushed to join her, but all they could do was watch, helpless, while the jet lined up an attack.

Flashes of blinding light stitched the sky above the hills. The jet vanished from sight, the sound receding then gaining again. More bolts hammered down, accompanied a few seconds later by rumbling thunder.

Oily smoke coiled into the sky beyond the ridge.

Anna staggered, saved from falling by someone's hands at her back. "Sarah," she gasped. "Ben."

"That's not possible," Nick muttered. "They couldn't have seen that crawler from down here, and they didn't come after *us*. What made them take off like that?"

The jet rose high in the sky, circled twice, then lazily banked to the south-west. The roar of its engines rose to a scream and it abruptly picked up speed, arrowing into the stratosphere and vanishing from sight.

A cold logic gripped Anna's mind. The answer was clear. "They were already leaving. They must have seen the crawler from the air and realized they could strand us here. But they were leaving." The circle of faces blurred through her tears.

"They finished their tests on the fake samples," Nick said. "They're reporting the results to Jorvick. We're too late."

Nick's words knifed through Anna's thoughts, but her gaze never left the ominous stain on the afternoon sky above the ridge. This couldn't be happening. She couldn't grasp it. Denial battled in her mind with the visible evidence, but the evidence was nothing more than a cloud of smoke. That could mean anything. Maybe the crawler up there was salvageable still. She had to see it.

Anna raced back to the crawler, squeezing past the car still jutting half-way out of the garage. Rough strips of heavy flax hanging in the entrance tunnel ripped her sleeve as she shouldered her way through.

Up in the cab, she rammed the crawler into reverse, heedless of the screech of panels against the side of the tunnel.

A tangle of disconnected thoughts battled inside her while she turned the vehicle around and guided it away from the garage. Sarah. Ben. The crawler. How would they get home? Maybe Sarah had escaped. Maybe she'd managed to drive to safety.

With the back of a hand she angrily brushed away more tears. People ran alongside and tried to flag her down. She was sure some had followed her into the tunnel too, but she'd been running too fast, heedless of the risks. Anna was barely aware of driving, of the dips and bumps in the terrain and the pitfalls she avoided without conscious thought.

Maybe the smoke was coming from Sponge itself. But she'd seen surface fires and none had ever looked like this. Black, greasy. The smoke rose and flattened, hanging like a pall over the valley.

A terrified part of her quailed at the risk she was taking. This vehicle was cranky to drive, but it was a working rig. It was their last hope. As long as it could make the travel from one way station to the next they could still get out of here. As long as the battered wheels and drive held up. It was no different from what she and Mikey and Georgie had planned to do, however slim the chance.

They could still make it.

But not if that jet returned and found her out here, her rational side screamed at her. Too risky!

But Anna had never heeded that voice before and she wasn't going to now. The urgent need to *know* overwhelmed her.

At least she had the sense to take a wide loop north of town and seek a gentle path to the ridge above. She was not that reckless. Close, but not quite.

At last, even that lonely voice of caution silenced as she emerged onto high ground and the smoldering forest came into sight.

It was as bad as she'd feared. Yellow panels, blackened at the edges, littered the ground ahead of her. It looked like the rear of the crawler had taken the brunt of the air strike. The rear two cars had been completely obliterated. Only twisted, smoking shells remained. The next car was gutted, its splayed sides cradled a wreckage of harvesting equipment.

Numb, Anna brought her own rig to a halt while she tried to take in the devastation.

Oily black smoke coiled through the shattered windows of the cab.

There was nothing salvageable here.

A pang, as she remembered this was *her* rig. Her cab. Gone now.

She jolted herself out of grief. Where was Sarah? Ben?

Ben would have been in the living quarters at the top of the cab. Could he have survived?

Sarah, she knew, was supposed to be keeping watch on the town from the ridge to her left. Once Anna was safely under cover, they'd agreed Sarah would join them in the northern garage. It was too late in the afternoon to leave for the way station, and she needed to get under cover before nightfall.

So where was she?

Anna scanned the ground around her, but there was no-one in sight. Last night's windstorm had scoured the ridge of yesterday's snow, and there weren't even tracks to follow. Now, ironically, her view was obscured by fresh flakes swirling white through the black eddies.

A wisp of smoke curled from the top of the cab. Anna frowned. The roof looked undamaged and there were no openings up there ... apart from the airlock.

She leapt from her seat and bolted for the outdoors. Tendrils of Sponge, the fringe of the forest, caught at her feet as she stumbled across the twenty meters of open ground to the burning crawler. Heart pounding, Anna clambered up the nearest outside ladder.

Smoke engulfed her as she passed the driver's level. The side of the cab radiated heat.

On top of the cab, she found the airlock hatch open. She peered down. There was Sarah, propping Ben up against the ladder. White faces, streamed in sweat, peered back at her.

Anna's legs buckled in relief. She wanted to weep, but they were all still in danger. With an effort she brought her trembling limbs back under control.

"Good to see you," Sarah gasped. "Only way out. Fresh air here, at least."

Made sense. With the cabin on fire and filling with smoke, the airlock offered a temporary shelter. "Can we get Ben up the ladder?" Getting down the outside was a problem for later.

"Maybe, with both of us."

"How long do we have? Can you hold out down there for a few minutes?"

"Fire's on the lower decks. At least we're sealed off from the smoke here."

Anna nodded and clambered back down to the ground. She returned a few minutes later with a coil of rope and a climbing harness. Thank the skies Seth kept his maintenance bay well stocked. A cold lump formed in her stomach at the thought of how lucky they were Ben and his girls hadn't plundered the stores for anything other than items of immediate use for the trek back at the way station.

With Ben strapped into the harness, Anna hauling from above while Sarah guided from below, they helped him out onto the roof. Anna was shocked by his appearance. Even allowing for the sickly light filtering through the spreading pall, his skin looked sallow. His breathing was labored and his movements weak. He needed to be resting, not hauling his ass up and down like he'd been doing for the past hours.

They needed to get him to a medical center.

Nearest working medical facility, three thousand kilometers south, and two weeks away by wonky crawler.

One problem at a time.

They rested a minute on top of the cab. Anna became aware of cloying smoke starting to work through her mask, and the roof was like an oven beneath the soles of her boots. Fat snowflakes fell and hissed on the decking.

Anna took the strain on the rope while Sarah went ahead, guiding Ben down the ten-meter drop to the ground.

Once again, they hauled Ben into the maintenance bay of her cab. "Home from home," he muttered as they settled him down.

The relief at finding Sarah and Ben alive faded as they rumbled away from the pyre and headed back to town. It was replaced by an aching emptiness. After all they'd been through, they were back to square one, facing deepening darkness as Sponge sank slowly into standard years of winter.

Their one good vehicle was gone, and, with the rattles and irregular lurches from its damaged wheels, Anna wondered how far this wreck would carry them. She was starting to wonder if they'd even make it the few kilometers down the hill back to town.

Her hands were starting to cramp on the twin joysticks, and a deep throb in her temples told of the relentless vigilance needed to keep this rig on course. Even if the vehicle could make the journey, could *they*?

There was no sign of life outside North One. Anna had thought they might leave someone on lookout, but the growing blizzard was a grim deterrent. Fat snowflakes up on the high ground had given way to ice-filled drops lashing the cab windows in a roaring gale.

She wondered what the others had been up to while she was gone. Not just sitting around on their backsides, she was sure of that.

With the jet gone, gone too were her ill-formed notions of setting Nick's plans for Elysium back on track. The goal now was back to simple survival. The others would surely have come to the same conclusion. Transport was one thing. There was also the small matter of any remaining hostiles in town.

She bypassed the northern garage and headed instead to East One, where she and Ben had entered town last time. Domes loomed ghostly grey shadows in swirling white.

With no threat of a jet breathing down her back, she took the vehicle lock slowly and carefully, threading through the tunnel with barely a scrape.

As they'd done before, they left Ben settled in the maintenance bay guarding the lower airlock. Working on a hunch, Anna led Sarah through town to the assay shed. That was where all the activity had centered. If anywhere, that was where the *vreemde* would be found, and where Seth, John, Mikey and the twins would likely be headed.

Anna carried the last spike gun and a measly pair of pitons. Sarah armed herself with a kitchen knife.

They crept forward until they reached the lock to the assay shed. Anna peered through the door, and listened. She heard low voices beyond, somewhere out of sight behind the row of offices.

She strained harder to make out the voices, and then risked cracking the door open. She flung it wide when she recognized Seth and John talking.

The workshop held an unexpected sight. John, Seth, Mikey and the twins stood in a circle with spike drivers loaded and menacing. In the middle of the floor lay the man Anna had killed. It seemed he was left in full view as a reminder of what their makeshift weapons could do.

It seemed the point was being made.

Huddled against the far workbench, three *vreemde* sat on the floor. They looked terrified.

"Anna!" Seth's voice held a mix of joy and anger. "What the kak did you take off like that for?" He glanced behind Anna. "Sarah! Thank the skies you're safe. Where's Ben?"

"Safe. For now." Sarah's voice held immeasurable weariness. "But he needs treatment. I don't know how long he'll last without proper attention. The crawler's toast, though. We're not driving out of here."

"All we've got left is that beaten-up wreck sitting in East One." Anna let that news sink in. She felt numbed by defeat. Waves of fatigue rolled through her. For a while, the only sound was the drumming of sleet against the dome high above their heads.

She risked a look at her friends, at their faces echoing her own despair. She caught Mikey's eye. Without being aware of how she got there, she found herself alongside him, pulling him into a hug.

A movement at the corner of her eye broke the spell. One of the prisoners had eased himself up from the floor. He blanched and lowered himself at Anna's glare.

Empty of emotion, Anna forced herself back to the here-and-now, to practicalities. She jerked her head towards the prisoners. "What's going on here?"

"These are the last three," said Seth, wearily. "Question is, what to do with them? They could still cause trouble."

"Would too, given half the chance," added Nick from the back of the circle. "They're in deep trouble when they get out of here. The Company won't take kindly to this *debeel* futzed-up mission."

"We felt it would be doing them a kindness to kill them now." John's voice was soft.

For a moment Anna thought he might be serious. This wasn't the John she knew. He turned towards her and quirked an eyebrow. She relaxed. He wouldn't kill in cold blood. But, she agreed, the three captives didn't need to know that. Better not, in fact. Nick was right, they'd try to regain the upper hand at the first opportunity, and they'd shown how little they cared for poor colonists' lives. Right now they seemed docile, but it was only a matter of time.

Kak! What to do with them? The more she thought about it, the less Anna liked the idea of having them anywhere nearby. For a brief moment, she wondered if *she* had it in her to execute them. She'd had to run for her life from these people. They'd have not hesitated, and they wouldn't hesitate now if the tables were turned. What did Anna owe them?

She raised her spike gun, finger twitching on the trigger, imagining the few millimeters' movement needed. The swirling in the pit of her stomach gave her the answer she needed. She gestured the three to stand.

"Put them in South Two. Leave them rations but take their masks." At Seth's questioning look, she said, "They've got power and clean air in there, and they can't go anywhere without masks. The garages either side are poisoned now, and the only other tunnel back into town is ruptured. Galloway put his last bullet through the skin."

———— ◆ ◆ ————

Jennifer Steel gazed sourly at the technician cowering in front of her. One of Galloway's lackeys, the woman was still in grubby outdoor wear, a face mask dangling from her neck, wringing wet and dripping on the floor. Jennifer grimaced as she took in streaks of grease up the front of the overalls, and she would swear that was blood staining the sleeves. This backwoods world had no police force to speak of, but she'd still have to bring in her own crew to ensure her suite held no incriminating traces.

"You have news."

The technician ... no, that was a pilot's insignia on her shoulders ... twisted her hands in front of her. Stupid little woman. She probably imagined she would simply pass on her message to someone way down the food chain. Someone less intimidating. Surely she realized the importance of this assignment. Whatever she had to say needed to be said to Jennifer, in person.

Jennifer ignored for now the impudence of sending a *pilot* to convey the results. It should have been Galloway in person, or at least the senior analyst. Someone who knew what they were talking about. This disrespect was intolerable! What were they thinking? And the suspense was tying her up in knots so tight she could barely mask her impatience.

"Speak."

The pilot gulped. "Supper is cold."

Nothing more.

An icy wash drenched Jennifer's mind. It took all of her schooling to hide her shock.

She was tempted to ask her to repeat the message, but stopped herself just in time. The code was unambiguous. It couldn't be misheard or mistaken for any casual utterance.

Galloway's search had failed.

Jennifer nodded once, then glanced at her guards. "Deal with this one." She tried to keep the ice out of her voice. There was no need for loose ends to realize they were being tidied up.

She turned away as the guards hustled the wretch through the door.

A part of her rejoiced in Galloway's come-uppance. Precocious little upstart. But against that, she realized she'd truly been excited at the possibilities. Even though the necessary climb-down in the negotiations would have signaled the end of her career, the discovery of a revolutionary new drug precursor hiding in the winter depths of Elysium would have made the Company rich beyond belief. She was sure she could have negotiated some crumbs from that lavish table.

Her mind flicked back to unfortunate Don Kozyr, her financial analyst who'd succumbed to the extremes of wormhole travel. Even their best drugs still made travel a dangerous prospect, and the dangers grew the further you tried to jump. Who wouldn't get excited at the thought of safely expanding their spacefaring reach?

It wasn't the sale of the drug itself. The Company would have—albeit short lived—exclusive access to volumes of space far beyond current boundaries.

But, like so many dreams, it was all in vain. An elusive promise that came to nothing.

For a moment, the emptiness, the disappointment, threatened to crush her. She steadied herself against the back of a chair and blinked away dark spots in her vision. She was dimly aware of her aide, Nikolai, hovering in the background with concern on his face. She waved him away.

Only then did the enormity of the message hit home, and its implications for her, personally. Galloway had failed. So she needed to make the traditional colonial agreement work. The one that she and her team had been so hopelessly outmaneuvered on.

She'd arrived on Elysium planning to take them to the cleaners and ensure an undisputed income stream for the next century. But with Galloway's bombshell she'd had to tread a fine line between two credible alternatives. That was bad enough. She'd been forced to pussy-foot around the terms in order to make that version of the agreement appear reasonable in comparison to the radical rewrite they'd placed on the table as an alternative. But add in the Company's woefully misleading intelligence on the true goals and values of the colonists, and they'd surrendered a far sweeter deal than the colonists had any right to expect. Jennifer could never live down this failure.

Sure, her team had spent the past few days surreptitiously reinforcing the dense tangle of clauses that surrounded the substantive terms themselves. All the criteria and conditions, the notwithstandings, heretofores and hereafters, the pegs to market conditions and acceptance criteria that the Company could game. The logical dependencies were so interwoven it would take an army of analysts to fathom out that a clause that seemed to promise one thing would actually have the opposite effect, or be so hemmed in that it could never take effect in the first place. There were enough loopholes and poison pills woven into the legalese that achieving independence would remain tantalizingly out of reach for a long time to come, but it was hardly her best work.

She squared her shoulders and tried to reassure herself that it was the best anyone could have managed given the constraints.

Now she had a negotiation to win.

"Ben's not doing too good." John's hoarse whisper jerked Anna out of a restless doze. She was curled in the driver's seat, a familiar place and somewhere she could usually sleep as well as in any bed.

John's shadowed face was unreadable, but his words and the alarm in his voice finally broke through her sleep-drugged confusion.

Kak!

They'd already been through their predicament endlessly while the night's gales roared across the valley far above their heads. They might be able to scavenge a few spare parts, tools, and supplies to keep the rig and themselves going for the long trek.

At least if they could make a few days' travel, to one of the way stations with a comms shed tapped into the landline, they could raise Laverne and maybe meet halfway.

It was a desperate chance, but seemed to be the only one they had.

Nick had pointed out that when the pilot reported in to Jorvick, the Company would surely send someone out to collect the remainder of their team. They must have had plans for cleaning up and leaving the town seemingly undisturbed. As far as Anna was concerned, that was all the more reason to leave, pronto. The Company would hardly rescue them, given the lengths they'd already gone to, to shut them up.

In short, they were futzed.

And on top of it all, even if they could save themselves, none of their choices would help Ben in time.

"The bullet went through." Anna was sure they'd gone over this already, but her mind was too muggy to be sure. "It's not still in there, is it?"

"For sure. There's an exit wound. But I don't know what it hit on the way. I'm really worried about internal bleeding."

Anna frowned. Her thinking came back into sharper focus. "He lost blood before we got a dressing on. He's getting plasma. No signs of sepsis?"

John shook his head. "He'd be dead by now."

This was more than about Ben, Anna realized. John was feeling responsible, and driving himself frantic with frustration. "I know you're the designated medic on Seth's crew, but we all have field training. We've all been over this for hours. You've made him as comfortable as you can. Anything else is beyond what we can treat out here."

John pottered morosely around the cab, poking at shattered screens as if he could magic a set of replacements through sheer force of worry.

"John!" Anna cringed inwardly at her sharp tone, but this needed firm handling. "You've done all you can for tonight. Whatever we decide to do tomorrow, you need to be sharp. Get some sleep."

Mikey stirred at her feet. She hadn't yet fathomed how he could make himself comfortable on the hard floor like that, but he seemed to take some cheer in the view from the sloping wraparound windows. Like a fabled king surveying his kingdom from a castle eyrie, he'd spent hours mesmerized by the flowing landscape on their travels.

Not that there was anything visible right now, in the dead of night. No lights broke the inky black of the powered-down garage. There weren't even multicolored console lights to lift the gloom in the wrecked cab. Only a dim red nightlight from the stairs gave a wash to show the way.

One of the twins shifted in the starboard nav seat and muttered something under her breath. The other was down below with Ben. There seemed to be nothing more to say. Eventually John made his way upstairs.

Anna tossed and turned in her seat. Sleep was clearly not on the cards tonight. Silence gradually descended as the night storm receded. She wondered how long they had until the turbulent atmosphere flipped fully into its early autumn pattern, a ferocious prelude to the calm and deadly deep freeze of winter. Maybe a few days, maybe a couple of weeks. The exact moment was impossible to predict, but when it did, all traffic at these latitudes would become impossible for months.

Crawlers nearing the calmer belt around the equator would be okay, but if they didn't make good progress they'd be caught in the violence and literally swept off the face of the planet.

Maybe they should take their chances with whatever craft the Company sent to pick up the remnants of their exploration team.

Maybe they could surprise and overpower the pilot. She reminded herself that the tables were turned from when the *vreemde* were chasing a scared and unarmed mother and son.

Then again, that pilot in the scramjet would report the debacle to her superiors. They'd come back ready for trouble. And Galloway had shown them they had access to proper weapons, and a readiness to use them. In her mind, the tables turned again.

Anna jerked awake. Somehow she'd dozed off after all, until a clear and blinding thought pierced her fitful dreams. Heart pounding, she crept from her seat, picked up her mask, a flashlight and a heavy out-door jacket, and tiptoed downstairs.

She had to step over–Clara? or Helga? She couldn't tell–curled up on the floor of the maintenance store next to Ben. Ben's eyes glittered in the red night light. Anna pressed a finger to her lips as she passed him and opened the airlock. It was hard to tell in the burgundy twilight, but it seemed he managed a faint smile.

Or was it a grimace of pain?

They had to get proper medical help tomorrow. Not weeks or even days.

———

Jennifer Steel froze. The room, the dome, the city around her had vanished. Far beneath her, hard bedrock was visible. The hundreds of meters in between was filled with nothing more substantial than soap bubbles. If she moved, they'd pop. She'd fall.

The planet watched her.

It was the same as when she'd stood on the surface and touched Sponge with her bare hand. That feeling of energy, alive and aware.

This was a dream, she realized, but so real. And was she dreaming that she was dreaming? Surely your true self was never really aware of the dream. That awareness itself was only ever an artifact of the dream world.

Her head hurt thinking about it.

She needed to wake up.

Her dream self thought she was already awake and was pondering the meaning of the dream-within-a-dream.

The precarious position, she could see, was a metaphor for her own career. Whatever happened now, whatever move she made, she was finished and she had a long way to fall.

Too obvious! C'mon, Steel, you used to be more subtle than that.

You ... need ... to ... fucking ... wake up!

The bubbles popped.

Jennifer Steel woke, drenched in sweat. It was real this time. She was back in the real world, and yet it felt less solid than the dream she'd just left. On shaking legs she hobbled to the shower room and sponged her face with cold water.

She shivered and tried to bring the world back into focus.

It wasn't all bad, she reflected. She gave herself a wry smile in the mirror, trying to bolster her own confidence.

It didn't work. The traditional colonial treaty was a pale shadow of the terms she could have screwed out of them given a free hand and complete information. On an absolute scale, it was a tolerably competent piece of work, but the Company didn't pay her for tolerably competent. The bitter truth was, it was a long way from anything she herself would deem acceptable, and the Company president would know it.

———

In the cold light of dawn, eight people lined up on Serendipity's east dock, breath steaming through their masks. Ice rimed the dock, making the footing treacherous. A blanket of white glowed in Big Red's sullen light reflected off the undersides of scudding clouds.

"You've got to be out of your *nutloos* mind." That was Nick's considered opinion.

Anna studied the others. Seemed Nick's opinion wasn't his alone. She'd expected nothing less. "I've been out of my mind living in fear this past week. I guess I'm getting used to dealing with insane situations thrown at me."

She turned to face the boxy survey craft snugged against the dock. She'd gone out to check on it last night while her wild thoughts formed into a plan. Her tracks were still plainly etched in the frosted ground. Too bulky to fit through a vehicle lock, it had been lashed down securely against the elements. Whatever else they may be, Anna reflected, the *vreemde* were competent explorers. They'd done a good job.

"We can split up. Whatever else happens, I'm taking Ben in this aircraft. That doesn't mean anyone else has to risk it. Sarah can drive the crawler. It's a long shot but maybe you'll make it that way."

Nick opened his mouth. Anna glared him to silence. She gave herself a mental high five. She'd always looked up to Nick, to his place in the town's pecking order, the one with all the wisdom, who always seemed to know best. A week ago, she'd never have dared argue with him. Of course, he was probably right too. She had to be out of her mind. "Or you can wait for the Company to drop by and take your chances with them. But here's the thing. Ben will be dead by then. John's done what he can for him, but he won't last another night. I'm not giving up on him."

The twins regarded her with disturbingly blank expressions. They were the ones she was most afraid of. Either they saw her as a threat, pointlessly risking their dad's life, or as his only chance. They would either be for her, up to the hilt and damn the others, or against. There were no half measures with the de Vries girls.

"You still have your choices. Nothing's changed since yesterday, and nothing I do will alter your chances whichever path you choose, but know this—my mind is set."

"You can't fly!" Nick's negativity was starting to get on her nerves.

"Never driven a cobbled-together crawler on manual sticks before either. First time for everything."

"Besides," John said, "I *do* know how to fly. Anna won't be alone."

She gave John a grateful smile. She hadn't talked this over with him, but he'd been crucial to any chance of success. Up to now, she'd consoled herself that a high-speed crash would be a quicker death than hypothermia.

As one, the twins nodded and took station on either side of Anna. They must have some kind of telepathy going, she thought. Would explain a lot.

"Room in that crate for one more?" Seth asked. "I'm not letting you out of my sight again."

"Two," said Sarah. "Sorry, Nick. If you like, I can teach you to drive. Not much to get the hang of."

Mikey had already sidled over to stand by Anna. No way were they getting separated again, no matter the odds.

Nick huffed. "What about those three in South Two?"

"What about them?"

"One of them might have piloting skills."

"Don't care. I'm not sharing a craft with any of them."

"So, we're leaving them here?"

"We'll notify the authorities when we get back. It's up to the Company whether or not they send a party in to pick them up."

———

"As we've made clear over the past few days, the Company is more than willing to accept reasonable terms." Jennifer ignored a contemptuous huff from someone in the administrative support and research team at the back of the Elysium negotiators. "We take the future of the people on this planet very seriously. If Elysium became independent and then failed to remain self-sufficient, that would paint a very bleak future for the millions of people who now call this home."

Jennifer wasn't really speaking to the colonists. Her audience was the group of ENCOA observers to her right–in particular the fastidious chief facilitator–and the media crews recording proceedings to her left.

"Accordingly, we feel that traditional measures of a colony's viability remain the best approach. We have concluded that we are not prepared to entertain the fixed term path to independence. That risks cutting the colony loose before it achieves financial self-sufficiency."

With their preferred door finally shut, after so long holding out faint hope, the members of the Elysium contingent showed a mixture of emotions. Sadness, disgust, resignation. Jennifer paused a moment to bring her own reactions under control. Her own feelings of failure, of complete disorientation and loss of control after being manipulated by Galloway into an untenable position, still threatened to drown her. But she remained professional, and was sure her own expression gave nothing away. She permitted herself a satisfying glimmer of contempt at the lack of control shown opposite. Those small-town negotiators really needed to curb their emotions.

"In recognition of the colony's long history with us, and as a token of goodwill, we will accede to the adjustment to section twenty-three regarding fair market rates for shipping, and we will allow the inclusion of section fifteen permitting the open sourcing of essential machinery. These are two key provisions that have been a clear source of contention in recent decades."

Again, she studied the faces opposite. She felt she could read them like an open book. She had them. These concessions had been allowed for in her thinking, and the agreement was still rife with legal traps that would keep them wriggling for the next century.

Seeing no other movement to address the assembly, she turned to the facilitator. "If both sides are in agreement with the substantive terms, I propose we finalize the treaty for signature without further delay."

The chief negotiator nodded, and gazed to the table opposite.

The head of the Elysium contingent cleared his throat. "The terms are acceptable to us, also. However, before we prepare the final document for signature, we noticed a few extremely minor irregularities in the wording of a few clauses. I'm sure these were simple oversights during the course of drafting and re-drafting. Bringing them back to more standard phrasing I'm sure is just a technicality, and one which, I'm equally sure, the Company can have no reasonable objections to."

With the media from two dozen planets focused on her response, Jennifer was at a loss for words. She felt the bottom drop out of her world.

Chapter 34

"So," Anna whispered, "how much flying time *did* you clock before you ..."

"Got sick?" John gave her a wry grin. "I was top of my class until then." He turned his attention back to the de-icing controls. Water trickled down the outside of the canopy.

He hadn't really answered the question. Anna decided this was not the time to pry. She perched on the armrest of the co-pilot's seat while John settled in the pilot's. At least, that's what she assumed. The layout here was nothing like a crawler's cab.

A smell of sawdust and stale food leaked through her mask, like a clan kitchen that hadn't been properly cleaned at the end of the previous season. John tapped the controls. A few screens came to life and a whiff of ozone caught at Anna's throat. She stared in dismay at the wrecked console. John had assured them all it was only navigation. All the essential flight controls were still working.

He turned to face Anna. "You realize, though, I've never flown anything like *this* before?"

"Keep it down, guys," Sarah muttered from behind her. "Everyone's nervous enough as it is."

Anna gave her a weak smile. To John she said, "But you do know what you're doing?"

"In theory ... yes. I can get this crate off the ground and flying in the right direction."

"But ...?"

"Getting down again might be a problem. Most of the instrumentation is shot, so we'll be flying entirely by eye."

Anna gazed at the panels Mikey had smashed, and exchanged looks with Sarah. She then glanced through the door to the cargo hold where the rest of their party were bracing themselves as best they could. They'd emptied the hold of most of the equipment, leaving a heap of survey, climbing, digging and cutting tools on the crawler dock.

Seth slammed the outer hatch shut and gave her a thumbs-up.

"One problem at a time," she muttered.

Sarah climbed up into the spotter's seat, with its observation bubble above and behind the pilot.

The engines roared to life. The craft shuddered around them.

"Here goes," John yelled. "Strap in and hold tight back there."

Without warning, the craft wallowed into the air. One landing strut clattered against the loading dock. John swore and corrected.

Anna's stomach did somersaults and she understood why John had abandoned his flying career.

They cleared the dock and hovered high above town, buffeted one way then the other in fitful gusts.

"We've got to make tracks. Taking off and landing burns a shitload of fuel compared to level flight. And I can't see how much we've got left, with all these gauges busted up." He circled the town, now little more than a rash of blisters covering the valley floor. He looked expectantly at Anna and up at Sarah. "You realize I'm depending on you to navigate us."

Anna peered out the cockpit window, taking in the ground already impossibly far below. Her stomach heaved again.

Sarah pointed the way over to where the crawler still smoldered. "Stick to the ridge. We'll have to look out for landmarks and follow the trail south."

John eased the controls forward and Anna felt herself pressed into her seat. The ground rolled past. Eerily, the roar of the engines faded to a soft rush of white noise and relative hush descended on the cabin.

"There," said John with a cheeky grin. "Not so bad now, is it?"

After a few minutes, the uplands of Sponge rose to meet them. John leveled off five hundred meters above the highest point and lined up their course along the back of the spine. Vast ribs the color of bleached bone meandered away to the south. From this elevation the network of Sponge's support and circulatory system was clear, long parallel hills kilometers wide rolled one after another to the western horizon.

A dark patch ahead caught Anna's eye, a fine comb of parallel shadows etched across the ground in the midmorning sun. With a shock she realized it was the first way station. Already?

Anna glanced back through the open door. Sporadic rumbles and rattles broke the steady hiss of rushing air. She couldn't see Ben from here, but the silhouettes of the twins hovered close by, keeping their dad comfortable against the bulkhead behind her. "How long, do you think?" she whispered.

John also glanced back for a moment and lowered his voice. "We can't make hypersonic like those scramjets. This tub's strictly subsonic. Maybe a thousand klicks?"

"So, about three hours to Laverne, maybe only another four to Jorvick." She chewed the inside of her cheek.

Sarah gaped down at her. "What do you mean, Jorvick? We need to get Ben to the closest city. That's Laverne by anyone's reckoning."

"But Jorvick is where the talks are happening."

"Are you out of your karking mind?" Sarah hissed.

Anna did a mental calculation. "If we cut south-west we'd shave a couple of hours off."

"With no navigation? You really have lost it. We lose sight of the trail we may never find our way back."

John shook his head. "You said this was to save Ben, not to help Nick's futzed-up plans."

"We can do both." But the protest was half-hearted. Guilt tore at Anna. They wouldn't be in this mess at all if it hadn't been for her. Ben got hurt because of her. If she hadn't faced off against Galloway, he'd still be alright. If she hadn't got so fired up about wrecking the Company's plans they'd be safe in a crawler half way to Laverne by now.

If ... if ... if ...

John seemed to sense her black mood. "Let the Company and the planners work out their own mess. After all, this is their doing, not yours. What's done is done, Anna. We gotta look after our own now."

"We've got to look after *ourselves* first." Sarah pointed ahead. A cold pit seemed to open up in Anna's belly. It was still only a faint smudge on the horizon, but she knew those cloud formations all too well.

Sarah and John did, too. Both outdoors people, they were familiar with all the atmospheric theatrics Sponge could produce.

Sarah swallowed hard. John blanched. "It's right in our path," he said.

At the speed they were traveling, the mass of cloud grew at a terrifying rate. Within minutes, they could pick out the vast swirling eddies as the turbulent layers of Sponge's atmosphere collided.

It stretched from one horizon to the other.

"No way around," John muttered. "We'll have to gain height."

Even as he spoke, he eased the controls back and the ground dropped away with dizzying speed.

"Hold tight back there," Anna yelled through the hatch. "Storms ahead." She belatedly reached for her seat's harness, seeing Sarah grappling with her own buckles. Only John had strapped in before takeoff. A pilot's habit, Anna guessed. Nobody had ever seen the need to fit harnesses in crawlers.

Just as the buckle clicked into place, an invisible hand flipped the craft into a barrel roll.

"Kak!" John yelped. "Was afraid of that." He wrestled with the controls. The ground whirled closer through the cockpit windows. Anna squeezed her eyes shut, fighting to keep her roiling stomach under control. It seemed an eternity before the mad gyrations eased, and John managed to break them out of the deadly spin.

Anna risked opening her eyes again, and wished she hadn't. The towering cloudbank was on top of them. John had brought the aircraft around to the west, keeping the clouds to their left. Grey tendrils whipped at them, rattling the cockpit windows with shards of ice. Lightning lit the depths.

"What happened?" Anna asked. "Why aren't we flying over that crap?"

"Wind shear," John muttered. "Somewhere up there we hit a ceiling. Layer of air moving supersonic compared to us. Some craft have doppler instruments to detect it. Doubt this one ever did."

A crack and a blinding flash. The cabin lights and the few remaining instruments went dark.

"Double kak," John said. "Another hazard up here. Lucky the engine electronics are well shielded."

More lighting split the sky around them. Those boiling clouds seemed to be getting closer.

John followed the line of Anna's gaze. "No use trying to outrun this. We're getting sucked into it, just a matter of picking our moment. Warn the passengers. It's going to get rougher before we're through and I need some help on the controls."

Anna leaned back in her seat to confer with Seth, who'd tied himself to the bulkhead with a makeshift harness improvised from climbing gear. They were as secure as could be expected, and Ben was hanging in there though the buffeting pained him. The stream of harvester invective from behind her told Anna he still had fight left in him.

It was only then that she processed John's last words. She turned back to him, feeling faint.

"I need a steady hand on the steering," he explained, "so I can focus on thrust vectors."

"But I've never flown before," Anna hissed.

"You've driven jury-rigged craft on manual sticks. This isn't much different, just with one extra dimension."

"Hardly a qualification," Anna muttered as she followed John's movements on the twin joysticks. She took her own set of controls in hand and gingerly took over. It took a few moments, and a dizzying lurch towards the ground, before she could hold the craft level.

"You're doing great. Just worry about level and line. Let me worry about the third dimension." John leaned over the engine controls, but his attention was on the grey frenzy that formed an endless wall alongside them. A slight adjustment to the thrust and the craft climbed half a kilometer.

John tensed. "When I say so, take us straight into that cloud face."

"What?"

"No hesitation. Straight in."

"You've got to be out of your karking mind!"

"Now."

Anna froze. He couldn't be serious. Spinning vortexes boiled a hundred meters to their left, a maelstrom. They'd be torn apart.

"Now, Anna!"

She eased the sticks over, gut clenching as she felt the craft respond. Sky and ground vanished. A storm giant picked up the craft and hurled it forward, pressing Anna deep into her seat. She gasped, but kept a steady hand on the sticks.

"Good, keep it up," John said. His own hands were busy on the engine attitude controls.

For a heart-stopping moment, the bottom dropped out of their world, then weight was restored and calm enveloped them.

The world outside the cockpit was a uniform blankness, lit by occasional flashes. Alongside her, John breathed a deep sigh. "So far, so good. We're high enough to stay out of trouble for a while flying blind, but we can't depend on that for too long."

"How can we navigate in this?" Anna muttered. The flickering grey out there felt like it was hemming her in. She expected the unyielding ground to appear at any moment through the cockpit canopy.

"We don't. We'll need to get above it."

"But you said–"

"I know what I said. That was out there in still air but the storm's carrying us along with it. Hopefully fast enough to lessen the shear up into the next layer."

He squeezed his eyes shut and clenched his fists tight. Anna panicked for a moment when he let go the engine controls, but nothing bad happened. They might as well be stationary for all she could see and feel. The craft seemed to exist in a bubble, separated from normal time and space.

At last, he took a deep breath and leaned over the console again. "Just keep us level. You're doing fine."

Anna's seat pressed against her backside, the only hint of movement in this eerie world. John was sweating and turning a sickly green, but his hands on the attitude and throttles never wavered.

The sky abruptly lightened above. Streaks of polished copper flashed through the grey. They hung, suspended in a marshmallow valley that could have swallowed a dozen Serendipities. The circling clouds around them seemed leisurely, at odds with the fury Anna had experienced at ground level from such storms.

"Here goes," John said. His calm voice jarred with her fluttering heartbeat. With a final push that tore Anna's breath away the storm spat them out into clear skies.

She suppressed a violent shiver and held the craft steady. Sarah quickly found her orientation by the position of Big Red, and directed Anna south once more.

They flew on in silence for an hour. The cloud banks beneath stretched from one horizon to the other. Anna's hands grew numb on the controls, but John still looked deathly ill. She decided she now had the steadier pair of hands between them.

From her vantage point on the observation bubble, Sarah swore under her breath. "Over there, ahead and right."

Anna peered into the distance. On the edge of visibility, sparkles of white glinted. She wondered if that was the edge of the storm, but nothing that she knew of on Sponge glinted like that. Realization dawned, and she blushed at how slow she was being. "Mountains?"

"That's what I figured," said Sarah. "We should be half way to Laverne by now, and I thought it might be Lamarck—"

"Not a chance," said John. "We're being blown west at a rate of knots—"

"So that has to be Kepler," Sarah finished off for him. "That's what I was afraid of."

Anna tried to hold the craft steady while building a mental picture of the equatorial belt. "But Kepler's way over to the west. How did we wind up there?"

"Told you," John muttered. "Rate of knots. We're probably being blown west as fast as we're motoring south."

"Anna, you need to head east. Keep those peaks to your right. John, we need to find a break in that storm and get out of this airstream."

Even as they talked, the white ridges came into ever sharper focus. There was no longer any mistaking their nature. Anna stared in fascination. A stray thought flitted through her mind that this was the first time she'd ever seen the raw uncloaked planet that lay hidden beneath Sponge.

John scanned the writhing blanket below and shook his head. "We can't head back down into that, and I don't know how to manage that shear layer. We were lucky to get through it on the way up. We've got to hit it again at some point on the way down and we need to hit an airflow heading the right way to survive it."

Anna's heart leaped with sudden hope. "If we're near the top of the Kepler range, that must make Jorvick as easy to reach from here as Laverne. Especially if we're still being carried so fast westward."

Sarah gaped at her. "You're still chasing that fantasy? What about Ben?"

"Anna's right." Ben's gravelly voice cut through the rush of air. He peered around the edge of the doorway. "There's bigger things at stake. We could still make this right."

"But–"

"Dinna fret, lass. I've got life in me yet."

Anna leaned back in her seat and studied Ben's face. He was grey, hanging by a thread. She locked eyes with his girls, trying to divine their thoughts behind those blank masks.

They seemed to reach some unvoiced accord. They nodded in unison. "Da's right," said Clara. "Let's stick it to the karking Company."

Anna needed no further prompting. She eased the controls over and faced them westwards, across the northern edge of the range. The aircraft seemed to leap forwards, the nearest rounded summits approaching with gut-wrenching speed.

"John," Sarah shrieked, "take over. She can't do this."

But John shook his head again. "We'll never make headway against this stream. For better or worse, we're committed."

Sarah slammed her fist against her armrest in frustration.

"Besides," said John, "I reckon Anna's right. With this wind at our heels it's as quick now to head on to Jorvick." With that pronouncement, he hurried from his seat and headed aft. From somewhere among the storage racks at the back of the hold came the sound of retching.

———————

Jennifer Steel stared at the closed door of the conference room. She was alone. She needed the time to retrieve some tatters of composure.

It was bad. It would take them time, time they'd run out of, to work through the implications. Her whole legal team was even now trying to unravel the interdependencies but they had weeks of work ahead of them to forecast the true impact of those few innocent changes. Their own handiwork was now working against them. The document was designed to be hard to unravel. Not obviously so, but subtly. That was the hell of it.

But those changes were far from the innocent corrections the colonists professed. The strike was far from random, it had been done with the deftness of brain surgery. They'd known exactly what they were doing and there wasn't a damned thing she could do about it. Not without revealing her own dark machinations.

She felt empty, gutted, like the agreement her team had pieced together so carefully.

If only Galloway had succeeded, they'd now be finalizing the alternative agreement, the one the President had wanted all along. The one that really wasn't all that complicated. Yes, it had its share of twisted logic but that wasn't the point. The prize was a clear title to all future drug discoveries between now and full independence.

In the end, Galloway had failed and she'd been out-maneuvered on an agreement she should have been able to wrap up in her sleep.

Dazed, she staggered to her feet. Blackness edged her vision. She blinked it away and straightened her jacket.

———

As the minutes ticked by, Anna's anxiety mounted. John had left her alone at the controls. With Sarah's eye on their heading, she held a steady course as best she could. The smooth ride of the last two hours was gone. The air had grown lumpy.

"Looks like the cloud's breaking up this side of the range."

Sarah's voice shattered Anna's concentration on the controls. She leveled the aircraft from its sudden lurch and risked a glance downwards, away from the horizon that she'd been aiming to keep still in the cockpit window. Sarah was right. Flashes of green showed through the grey.

Anna switched her attention back to their flight, correcting again. Where the kak was John? She could steer, but they were locked in headlong flight and she had no idea how to manage the engine controls.

Another bump, more violent this time, then more judders like she was driving a crawler through forest.

They seemed to fall into an invisible hole. Cloud tops rushed closer. Up in the observation bubble, Sarah shrieked. Anna tasted blood where she'd bitten her tongue.

The craft tumbled in turbulence spilling over the top of the mountain range behind them. A grey blanket cloaked them once more. They were flying blind. In the bumps and dips Anna had only the vaguest sense of which way was up. She tried to level off the craft but whether they were climbing again or steering down into the ground she couldn't tell. Again and again she tensed on the controls as the grey outside darkened and lightened, bracing herself for a messy landing.

Dark shadows flickered beneath them. That must be the ground. The darkness deepened, then suddenly they broke through into clear air.

As Anna's eyes adjusted to the shift in perspective, she let out a giddy laugh. They were still high up, maybe a thousand meters. Patches of sunlight checkered the ground in the distance. The swell of a structural rib rose ahead, not quite meeting the cloud ceiling. Anna lined up their course along its top.

"Any idea how far we've come? I assumed we were still some way north and I turned what I hoped was south." Anna chewed her lip as she thought about that. There was nothing down here to get her bearings, and they could easily have got turned around in all that turbulence.

"Head over to the right. There's patches of sunlight over there. I should be able to get an idea of where in the sky Big Red is."

Anna turned towards the brightness. The network of ribs stretched away in both directions like a giant string of noodles. She called out to Sarah, "Is that a way station up ahead?"

Sarah confirmed her guess. "And you were heading the right way, too. I can see how the sunlight's slanting in through that gap up ahead."

Anna resumed her original line. Ten minutes later, another way station appeared in the distance. "We must be on the road to Killarney."

From the corner of her eye, Anna saw Sarah tense. She studied the ground and grabbed a pair of binocs hung on the cockpit side. "Take us lower."

"What can you see?" Anna asked.

Sarah pointed. "Those are vehicle tracks."

"Well worn," Anna conceded as they got closer. "And running *across* the ribs, not along. I think we've just found the link road." She let out a cry of joy. "Straight run in to Jorvick."

Chapter 35

Mikel wrapped his arms tighter around a stanchion as the aircraft lurched again. His knuckles were white and his arms numb, but this grey-painted pole had become his support and companion through this nightmare flight. He was intimately familiar with every square millimeter of its semi-gloss finish. Every pit and ridge, the brush strokes and congealed drips where an over-eager workman had applied too thick a coat, the bumps and scrapes of industrial wear.

Somewhere along the way, John had stumbled past Mikel. He tried to block out the sound of tigering just the other side of the bulkhead. Wet splashes with each fresh heave almost set Mikel off. Like Anna, John must have mastered the art of throwing up and getting his mask back on before breathing in again. Not something Mikel wanted to try. He focused back on the stanchion, barely noticing when John eventually lurched back to the cockpit.

A few tiny flakes of paint had come loose, revealing an off-white undercoat and forming a universe of detail. Mikel imagined them as islands in an alien sea, like he'd read existed on other planets. His eyes roved the shoreline and pictured towns and roads too small to make out. Anything to keep his mind off the shakes and gyrations in the real world around him.

He swore he'd never again complain about leaving town in a crawler.

One more bone-shaking crunch. A low chorus of groans from inside the cargo hold was counterpointed by a descant shriek of metal outside. It seemed to last forever, drilling deep into Mikel's mind.

At long last, the noise and movement stilled.

He cracked open gummed-up eyes, but his stranglehold on the stanchion stayed put. His body tensed, waiting for another violent shake. He'd been lulled into false security too often in the past few hours, and he had the bruises to prove it.

People around him stirred from their braced positions.

They really had stopped.

Across from him, Seth staggered to his feet. He glanced through the forward door to the cockpit, then managed a drunken walk to the loading hatch.

It opened, letting in a sullen light and a blast of hot and humid air. Outside, rain sheeted in a vertical curtain. Yellow lights flashed in the distance, drawing closer.

Mikel tumbled to the sodden ground, his knees unable to hold his weight. Everything became a jumble of unfamiliar lights and sounds. Burly grown-ups hustled everyone through the rain into waiting trucks. He got separated from both Anna and Clara. Clara and Helga stuck close by Ben. At least they seemed to be carrying him gently into the bed of a truck. They were far from gentle with everyone else, including Mikel.

He couldn't understand it. They seemed angry. Voices raised, barking orders.

"Look at this damage. There'll be hell to pay when the Company accountants get a hold of this mess."

"Count them. Check no-one's hiding in the back there."

"Where the kak did this lot appear from?"

"Has to be a Company craft, with all their *nutloos* travels this season, but these are Sponge folk."

"We need somewhere to hold them until the council has time to decide what to do with them."

Mikel glanced over his shoulder. He spotted Anna in another truck alongside Sarah and John. Their eyes met, and she gave a nod and a weak smile behind her rain-spattered mask.

Seth settled alongside Mikel. Nick was in front with one of the workmen. Mikel shrank back in his seat. It was the angry one who'd been doing most of the shouting.

" 'S okay, Mikey," Seth murmured. "Things will come right when they hear what we have to say."

"Glad you think so." The workman turned in his seat and glowered at Seth. "Wrecking an aircraft *and* tearing up our landing strip, that's goin' to take some explaining."

The cars pulled away. Soon, a shadow loomed through the deluge. A dome. Looked like a garage or warehouse. Hard to say. As they neared, more came into sight on either side, stretching into the distance. Mikel stared, wide-eyed.

"We've had enough of these *vreemde* popping in and out at all hours," their driver muttered. "Not supposed to be flying this time of year but try telling those Company folks." He shook his head. "Never thought our own folks would be *debeel* enough to hijack a craft and take it for a joyride."

"It's a long story," Nick said. "We need to talk to the Jorvick council."

A grunt. "Council's busy. They're finishing their talks with the Company."

The cars entered a vehicle lock, then a long tunnel that curved away out of sight. As they rattled along, Mikel gave up trying to make sense of what was happening. There was a glimmer of familiarity inside the city, the same sheds and airlocks, with the same telltale panels alongside. But after so many days in a dead town the brash lighting was overwhelming, and his mind tied itself in knots trying to absorb the size of this place. They must have driven the width of Serendipity several times over already and there seemed to be no end in sight.

He closed his eyes in misery and tried to wedge himself in his seat more securely against the rocking of the car.

At last, it stopped.

More shouting.

One of the voices was Anna's. Mikel's eyes flew open. He clambered from the car and pushed his way after Seth through a narrow and crowded hall. Seemed to be a habitat dome. Why would they bring a line of cars into a dome like this?

With a small cry he pushed past a knot of dark-skinned *vreemde*, barely registering them enough to be scared, but they didn't seem threatening and Anna was in trouble.

"I need to see the Company negotiators," she pleaded.

The stone-faced driver was unmoved, shoving Anna through the door. Mikel wormed past him, giving the man a furious look as he passed.

"Please," Anna whispered. "I've got an important message for them."

"The council will see you lot tomorrow. They've got more important things to deal with right now."

Anna wandered the accommodation area in a state of disbelief. She'd made sure Mikey was okay, but he'd seemed more worried about her than anything. As soon as they'd reassured each other, he'd settled down to playing *Rib Flax Shears* with Seth.

Now they were out of physical danger, the unreality of their situation hit her like a dusk storm. They'd come so close. If she could only find and talk to Galloway's boss, pass on the message that should have been conveyed in the first place, all would be well.

But she was trapped. They'd been placed in some empty clan quarters. Prime location, too, which puzzled her. Out in the hallway, she'd decided they must be somewhere near the heart of the city judging by the resounding clamor of people through long hallways in all directions. Conversations, laughter, music.

Familiar.

Her heart ached at all that life so close yet unreachable. Strange, although she relished her time alone out on the surface far from other people, she'd never properly admitted to herself how much she needed company at times. Her life was a fine balancing act. After days, and sometimes weeks, alone she was glad to be back in the hubbub of the town. But before long, she'd find the confines oppressive and seek the outdoors once more. Neither one nor the other would do for long.

This unaccustomed solitude in the middle of a city was neither one nor the other, which brought her back to her puzzlement. Why was a dome in the city center lying empty like this?

More to the point, why couldn't she leave? There were people, Jorvick locals and presumably the council's chosen enforcers, stationed at the main doors who refused all questions and entreaties. Of course, there were lots of ways into and out of the sprawling interconnected quarters but, frustrating and shocking at the same time, the doors wouldn't open. She recognized the technology, had read about it on other worlds, as old as human civilization. Locks on the doors. She stared at the door in front of her, appalled by this alien intrusion into her world.

As she wandered up to another level and began another fruitless search for a way out, she came to the conclusion that this must be something to do with the aliens. She closed her eyes and leaned her forehead against the cold, hard wall. A tear squeezed through her lashes. She whimpered and slammed a fist into the wall. Again. And again, the pain a welcome distraction from the ache of failure.

"I usually find the wall comes off best in these kinds of encounters." A soft voice at her side startled her.

Anna whirled around, self-consciously wiping her face on the back of her sleeve. Her face ended up wetter than before. One of the aliens stood there, hands clasped in front of him, gazing at her with a faint smile on his face.

"Who are you?"

"My name is unimportant. What matters is that I can help you."

"Well, *Meneer Unimportant*, can you get me out of here?"

"Better than that. I heard you speak, outside. You have a message for the Company negotiators. I can take you to them."

Anna's heart leaped, stilling the urge to run, the panic that had gripped her at his sudden appearance. "What do you know of it?"

"I know there was work happening elsewhere on this planet, something of great significance, to be reported back here." He shrugged. "You appeared eager to convey the results of that exploration."

"Why would you want to help me?"

"It seems you wish to help the Company. I am in the Company's employ. A more insightful question is—why would *you* want to help *them*?"

Anna studied the man in front of her. Skin the color of well-oiled rimwood, at least his eyes were a healthy brown, not those ghostly pale orbs that gave Galloway such a disconcerting appearance. She tried to see past his alien features and read the man beneath the skin.

He was old, self-assured, and calm. Fine lines around his eyes suggested much greater age, in fact, than she would have first guessed from his otherwise smooth features and graceful poise.

There was no hint of threat in his manner, or of suspicion. She wondered how much he knew of what had happened in Serendipity.

"A friend of mine was helping the Company. Things didn't go as intended. I am trying to help *him* more than the Company." Before the stranger could pursue the question she asked, "How did you get in here?"

He laughed. "You people have lost all notions of how to secure a place. Guards on the main doors, and locks on the rest. But who accounted for the keys to those locks?" He stepped forward and did something she couldn't see. The door swung open. "There is a way through the adjoining quarters and back down the other side of the dome, out of sight of those vigilant guards."

———— ·•·——

An eerie sense of unreality gripped Jennifer Steel as she took her seat in the middle of the negotiating table. The room, the table, the people were real enough, but they felt distant, like a story within a story. She seemed frozen in space while the chair rose to meet her of its own accord.

Somehow she managed to settle herself and stay upright.

She was fairly sure, anyway.

Someone placed a thick document in front of her, in a binder bearing the Company crest embossed in platinum on a background of deepest azure. The fibrous texture of the pages came into sharp focus, the only reality in this ethereal nightmare.

She should have let that pilot live long enough for a thorough debrief. Her security team had questioned her, but had only established a few brief facts before terminating her. Damn them for their shortsightedness! She'd only just heard about Galloway's demise and harvesters returning unannounced from the town. That brought a whole new tangle of unwanted loose ends into the picture.

Too many witnesses! How in all the darkest heavens was she going to clean this mess up? Or, were there ways to distance herself from the underhand dealings that must surely be coming to light out there?

Yes, that seemed like the only possible course. Galloway was a rogue operative. Nobody here in Jorvick had had any contact with him since he took off on his covert mission. There was nothing tangible to link her to his activity. No proof of involvement. She could swing that line, surely?

Of course, there would be hell to pay when she returned to Earth. And the other senior members of the negotiating team knew about the mission.

But–Jennifer's heart leapt at the thought–they would be just as keen to distance themselves. If they all kept their stories straight, that would actually lend strength to her own denial. They would all sink or swim together, and if there was one thing Jennifer was good at, it was bending people to her will.

The binder opened at the last page. Some lackey must have opened it for her, but she hadn't registered the hand. The binder seemed to have a life of its own.

She still couldn't believe it. At the last minute, those accursed colonists had sniffed out and closed three of the most secretive loopholes she'd inserted into the document. Taken individually, they looked innocuous enough, although worded slightly differently from standard. Collectively, those subtle differences gave the Company leeway to adjust required profit margins to suit its own ends. It had taken her own legal team months of research to find the right pressure points to make those tweaks in the dense maze of wording. How in all of Space had these bumpkins spotted the maneuver?

She'd been caught off guard, unwilling to admit to outright dirty tactics and unable to defend the clauses under the gimlet glare of the ENCOA observers. Her world was unraveling. Now, trapped in this nightmare unreality, she just wanted an end to it all.

Her signature joined that of the colonial negotiation lead, although she didn't recall picking up a pen.

The document passed along the ENCOA table for witnessing signatures. Jennifer sagged back into her chair. It was done.

The room span around her as she absorbed the implications. *Jennifer Steel, the great negotiator.* She recalled with growing dread that those clauses had also been pivotal in several other poison pills scattered throughout the new treaty. Her careful work had been almost entirely defanged. Even without Galloway's interference and plotting, her days as a senior executive were surely numbered after this debacle.

She looked up and found Maximillian Kyari, the ENCOA legal counsel to Elysium, staring at her. His dark baby face held the hint of a smile. Damn him! He must have pointed out those clauses to the colonists. He was supposed to be her agent, her snake in the midst of her foes, pointing them in the wrong direction. He'd pay for this ... if she retained enough power to do him harm.

Who else might have betrayed her?

Her eyes flicked sideways, studying the others at her table. Nobody met her gaze. The guilt of treachery, or hurried distancing from her inevitable fall?

Burning rage overcame her. All that she'd worked for on this hellhole, all she'd worked for her whole life, lay in ruins because of an over-ambitious young hellion overreaching himself.

A commotion in the doorway behind the media table caught her attention. From the corner of her eye, she also noted a growing gathering of ENCOA enforcement agents at each doorway.

Unease battled with fury. What the hell were they doing in the negotiation chamber? The sense of unreality deepened. This had to be some bizarre and frighteningly real dream. She would wake up soon and find herself back at the negotiations, her precious legal traps still intact. This time around she'd have answers to satisfy the observers.

A woman strode to the center of the room and faced her, mussed brown hair framing a pale, blue-tinted face. She wore grubby outdoor clothing, dripping onto the floor. A mask dangled at her neck.

For a moment, Jennifer was seized by a powerful *deja-vu*. That pilot, who'd brought the news that derailed everything. But she was dead. This was an unknown woman. A colonist. A nothing.

The woman cleared her throat and spoke into the sudden silence. "The cows have come home."

The words jolted Jennifer like an electric shock. She stared at the woman, dumbstruck, then lurched to her feet. "What? That's not possible. I already had ..."

Too late, she saw the trap she'd sprung. "Who *are* you?"

"The more interesting question is"–the deep tones of the chief facilitator rolled across the room–"why would that meaningless phrase provoke such a reaction?"

Behind the media podium, where all cameras seemed to be focused on her, she noticed her aide, Nikolai Shevchenko, standing in the far doorway with a grim smile on his face.

Her knees buckled. She had no answer to offer.

An enforcement agent took hold of her elbow. "Jennifer Steel, I am placing you in custody pending a formal investigation into charges of insider dealing, theft of intellectual property, and accessory to murder."

Chapter 36

Back in the empty clan quarters, Anna slumped onto a bench and buried her head in her hands. The others crowded around, besieging her with questions.

A hand on her shoulders, and a surreal warmth suffused the air. Her churning thoughts calmed, a sense of peace washed around the edge of her mind. She cracked open her eyes, knowing who she'd find there.

She gazed deep into Mikey's eyes. He'd never uttered a word in his life, and his thoughts were wordless still but utterly clear. *It's okay, mom.*

Seth settled alongside her. "What can I do to stop you disappearing on me like that?" His voice was a hoarse whisper, but she heard the pain and pleading in it.

"You can't. It's what I do. I see what needs to be done and I do it. No questions asked." She paused, knowing what she needed to ask, but dreading where this line of thinking might lead. "Is that something you think you could live with?"

"Like I'll always be an outdoorsman, dicing with the Deep. Could you ever live with that?"

Again. The unspoken word hung in the air between them. That was the question, wasn't it?

Past Mikey's shoulder, past the ring of concerned friends, she noted her escort leave with unreadable expressions as they glanced back before closing the door. They'd manhandled her out of the community hall, something so unheard of on Sponge she was outside in shock before she'd even processed what was happening. Then a moment of panic struck her, wondering if they were about to shove her out the nearest lock onto the surface. But they'd loosed their grip as soon as she'd stopped struggling, and marched her silently back to her companions.

And what now? The circle of faces begged questions she wasn't sure she could answer.

"Give me a moment. Not sure what the kak just happened."

Mikey pressed a flask of water into her hands. She glanced at him in surprise. She hadn't asked for a drink but she suddenly felt how dry her throat had become.

"Thanks," she croaked.

"Take it easy, lass." A familiar growl. "We're goin' nowhere."

Anna stared past the press of bodies. She had been so stunned when she'd been returned to the common room she hadn't noticed Ben propped up on a bench in the corner. John stepped to one side to make a gap. The circle widened respectfully to include Ben in the conversation. He waved aside a medic and winced as he eased himself further upright, but at least his face had taken on a healthier color.

"From the beginning." His voice was kindly, but his expression betrayed concern bordering on fear.

Anna rolled a mouthful of water around her tongue, and swallowed. "I was looking for a way out of here. This off-worlder sneaked me out and told me I could make everything right."

"And you trusted him?"

"He said I could put things back on track. Deliver the message to Galloway's boss directly." She glanced at Nick. "That was what you wanted, wasn't it? We kakked up your plans when we stopped Galloway."

Nick grimaced. "Years of delicate planning, started long before my limited involvement. But, heck, it was always a long shot at best."

She turned her attention back to Ben. "Couldn't see it doing any harm. Besides, I wasn't trusting the *vreemde*. I was trusting that *Nick* knew what he'd been doing, even though I don't understand any part of it."

Nick frowned. "We wondered what had happened to you."

"Wondered?" Seth burst out. "Kak, Anna! we had no idea what had become of you." He speared Nick with a furious glare.

His outburst subsided when Anna placed a hand on his knee. "It's what needed doing."

Ben looked deep in thought. "Tell me more about this off-worlder, this unlikely helper."

"I think he works for the Company boss, but he hates her with a passion. Just the way he talked while he briefed me on what I needed to do. He'd heard what happened out at Serendipity. I wonder if he was part of your plans, Nick, somewhere in the background. He seemed to know all about Galloway. More than he was letting on, for sure."

Nick shrugged. "I never met any of the off-worlders."

"He told me who to look for, where she'd be." Anna huffed and shuddered. "He didn't mention anything about it being in the middle of a community hall in front of an audience."

"Those words we heard Galloway say, back in the assay shed, that was the message?"

Anna nodded.

"So you gave the boss that coded message. In front of everyone."

"By the time I stepped through the door and realized it, I was already the center of attention. Didn't seem much point in backing out by then." Anna screwed her eyes in concentration, trying to see past the blur of events and emotions. "It looked like the negotiations had finished. I was there too late. I delivered the message, but I don't think it made any difference."

Anna's shoulders slumped. Tears of frustration welled again. This was not like her to fall into despair, to tear up so often, but events swirled around her too big to understand. She longed for the comfort of her familiar cab and the wide outdoors. "After everything we went through, I was still too late."

Ben gave a tiny shake of his head. "Makes no sense, lass. This mysterious off-worlder sounds too organized for that. Somehow I think he took you there exactly when he wanted you there."

"Why? What good would it do to deliver a message too late?"

"Depends." Ben chewed his cheek, deep in thought. "What happened afterwards? Think now. Details."

Anna closed her eyes again, trying to piece the jumble of images together. She sighed. It was all too much of a blur. In her mind's eye she homed in on the leader of the Company representatives, the one the strange man had been so careful to describe. "That white-haired *vreemde*, the one in charge, it seemed to shock her. And there was a lot of commotion and shouting after that but I didn't take it all in. Then I was hustled out of the room."

"So he shocked his boss. So what? What does it mean?" Ben wondered.

"I don't know." Anna pressed her face into her hands again. "I don't even know what's supposed to happen now. I mean, we're in big trouble, aren't we?"

"Maybe. Maybe not." Anna and everyone else looked around, startled, at the alien accent. A short, round man stood in the doorway. "It rather depends on you." Teeth flashed in a face as dark as charcoal. He was another *vreemde*, like Galloway and his cronies.

Except ... he was dressed in Elysium fashion, not like an off-worlder.

And he seemed ... benign. Like a favorite aunt. Not threatening like so many people she'd encountered recently. Not the immediate, physical kind of threat, at least. Anna had met some kindly aunts with cores of steel. She decided to reserve judgment on this newcomer.

His face creased in a broad smile. "Maximillian Kyari. I'm a lawyer."

Anna stared blankly at him. "A what?"

Nick's eyes widened. "You're our off-world counsel, aren't you?"

His smile broadened. "My fame precedes me. But let's not stand on ceremony. Elysium is known for its casual culture, so when in Rome etc. Call me Max."

"And what would a high-standin' legal person be doing wi' a bunch of miscreants?" Ben growled. "We must be in worse trouble than even I imagined."

"As I said, maybe, maybe not. First, I think I can help untangle some of the questions you've ensnared yourself in."

With a maddening unhurried air, he gazed around the room and pulled a chair over from the far wall. "That's better." He blessed them all with a beatific smile that Anna longed to drive a piton through. She was boiling over with impatience.

As he sat, he said "So, Anna 't Hooft, let's start with this mysterious benefactor of yours."

A cold tingle up her spine sobered her like an ice bath. "How ..."

"Oh, I think your name is on everyone's lips after your brief but powerful performance."

Oh kak!

"You guessed correctly that he did indeed work for Jennifer Steel—the lead negotiator. That was Nikolai Shevchenko, her personal assistant." Max looked grave. "A very dangerous character. Probably as well for you that you chose to go along with his suggestion."

"He wasn't helping Nick with his plan, was he?"

Max shook his head. "His only interest was in bringing Steel down. As you suspected, the negotiations had concluded, the deal was signed."

A queasy sensation formed in Anna's gut. "We did fail, then."

Max cocked his head to one side, studying her. "What counts as success or failure here?"

That was a strange question. With shocking vividness, Anna's mind went back to those moments of despair watching Galloway's jet hover outside the garage, taunting them, unreachable. Her thoughts back then, acceptance of things beyond her reach and focus on the things they had, still made sense. Is that what this lawyer meant? But wouldn't that mean everything they'd gone through was pretty much irrelevant? Maybe. She was tired of the whole business, and just wanted to get back to normal life.

Maybe that *was* it, after all. "We already have a good life, don't we?" She glanced around, looking for some affirmation. "It would help to be able to maintain our equipment properly, not having to salvage and patch up every last item, but we have food, shelter ... and each other."

"You have a way of living that would be the envy of most colonies, and certainly of most people on Earth, if only they could see past the reputation this planet has for its hostile environment." Max sat back and folded his hands across his ample belly. "But you manage the risks, and as you say, you have an abundance of the essentials. And whichever way the negotiations went, I doubt that many people would notice a material difference in their lives. So ... success or failure? What, really, have you gained or lost?"

"We're all still here, aren't we?" said John.

"Mostly." Anna trembled.

"Aye, Georgina will be a-sorely missed," Ben grated.

"And we still don't know what's going to happen to us."

"Ah, yes." Max gave another of those beaming smiles. "All in good time, I'm sure. You've been through an ordeal, but, as you say, you still have each other and life will go on. The real success is the new drug discovery. Not for Elysium or the Company, but for the whole of humanity. Elysium scientists long ago suspected it was there to be found, the big question became—what to do about it?"

"How long has this plot been cookin'?" Ben muttered.

"Long enough. We know how the Company operates. Our biggest worry was the Company finding a way to make off with the proceeds of the discovery once it became known, hence the deception. Let them keep the profits–for something we weren't supposed to know about–in return for a quick escape from their clutches. Something we never thought to see in our lifetimes.

"In the end, things went better than any of us could have hoped. They overreached themselves. The deal we actually signed was better than anything Elysium had any right to expect. Steel was off balance by then, and we'd already sprung a trap of our own. She thought I was her man on the inside. She was sadly mistaken. I'm quite relieved that you were too late with your message. That would have ruined everything. As it is, your announcement pushed Steel over the edge, as I think Shevchenko planned. His timing was exquisite. She implicated herself before she realized what she was saying."

There was a long silence. Anna studied Max, who seemed lost in a world of his own. Her mind rebelled once again at the twisted thinking going on here. How did people cope with such deception? They must have way too much time on their hands. Sponge taught its populace to keep things simple. There was only a short step between safety and death, and no room for misunderstandings.

Max stirred. "And so, we come back to the question of you people, here. The Company's covert operation has been exposed, and they will pay dearly for that. But one thing I must be sure of. We cannot allow Elysium's part in this to become known."

"Because of the legal implications?" Nick asked.

"Partly, but also think about the effect on your own society. To think that your own planners, leaders you trust, can act with such duplicity? Could you ever fully trust them again?"

"But surely someone involved will say something, let something slip, bargain with information in return for more lenient treatment?"

"Who would talk, I wonder? The Company executives here had no knowledge of the plan until their arrival here, and they only knew about the Company connection. People might well suspect they had local help, but suspicion falls short of proof. Their best choice for survival is to maintain ignorance.

"Obviously there must be a large network inside the Company back on Earth, but they will have ensured they are even more distanced from the whole thing. And as far as they are concerned, it was a Company conspiracy pure and simple. We made sure they had no hint of local involvement beyond a few paid lackeys."

Anna puzzled over that. Her confusion must have shown on her face because Max gave a twisted smile. "Yes. Something of an Earth concept, but so ingrained they'll have no trouble accepting it."

"What about the ground team that landed at Serendipity? They clearly knew they had contacts here on Sponge. In Serendipity." Anna glanced at Nick, who winced.

A shadow crossed Max's eyes. "Ah, yes. The Company dispatched a rescue team as soon as you landed. They arrived too late."

"What?" Anna's mind reeled. "We left them in a working dome, with supplies to last for weeks ..." Her voice trailed off under Max's gaze.

"They discovered that the survivors had ... how did they put it? ... grown careless with their airlock discipline."

There was a long silence as the implications settled in.

Anna studied Max's suddenly bland expression. A chill raced up and down her spine, deepening with a sudden realization. "That leaves *us*."

"Precisely."

"I hope I can speak for everyone in this room in saying all I want to do is forget the whole thing. I'm certainly not saying anything." Anna looked to Ben for support. He nodded.

"I assumed as such, but I had to hear it from you." Max's gaze seemed to skewer Anna where she sat. He seemed to flip between soft geniality and tungsten steel without moving a muscle. "For my part, I'm satisfied."

"Meaning ...?"

"The rest, I think that will be left to the Elysium authorities to decide."

Anna squeezed her eyes shut. She couldn't face the looks on her friends' faces. "Then we really are futzed. Might as well take a walk to the nearest airlock."

"What makes you think so?"

Anna glared at him. "Where the kak do I start? I got left behind, wrecked a crawler trying to escape ..."

"We went against policy turning back from the trek." Ben's voice was grave.

Max looked from one to another, with a quizzical expression. He nodded. "True enough. Thing is, Elysium has no codified laws as such, so nothing for you to contravene in the usual sense. At least, that's what a good lawyer would argue." His voice took on a tone hard as knotwood. "And, remember, I *am* the best lawyer on the planet."

"So, you'll put in a word for us, then? I hope they listen."

"I think they will. Besides, they can hardly do anything too drastic to their new national heroes."

"What?" Anna realized her jaw was hanging open. She willed it shut.

"After today's revelations, with corrupt Company officials caught red-handed trying to rob Elysium of its natural wealth, I'll be placing a motion for ENCOA to conduct an external audit of its stewardship since inception."

"I think plain language is in order here." Nick grinned.

Max gave a graceful bow of his head. "I keep forgetting, so many money-related concepts have no meaning here. Something I'll have to get more used to. In plain terms, I'm threatening the Company with action that will cost them so dearly that today's debacle will seem but a down payment, and I believe they'll be more than ready to cut their losses."

Nick's grin widened. Somehow, Max seemed to be talking a language he understood. Good for him.

"Still waiting for the 'plain language' part of all this," Anna ground out.

Max sighed. "I expect Elysium to be free from Company control within a standard year."

"Now, *that* I can understand," said Ben.

"I still don't understand how I can get away with so much equipment damage."

Old habits were hard to dispel. It seemed that Max realized this. "Many of the ways you're used to are Company policies, designed to preserve assets and profits. I think there is a new wind blowing through Elysium. It's time people were valued ahead of profits. Something I think the people of Sponge already know."

Anna thought back to her years of rebellion, of rules broken. The games all field crews and operations controllers played to skirt the rules and do the right thing.

She smiled.

Chapter 37

People and vehicles, little more than specks in the distance, scurried around a squadron of scramjets on Jorvick's landing field. Floodlights cast a pool of radiance in the dawn shadows around town. The forecasters had given them a brief window of opportunity to land and take off again.

The word in the kitchens was that the longship had taken up orbit again some time in the past week, after a month riding out Big Red's flares in the shelter of the Lagrange point.

The word also was that the visiting negotiation team and neutral observers were going quietly mad with frustration at the delay caused by Sponge's turbulence. Someone back on Earth would no doubt have to come up with creative explanations why the negotiations had been held at this time of year. Anna knew why, of course, but the real explanation would never become public.

She squirmed a bit as she thought of the deception involved. She felt grubby, just from that fleeting contact with such profound duplicity. The *vreemde* had come for reasons beyond negotiating a release from colonial debt, and Sponge had exacted a heavy price, not the least of which was a prolonged stay while the atmosphere shrugged its shoulders and settled itself into the new season.

Serves 'em right.

In fact, they were lucky to get even this gap in the equatorial storms. The violent about-turn in the wind patterns from one hemisphere to the other usually had everyone hunkered down in the cities ringing the equator, partying and making new alliances ahead of the onward trek to the new harvesting season. To see so many people outdoors was unheard-of.

Although she'd not come across one of the off-worlders—other than Max, and he didn't really count—since that last confrontation, she was glad to see the back of them. She and most the population of Jorvick, judging by the crowds thronging the hills surrounding the city.

Crawlers picked their way gingerly through droves of people, seeking a vantage point. Anna had negotiated with one of the local clans to bring her and her friends out. She'd also bagged a coveted spot on the roof of a crew car. Prime viewing.

Over the years she'd been so used to the life of a loner, regarded with caution outside her immediate family group. Good at her job, solid, reliable, someone you wanted by your side in a tight spot, and yet still apart.

Celebrity status didn't sit well. The endless invitations in the past weeks, subtle and not-so-subtle overtures to tempt her into a clan marriage, it was all getting too much. But at times like this it had its perks and Anna was not above cashing in just this once. The sight of the Company fleeing the planet, cowed by the poor colonials, was a once-in-a-lifetime event. And for Anna it was personal.

Sheet lightning cracked the sky way out to the west. *They'd better hurry.* Mikey snuggled into her side. On her other side, Seth's bulky silhouette was a comforting presence.

She leaned into his warmth. "You sure you want to hang up your harvesting tackle?"

He grunted. "Sarah will make a good crew boss, and John's still there to keep her in line."

"That's not what I asked."

"Someone needs to keep *you* in line."

"You really think they'll give me another crawler after losing three in a matter of days?" But she was joking, and Seth knew it. "And that *still* isn't what I asked."

"Yes, I'm sure." He sighed. "For all sorts of reasons. Where do you want me to start?"

"Stop futzing around and pick one," Anna growled.

Seth paused in thought, then reached over and ruffled Mikey's hair. "Mikey's got a talent. We need to work out how to use it, to everyone's benefit."

"*That's* what you're leading with?"

"I don't think you see yet how much this means."

Kak! He was serious.

"For all that we've learned of Sponge, much of it's still a mystery. You already know that wayfinding on the surface is more an art than a science, but it's ten times more so down in the depths. Just think what a difference it could make with someone who can read Sponge the way Mikey can."

"So, a combined surface and deep survey team?" He'd hinted at this, but it was so far removed from how the teams operated today that it was taking a while for the pieces to click. "Never been done before. The harvest teams will think we're treading on their turf."

Seth huffed. "They'll be all for it, believe me. Being able to home in on ripe tubers in a fraction of the time? This is exciting stuff, Anna. This is where the future lies. Who wouldn't want to be part of that?" He paused, then continued in an off-hand tone. "Besides, I don't want to let you out of my sight again."

She gasped in mock outrage and punched him on the arm. But it was what she wanted to hear. She snuggled close again and pulled Mikey in beside her. "What do you think, Mikey? Ride the surface with me and Seth?"

He grinned and gave her a thumbs-up.

"And," she said, "you got no problems with the next leg of the trek? Don't want a repeat performance."

He waggled his hand, non-committal. His cheeky grin said he, too, was joking. It felt good to be able to relax and laugh at last. The memories still hurt, they probably always would, but the nightmare was over.

"It won't be like last time. I know all the crowds here are hard to handle, you'll be glad to get away. But we've got a long haul ahead of us just to get back to Laverne, and then we'll have to trek south on our own. Everyone else will have left before we make Laverne."

"You're sure about this?" Seth asked. "There's lots of tempting offers to join clans in the Jorvick sector."

"Ben would never forgive me if I jumped rig. Besides, Serendipity North and South have always been my home. I'm like Mikey, don't take too well to too much novelty."

Mikey gave a faint "Hnnhh" and pointed. Two kilometers away, the scramjets were maneuvering away from the attending vehicles and lining up on the taxiway.

"Seriously, though," Anna said, "how much difference can one person make?"

"There must be others. Ben's girls say they can *feel* Sponge. Not as deep as Mikey, but it's there."

"Their harvest teams always do seem to strike lucky more often than most."

They sat in silence for a few minutes, watching the distant craft maneuver.

"Max was right about one thing." Anna lowered her voice to a whisper, aware of the dozens of strangers crowding the car roof. "If people knew the *stiig* things the planners did in their dealings with off-worlders, they'd never trust our own council again."

"Like you never really forgave Nick, you mean?"

She shook her head. "Is that what you think? I can't blame Nick for leaving us behind, but knowing all the secrets he's been keeping? I can never look at him the same way again. And I think it would do real damage if more people realized what went on in those council meetings."

"Well, Max has taken him in tow. I think he'll be happy staying here in Jorvick."

"Probably just as well. Seems to me that our whole way of life depends on a way of thinking. Something that sounds like it might be unique to Sponge. I can't help feeling that what we have here is fragile still."

"Still? You think things will change?"

"Sponge is changing us." Anna shivered. "For good or for ill. It's got to be more than skin deep, too. Generations born here exposed to traces of alien drugs? Even with the best filters, it's in the air all around us. That has to have an effect. What if it's changing the way we think, too?"

A scream high overhead echoed around the valley. One after another, the jets climbed and blazed streaks across the sky.

The planet was theirs once more.

Afterword

More about Anna's world

For a behind-the-scenes dive into the worldbuilding for this story, visit my website:

www.iansbott.com/anna-s-world

The site contains a wealth of detail about Elysium and the colonists' life on Sponge – maps, pictures, terminology, technical information and more.

The fact that this is a world where masks are an ever-present feature is entirely co-incidental. I started writing this story in 2017, and the first draft was finished in March 2019, long before COVID-19 made its unwelcome appearance and before the humble face mask became a political flashpoint.

A final word from the author

If you've enjoyed reading a book – any book, not just this one – please consider leaving a review where other readers can find it.

One of the greatest challenges Indie authors face is gaining visibility in the immense marketplace of online publishing. Indies can't hope to compete with big publishers for shelf space or advertising copy or magazine column-inches. Our visibility to readers, our ability to be found, rests on ranking algorithms at online stores. Those algorithms rank books on sales and reviews.

You've got this book in your hands. You've already made me happy. The best way to make me even happier is to leave an honest review wherever you bought the book, or on a readers' forum where you hang out.

Thank you!